VALLEY OF THE SMOKES

To my good friend George

First Edit

A NOVEL

Durward C. Bynum

by Durward C. Bynum

Book design by Amanda Koo
Cover design and imaging by Amanda Koo

ISBN-13: 978-1-934379-32-5

This book is dedicated to my family

ACKNOWLEDGEMENTS

I owe a debt of thanks to many precious people whose invaluable experience, assistance, advice and encouragement helped make this project possible:

Mary P. Seigman, a particularly helpful librarian at the San Bernardino Public Library in Hesperia, California for help with my research.

My brother, Jack Bynum, who always encouraged me throughout my life to write a book.

My daughter-in-law Jennifer Bynum, Joyce Mayes, and Sally Hale for their advice and encouragement to submit this work for publication.

My son, John Bynum, for his devotion in preparing the final work for publication.

And many others unnamed who have also encouraged me in my writing.

Most of all, my dear wife, Lucille, for her love, encouragement, and countless hours of selfless work in editing, typing and retyping the original manuscripts. It would not have been possible without her support.

Valley of the Smokes

CHAPTER ONE

Michael Ross was born a few minutes ahead of his identical twin brother, Gabriel, in the rustic three-bedroom mountain cottage built by his grandparents. The babies came into the world vigorously protesting leaving their warm nest, early on the frosty morning of November 1, 1777.

The cabin was perched on a treeless knoll about thirty yards from the west bank of the Northern Lake of Killarney. It had been built there to reap the full benefit of what little sun was available. It rained almost every day in this part of Ireland, except for a very short time in midsummer, but the sun came out for an hour or two almost every day just before sunset.

Behind the cottage rose the highest mountain peak in Ireland, Mount Carrantuohill, with its majestic trees, evergreen foliage and brightly colored rhododendrons. The low-hanging clouds and the rays of the setting sun over the Atlantic Ocean cast a shadow into the lake, mirroring the mountain and the cottage in the clear blue-green waters. The family would often sit on the verandah of the cottage in the late afternoon to enjoy the beautiful mural in the lake, as they discussed the events of the day and their plans for the next. The green meadows and forest glades along the mountainside made this the most beautiful place in all the Emerald Isles. When fishing along the shore or hunting in the woods, if you sat quietly it seemed as though you could hear the angels singing and playing their heavenly music as the wind came whispering through the trees.

Irish folklore is full of legends concerning angels and the little people they call Leprechauns, and it was in these mountain forests they were reputed to be found.

The temperature of Ireland ranges from forty to seventy degrees the year round and the almost constant rainfall keeps it forever green, hence the name "The Emerald Isle." Frost is found only in the mountain areas.

Michael and Gabriel lived here with their parents, Riley and Patricia, and their sister, Esther, who was two years younger and adored by all. Theirs was a devoted family and Riley and Patricia demanded strict obedience from their children. Riley spanked them when warranted, which was seldom, and the children grew up with a deep respect for their elders and the laws that governed them.

There were so many rivers, lakes and canals in Ireland people could travel from one side of the country to the other without losing sight of water for very long. There were no coal mines and so few forests that nearly everyone cooked or heated their cottages by burning peat. They would cut the peat out of the bogs and lay them out to dry before burning.

The main diet of the day was Irish potatoes, fish and cabbage, with a treat of mutton or beef once in a while, and everything was boiled.

There were three great lakes called Lakes of Killarney; Upper, Middle and Lower, which were connected by natural waterways, and there were forested islands out in the lakes, on an island in Middle Lake there was the ruins of an old monastery.

On an island in Lower Lake stood the ruins of an old castle called, "Ross Castle". The Ross family didn't know if they were the offspring of the owner of this ancient castle, but the children liked to think they were.

Transportation to the islands was via small boats built out of strong canvas covered with pitch stretched over a sturdy wood frame. They were moved over the waters by oars, and a crude sail. Nearly all Irishmen were great sailors and most of their livelihood came from the sea, or large lakes. The weapons they used were bow and arrows, spears, swords, broadswords, knives and a sturdy stick that fit the hands well, about seven or eight feet long which doubled as a walking staff, but it was a formidable weapon in skilled hands.

Riley was a master of all these weapons, as well as a skilled boxer and rough and tumble wrestler. He had taught his twins so well that at the age of eighteen they had surpassed his own skills.

They had not been to sea because they raised fine thoroughbred horses, beef cattle and a small dairy herd. Most of their horses and beef cattle were sent to the huge markets of the British Isles, but their dairy products were sold locally.

The Irish were fun-loving people, but their quick tempers prompted frequent fights, as much for the joy of it as for satisfying a grudge or to right a wrong.

Many of the Irish lads joined the Spanish and French armies and navies to fight the English. Many of them hated the English, they thought justly, and they fought them any way they could. The Ross family was not consumed with this hatred, but they understood it. They sold nearly everything they raised to the English markets and they fared well. They were well known and highly respected by both the upper and lower class. They were somewhere in the middle, not considered wealthy, but far from being poor.

Riley thought he was the richest man on earth. He had a wife who adored him and showed it in every way, and he cherished his three offspring, none of whom seemed eager to leave the nest.

The Kerry Mountains and the forest were inhabited by large timber wolves, elk and deer, and the wolves often invaded the meadows and killed calves, colts, and sometimes a grown horse or cow. This cut deeply into their profit.

Over two thousand years ago the Irish interbred dogs to develop a large wolfhound that was a strong, fierce fighter, but was gentle and loyal to its master. These dogs could reach thirty inches high at the shoulder and weigh up to a hundred and forty pounds. They could kill the Irish wolf with ease and were capable of bringing down a grown elk.

Ranchers in the United States used these animals to rid their range of wolves and for hunting bear and mountain lions. The only animal faster is the cheetah, but the hound could still run them to ground because they could outlast them.

The Ross family never lost any of their stock because they had these dogs trained to watch the stock night and day. Riley and Patricia never worried about their three children because they were all well trained in weaponry and each of them had their own hound dog that went with them everywhere, except to school.

When the children were growing up they loved to sail their small craft across the lakes to explore around the old monastery and Ross Castle on Middle and Lower Islands. They pretended to be great fishermen and great hunters who supplied the meat for the castle and monastery.

Michael often pretended to be King Ross, Gabriel was his favorite knight in shining armor, and Esther was the beautiful princess decked out in her finery to whom all the knights of the kingdom would come running at her command.

As they grew older they started dreaming about finding buried treasure and they began digging holes around old Ross Castle. One Saturday morning after they had finished their chores they told their parents they were going over to old Ross Castle to look for buried treasure.

"Be careful digging around those ruins," Riley said, "You could drop into an old dungeon and get yourselves buried under a ton of dirt and rock, and be sure to be home in time to milk the cows and feed the stock. Your mother and I are going into Killarney shopping today."

The gold seeking adventurers loaded their boat with the tools they would need, took their dogs and set sail for the island in Lower Lake, headed for Ross Castle. They sailed across to the island in Middle Lake, then down to Lower Lake. It was much further that way, but safer because the water was calmer than it was out in the deeper part. They knew that these waters could become very dangerous when the wind came howling down the mountain.

When they reached the old castle King Michael said, "Princess Esther, you take our lunch to the parlor, and Sir Gabriel and I will get the tools and start unearthing our fortune."

Sixteen-year-old Esther giggled grabbed the lunch bucket and went skipping toward the old castle. Once she placed their lunch on the table in one of the rooms she ran back to help her brothers dig.

As the brothers approached the castle Gabriel looked around, then said, "I think I'll start digging right here." He stuck his shovel in the soft earth about six feet from one of the old walls.

"One place is as good as the other," Michael replied. "We've dug holes all over this place, wherever your urges dictated. We haven't found anything yet."

"This is the day," Gabriel said, "I just know it." Michael shook his head, and then looked up at the old wall. He said, "Gabriel, I don't like the looks of that wall, look how it's leaning. It could come down on us, let's dig somewhere else."

"No! Michael, that old wall's been there hundreds of years like that. This is the place, I'm telling you."

"Sure," Michael replied.

Esther walked up and said, "He's right this time, King Michael."

"That settles it, I'm outnumbered." Michael replied. "I guess we dig here."

The siblings began digging energetically and Gabriel struck a stone surface about two feet down. They dug a trench and found it to be an arched roof about eight feet across, adjoining the old leaning wall. They went back to the center of the roof and dug east about six feet, where they found the edge of the arched roof.

Their excitement grew as they dug downward, clearing the dirt from the wall. About four feet down they found a hardwood door with large iron hinges that were almost rusted away. By the time they had all the dirt cleared away from the door they were all soaked in perspiration. Michael and Gabriel had kept Esther busy running for water, and when Michael told her to go for still more she said. "You two better come eat your lunch, then cover the hole and get ready to go. Dad will be mad as hops if we're late for chores."

The boys climbed out of the hole and went down to the lake to wash. When they returned, Princess Esther had their lunch ready and they ate quickly.

Michael and Gabriel trudged into the woods, cut down some small trees, and dragged them back to cover the hole. When they reached it, Esther was in the hole. She looked up at them, her bright blue eyes dancing with excitement. She held up an ancient sword and said, "Look!"

She handed it to Michael and he and Gabriel examined it carefully. It had been wrapped in some kind of tapestry and it was made out of a type of metal that miraculously had not rusted over the years. The golden handle was inlaid with diamonds, rubies and sapphires. The hand guard was of hard silver.

Speaking in a whisper, as though he was afraid someone else might hear him, Michael said, "Gabriel, there's no telling how much this is worth."

Gabriel said, "Michael, Esther, we can't let anyone know about this until we find out what else is down here. Let's rebury this until next Saturday when we'll come back."

They trimmed the trees and laid the trunks across the hole, and then laid branches and brush across them, covering them with a thick layer of dirt, scattering dead leaves and twigs over the entire area until they were finally satisfied that the area looked undisturbed.

They hid their tools in some brush, called their dogs and sailed for home. It was getting late, so they sailed straight for home across the widest expanse of the lake instead of along the shore of Middle Lake. When they were about halfway home the wind began to howl, whipping up the water. The small boat was tossing so badly they had to lower the sail to keep from capsizing, but the boys were strong oarsmen and they sent the small craft gliding over the waves as Esther bailed as quickly as she could.

They were sure they were going to make the dock when a seam in the canvas suddenly ripped apart. The boat started sinking fast and they had to abandon it. They were all good swimmers and always wore swimsuits under their clothing when they were out on the water. They just had time to strip their clothes off and dive into the water before the boat sank.

Esther always wore her favorite tight-fitting leather jacket when in the boat. She was as good a swimmer as the boys were, but the coat hindered her some. The boys swam out ahead of her, reaching the shore far out in front of her. They climbed out and lay down on the green grass to rest.

When Esther didn't appear they became concerned and swam out to find her. As they swam they saw their own two dogs swimming side-by-side in front of Esther's hound. Esther was lying on her back and her big hound had hold of the collar of her leather jacket, pulling her toward the shore. The other two hounds were breaking the water right in front, making it easier for Esther's hound to drag her through the choppy water.

The boys could see that Esther was conscious and as they approached she called, "I got a cramp. I whistled for Wolf and just as I started to go under he latched onto my jacket and pulled me along."

"Thank heaven," said Michael, and he and Gabriel helped their sister to shore.

CHAPTER TWO

The three young people could hardly contain themselves until Saturday, when they could get back to their exploring. They had agreed not to tell their parents about their find until they could explore the underground room more thoroughly.

They thought Saturday would never come. When it finally did, it did not bring with it quite the excitement they had been expecting. As they were at the breakfast table Riley said, "Michael, I bought a stud from a breeder over in County Cork and I want you to go with me to get him."

Michael was desperately disappointed, but he wouldn't let his father know it. Gabriel said, "Dad, you enjoy another cup of tea and we'll saddle the horses." He motioned his brother to meet him outside.

Esther said, "I'll feed the chickens," and ran after her brothers.

When they conferred in the barn, Gabriel and Esther agreed to wait another week so Michael could go with them.

"I would dearly love to go with you," Michael said, appreciative of his siblings' kindness, "but you go on. You two wouldn't be fit to live with if you had to wait another week. Just remember...we split whatever you find, equally."

Esther fed the chickens and gathered the eggs while the boys saddled the horses and took them to the house. She and Gabriel watched as Michael and their dad rode away, knowing how upset Michael was. They headed to the dock where they had their other small sailboat ready to go. They had prepared it before breakfast and would have left then, but they knew Riley would not allow it before their daily devotions and prayer.

CHAPTER THREE

As they loped along Riley noticed that Michael wasn't his usual happy-go-lucky self. He hadn't said a word since they'd told Patricia and the others good by.

"What's bothering you, Michael?" Riley said, "Did you have a date to go riding with that pretty little waitress, Molly O'Casey, today?"

"No, dad, I've dated her a few times, but it's nothing serious, I just kind of wanted to go with Gabriel and Esther to old Ross Castle. We found an underground room that looked interesting last Saturday, but we didn't have time to explore it. They're going to have a look today. I'd like to see what's in there, but taking care of business is more important than having a good time."

Riley knew that Gabriel and Esther had nicknamed Michael "King Ross," so he said, "You're a good son, Michael, and I'm glad you feel that way. But I wish you had told me, son. I could have gone alone, but I like to have one of my sons with me sometimes."

"I like being with you too, Dad. I learn a lot when we're together; I just wanted to be with Gabriel and Esther when they found our fortune." Riley laughed.

They picked up the stud and rode back to the inn at Killarney and ate a late lunch. Molly waited on them.

When she set their corned beef and cabbage, with boiled potatoes and a pot of tea, in front of them she said, "Aren't you taking me to the dance tonight, Michael Ross?"

"What would Pat Donahue say about that? I thought he was your steady," Michael said, smiling.

"Only when you're not around, she said. Are you going to take me or not?"

Sure, I'd be happy to, but I've got to go home and take a bath first. You do want me smelling nice, don't you?"

"I want you any way I can get you, Michael, you know that." She kissed him lightly on the cheek just as Pat Donahue walked in the door.

Pat was big and rawboned, about an inch taller than Michael and twenty pounds heavier. He was also the banker's son, and because of that, acted as if he were better than any of the farmers.

"Michael Ross, you stay away from my lass," he shouted as he approached Michael's table.

Michael said, "I will, Pat, until tonight. I'm taking her to the dance."

Pat turned to Molly and said, "We had a date for tonight! Nobody breaks a date with me and gets away with it."

"You don't own me, Patrick, and I'll go with Michael anywhere I like and any time I like. Now, unless you're going to order something, you get out of here."

Patrick turned back to Michael and said, "Ross, don't you show your face in town tonight if you know what's good for you." Then he stalked out, murmuring all kinds of threats.

When they left the inn Riley said, "She's a bold one, isn't she?"

"She sure is," Michael replied, "and she can really do the Irish jig."

"Is it worth getting your ears boxed off for?" Riley asked, "He's a big lad."

"He never saw the day he could beat me, Dad, after all, look who taught me."

Riley smiled proudly and said, "Maybe we should put the mitts on and spar a few rounds when we get home. To sharpen you up, like."

"Let's do that."

When they got home they did spar a few rounds as Patricia watched. Finally she said, "You can't beat the boys anymore. They're too fast for you."

"True," he said. "I don't think you have to worry too much about the banker's son, Michael, he's big, but he's soft. He won't touch you if you box him right. Patricia, how would you like to go jigging tonight?"

"I'd like it. But I'd much rather see our son whip Pat Donahue."

Riley said, "We'll do the chores and go in early and eat at the inn tonight. We can walk around town for a while until it's time to go to the ball room."

* * * * *

When they walked into the inn at six o'clock, Molly had her bag over her shoulder and she was just leaving. "Mr. and Mrs. Ross, you sure have a couple of handsome sons," she said as she winked at Michael. "Trouble is you never know which one you're out with; they look so much alike."

"We have a daughter who's almost as beautiful as her mother, too," Riley said.

"I see where you get your blarney from, Michael," Molly replied as she slung her bag over her shoulder and walked out the door, swinging her hips.

Patricia remarked, "She doesn't know the half of it. Michael, are you really interested in that floozy?"

"Only to dance with, Mother. And you'll see why tonight. She sure can do the jig."

"Don't judge her too harshly, Mother, I can remember you twisted yours pretty well when you knew I was looking," Riley quipped. They all had a good laugh.

Michael said, "Mother, you're blushing."

"Your Father always did make me blush. And I hope he never stops trying."

"Don't you worry, my sweet; you'll always be the most beautiful lass in the whole wide world. Where you are is where I'll be content to be."

"Take a lesson from your father, Michael," Patricia said, "Never stop feeding your chosen one the blarney even after she's all yours. Can't you see why I still adore this big bruiser of mine? He's been all mine, since the day we met, and we were just little tykes then."

"I hate to admit it, but truer words were never spoken, my love, and I'm eternally grateful I've never known another."

"You two are a treasure," Michael said, "I hope it will be that way for me, but I'm sure not ready for that."

"Be patient, Michael, be patient, you have a lot of living to do. You're too young to take on those responsibilities," Riley said.

At the dance Riley and Patricia danced a few times, and then sat along the wall and watched Michael and Molly.

"Riley, that little floozy can jig, but I sure would hate to see Michael tie up with her."

"They're by far the best dancers on the floor. I can see why Michael likes to dance with her," Riley replied. "You don't have to worry about any of our youngsters, we've taught them right, and they have their feet on the ground, and they'll make us proud. Now, how about you and I go home to see if Gabriel and Esther have made us all rich?"

"We're rich already, as far as I'm concerned."

"Well, yes, but not money wise."

Riley told Michael and Molly that they were going to call it a day and they would see them in church in the morning.

When they started to leave they heard Molly say, "I don't go to church because I usually work on Sunday. But I'm off tomorrow, so if you'll pick me up, I'll go with you."

"I'll pick you up at ten," Michael told her.

"Michael, I've been working here a long time and I get some privileges. If you promise to be my steady boyfriend I'll go to church with you every Sunday."

"I don't go with anyone else now, Molly."

"I know, but you only come to see me when you feel like dancing, I want to be with you all the time."

"I'm sorry, Molly, but I'm just not ready to make that kind of commitment."

"How long would a girl have to wait, Michael Ross?"

"Don't wait for me, Molly, I'm only eighteen and I have a lot of growing up to do before I want to take on that kind of responsibility."

Just then Pat Donahue appeared, trying to cut in on Michael. It was obvious that Pat had too much to drink. His face was flushed, his speech slurred, and his gait was unsteady.

Molly said, "Get lost, Patrick."

Pat almost screamed when he said, "Don't tell me what to do, you little bitch!"

All eyes turned on them, and the room became eerily quiet.

"Go home, Pat, and sleep it off," Michael said calmly, "and hold your filthy tongue."

"Michael Ross, you just come outside and I'll show you what you get for stealing my girl," Pat said

"I'm not your girl, Pat Donahue!" Molly cried.

She followed Pat and Michael outside, obviously thrilled that two big handsome men were fighting over her.

When they got out in the middle of the street Michael said charitably, "Pat, you're drunk. Just apologize to Molly and I won't have to beat the hell out of you."

Pat charged Michael like a raging bull, his head down, fists flailing.

Michael stepped quickly to one side and clipped Pat behind the head. Pat went to his knees. He came up fast, shaking his head to clear it, and approached Michael again.

Michael then threw three quick jabs to Pat's chin, but Pat's chin and jaw were like rock. Pat swung a hard overhand right that caught Michael high on his forehead, and he catapulted backward. Pat threw himself to the ground, hoping to land atop Michael, but Michael was too quick for him. He rolled to his right and when Pat came slowly off the ground Michael hit him with an uppercut that knocked the bigger man back on his rear.

Pat got up on all fours and dove, but Michael danced nimbly away, waiting for Pat to gain his feet. Then he walked in with two quick jabs to the chin, followed with a fist in Pat's solar plexus, which took his breath away. It didn't knock Pat out, but it sobered him up enough that he knew he was licked.

Pat stood up, and when Michael came at him again, Pat held up his hand and said, "You win, Michael."

He turned and looked up at Molly who was sitting on the banister and said, "You have my apology, Molly. You too, Michael, I made a fool of myself. Will you shake my hand?"

He extended his hand and Michael took it. Pat hugged Michael close for a moment then disappeared into the crowd.

Everyone went back to the dance for more fun. Molly said, "Michael, will you take me home now"?

They walked the few blocks to Molly's house and sat on the swing on her front porch. Michael hadn't said a word since he agreed to take her home. He still had a headache from the one time that Pat had hit him high on his head.

Molly slid her arm around Michael's neck and whispered, "Michael, I'll give you anything you want."

Looking deeply into her eyes, Michael said gently, "Molly, you don't have anything I want". He kissed her lightly on the cheek and headed for his horse.

Molly was so shocked that she stood there for a moment. Then she hollered after him, "Run, Michael Ross, you're not a man anyway, you're just a mama's boy."

Michael heard her but ignored it, he knew she'd said it to save her pride, and also knew he'd be every bit a man when the right woman came along. He wanted to have the same loving respect for his wife that his father had for his mother. And he wanted to see the look of love from his wife when they grew old that he saw in his mother's eyes when she looked at Riley tonight, when she blushed like a rose through the wrinkles that were beginning to appear around her eyes and mouth. That was the kind of love Michael longed for from a woman, and he knew he couldn't get it from Molly.

He was pleased with himself as he rode slowly home, singing softly. As he rode along the shore of the lake watching the moon rays dancing across the water, and listening to the music of the waves as they lapped over the rocks along the shore, he felt at peace with the world.

CHAPTER FOUR

When Riley and Patricia got home they weren't overly concerned that Gabriel and Esther weren't there. They knew that sometimes they spent the night on the island and they had their hounds with them. They would sail in early in the morning, soon enough to help with the chores and go to church. They always had before.

They had no close neighbors and no one ever came here this time of night, so Patricia had no shame or fear when she walked nude from her bath into the bedroom. Riley was lying on his back, looking at her as she walked toward him. She crawled up beside her husband and snuffed out the candle.

About two hours later they heard the clippity clop, clippity clop of Michael's horse as he rode up to the stable.

Patricia murmured, "Well, I wonder if he'll be sporting a black eye in the morning."

Riley replied, "I think Pat hit him only the one time he knocked him down, Michael and Gabriel both have beaten him in the ring so many times he won't box them anymore.

"He wouldn't have challenged Michael tonight if he had been sober." They both rolled over and slept soundly.

Michael awoke with a start early the next morning when he heard his father hollering, "Michael, get up, we've got to find Gabriel and Esther."

Michel's hound had awakened Riley and Patricia as he stood whimpering by their bedside. When Riley placed his hand on his wet head he fell to the floor, whimpering like a child, wet and exhausted. Patricia lit a light and they examined the hound and found his paws cut to ribbons and most of his claws were ripped from his paws.

Riley said, "That dog must have been swimming most of the night, and look at his paws—he looks like he's been digging for hours."

Michael's heart beat wildly in his chest. Fear gripped him so he couldn't speak.

Seeing the shock on Michael's face, Riley shook him and said, "What's wrong?"

Michael said, "Ross Castle... hurry! Get the boat ready to sail and I'll get the pickaxes and shovels, we must go now! I'll explain later."

Patricia wanted to go too, but Riley said, "No, mother. You turn the calves into the cows; we'll not be milking this morning."

He turned and ran to get the boat ready to sail. Michael had already gone for the tools.

Patricia handed Riley a basket of bread, cheese and fruit and a jug of water and said, "Hurry!"

As Michael untied the boat, Michael's faithful hound was trying to climb over the side of the boat. Michael picked him up and placed him on a mat in the bow. They cast off and sailed as straight to Ross Castle as they could. There was a good wind blowing and Michael and Riley were gliding over the waves of the lake faster than they ever had before. Soon they were tying up at the dock at old Ross Castle. When Michael and Riley reached the hole they found the other two dogs at the bottom, still, in death. They had cut their paws down to the bone trying to get to their loving masters.

Michael pulled them out of the hole and laid them to one side and Shep lay down beside them whimpering. Michael started enlarging the hole while Riley shoveled the dirt back further.

"Dad, their shovels are missing. If they have them, they'll be digging from the other side. That means we're going to get them out."

"Yes, son, but we must hurry; the air may be almost gone down there."

They worked furiously until they broke through to the bottom of the hole Michael and Gabriel had dug in front of the dungeon door the week before.

There was an old steamer trunk on the floor and Gabriel was holding on to one handle and Esther the other. They must have been almost out of the hole when the old wall came crashing down on top of them, knocking them back down to the bottom of the hole. Riley found them while Michael was keeping the tunnel clear. Michael heard Riley cry, "Oh no! Not my beautiful children!" Then he said, "Get out of here, Michael," and he turned and started pushing Michael out of the tunnel. When they got out into the clean, fresh air, Michael could see his dad's face, white and pasty looking.

Michael said, "Dad, what's wrong? Tell me, what did you find, are they going to be all right?"

Riley didn't answer right away, but he kept gasping as though he were having difficulty getting his breath. Then he crushed Michael to his chest and said, "Oh, Michael, when I found them I went crazy, and the only thing I could think of was getting you out of there. They are gone, Michael. If that tunnel had collapsed on you and we'd lost all three of you, your mother and I would have no reason for living."

These two big men clung together as they poured out the grief that seemed to be suffocating them.

Michael sobbed, "We have to get them out and take them home for burial."

Shep stayed by his two dead companions as Riley went back to the boat and Michael followed him. Michael watched as his father reached under the seat near the tiller and pulled out a bottle of Irish whiskey. He turned it up and took a huge swallow, then offered it to Michael.

Michael had been drunk a few times, but had decided long ago that he didn't much like it. He hadn't had anything alcoholic to drink in over a year. When he hesitated to take the bottle his father commanded, "Drink the rest of it!"

Michael grabbed the bottle, and emptied it. As the burning liquid hit his stomach he was glad the bottle had nearly been empty when his dad handed it to him.

Riley said, "Michael, sit down. I wish you didn't have to see this, son, but I need your help. I don't want your mother to see them this way. She'll probably be angry with me for a while for not bringing them home, but at least she can remember them as they were."

He reached and took both of Michael's hands in his, "Michael, they found an iron chest and they were bringing it out when the wall fell, crushing both of their heads as flat as your hand between the chest and the wall."

As a cry escaped Michael's lips, Riley embraced his son and said, "It's all right, son, let it out, let it all out." And he did; he sobbed so hard Riley could barely hold him. When he finally got some control he stammered, "Dad, what do you want me to do?"

"Come," Riley said, and he led Michael back and they picked up two shovels and walked away from the castle about a hundred yards, and under the branches of a large maple tree, dug a grave. When they finished they went to the boat and retrieved their spare sail and ripped it in half.

They took it back to the hole, where they lovingly removed the bodies. Then they wrapped each of them in the canvas. They covered the bottom of the grave with stones, and then gently lowered Gabriel and Esther into the grave, side by side. They placed stones all around their bodies, covering them completely. As they were shoveling the dirt back into the grave, Michael asked, "Dad, why did you cover them with rocks?"

"If a pack of hungry wolves dig down this deep, I don't want them to be able to mutilate their bodies."

When they finished filling the grave they took two of the largest stones they could carry and placed them as headstones.

As they started to leave Michael asked, "Dad, aren't you going to pray over them?"

"Not now, son, I just can't do it."

Riley turned wearily and trudged back to the boat, carrying the weight of his sorrow on his drooping head and shoulders.

Michael removed his hat, bowed his head, and prayed quietly, "Lord God, let the breeze blow softly here and may the birds sing sweetly, and may they hear the angels sing as the wind whispers through the trees."

Then he said, "Good bye, Gabriel, good bye, little sister," and he went to where Riley was waiting for him in the boat.

"Wait a little longer, dad, I'm going to bury Rover and Daisy at Gabriel and Esther's feet."

Riley nodded.

Michael buried the dogs and when he returned to the boat he noticed that while he was burying the dogs Riley had gone back into the hole and had drug the chest onto the boat. Lying beside it was the sword Gabriel had re-wrapped in the tapestry.

As soon as he stepped into the boat Riley steered it out into the lake and the wind filled the sails, carrying them home.

CHAPTER FIVE

After Patricia watched Riley and Michael sail out of sight as they went to search for Gabriel and Esther, she went into the house and dropped to her knees. After praying, she forced herself to eat. She knew that if the calves got too much rich milk it would make them sick and the cream and milk they sold was their source of ready cash. She hoped that if she kept busy she wouldn't worry herself sick.

She milked all thirty cows, fed the chickens and gathered the eggs, then she went into the kitchen to prepare the soup Riley had requested, but her heart wasn't in it. She went back into her bedroom, threw herself down on the bed and cried herself into exhaustion.

She stood for hours on the shore, staring out across the lake, seeing nothing. It started to rain, but she stood there until she was wet to her skin and chilled to the marrow. Finally she turned and trudged wearily up to the house. Her brain was dull from worry as she automatically undressed, bathed her aching body, and put on her warmest clothes. When she walked out on the porch the sun was shining and a glimmer of hope sprang anew in her heart when she saw the boat skimming across the water, headed straight for the dock

She flew down the steps and stood bathed in the late afternoon sun, waiting for her beloved Riley and Michael to bring her news. She saw Riley drop the sail and watched as Michael rowed the boat in to be tied up at the dock.

Michael's old hound struggled out of the boat and limped up to her, collapsing at her feet.

Riley came up and took her in his arms. Before he could speak she said, "I know, Riley, and I have already shed all the tears. My children are gone."

"Yes, my love," he said, and led her back to the house.

When Riley walked away from the dock, half carrying Patricia, Michael took all the tools and put them in their proper place, then dragged the old chest into the tool shed and covered it with canvas. The sword he hid under his bed.

Michael marveled at the strength of his father, and the love that flooded his heart for his mother and father almost choked him. He knew that his father's heart was breaking, but he had held Michael close as he sobbed his heart out. Now he was supporting his mother. So far, he himself had not shed a tear. Michael knew it would come like a river in flood, but it would be some time when Riley was where his family wouldn't witness it.

Michael whispered, "Dear God, make me half the man he is and I'll be grateful."

His dog hadn't moved since he lay down on the dock and now Michael picked him up and took him to the house. There he heated water and cleaned his cutup front paws and put a soothing ointment on them. Wrapping them in clean white sheeting, Michael laid his beloved dog on a blanket near the stove to warm his chilled, worn out body.

When sleep finally came to the three Ross's, it came because their exhausted bodies demanded it.

When the roosters awoke them, the first thing Michael did was to check on his dog. Shep had been his constant companion since he was six years old. Michael had camped out many nights and slept without fear of anything because he knew Shep was near. He had rolled on the floor as a boy with Shep when he was a pup. The bond of love between them was a beautiful thing to behold. Now Michael's grief was compounded because Shep didn't respond to his call. Like his two companions, he had given his life trying to save Gabriel and Esther.

Michael picked him up gently and carried him up on the mountainside and buried him alongside mother and father, two Wolfhounds who had served the Ross family as faithfully as Shep had. The dog grave site was filling up.

Michael went about his morning chores in a stupor. He did his work, not really caring about any of it. It was something he had to do. He could hardly bear the thought of staying here without Gabriel and Esther.

When he poured the milk into the water separator on the back porch, his father stepped off the porch with his crossbow in his hand, and his knife in its sheath on his belt, and started for the woods up on the mountain.

Minutes later Patricia came out on the porch and said, "Michael, dear, get your weapons and follow your dad, but don't let him know. I know he'd never hurt himself, but the load of grief he's carrying right now might cause him to become careless and fall off a cliff or something. I couldn't bear to lose one of you, too."

"All right, mother, but don't worry about dad, he's the strongest man I know."

"I know he is, son, but go."

Michael was already going down the back steps. He saw his dad enter a thick stand of pines on the trail that ran along the creek where they often went fishing. He was sure he knew where his father was going to pour out his grief and anger. He would circle around and watch over Riley from the top of Bee Rock Cliff that overlooked the forest glade where he was sure he would find him.

When Michael finally reached his destination he took his knife from its sheath and stuck it in the ground and sat down next to it with his back to a tree. His crossbow lay just in front of him with a new arrow in place.

He saw his dad a hundred and fifty feet away, with his back to a large cottonwood tree with his weapons exactly like Michael had his. After all, Michael thought, it was Riley who had taught him to do this.

Michael would never let his dad know that he'd seen his massive shoulders shaking as he sobbed out his grief. All of a sudden he saw his dad stand up and shake his fist at the sky. Riley's booming voice echoed back from the canyon walls when he shouted, "God, I hate you for taking our beautiful children from us and casting my beautiful Patricia and Michael into such despair!"

Then he fell on his face and dug his big work-worn hands into the leafy soil and sobbed out his misery. When he finally got up and went down to the stream to wash his face, Michael looked up and said, "Father God, I know you understand."

When Riley came back and retrieved his weapons he looked up to where Michael was sitting and called, "You can come down now, son."

Shocked, Michael hurried to where his father was waiting for him. "How did you know I was up there?" he said. "I was very quiet and I was never going to let you know I was watching over you."

"Michael, I knew your mother would send you. Mothers are like that, and she is the best, Michael boy."

"I know, dad. I'm so blessed to have you both. I don't think I could get through this without you."

"You would, Michael, you are as strong as these mountains, and don't ever doubt yourself."

When they got back to the house Patricia set a platter of ham and eggs on the table and they ate.

CHAPTER SIX

The days seemed to drag by as the three of them went about their daily tasks. Riley tried to convince Michael that hard work was what he needed and that time would help heal the wounds, but Michael was struggling.

One day when he and his dad were hauling hay to the feedlot, Riley noticed that Michael was staring off into space. Then suddenly, Michael screamed and leaped off the wagon and started running toward the lake.

Riley jumped off the wagon and ran after him, but soon realized he couldn't catch him. "Michael! We've lost two of our children already, we can't lose you too!"

Michael stopped and walked slowly back into his father's outstretched arms. Riley held him as he broke down. When Michael had composed himself he said, "Dad, I killed them! I killed my twin brother and my little sister! How can you and mother forgive me? How can I ever forgive myself? They offered to wait for me and I told them to go ahead and make us all rich. They'd have waited if I'd told them to. I killed them, Dad, it's all my fault."

Riley shook him hard and said, "Michael! You have nothing to feel guilty about. I've asked myself over and over again why I asked you to go with me that day instead of Gabriel. If I hadn't asked you to go with me we might have lost all three of you. That would surely have killed your mother and me. You give us something to live for. Your mother is doing a better job than we are of putting our loss in perspective. She's put it behind her enough to start looking to the future and we must too. Can't you see, son... losing you would kill her?"

"I'm sorry, dad. I've been so wrapped up in my own pain I didn't give much thought to what you and mother were going through."

"Michael, you heard me tell God I hated him, but I don't, I love Him above all else. He's a father too and he understood my anger, just like he understands yours. I've asked his forgiveness, and you must too. We don't understand why God allows one to die and the other to live, but there has to be a reason. We're still alive, Michael, you and me and your mother. It's time we started acting like it."

Six miserable, soul-searching and heart-wrenching months had gone by when Michael went to Riley and asked him why he had gone back into the hole and dragged the chest out.

Riley said, "I forgot about that chest. Gabriel and Esther gave their lives to get that chest out of there, so I thought we should at least see what they died for. Where is the chest? I've not seen it since it was on the boat."

"I put it in the tool shed and covered it with a piece of canvas."

"Michael, it'll take us a couple more days to get this hay stacked. When we finish, we'll go back and see if there is anything else in that underground room. If there's nothing else, we'll fill the hole in. But don't tell your mother what we're going to do. She hasn't mentioned going there, and I don't want her to unless she tells me otherwise."

Three days later Patricia said to Riley, "Sweetheart, would you hitch old Dolly to the cart? I want to go shopping today."

As soon as she was out of sight, Riley and Michael put the tools in the boat and sailed to Ross Castle.

When they got there they wasted no time, but went right to the hole and found it just as they'd left it. There was evidence that wolves had been there, but it was undisturbed otherwise.

Riley firmly forbade Michael from going into the place, but he took a torch and searched the underground room thoroughly. He found nothing except an old helmet and shield. He told Michael it looked like it was a storeroom where armor was kept.

They went to work and filled the hole as quickly as they could. When they went to the grave they found it just as they had left it. Michael said, "Listen, dad, it sounds like soft music and singing."

"That's the wind passing through the pines. One of our poets wrote that it's so beautiful here the angels come here to play. If you let your imagination run wild you can hear your favorite hymn set to music."

They stood in comfortable silence for a while until Michael said, "Dad, why don't we throw some lines out and troll a while on our way back. We haven't had any fresh fish for a long time."

"Good idea, you row slowly along the shore for a ways and I'll net us some fresh bait," Riley said.

It wasn't long before they had a couple of lines strung out behind the boat, baited with live perch. They were sailing at a pretty good clip when a large bass took the bait. Michael pulled him alongside the boat and Riley had just hooked and pulled him in, when another even larger bass sailed out of the water, hooked to the other line.

When they got it safely aboard Michael cleaned them and Riley turned the sails to catch more wind. They were tying up at their home dock in what seemed like no time at all.

* * * * *

Patricia hadn't been in town in a long time, so she treated herself to a good meal at the pub and bought herself a new dress before she did her grocery shopping. When she drove up to the house and tied her mare to the hitching rail at about six o'clock, Michael met her and took the groceries into the house. She retrieved her new dress and said, "Smells like your dad's cooking fish. You men go fishing today?"

"Yup, we decided if you were going to leave us all day we'd play hooky."

When she went into the house she kissed Riley on the cheek and he said, "Supper will be ready in about twenty minutes."

She disappeared into the bedroom and donned her new dress, pinched her cheeks for color, and walked into the kitchen.

Michael said, "Well, look at you, mum! Don't you look great?"

Riley had just put a bowl of cream gravy on the table and he turned around. Forgetting that his son was in the room, he walked toward his wife, took her in his arms and gave her a long, lingering kiss...the first in six months. They came untangled when Michael let out a long whistle.

After supper Michael said, "The chores are all done, you two love birds sit on the porch and watch the sunset and I'll wash the dishes and clean the kitchen."

When he finished he went in and took a bath, put on his best clothes and walked out onto the porch. His mother and dad were standing near the porch banister holding hands, looking out over the water as the rays from the setting sun danced over them.

His mother said, "I'd forgotten how beautiful our sunsets are."

Michael slipped between them and put an arm around each of them saying, "I think I'll go to the dance tonight."

Riley said, "I was your age when I reached for the moon, but the night your mother agreed to be mine, I caught a star and it has never grown dim. Michael, go find your star."

"It's time, Michael," his mother said.

As he rode his horse by the porch Riley hollered, "Have a good time, son."

When he was gone, Riley and Patricia strolled along the shore of the lake, holding hands as they had so many times over the years. It was the first time in a long time now, and as they turned to go back to the house, Patricia said, "I feel like a bride again."

Riley said, "Welcome home, my love."

Later, as they lay in each other's arms, Patricia said, "I bought iris bulbs today, tomorrow I'd like you to take me to Ross Castle so I can plant them over Gabriel and Esther."

Riley kissed her and said, "Done." Then smiling roguishly he added, "Honey, it's been a long while; How about one more and then we'll get some sleep?"

She nestled in his arms and said, "I was wondering if you still had it in you."

"Never fear, dear," he said, and he proved his point.

When morning came Michael went into the kitchen just before breakfast and said, "Old Belle is getting ready to drop her foal."

Riley said, "Patricia, we'll have to put off our trip for a few days."

"It's just as well. I have a few more beans to put up and the bulbs will keep."

Michael and Riley stayed with Belle until she dropped her foal, a beautiful bay filly.

Patricia watched it frolic around the corral a bit, and then called her men in for lunch.

While they were eating they decided to go out and open the iron chest they'd brought from old Ross Castle. Eager to see what was in the chest, Patricia didn't even clear the table.

They went to the shed and Michael slid the chest up close to the workbench. Riley took a hammer and chisel and broke the old rusty lock and then pried off the lid with a crowbar.

Riley said, "Mother we're going to give you the privilege of discovering the contents of the chest."

Patricia carefully laid a number of folded strips of fine, colorful tapestry on the workbench. Then she lifted a small wooden box from the bottom of the chest. When she lifted the lid she gasped, and she couldn't keep the thrill out of her voice when she poured out fifty gold coins with Julius Caesar's image on them and said, "Look! Look!"

Michael scooped them up in his hands and let them trickle slowly back onto the tapestry and said in awe, "Would you look at that! And they look like they were minted yesterday."

Riley said, almost in a whisper, as though he was afraid someone else might hear, "We must tell no one about this discovery. We have a small fortune in our hands and there are many men and women that would kill for much less. Our good friend, William O'Casey, deals in rare coins and all kinds of old things. He's an honest man and he'll handle these things for us for a fair price." He took a clean white handkerchief from his pocket and wrapped the coins in it carefully.

"We'll get someone to take care of our stock for a few days and take these things to William and get them sold as soon as possible." Excitement started to build in Riley and he grabbed Patricia and hugged her, and then turned and squeezed Michael and said, "Folks, we are rich beyond our fondest dreams!"

"Thanks to Gabriel and Esther; I wish they were here to help us spend it," Michael remarked.

* * * * *

Two days later they entered O'Casey's shop in Dublin, but when they walked in there wasn't anyone in sight. They walked up to the counter and Riley boomed out, "Is William O'Casey here?"

A short, pudgy man in his early sixties walked in from a back room. His head was as bald as a billiard ball. When he saw who was in his shop, a broad smile spread across his face and he cried, "Riley Ross, and Patricia, what a sight you are to these old eyes of mine! And here's Michael, or is it Gabriel? I never could tell them apart. Callie and I was just discussin' yesterday payin' you a visit. We're thinkin' about retirin' to a little place near Killarney."

He lifted the swinging part of the counter and said, "Good friends, come into the parlor where we'll be more comfortable."

When they were in the small sitting room, O'Casey said, "Callie, come out and see whose come callin'."

When she came out she looked like she was his twin sister instead of his wife. She and Patricia hugged and Callie said, "You're just in time for tea and scones." Then she disappeared back into the kitchen.

After the tea and scones, Callie and Patricia disappeared into a bedroom where Patricia told Callie about the loss of Gabriel and Esther.

Callie said, "You poor dear," and she held Patricia as they both had a good cry.

Riley told O'Casey about their loss, and then got down to business. "William, we think that Gabriel and Esther discovered something at old Fort Ross that may be very valuable." Riley showed his friend the pieces of fabric.

O'Casey studied them carefully, then said, "Riley, I've never dealt in fabrics, but I'm sure there is a market for them. I've a friend in London that can tell us what they're worth."

"You haven't seen it all yet," Michael said, and he pulled a leather pouch out of his coat pocket and poured the fifty gold coins onto the fabric.

O'Casey took a magnifying glass and his excitement mounted as he studied the coins. His eyes were bulging, and when he could get his voice he said, "Riley, you're a rich man! There's a fast sailing ship in the harbor that's sailin' for London in the mornin'. You and I should be on her. We need to get these in safe keeping as soon as possible. I've handled coins like these before, but nothing in such mint condition as these are. I really don't know what these are worth, but they will at the exchange in London. I do know that my ten percent will make it possible for Callie and me to retire and enjoy life to its fullest!"

Riley said, "How long will it take us to get back here?"

"Three weeks at least; maybe longer."

The women rejoined them and Riley told Patricia that he'd be leaving in the morning with O'Casey for London and he would be home as soon as possible. "I want you and Michael to go home and wait for me there, and if anybody asks for me, tell them I've gone to London on business. That's no lie, either."

Callie said, "William, Patricia has invited us to spend some time with them, so I'll go home with them and wait for you there."

"That's fine, and when we get back from London I'll call the broker and tell him to sell this place to O'Shannon at his price, and when that transaction is completed I'll join you there."

Michael, Patricia and Callie saw them off for London early the next morning and an hour later they were sailing back down the canal for the Shannon River and home.

* * * * *

When Riley and O'Casey had the items appraised, Riley was astounded at the price. They were offered a fair amount then and there, but O'Casey was a wise dealer. They left them at the Antique Exchange for safekeeping and O'Casey took Riley to his most trusted counterpart in London to show him the appraised value for the items. O'Casey introduced him to Riley as Robert Ryan, the most honorable antique dealer in London.

Ryan suggested they let him contact twenty of the wealthiest dealers in London and auction off the coins and tapestries, starting at the appraised price. "My fee will be twenty percent of anything over the appraised price." He added, "It will take me two or three weeks to set this up."

Riley said, "That sounds good to me, and that'll give William time to show me some of the sights. We'll keep in touch so you can advise us when and where to appear for the auction."

It was three weeks to the day when the auction was held at the Exchange where they had left their wares.

The Ross family became moderately wealthy at the stroke of a gavel.

Riley had a comfortable nest egg already, so he invested the money at a couple of investment houses in Dublin. When Riley and William got home and showed Michael and their wives how much money they had, it made them a little giddy thinking about it.

Michael said, "Dad, mother, there's something I haven't shown you," and he went to his bedroom and brought out the sword. "Gabriel and Esther gave their lives for these things. I'd like to keep the sword for myself." They marveled at the beauty of this magnificent piece of artistic craftsmanship and agreed that by all means Michael should have it to treasure.

CHAPTER SEVEN

Michael walked up the stream that flowed off the mountain in back of their home, and sat down with his back against the same cottonwood his dad had when he'd roared out his anger over the loss of his children. Michael had come here in the solitude of this beautiful place to contemplate what all these riches would mean, and how it would change their lives. Finally, after much soul searching, he resolved that he would live his life as though he had no more than his grandfather had when he'd bought this acreage and built the cottage they lived in.

The O'Casey's decided to stay with the Ross's a few weeks to look over the lay of the land. Their fee for the transaction meant they could retire, and William and Callie had fervently expressed their desire to live somewhere around Killarney near their good friends. This would give them the time to find what they wanted. Maybe they would buy a small place where William could run a few sheep

The following morning two marble tombstones were delivered to the farm, with Gabriel's and Esther's names, and dates of their births and deaths engraved upon them.

Patricia wanted to go to old Ross Castle the next day to place the stones and plant the irises on the grave site. She hadn't gone there to grieve over her lost children, but knew that the emotional scars had healed enough that she could do it now without going all to pieces.

That evening Riley said to Michael, "Son, do you think you could take care of things for a few days while your mother and I tend to the grave site?"

"I would be happy to, but we might want to get someone else to take care of things here. Then I could go and help you with those head stones—they're pretty heavy."

"I can handle them, son, and I would feel more at ease if you were here. Besides, your mother and I kind of want to be alone for a few days."

"I understand, dad. The O'Casey's will need a guide while they're here anyway. I'll enjoy that."

The next morning as Michael and Riley were loading the boat Riley said, "We'll be home the morning of the fifth day, if not sooner."

Presently Michael and the O'Casey's stood on the shore and waved as Patricia and Riley sailed away over smooth waters.

As they got out on the water what little wind there had been died. This was almost unheard of on these lakes. Riley had to row most of the way but he was a strong oarsman and they reached the castle long before dark. Riley took one of the gravestones on his massive shoulders and led Patricia to the grave site. He placed the stone near the rock that he and Michael had placed, then stood and put his arms around Patricia as she wept softly. She reached up and kissed him and said, "You go get the other headstone and let me talk to my babies for a while."

He squeezed her shoulder and went back to the boat. Before he picked up the stone, he swung the sack of Iris bulbs and a small shovel over one shoulder, lifted the stone onto the other, and went back to Patricia.

She was on her knees cleaning the leaves and twigs from the grave. While Riley was placing the headstones, Patricia started planting the Iris bulbs. He left her there and went and pitched their small tent, set up the camp stove, and put water on to boil for tea.

When he went back to Patricia he saw the pattern she had made in planting the bulbs, so he took the shovel and dug the rest of the holes. The planting went quickly.

Wiping soil from her hands, Patricia stood up and said, "It will be lovely in a couple of years; you picked a beautiful spot for our babies to rest."

They fished on and off for three days, but mostly walked through the woods hand-in-hand, content just to be together. They sat in a grove of tall pine trees, watching in awe as the sun sifted down through the branches, casting changing shadows and small spots of bright light that hit the wet leaves, shimmering like sparkling diamonds.

They were sitting quietly, feasting on the beauty all around them, when Patricia softly said, "The wind passing through the trees sounds like music keeping time with the singing of the birds." It's so peaceful here." She squeezed Riley's hand and added, "I'm so glad that you buried them here on this island they loved so much. I know we have to go home tomorrow, and I'd ask you to stay a few more days, but Michael would worry too much. He's lost so much and he's nowhere near over the hurt yet, I still see him staring into space, and if you hadn't been so strong and kept him working hard and long, he might never have gotten over it."

"Don't underestimate him, mother, he's your son, and he has your quiet gentle nature, but he has strength from both of us. No matter what comes his way, his deep faith in God will help him handle it. There'll be other lows in his life, but he'll pass through the valleys, to come out on the mountaintops, stronger for them. Don't you worry about Michael, but if you want to go home tomorrow, its home we go."

They had discussed what they would do with their riches and decided they would lease out their land and travel for the next few years, if this pleased Michael, but this was where they wanted to grow old and live out their lives.

They ate a leisurely breakfast the next morning and lingered over their last cup of tea. While Patricia cleaned up the camp, Riley struck the tent and loaded the boat.

When Riley stepped into the boat to cast off, he was unaware that a nail had torn a hole in the side of the boat inside of the fish tank that held a hundred gallons of water. When he pushed the boat away from the dock the nail ripped a six-inch tear and the water gushed in. There was a good wind blowing and the sails caught the wind, moving Riley and Patricia swiftly out into deep water. As the waves got larger, so did the tear in the fish tank. By the time the water overflowed the fish tank it was too late, the tear had ripped wide open and there was no way they could bail the water out fast enough.

Riley tried to steer the boat back to the island, but it was sinking rapidly.

A large wave hit them and the rope on the sail arm broke. It swung around viciously, striking Patricia in the head, knocking her unconscious into the water. Riley dove in after her. She had gone under, but he saw her long strands of red hair floating up like ferns. He swam toward her and grasped her collar, then started swimming back toward Ross Castle. Rough waves pounded his face and water forced its way into his laboring lungs. His mighty strength failed as he pressed on, murmuring to Patricia and begging God's help. He felt his legs go numb, then his arms. He whispered, "God, give Michael strength," as he and his beloved Patricia sank into the depths of the lake.

* * * * *

Michael went into Killarney the day his parents left and bought two nine-month-old Irish wolfhounds. They were already house broken, so he began teaching them to sit, stay, heel and fetch. He took them into the mountains with the old dogs to teach them to hunt the wolf and elk.

When his mother and dad failed to show by the sixth day, Michael and the O'Casey's became concerned. The only boat they had left was a one-man skiff, which was far too small to go to the island in. The waves were tossing high on the lake and Michael figured perhaps Riley had decided to wait for calmer waters. But when his parents didn't return the next day when the lake was calm, he couldn't wait any longer. Fear gripped him.

Knowing that his friend, Joseph O'Callahan, had a sturdy fishing vessel, Michael saddled his horse to go ask Joseph to take him to look for his parents. Mister O'Callahan was just approaching the boat when Michael rode up and explained his concern.

Joseph said, "Take your horse home and we'll be tying up to your dock by the time you get him unsaddled."

Michael and William took food and plenty of drinking water and their dogs, and stepped in the boat. Soon they were skimming over the water faster than Michael ever had. He congratulated Joseph for his wisdom in purchasing the schooner.

"Thanks, Michael, the salesman said this was the fastest boat ever built for river and lake travel, and I believe him. I'm very pleased with it so far."

When they reached the dock at old Ross Castle and there was no boat visible, Michael felt terror seize him again. They tied up and went to the grave site, where they found the headstones in place and the iris bulbs planted around the grave. His parents' tent and camp gear was gone, so Michael knew that meant they had headed home. Each of the four men took a dog and went in opposite directions. They spent the better part of the day combing the whole island. They found no evidence of them anywhere.

When Michael gave up the search and returned to the dock, Joseph was down on his knees reaching into the water. When he stood up he was holding a small piece of soaked pitch-covered canvas in his hand. When Michael saw it his heart sank. They sailed quickly to Middle Island where the old monastery was, and Michael sent the dogs out to find his parents.

They walked the island until it was too dark to see, but all the dogs had returned and Michael was satisfied that they weren't on this island either.

Joseph placed his hand on Michael's shoulder and said softly, "We'll have to come back in the morning and run the shorelines to see if we can find a capsized boat somewhere."

Michael spent a restless night, praying most of the time that by some miracle they would find them safe somewhere. He knew that there were old dead trees sticking out of the water in some places, maybe they were in one of those.

They were out by daylight the next morning. They circled the island in Middle Lake, but found nothing. When they were sailing on the backside of the island in Lower Lake they saw the sails from the boat tangled up in stubs of an old tree that was almost completely submerged.

Michael dropped to his knees and cried, "Lord, how can I bear this?"

William O'Casey put his arms around Michael and said, "Callie and I will help you through this."

Joseph said, "I'll take you home, Michael, and you do what you have to do. Leave the finding of them to me. Rest assured I'll find them."

"Thank you. Please let me know as soon as you know anything. We'll bury them alongside of Gabriel and Esther, where mom's irises will grow."

Joseph dropped Michael and William at the dock and Michael went straight to his room and threw his tired, aching body across the bed and cried himself to sleep.

The O'Casey's never disturbed him, but there was one of them near his door at all times.

Two days later Michael came out of his bedroom. He hadn't shaved for nearly a week, but even the heavy beard couldn't hide how haggard he looked. "It's time I started acting like a man," he told Callie. "I'm going to walk up stream and take a bath and shave off this miserable beard. When I get back I'm going to cook a slab of ham and a dozen eggs and drink a gallon of hot tea with about a cup of honey in it, and fried bread, if we have any."

"We have," Callie said, "And Michael, you tell me how long it'll be before you're ready, and I'll have your food ready."

When Michael was devouring the good food that Callie set before him, she told him that William had hired two men to take care of Michael's stock and bring in the last of the hay.

"Bless him," Michael replied, "The cows' udders would have been ruined if they hadn't been milked."

"William knew that. He's no farmer, so he hired these men, and he said they seemed to know what they're doing."

Joseph O'Callahan sailed up to Michael's dock the next morning and Michael and William went down to meet him. The look on his face told Michael he'd found his parents' bodies.

Michael said, "Can I see them?"

"No, Michael, you don't want to see them. They were in the water too long . . .you wouldn't recognize them. I have them wrapped and bound in rolls of new canvas, and my sons are digging a common grave like the one you and your father dug for Gabriel and Esther. By the time we get there the grave will be ready."

Michael took a moment to tell Callie and she wanted to go too, so as soon as she donned her bonnet, they sailed. Before the sun set Michael had buried all that remained of his family.

They returned to Michael's dock where he turned to William and Callie and said, "I thought I had no more tears, but, but...can you stay for a few days?"

Callie hugged him and said, "As long as you need us."

Michael went into his room and poured his heart out to his Heavenly Father. "Thank you, Lord, for the years you gave me Gabriel and Esther to grow up with, and for my mother and father who guided me to your loving care. Now you are the only father I have and I'll be calling on you often."

He knew it would take time for peace to come, but at least he felt like he was ready to face the world. He was only nineteen years old, but he had grown up considerably in the last few months. He resolved to become as much of a man as his dad had been. He doubted he would ever reach that lofty goal, but he was determined to give it his best.

He could smell the corned beef and cabbage Callie was cooking, and he realized he hadn't been able to eat much for days now, and he was ravishingly hungry.

Callie had cooked Michael's favorite meal, with a creamy chocolate pie for dessert, hoping it would bring him out of his room, but he really came out because he had resolved to be the best man he could be.

Michael tore into the meal with gusto, and after the dishes were put away, the three of them sat on the verandah and enjoyed the beautiful picture nature painted in the lake every afternoon. Callie said, "I could spend the rest of my life here. I could never get tired of viewing this scene."

"I know what you mean, dear," William said. Then, turning to Michael he said, "I know this may not be the best time, but I was wondering if you'd consider selling us a small plot of your land."

Michael said, "I was just going to tell you that I've been selfish long enough in keeping you away from your home and that you should feel free to go or stay. It would please me no end if you'd move in here with me until I get my feet on the ground and figure out what I'm going to do with the rest of my life."

"Nothing would make me happier," Callie said. "I love to cook, and any cook likes to see someone enjoy her cooking. And the way you two ate tonight, I'd say you definitely like my cooking."

William said, "Callie and I have always wanted to live around Killarney, and you offer us free rent in the most beautiful place on earth, who could ask for more? Callie, is there any of our old furniture that you just can't live without?"

"Just my spinet."

William said, "Michael, there's a fellow who has made me an offer on our place and everything in it. And it's really more than it's worth. If we left in the morning we could have everything taken care of in two or three weeks."

"The sooner the better, I'll get mighty tired of my cooking long before that."

The next day they left for home, promising to be back soon.

Michael went to the boat yard and purchased a sleek little craft that, though not new, was in excellent condition and exactly what he wanted. It was delivered to his dock the next morning.

He went to the marble mason and ordered two headstones just like the ones his mother had ordered for her children. Then he went to the inn for lunch and Molly came to wait on him. He noticed she was with child and she was wearing a gold wedding band. "Who's the lucky man, Molly?"

"Do you really think he's lucky, Michael?"

"Yes, and I hope he's making you happy."

"I once thought it was you who'd fulfill all my dreams, Michael. But I knew I could never have you, so I settled for Pat Donahue. Oh, I don't mean that. Pat is good to me and he deserves more. I'll be as happy with him as I could be with any man. But I'll always love you, Michael."

"I'm sorry. But right now I'm not fit for anyone."

"I know" she said, "I heard what happened to your family and I'm so sorry. But I have faith in you. You'll do great things some day, Michael."

"I wish I had your faith. I don't know what I'm going to do."

Molly smiled warmly, "Right now, why don't you have some of our good corned beef and cabbage?"

After she had turned in his order and brought his tea, she said, "Pat's been after me to quit here, saying my working undermines his status at the counting house."

"He's right, Molly. You should quit and take care of your home and baby."

"You're right. But I'll miss this; it's all I know. Still, I've given notice and I'm training a girl to take my place. In fact, she's ready now and I could leave anytime. I've just been putting it off. Here she comes now to relieve me. This meal's on me...for old time's sake," she added.

"Thanks, Molly. And tell Pat hello for me, he's a good man."

"I know. You know, he's never had another drink since the night you beat the devil out of him."

"You tell him I didn't get over the headache he gave me for a week."

"I'll tell him."

She walked away and Michael savored his meal before heading slowly back to his empty cottage. It was almost milking time and he went out to get the push cart that held the cream cans and buckets and was pushing the cart into the milk shed when he saw the hired men coming with the last load of hay. After they put the hay in the loft they put feed in the trough to get ready to milk the cows. Michael didn't even know their names, and he couldn't remember ever seeing them up close before.

He walked into the hallway where they were putting the feed out and introduced himself.

The older man said, "Our sympathies, Mr. Ross. I'm Jack Culpepper, and this is my son, Earl. Mister O'Casey told us that this was a temporary job that might become permanent, and we sure could use the work."

"Mr. Culpepper, I can't do all the work around here myself. Are you satisfied with the arrangements you made with Mr. O'Casey?"

"We haven't been paid anything yet, he said we would have to take that up with you when you got over your grieving."

"If you waited for that you might never get paid."

"Well, Mr. Ross, if we don't get some money soon, we and my wife and the other kids are going to go hungry."

Michael said, "I could use one more hand, do you know of a good man for hire?"

"I have an eighteen-year-old, James, who'll graduate from high school in a week. He's worked in the fields since he was a little tot, and can milk a cow with the best of them.

"Mr. O'Casey tells me that you two are good workers. So, Mr. Culpepper, I'll pay you overseer's wages and your boy's journeyman wages at the going rate. How's that sound?"

"It's a very generous offer, sir, and I accept it gratefully."

They figured out how much they had coming, and Michael went to the house and got cash and paid each man. When they finished settling up Michael said, "Where do you live, anyway?"

"We live in a rented house in Killarney."

"How have you been getting out here each day?"

"Walking."

"Is there some place you can keep horses at night?"

"There's an old stable behind our house."

"Then why don't you take the wagon home with you each night?"

"Mr. Ross, we've looked over the old house that's standing empty in your upper meadow, and there's a good well there. There are three bedrooms in that house, the roof doesn't leak, and there are only two or three cracked windowpanes. That house could be made livable for very little money. If we could move in there we would pay you the same rent we pay where we are."

"As you know, milking is a seven-day-a-week job. If you want to get your family out there and fix the place up you can live there free of charge. I only expect you to work five days a week, except for the chores that just have to be done on Saturday and Sunday. I don't care how you divide up the work. Or, if your younger two who are still in school want to milk the cows weekends and give the rest of you a break, that's all right too, as long as you or Earl is here to see that they do it right and you do the stripping."

Jack was almost speechless when he reached for Michael's hand and said, "Thank you, sir."

Michael helped them milk the cows, and told them he would help them at times, and said, "Jack, tomorrow I want you to go into town with me and I'll show you where to take the cream and eggs to market. There'll be times I won't be able to. When I'm not here, that will be your responsibility."

CHAPTER EIGHT

Three days later the marble headstones were delivered and Michael had the delivery man put them in his boat, and the next day he had James go with him to help him put them in place.

Saturday morning Michael went into his father's study and started going through his desk. He found his account books and saw they were kept in a neat hand with big, bold letters and numbers. After spending six hours going over the books, he learned that the income from the farm would cover the wages he had agreed to pay the Culpeppers, take care of the expenses for him and the O'Caseys, with a little left over, even after taxes. He wouldn't have to touch the sizable sum that Riley had accumulated unless something unforeseen occurred. He also found the records indicating the amount he had in the investment house in Dublin. He realized that his family had left him very well off.

He decided he would rebuild their church. The old building had become an eyesore in the countryside. It would take a bit of the money they received for the coins and tapestry, but he could afford it. He began to have second thoughts about giving the church so much, but the Lord had laid it on his heart, and he would obey the Master.

He found a will handwritten by Riley, leaving everything to Michael if anything happened to him and Patricia, and a note saying that the will was recorded in the Killarney Town House.

Michael knew he should keep busy, but he was going to let the Culpepper's run things for a while and take some time to reflect and try to figure out what he wanted to do with his life. Marriage some day, of course, but right now that was on the back roads of his mind. Tomorrow he was going to take his dogs and go fishing.

The next morning broke bright and clear, which was rare this time of year in southern Ireland. There was a good wind and by daybreak he was skimming over the bluish-green water, headed for Ross Castle.

He went to the grave site and gave in to self-pity. He cried out, "Dear Lord, I have never gone fishing without one or all of my family," and the tears began to flow. He didn't know how long he sat here crying, but he felt better.

Michael had loved the work on the farm—the tilling of the soil and the sowing of the fields. He loved to watch the crops grow to maturity.

He strolled through the pine forest where he, Gabriel and Esther spent so many happy hours reminiscing about days gone by. This is where he would come when he wanted to be alone, just to commune with nature, and his God, to listen to nature sing. He sat down on a log and tried to bring the good times back, and the singing in the trees, but he couldn't hear it any more. The light had gone out of his life. He wondered if he could really stay here where everything he saw or touched reminded him of what he could never have again.

Shaking himself, he got up from the log and trudged back to his boat. He halfheartedly got out his fishing gear, drifted out on the lake, and sailed around the island, trailing two lines behind him.

The fish were feeding with frenzy and they kept him busy for a while, but it wasn't fun any more. He didn't hear Esther squealing with glee, or the hearty peal of Gabriel's laughter.

When he pulled his lines in and cleaned the fish and put them away, he had a number of good lake trout and a few bass. He headed home to give the fish to the Culpeppers; he didn't feel like cooking them.

The O'Caseys returned and they, with their happy spirits, made life a little easier, but Michael couldn't shake himself out of his grief. He saw his loved ones everywhere he went. And the pain of knowing he could never be with them again frequently overwhelmed him.

CHAPTER NINE

A year passed and the farm prospered, but Michael knew it was because of the O'Caseys and the Culpeppers, not anything he'd done. Even with all his wealth, he was lost and miserable.

He no longer saw the beauty that was all around him. Everywhere he went he heard Gabriel and Esther laughing gaily. He often caught himself listening for his mother's "come and get it!" at suppertime. Other times he was sure he heard Riley's booming laughter floating over the waves of the lake. He became so silent and withdrawn that his young hounds began to ignore him. He decided he had to get away from this place before he went mad.

He thought about selling the place to the O'Caseys. He knew they'd love to have it, but he couldn't bring himself to do it. He might want to come back some day.

One morning at the breakfast table Michael said to Callie and William, "You've been like a mother and father to me, and I don't think I could have gotten through this last year without you. I'll always love you for that. I've been giving this a lot of thought and I've decided to go to America and explore the frontier. I'd like you to stay here and run the farm until I get back. You'd have full control and the profit from the farm would be yours. I want to retain ownership though, just in case I want to come back some day."

Callie said, "Oh! Michael, I've read that the Indians on the frontier of

America are very savage, and will kill a white man just for his scalp. Must you go?"

"Michael, I've seen this coming, and it might be wise for you to get away for a while, but come back soon. You have become a son to us. We'll be happy to run the farm for you, but you are too generous," William said.

Michael said, "No, I'm not. I'll feel better having someone I know and love taking care of things, and there's always the possibility I might never return and there isn't anyone I'd rather have the place than you."

They went into Killarney and had a solicitor draw up legal papers for them to sign. Then Michael wrote to the investment house and advised them he was going to America and that when he got established he would let them know where to transfer his account.

He took his two young wolf hounds and his young coal-black Arabian stallion, all of his weapons, a few good books, including his leather-bound Bible, and booked passage on a sturdy sailing vessel for Richmond, Virginia, in the new world called America.

As Michael stood on the deck waving good-bye to the O'Casey's and his beloved Ireland he couldn't keep the tears from slipping down his cheeks.

* * * * *

The ship was well out to sea when Captain Angus Alcott, the owner of the vessel, noticed a young man standing like a statue, looking back at the land that was fading away. Six feet two, he guessed, with broad shoulders, a massive chest, slim waist and narrow hips. His head was bare, revealing a mop of auburn hair that curled over his head.

There is a powerful man, Alcott thought, I wonder what he's running from. As he approached him, Michael turned and Captain Alcott extended his rough seafaring hand and said, "I'm Captain Alcott, owner of this vessel, and I'm glad to have you on board."

Michael shook his hand, surprised at the firm grip coming from a man so small. The Captain was thin, but Michael recognized the man's strength as he looked into the Scotsman's deep blue eyes. The handshake indicated that he was as tough as iron, and as they each took the measure of the other, the captain's gaze never wavered from Michael's sorrowful dark brown eyes.

Michael decided he liked this man as he said, "I'm Michael Ross, and I'm glad to be on board."

Angus was a kindhearted, God-fearing man, and he thought he had never in his life looked into eyes that revealed so much hurt and sadness, but he resolved that before they reached Virginia he would see them smile.

He said, "Son, we could stand here all day trying to see who could out-grip the other, but we have work to do. Would you come to my office? I have something to discuss with you."

He turned and walked swiftly to his quarters. Michael followed him and marveled that even with his own long stride he had difficulty keeping up with the Captain.

When they reached the Captain's quarters, Angus shoved a chair at Michael and said, "Have a seat." Then he swung his chair around to face Michael. "I want to know a little something about you before I offer you a proposition. From the weapons you carry and the clothes you wear I'd judge you come from a well off, well-educated family. I'd also guess your father has spent a considerable amount of time teaching you to use those weapons."

"Captain, the only weapons I've ever used against another human being are these," Michael said, holding up his fists. "And I've never been beaten since my father beat me in the ring when I was seventeen. I'll turn twenty-one before we reach America. I've killed timber wolves and Irish elk with the bow—I never miss what I shoot at. My father said that his prayer was that none of his children would ever have to kill a man, but he also made sure we could do it if we had to."

"Michael, there's a deep sadness in your eyes. What are you running from? Your secret is safe with me, but I must know."

"It'll take some time to tell you the whole story."

"I have a fine Irish first mate by the name of Bill Sweeney who can run this ship as well as I can. It'll take weeks to reach Virginia, I have time."

So Michael told this stranger the whole story; how he lost his family and how he felt responsible for their deaths.

"Michael, you're not responsible," the Captain said sympathetically. "It was their fate—the way they were meant to die."

"That's what my mother and father said when I told them I'd killed Gabriel and Esther. But I haven't been able to shake the guilt."

"I know how you feel, son. I had a son, and if he had lived he would be just your age. Evelyn, my wife, begged me not to leave on a voyage when he came down with a cold. But I had just put every pound I had into purchasing my first ship and it was loaded with goods bound for Portugal, where I was to pick up a load for the West Indies.

"I felt I had to go, and I assured her the boy would be all right. She was carrying our second child at the time and I told her I'd be back before the baby came, that Jacob would be fine.

"Michael, I left her in tears. Jacob didn't get well, his cold developed into pneumonia and she got it from him. When I returned I found they had buried my entire family.

"I blamed myself for years until one day on board ship, when the sea was calm, I was reading my Bible. Romans eight twenty-eight says that all things work together for good to them that love God. My wife loved Him and I love Him and I know I'll see my family in heaven some day. I've never forgotten that verse. I claimed it that day and then I found peace. I've never remarried. Give your life to God, Michael, so you can claim that verse and you will find peace."

"My father read the Bible to us around the breakfast table nearly every day and taught us to love God, and I know I'll see them again some day also. I know that verse well, but I'm afraid I neglected to apply it to my own life. Thank you, Captain."

"Now for my proposition, Michael; I can use a good man and if you'll work on our way across you won't have to pay your fare, or for your animals."

"That's fine with me, Captain, but I must warn you, I know very little about ships. I'm going to the far western lands of America; Virginia is only a stopping place to supply myself for the journey"

"I'll teach you what you need to know. Seeking your fortune, eh, Michael?"

"No sir." He told him what Gabriel and Esther found. "I'm not filthy rich, but I have all I need and a beautiful stock farm bordering the Lakes of Killarney. I'm going to America to try to find myself; I've only taken my weapons, my horse, my two dogs and five thousand pounds."

"That should be all you'll need out there, if you can keep it.
There are many men that would have your life for your horse and
saddle—but that much money! Don't flash it, Michael."

The Captain showed him to his small cabin and said, "Get a good night's sleep, Michael. Tomorrow you start learning how to navigate a ship. By the way, that's a fine looking sword you're carrying, and I noticed your bill of lading indicated you have a broadsword. Are you skilled with them?"

"As I said before, Captain, I've never actually faced a man in combat, but my father told me I could hold my own with the best of them, with all kinds of weapons."

"We'll see tomorrow. I employ some of the best swordsmen in the world and the crew fences a half hour every day to keep sharp. I'll put you with my best man. On the open seas it's as important to have good fighting men as it is it is to have good sailors, these days. There are pirate ships running these waters and they're well armed and manned with the worst cutthroats that ever sailed the seven seas. They'd slit your throat for a farthing."

The next day Captain Alcott put Michael with his first mate, who was his best swordsman, and stood back and watched the two men fence. When they removed their headgear, Sweeney said, "Captain, this lad will do to sail the seas with. I'm not sure I could beat him. He's the fastest man I've ever met."

When the men went back to their respective duties, Captain Alcott slapped Michael on the back and said, "You will do, lad, you surely will. Michael, Bill Sweeney and I have a Bible study in my cabin once a week when we're on the open seas, and it's tonight. You're welcome to join us if you like."

"I would like that very much; I've been neglecting my Bible reading." So this became a weekly study that drew these three men closer together.

Captain Alcott became fond of Michael and started calling him son, and he started teaching him navigation, and he found Michael to be highly intelligent and he learned fast.

One evening after their Bible study Michael lingered after Sweeney left. There were some things he wanted to ask the Captain.

"Captain, are you attacked often, and whom do you fear the most?'

"We don't fear any of them, Michael, but we respect them all. The English, Spanish, French and Portuguese fleets have the best ships and fighting men, and they will attack one another's merchants, as a pirate ship will. I fly the Irish flag and if we see an English ship we run up the English flag. There are so many Irish lads serving on the Spanish, French, and Portuguese ships they've left us pretty much alone, so far.

"The pirate ships are something else. They'll attack any ship they think they can take. But every one that's attacked us has come off badly and we haven't had an encounter in over a year. But we don't let that keep us from being alert always—this is a big ship and the prize would be a great one for them. Sooner or later they'll try to board us again, or some new upstart will come along, so we're forever watchful."

When they were about two days from the mouth of the James River that led from the ocean up to the City of Richmond, they were called out in the wee hours of the morning. When Michael came up on deck, Captain Alcott was passing out single-shot pistols that the sailors shoved down in their waistbands. Every man had a sword or a broadsword.

The night watch had discovered a longboat with twenty men in it. Captain Alcott put watchmen all around the ship to make sure other boats weren't flanking them. Then he instructed his men to hold back in the shadows until the pirates were all on board, unless they started forward singularly as they came over the side.

The Captain pulled Michael aside and told him to stay near him. "Remember, these men are coming aboard to kill us and steal our merchandise. If you become engaged, don't hesitate to kill, because it's either that or get killed yourself."

Michael heard rather than saw half a dozen hooks hit the deck. As each man came up on deck he strung out along the deck, keeping down low until all twenty men were on board. When they started to move away from the rail, Captain Alcott cried, "Take them!"

Michael was surprised to see the Captain lead the charge, but didn't have much time to think about it as he found himself face-to-face with a burly fellow with a sword in one hand and a knife in the other. They engaged in the pale moonlight, fighting furiously. Michael heard the clashing of swords all around him, but to look anywhere but at the man he was engaged with would be certain death.

The man brought first blood with a shallow stab just above Michael's elbow on his sword arm. Then their swords ran together up to the hand guards and the man swung at Michael's side. Michael sprang back and the knife ripped the front of his shirt wide open, nicking his chest. Michael twisted his sword as he sprang back. His assailant dropped his sword and withdrew a pistol from his waistband. Michael swung his sword downward cutting off the man's hand just above his wrist as the pistol exploded. The ball tore into the deck at Michael's feet. Before Michael could strike again the man turned and leaped into the sea.

Michael turned to see a big fellow knock Captain Alcott to the deck with the butt of a broadsword. Stunned, the captain lay on his back looking up as the man started to bring the sword down on him. Michael drew his pistol and shot the man and he fell over backwards before he could make contact with the Captain.

The pirates broke off the attack and leaped overboard.

When it was all over, seven of the pirates lay dead on the deck, and Captain Alcott had lost one man. Several of them had some mean lacerations and the Captain had a severe headache and a large knot high on his forehead.

They threw the dead pirates overboard, then wrapped their comrade's body and gave him a proper burial at sea.

Michael went to his cabin and fell prone on his bunk, contemplating what had happened. He had just cut one man's hand off and killed another, something he had fervently hoped he would never have to do. It hurt deep down inside, and his stomach was tied in knots; he felt as though a little piece of his soul had died. Was it fear or remorse that possessed him? Suddenly he leaped from his bunk and rushed to the rail of the ship and heaved. Captain Alcott walked up and put his arm across Michael's shoulders and said, "Killing a man never comes easy, and you don't want it to."

"I don't want it to ever happen again," Michael replied.

They had taken care of their wounded and were well underway by the time the morning broke bright and clear.

Captain Alcott said "Look," and he handed Michael his field glass and pointed at a ship much smaller than his own. There was a longboat alongside and men on board were helping their wounded on board.

Michael said, "Is there any danger of them regrouping and attacking again?"

"Not unless they are bigger fools than I take them for. No, they'll go off and lick their wounds and attack smaller vessels from now on. Michael, you saved my life last night and I'll never forget it. I wish you would change your mind and stay with me. You've lost your family and I've lost mine. We could become a family, just you and I."

"Maybe some day, Captain, but I'm determined to see America."

Well, son, it's something to see and it would take a lifetime to see it all. But if you ever change your mind, I put into Richmond three or four times a year. I do all my business here with a Mister Chambers who owns the docks where we'll tie up. He owns the warehouses nearby where he conducts his import/export business. Contact him if you ever want to contact me. He knows my schedule at all times."

The ship was a beehive of activity when they hit the mouth of the James River, and they slowed noticeably when they hit the current of the swift flow of the fresh water coming down from the Blue Ridge Mountains.

CHAPTER TEN

Michael liked what he saw as they sailed between the banks of the river. It was lined with a thick forest of trees, and farmhouses dotted the landscape. Beautiful horses and cattle were grazing in green meadows and crops were growing in well-kept fields.

Michael had discussed with the captain about going on down the coast with him to Atlanta, Georgia, but he decided he would debark here after all. He went to the Captain and said, "I have decided to debark here after all."

"I think that's a wise choice, son. Come to my quarters, please."

When they were seated Angus reached into a small cubbyhole on his desk and pulled out a small leather pouch of gold coins. "Michael, I know we agreed you'd work for only your passage, but I want you to have this. I have no one to call my own, and if my son had lived I'd have wanted him to be just like you. I'll be sailing in and out of the ports and rivers from Quebec to New Orleans. If you ever see my ship, come and see me. And if you ever need a friend, let me know. Remember, Mr. Chambers always knows how to get in touch with me."

Michael took the gold, more to please Captain Alcott than from need, and he reached out and gripped his hand in a firm handshake. He was leaving him with deep regret—he had become very fond of the Captain.

When they tied up at the dock Michael stood at the rail, marveling at the scene below. He was surprised to see that all the stevedores were black men. Most of them were tall, broad shouldered men with bulging muscles, and their hair was kinky and lay close to their head. They were all bare to the waist.

As he stood there he noticed that the perspiration ran down their bodies in little streams as they hoisted large, heavy containers onto the drays, to be delivered to customers or to the warehouse for storage. He thought he had never seen men so handsome and strong before.

He continued to watch as he walked down the gangplank. One of the men stopped for a moment to wipe the sweat from his eyes and to get a drink of water. Michael heard a man, the owner, he thought, call out, "You get back to lifting those bales, you black son of a bitch." Then he struck the man across the face with a leather strap.

The Black man threw his hands up to protect his face and said, "Yassa, boss, yassa," as the man kept applying the strap to his back.

Michael rushed forward and knocked the white man flat on his back, ripping the whip from his hand, "I wouldn't treat one of my animals like this! How could you do this to a human being? How would you like it if I used this strap on you?"

Michael had been taught to respect the law and he handed it over when an officer said, "Young man, give me that strap, you're under arrest."

Captain Alcott had witnessed this exchange and came charging down the gangplank in time to hear the officer say, "You're under arrest."

Angus said, "Officer, this is Michael Ross, and he just arrived in your country and is not aware of your customs here. I'm sure he wouldn't interfere if he had been. Would you be so kind as to call Mister Chambers, and see if we can straighten this out without my friend going to jail?"

When Mr. Chambers arrived, Captain Alcott introduced him to Michael and explained what happened. Mr. Chambers advised the officer to let Michael go and he fired his overseer on the spot. He said, "Angus, you know I don't, and never will, treat my slaves unkindly, or tolerate my overseers doing so. My slaves have warm houses to live in and they are fed and clothed well. This man will never work for me again."

After Mr. Chambers left, Angus said, "Michael, you were fortunate that Ted is the kind of man he is. Many slave owners would have prosecuted you and you'd have spent some time in jail. I know you meant well and I admire what you did, but if Ted were a cruel master you'd have done more harm than good. These black people are property and in many cases are treated worse than animals. The only way they can become free is if their masters give them their freedom or buy their freedom."

"Are you telling me that they are bought and sold like horses?" Michael said.

"Yes, Michael, they are."

"Could I buy this man?"

"I doubt if Ted would part with him. He's a strong lad and they need strong backs for this job."

They went to Mr. Chamber's office and were invited in to see him.

They went in and Mr. Chambers got up and extended his hand saying, "Angus, this is a surprise, seeing you again so soon. I thought you would be busy supervising the unloading of your cargo. What can I do for you?"

"Bill can handle that as well as I can. Ted, Michael is like a son to me. He's unfamiliar with your laws here and I'm afraid his indiscretion this afternoon may have put one of your slaves in great danger. As a favor to me, I'd like to buy the man as a gift to Michael."

"Angus, you are my friend. But business is business. Kabuta will cost you a thousand dollars."

"Seems rather high; I thought good work hands were going for five hundred."

"Not dock hands as young and stout as Kabuta is, he's the best hand I've got. You wouldn't get him at all if you weren't who you are."

"Make out the papers to Michael Ross and take the cost out of my bill of lading."

* * * * *

Michael found himself a slave owner his first day in America—an idea which was repugnant to him. He was determined to give Kabuta his freedom papers as soon as he could.

Before they left Mr. Chambers' office they made out the freedom papers and Mr. Chambers and the Captain witnessed the transaction. There was a place for Michael to sign, but he decided not to until he could determine how best to help the man.

Ted said, "Michael, any friend of Angus's is a friend of mine, call me Ted from now on and I'll feel free to call you Michael. Here's a leather case you can keep important papers in."

"Thank you, Ted. Can you tell me where I can buy some fine horses and a good wagon?"

"Paul Whitlock has the finest horses around Richmond," and he directed Michael on how to find the place.

"Captain, you have further business with Ted, so I'll bid you good day."

He took the papers and went down and presented them to the dock master, who called Kabuta and introduced him to his new master.

Michael said, "Kabuta, I don't believe in slavery and I'll set you free when you think the time is right."

Kabuta said, "Free! You mean you would give me papers and I could go anywhere I wanted to?"

"Well, anywhere the people would let you go."

"Not yet," Kabuta said, and Michael understood his reluctance. After all, the man had no money, no job, and no prospect yet.

Michael and Kabuta went to a livery stable and bought a team of fine young black mares and a sturdy wagon. Kabuta was a good teamster and he loved horses as much as Michael did.

Michael gave Kabuta the reins and said, "Let's go back to the docks and see if my gear and animals have been unloaded yet."

When Kabuta rode onto the dock sitting on the seat alongside of Michael, all the other slaves looked at him with envy—if only they could get such a break from the hard dock labor!

Blackie, Michael's stallion, had just been unloaded and tied to a post. And the two big Irish wolfhounds, Shep and Daisy, sat waiting patiently. The rest of his belongings lay in a pile nearby.

When Michael and Kabuta started to approach them, Shep and Daisy bounded forward, and Kabuta leaped back onto the wagon. He'd never seen dogs as big as these bruisers and he wasn't anxious to make their acquaintance.

Michael laughed and said, "Come, Kabuta, and meet Shep and Daisy. They are very gentle dogs and would never hurt anybody unless they were ordered to, or someone was hurting me. Call them by name and pet them on the head and scratch behind their ears and along their sides."

Kabuta really didn't want to do this, but he had become accustomed to obeying the white man's wishes, so he did what he was told. When the dogs wagged their tails and licked his big black hands, a wide smile broke across Kabuta's face. "Kabuta," Michael blurted, "you have the most beautiful teeth I've ever seen."

Kabuta looked at his new owner with shock, then stammered, "Thank you, Boss, that's the nicest thing anybody has said to me since a neighboring tribe in Africa captured me and sold me to the slave trader who brought me to America when I was twelve years old—nine years ago. You surprise me, but I like what you do and say. You defended me and bought me, and you said you would set me free any time I wish."

He had decided, however, that he would stay with his new owner and see what developed.

They drove to the slave quarters and picked up his clothing, then left the city and leisurely traveled the beautiful countryside. They passed a number of plantations with fine horses and grand houses, with slave quarters out in the back.

Michael was appalled when they rode by a field where about thirty men, women and children were thinning cotton under the watchful eye of a white man dressed in an all-white riding habit, with high-topped black riding boots that shone like new money. He was wearing a wide-brimmed white straw hat with a flat crown. He looked like a king sitting up on a beautiful bay horse. He had a cigar in his mouth and he carried a long whip, hanging by a strap from his right hand. Occasionally he cracked it close to the back of the field hands—man, woman or child, it made no difference. When a slave jumped he would laugh cruelly.

Michael wondered if there was anywhere in this country he could get away from this. If he understood his Bible correctly, God allowed slavery when Christ was on the earth, but according to the Scriptures, he never condoned it. It repelled Michael and he vowed he would have nothing to do with it.

When they reached the stock farm a gray-headed black man came out to the front gate to greet them. Michael said, "Sir, I'd like to speak to Mr. Paul Whitlock."

The man said to Kabuta, "Boy, you take that team down to the stables, and

Mister, let your boy tie that fine animal to the hitching post and you come with me. Follow me."

Michael followed him up the gravel walk lined with beautiful roses, climbed a flight of eight wide steps to a spacious verandah that stretched completely around the house, and entered the house when the servant opened the large, stained glass door.

They entered a long, wide hallway with a mahogany wainscoting that reached about four feet up from the floor, from there up to the ceiling was flowered wallpaper. They turned right into a large parlor where the servant invited Michael to sit on a soft cushioned chair. He took Michael's hat and placed it on a beautifully carved table and disappeared back into the hall. After a few moments he returned and said, "The master will see you now. Follow me, please."

They walked down the hallway to the back of the house and entered a large, impressively decorated study where floor-to-ceiling bookshelves dominated the room. A little man sat behind a large walnut desk. He had dark hair just showing a bit gray at the temples. His face was tan, showing that he spent a lot of time outdoors in the sun. He was surprisingly agile as he sprang out of his chair and walked around the desk to shake Michael's hand. "Paul Whitlock, how can I be of service to you?"

"Michael Ross. Well, Ted Chambers told me you have the best horses in the Colonies and, looking at the ones I saw in the paddock, I don't dispute that. I want to buy one now and maybe some more later. I'd like a mare about two years old and broken to saddle, if possible."

"I have a fine appaloosa, but she still needs some work."

"Let's have a look at her."

They retrieved their hats and walked to the stables, where Mister Whitlock told his trainer to put new blankets, saddle and bridle on the horse and bring her out.

Michael said, "May I examined her before you saddle her?"

"Sure thing; Bring her out, Ralph."

Michael called Kabuta over and said, "What do you think of her, Kabuta?"

Kabuta examined her teeth, picked up her feet and examined them closely, slapped her gently on the withers and ran his hands lovingly along her neck, speaking softly to her as he worked with her. He turned to Mr. Whitlock and Michael and said, "May I try her out?"

Michael said, "Kabuta, she isn't fully broken yet."

"She won't buck with me, Boss."

He took a handful of mane and swung up on her back. She shivered a little, but stood until Kabuta spoke to her. Then she bolted across the paddock. Kabuta guided her with pressure with his knees and a slight tap on the side of her neck. When he rode her back to where Michael and Mr. Whitlock stood, she stopped at Kabuta's command. He leaped off the horse and said, "She's a fine horse, boss."

Mr. Whitlock said, "I'll give you the horse with new gear and five hundred dollars for your boy."

"Kabuta isn't for sale," Michael said firmly.

"Four hundred dollars hard cash, then," Mr. Whitlock responded.

"Fine," Michael said, "bring out the gear." He was pleasantly surprised when the stable boy laid a pair of saddlebags on the saddle, as good as his own. Michael said, "Saddle your horse, Kabuta."

When Kabuta finished saddling the horse, Mr. Whitlock said, "That boy knows horses, and they take to him. I've never seen anything like it. That mare unseated almost everybody who's been on her, and she has never failed to pitch before." Looking from Kabuta back to Michael, Mr. Whitlock said, "I'll give you two thousand for the boy."

Michael said, "That's a fine offer, Mr. Whitlock, but Kabuta will never be sold again."

Kabuta tied the mare behind the wagon and climbed up on the seat and followed Michael back to town.

They went to the mercantile store where Michael bought two complete bedrolls, night sheet and camping gear, flour, cornmeal, salt, pepper, sugar, tea and other staple goods, and a large tarpaulin. He said to the proprietor, "I'm Michael Ross, just over from Ireland, and I know nothing about the country-side. Can you direct me to a place where we can camp out for a few days?"

"Mr. Ross, I'm Jim Cottle, and I appreciate your business. You can camp anywhere along the James River west of town. We deliver any big order for the convenience of our customers. Where do you plan to locate?"

"I plan to go to the western frontier and settle out there somewhere."

Mr. Cottle let his gaze travel over Michael from head to toe and said, "I don't see any weapons."

"I have a sword, broadsword, knife, crossbow and a fine staff."

"You'll need guns out there, and you'd better learn to use them quickly if you're going very far west. I have the best money can buy in double-barrel, twelve-gauge shotguns, Hawking Rifle, and Russian pistols, and plenty of ammunition."

Michael said, "I've never used them."

"Well, if you camp this side of the river I'll drive out early in the morning and demonstrate them for you."

"Done," Michael said, and he and Kabuta loaded their supplies into the wagon. They rode west out of town and about a mile out they came to a small creek running into the James River. They staked their horses in a small meadow and made their camp in the shade of a grove of Virginia live oaks and started to prepare their evening meal. Michael said, "I'll gather wood for the fire if you'll slice some bacon."

Kabuta said, "I think we can do better than that," and he waded out in the creek.

Michael walked along the banks of the James picking up dead wood for the fire and when he came back he saw Kabuta toss a fish out on the bank. He stood and watched him reach under the bank and toss another on the bank, and then he went and built the fire. Just as Michael got the fire going, Kabuta walked up with a string of four small-mouth bass and said, "Supper, boss."

"That's great, Kabuta, but let's get something straight, you don't have to call me 'boss,' my name's Michael."

"Yes sir, Mr. Mike."

"Okay," Michael said, smiling, "I guess I can get used to Mr. Mike for now."

As they sat by the fire eating their supper, Mike said, "Kabuta, I don't need a slave, nor do I want one." He handed him his freedom papers and said, "You're free." Kabuta said, "Mr. Mike, what if I don't want to be free? How's a black man suppose to make a living in this country?"

Michael thought for a moment, and then said, "Kabuta, I need a friend, why don't you come with me to the western lands as a free man? Whatever we find or earn we'll split evenly."

Kabuta opened his mouth to reply, but before he could say anything Michael said," Wait, there's something I want to give you, and then you can decide what you want to do. The bedroll, the mare and gear are yours."

Kabuta was silent, and Michael began to wonder whether he had understood what he said. Finally, Kabuta said, "Mr. Mike, are you telling me that you are giving me my freedom and this fine horse and gear? That I can just ride away?"

"Yes, Kabuta, just be sure you keep your freedom papers and the bill of sale that I'll give you showing that you are the legal owner of the horse. You must keep these papers in your saddlebags or on your person at all times. If anyone stops and questions you, you show them these papers."

"Mr. Mike, why are you doing this?"

"I told you I could use a friend. So what do you say, Kabuta? Will you go with me?"

"To the end of the earth, Mr. Mike."

Early the next morning Jim Cottle drove into camp with his buckboard loaded with guns and ammunition. They spent the first hour tearing the guns down and putting them back together until they both could do it, even in the dark. Jim also taught them how to clean the guns and to aim and fire them. They set up targets and fired many rounds until Jim was satisfied they would become proficient with all of the guns. He said, "The shotgun is good for bringing down birds on the wing, and the Hawking will bring down any big game, even the grizzly from a long ways, and all of the guns are good for defending yourselves from man or beast; snakes too."

Michael said, "We can't thank you enough. We'll take four shotguns and four rifles and eight of the pistols, and leather scabbards for each gun."

"If you go far west ammunition might not be available. You should take a couple of cases for each caliber of gun you own. I'll throw in a belt for your pistols and what ammunition I brought with me, and you can come into the store when you need more. You should practice until you're as good and fast as you can get before you set out on your journey. Now I've got to get back."

Mike paid the man and said; "We'll be seeing you soon."

Kabuta said, "Mr. Mike, Mister Chambers owns a cabin about ten miles further west where he took me sometimes to cook for him when he'd go fishing and hunting. He said he needed to get away from the grind of the business world two or three times a year to unwind. I'm sure he'd let us camp on his place until you're ready to go over the mountain. It's a big cabin with clear water running right near the back door. There are corrals for the horses and the place is shaded with giant hickory nut trees."

Mike said, "Sounds like a good idea, Kabuta, if you'll stay in camp and water the horses and move them to fresh grass, I'll take the wagon to town and see Ted and buy some more supplies. We need some fishing lines and a good sewing kit with a lot of extra needles of all sizes."

"We don't need any fresh meat, we can get all we need right here."

Michael drove straight to Ted's office and after some pleasantries, he said, "Kabuta tells me that you have some property out on the James, and he said he thought you wouldn't mind if we camped out there until we get our things together to go over the mountains."

Ted said, "Michael, because Angus spoke so highly of you, and knowing that Kabuta will leave the place cleaner than he found it, you are welcome to use the cabin as long as you like. I only get out there two or three times a year. The fishing's good, but I ask you not to shoot any of the wild turkey and deer on the place. I'm not as agile as I once was, so I like my game in close when I go hunting.

"I'd advise you to get a good span of mules and a sturdy wagon with wide flat tires if you're going to haul very much over those mountains. You'll need a number of sharp axes and a couple sledgehammers and a heavy block and tackle with plenty of rope; you're bound to run into places where you'll have to cut your way through and bust up some big boulders. There may be places you need the block and tackle to draw your wagons over some steep inclines, and you can always use it to raise logs if needed.

"And by all means, take the latest cast iron cook stove, bolted down in a sandbox in the tail end of your wagon. You'll thank your lucky stars if you do. I took a trip out far enough to know how rough it is to cook on open fires all the time and that I wasn't cut out to be a pioneer. Take a couple of buckets with tight lids and get milk and eggs every chance you get. Those are the foods you'll miss most. Take plenty of warm clothing and heavy blankets, as well as light summer clothing. The desert is extremely hot in the summer months and cold at night. Be sure you get the best rain gear you can find, and at least one big tarpaulin."

Michael made notes of all Ted's advice. "Thank you, Ted, that's good advice and I'll heed it. I know I have so much to learn."

When he left Ted's office he went straight to the carriage and wagon maker and looked at all the wagons he had. He picked out one and said, "If you could make me two wagons just like this one, only make the coupling pole, rocking arms, tongue, axle and wheels twice as strong. And if you make the sideboards five feet high and tight enough to keep the water out when we cross the rivers, I'll take them. Can you do that?"

"I can do it, but I've got several orders ahead of you. It'll take five or six months. And if it's loaded like you indicated it will be, you'll need two good teams to pull it."

"That was my thinking too," Michael said. "I'll be back for the wagon later."

He went to the land office and inquired if there was any land available along the James River between town and the Blue Ridge Mountains. The clerk went back and perused the files. When he returned with a ledger in his hand he said, "There's a fifty-acre plot just west of Mr. Chambers' cabin. It's the only one left on the river and it's a mystery to me why it hasn't been taken. Too rugged, I guess; you might not be able to build on it."

"What do I have to do to become the owner of that plot?"

"Pay the filing fee and I'll issue you a deed right now. But are you sure you want it sight unseen?"

"Yes, I do, at least I can say I own a piece of America, and there is a possibility that someone has checked it out and is on his way here to file on it right now."

"That's not likely, but I'll issue you the deed."

Michael paid the fee and put the deed in his leather case and went back to pick up his wagon.

As he approached the camp he heard a horrible howling sound. He stopped to listen, and then felt his heart begin to pound as he realized it was Kabuta's voice. He rode in quietly and saw Kabuta tied to a tree and two men standing laughing at him. Kabuta cried, "I'm a free man! Look in the saddlebag on the saddle that's lying over that log near that tree."

One of the men rifled through the bag, pulled out Kabuta's papers and dangled them over his fire.

Riding up close with his shotgun ready, Michael shouted, "Put those papers back "

The man turned toward Michael and fired. Just as he did, the wagon ran over a fair-sized stone, knocking Michael off balance and against the sideboard of the wagon. The bullet whizzed by, missing him by inches. Michael stopped the team and regained his balance as the man finished reloading his single-shot pistol. When he started to raise it for another shot, Michael cut him in half with both barrels of the shotgun. The other man's shot had lodged in a board in the front of the wagon.

With adrenaline pumping through his veins, Kabuta broke the rope that bound him to the tree as though it were a thread, and before the man could reload he was crushing the life out of him with his strong muscular arms.

Michael leaped from the wagon and sprinted to Kabuta and said, "Let him go, my friend!"

The man screamed when Kabuta gave him one more squeeze and dropped him to the ground, groaning.

Michael said, "Kabuta, gather up all of their weapons and put them in the wagon."

While Kabuta hastened to do as Michael asked, Michael told the man to put his dead partner on his horse and get out. "If you ever bother us again, I'll let Kabuta finish the job he started," he warned.

"I can't," the man whined, "He broke my ribs."

Michael and Kabuta loaded the dead man on his horse and tied it to the tail of the other man's horse, then helped the wounded man onto his horse.

Michael dropped to the ground in relief and Kabuta sat beside him, rubbing his chafed wrists.

"Kabuta, unless it's impossible to do so, let's stay together from now on."

Kabuta said, "This is a tough country, Mr. Mike, and there are a lot of mean people in it. But you'll surely do to travel through life with—I'm sure glad you came along when you did."

CHAPTER ELEVEN

They loaded the wagon and drove ten miles up the James and crossed it at a wide place where the water was about two feet deep, just west of a deep hole of water. About a half-mile south of the river they saw the headquarters of a large plantation sitting up on a low hill, with lush green fields spreading out all around the buildings.

When they crossed the river they were on the west side of their fifty acres and could just see the Chambers cabin tucked back under a grove of hickory trees. They put their things in the cabin, staked their animals and went to the river to fish for their supper. They caught some adobe grasshoppers for bait and Michael started fishing with his hook just below the surface of the water. He was fishing for bass, but Kabuta preferred catfish and he was fishing close to the bottom near an old rotten log half buried in the water.

Michael had caught a couple of small bass when he saw Kabuta's cork moving slowly back and forth across the water, and once in a while it would go under a little ways and right back up again. Michael laughed and said, "Kabuta, you've got a minnow or a mighty small perch playing with that thing."

Kabuta said, "You just wait until you taste this minnow."

With the patience of Job, Kabuta let the cork float around for at least twenty minutes. Suddenly it went under and started moving along the log. Kabuta set the hook and pulled out a five-pound yellow cat. As he reeled it in Michael was walking down the river. He hollered, "Mr. Mike, take a look at this minnow we're going have for supper!"

"Man! That's a beauty. With my two bass that's all we need. I'm starved."

When they got back to the cabin Kabuta said, "Mr. Mike, just lay back and have a good rest and I'll cook you a meal you'll never forget."

"I don't need the rest, but I'm a poor cook, so I'll leave it to you. Think I'll walk over our property and see if it's worth anything."

"Supper in about an hour."

Michael walked over to the survey stake sticking up out of the ground at the corner of the Chambers property and theirs. It surprised him to discover that he was beginning to think of everything he had obtained since he met Kabuta as being theirs instead of as just his; strange.

He walked due west until he found the other boundary line survey stake. For the life of him he couldn't understand why this property hadn't been filed on long ago. It did slope up from the river to a bluff at the back of the property much faster and steeper than the other, and it was rather rocky. But it had some good stands of straight pines that they could build a cabin with and rails for fencing. It would take a lot of hard work, but Michael could see some great possibilities for the place.

There was a clear-running, spring-fed creek about six feet wide that flowed right on the property line between their property and the Chambers place. It was as straight as a string from where it flowed off the bluff until it emptied into the James.

An idea was already forming in Michael's brain as to what he would do with all the rocks on the place. He picked up a dead stick and probed the bottom of the creek and found it to be two to four feet deep in holes, with three small waterfalls below the eight-foot waterfall that flowed off the bluff.

He washed up at the creek and started for the cabin when Kabuta stuck his head out the door and hollered, "Come and get it!"

Kabuta had been busy in his absence. He had found some poke salad in the river bottom when they were fishing. He built a fire outside and placed the salad leaves on the hot ashes, laid the fish on the leaves, and seasoned it with salt and pepper whipped into a little butter which he had rubbed all over the fish. Then he covered the fish with a thick layer of the salad leaves and covered it with hot coals.

He had buried two big Irish potatoes in the hot ashes earlier. Thanks to the cook stove that Mr. Chambers had in the cabin, and the milk and butter Michael had brought, there were fluffy hot biscuits. He mashed the potatoes and then quickly fried a dozen fresh eggs, sliding them onto their plates just before he took the biscuits out of the oven.

"Mr. Mike, you'll want to butter your biscuits while they're hot."

Michael said grace quickly and they dug in.

After everything was devoured, Michael said, "What a meal, Kabuta! How did you learn to cook like that?"

"Well, slave masters seldom allow their slaves to learn to read and write, but Mr. Chambers taught his house people how so they could read and write down recipes.

"When I was a little boy in Africa my mother taught me how to cook on an open fire. Mr. Chambers put me in his kitchen until I got so big he sent me to the docks. It was in his kitchen that I learned to bake all kinds of things. Wait until you eat some of my cakes and pies. I'll bake some tomorrow after we walk over your land."

* * * * *

The next morning after a quick breakfast of bacon, pancakes and eggs with ribbon cane syrup and a pot of hot tea, they went out and inspected the fifty acres. By mid-morning they had their axes as sharp as a razor and were clearing the trees and brush back about ten feet from their side of the creek. They trimmed the straight bigger trees to use in building their cabin and the smaller ones for fence rails. The crooked branches they cut into firewood. The trees that were too big for the team to pull out of the ground they cut down as low to the ground as they could with a crosscut saw. They were going to use this space for a wagon road. By the end of the first week they had reached the bluff where the creek tumbled down off the mountain creating a series of small waterfalls until it dropped into a pool about six feet deep at its deepest point, and about twenty feet across. The rocks in the pool were manageable, so they used them to erect a four-foot wall around the pool, except for the six-foot outlet for the creek. At that point the wall dropped two feet.

These two men worked hard from dawn to dusk six days a week. Michael flatly refused to work on Sunday, but he and Kabuta passed the hours fishing, swimming or hunting. This was pure joy after a week of hard labor.

Michael spent thirty or forty minutes every Sunday morning in Bible study and prayer before he left the cabin, and after a few weeks Kabuta said, "Mr. Mike, could I join you?"

"I'd be delighted, Kabuta, I just didn't want to impose my beliefs on you."

"Oh, Massa Ted taught us about Jesus."

Michael remembered that his father always read a few verses from the Bible and prayed every morning before they went about their daily task, and now that Kabuta indicated he wanted to participate, he started doing the same. He was trying hard to be the kind of man his father had been

Kabuta did all the cooking, which pleased Michael immensely. What a find Kabuta was. Michael was developing a heartfelt brotherly love for him and he knew that Kabuta felt the same way. Much of the loneliness and despair he had felt by the loss of his family was beginning to fade.

It took them three months to build the two-foot-high rock walls, three feet from the banks on both sides of the creek, and a two-foot rock wall across the lower side of the property. They built this wall to catch the topsoil as it washed down the slope during the rains.

Summer and fall passed and they worked on. When winter set, in earnest it was too wet and slippery for them to start building their cabin, so they started fencing the place. When they tied the last rail to the post they stood and stretched their weary muscles and wiped the sweat from their brow.

Kabuta said, "I'm sure glad that's done. Now we won't have to stake the horses any more."

"They'll be just as glad as we are. Now they can romp and play without being encumbered by the ropes," Michael said. "I'm thankful for the bluff because we won't have to build a fence there."

Kabuta said, "Mr. Mike, how about we put a fence across the lower half so we can plant corn for our horses. Spring is almost here and I'd like to plant a garden. We could grow English peas, radishes, onions, lettuce and other greens soon after the ground thaws."

"Well, let's see. This is Saturday, and it's still pretty early. Why don't we take the rest of the day off and go to town. We can eat someone else's cooking and sleep in a hotel tonight. If we hurry we can get there in time to buy a couple teams of mules. Our wagons must be ready by now."

"We can start the fence Monday, Mr. Mike. You can sleep in a hotel, but I'll have to sleep in the slave quarters at Massa Ted's place."

"I'm sorry, Kabuta, I forgot about that."

They went to the cabin and cleaned up, put on their best clothes and by noon they were on their horses making the eleven-mile ride into town.

As soon as they got in, Michael went to a cafe and bought sandwiches and milk and they ate in a park under the trees.

Mike said, "Let's go buy some mules."

They went to the wagon master's and Mike was thrilled to find that the wagons were exactly as he pictured.

"They've only been ready a week," the man said. "Come out in back, I want to show you something I picked up a few days ago." In a corral there were eight big, black mules.

"Are they broken to harness?" Michael asked.

"I hitched four of them to your wagon and drove out to Whitlock's plantation and hauled a load of corn to my crib. They're young and a little feisty, but they handle well, and man, can they pull a load! Come in the tack room."

He showed Michael eight sets of nearly new harness. "You can drive those teams out of here today for a fair price."

They went into the man's office and when he showed Michael the total price for everything, Michael studied the bill carefully.

"This seems to be rather high to me. If you'll fill those wagons with corn you have a deal."

The man took his hat off and ran his fingers through his hair, frowned and looked Michael straight in the eye for a moment. Then a smile broke across his rugged face. He reached across his desk to shake Michael's hand and said, "It's good doing business with a wise man."

Michael paid him, with the understanding he could pick them up Monday morning.

* * * * *

When they hitched up the mules early Monday morning Kabuta said, "These sure are mighty fine wagons and mules, Mr. Mike."

"Kabuta, I wish you'd knock off this mister stuff. As I told you before, my name is Michael, but I do like the nickname Mike." You could detect the thrill in Michael's voice when he said. "I agree with you, I'm very pleased with our purchases this trip."

The mules had no trouble pulling the loads until they reached the slope going up to the bluff. The wheels sank down into the soft earth along their new dirt road bordering the creek. When they pulled the teams to a stop to let them rest a spell, Michael said, "Kabuta, we're going to haul some heavy loads over this road, maybe we should put a thick layer of gravel on it."

"It's sure to keep from cutting deep ruts in the road during rainy weather."

They spoke to the teams and they eased into their collars and moved up the grade. Mike and Kabuta parked the wagons side-by-side underneath a large live oak and covered them with the tarpaulin.

When Kabuta awoke the next morning he heard the ring of Mike's ax as he started shaping logs to build a shed for the stock, with a corncrib in back of the shed.

Kabuta leaped out of bed and started a fire in the cook stove, singing softly. He was happy for the supplies they picked up in town. He had all the things he needed to set a fine breakfast in front of Mike. He stuck his head out the kitchen door and called, "Come and get it!"

Mike washed up at the creek and walked into the kitchen and said, "Brrr. It's cold out this morning, and there's a thin layer of ice on the edges of the creek."

"Why didn't you wake me, Mr. Mike?"

"You looked so peaceful lying there, I just didn't have the heart to route you out of that warm bed. Kabuta, if you don't stop calling me mister, I'm going to start calling you Mr. Kabuta and see how you like it. It makes me sound old, and I'm no older than you are."

"All right, Mike, I sure don't want you calling me mister. But it's going to take some getting used to. You may have to correct me once in a while"

"If you'll do the dishes, I'll get back to cutting logs for our cribs and shed and you can join me later," Mike said.

"I'll be there in a few minutes."

Mike was laying out the dimensions of the cribs and the sheds when Kabuta walked up and said, "It looks like they'll be big enough for many more animals than we have."

"I thought we might as well build a couple of pens and sheds for a couple of milk cows and their calves while we're at it. I thought I'd ride over to the plantation across the river and see if I could buy a couple of fresh cows so we could have butter for our bread and cream for our coffee and tea."

"That sounds good to me. If you'll show me where to dig the holes for the posts we'll need for this thing, I'll do that. Why don't you ride over today? I can taste that cool sweet milk right out of our spring house right now."

"What spring house?"

"The one we're going to build."

"I'll mark the holes. Dig the corner holes four feet deep and the stall holes three and I'll ride over right away."

Kabuta was tamping the last corner post in place when Michael came back leading a young cow that looked like she would drop a calf any day, and an older cow with a young heifer calf tagging along.

Kabuta said, "Sweet milk for supper, I can't wait!"

"You don't have to; I just put a gallon syrup can full in the creek to cool. There are a couple pounds of sweet butter too."

"I'm going to the house and make a pan of cornbread for lunch; you coming?"

"Not now, I'll tamp the stall post in while you're cooking. A man by the name of O'Flannery owns that fine place across the river, and he said he'd give us a couple of setting hens and plenty of fresh eggs for them to set on and we could have fryers pretty soon. I told him to wait until I could get a pen built. We have the wire for it and I'll do that while you're building the fence for our cornfield. I'll buy us some laying hens and a rooster too."

Two weeks later the cribs and sheds were finished and the corn was in the crib.

Kabuta was building his fence and Michael built the chicken coop and pen. Then he started breaking the land to plant the corn and garden. As soon as that was finished they started building their cabin. After it was framed in Michael said, "It's time to plant the corn and garden. Why don't you start that in the morning? I'll take a four-mule team and one of the big wagons in tomorrow and purchase the things we need to finish the cabin. Is there anything you need?"

"Tonight I'll make out a list of staples we need for the kitchen, and we both could use some new work gloves."

"I have those on my list. And Kabuta, if you can handle the things I mentioned, I'll finish the cabin."

"I have the easy end of the job, Mike, there's nothing I like better than planting and seeing things grow. That is, except eating what I grow."

The weeks passed quickly. Kabuta tended his garden. Michael continued his work on the cabin, and by the time the radishes and onions were ready for harvest they were moving in.

CHAPTER TWELVE

One morning Kabuta said, "Mike, my butt's dragging, let's go fishing."
"You took the words right out of my mouth. You get the lines and a
bucket and I'll get the seine and catch some minnows."

They went to their favorite fishing hole by the old dead log that protruded
out into the river. The fish weren't biting, so they lay back on the grass
and talked.

Kabuta said, "Mike, what prompted you to come to America?"

Michael told him the story of how he'd lost his family and how the discovery
of antique swords and gold coins had made him wealthy enough to make it
all possible. "I also own a fine stock farm in the most beautiful place in all
of Ireland," Michael said, "maybe I'll take you there some day. What about
you—what was your life like in Africa? How did you become a slave?"

"We lived in a small village on the Congo River about ten miles from the
Great Waters, that you call the Atlantic Ocean. We lived off the land. The
jungle supplied us with all kinds of fruits and wild meat. Fish was plentiful.
We lived well and were very happy; Then one day a large force of warriors
from a much larger tribe raided our small village.

"They struck in the middle of the night and killed all of our older men
and women, most of them in their sleep. All of the younger men and women
and boys and girls from the age of about eight and up had their hands

tied to a long rope. They pierced the hearts of all the younger children.

"They led us away and left the dead for the scavengers to eat, including my two little brothers and my mother and father. They marched us to the Great Waters and sold us to slave traders. We were put into long boats and rowed out to a large sailing ship.

"They put us down in the hold of the ship—packed in there like rats. We were fed very little and many of the weaker ones died. They even made us throw our own people overboard. Many of the people got sick and had dysentery and threw up everywhere, and the stench was almost unbearable.

"Mike, I was a husky boy of twelve. I never got sick. There was a pretty little girl about nine years old that I shared my food with. She never got sick either; I'd hide her when the crew came down to get a woman to share their bed. They liked the young girls, but I made sure they never took Swanna.

"When we reached Richmond they cleaned us up and fed us real good for about a month and then took us to the auction block. Mr. Ted bought me for a houseboy. I was nineteen when he transferred me to the docks. A pretty young girl and her papa bought Swanna.

"She clung to me and screamed as they dragged her away. Mr. Ted said he heard the man say he bought her to be his daughter's companion, and he thought he was a plantation owner up river. I'd love to find her, Mike, and set her free. If we could find her she could cook and keep our house for us, boss, and that would free me to work with you all the time."

"Kabuta, if you promise to never call me boss again, I'll try to find her for you."

Kabuta said, "I hope her master is as good to her as Massa Chambers was to me. He treated me real well, fed well, and most of his overseers were all right. He even taught me to read and write, although we had to keep that a secret, since it was definitely illegal. Massa Chambers could have been sent to jail and fined severely."

"I noticed how refined you were, compared with other Blacks I've seen and heard."

"The man that whipped me was new on the dock. I'd never been struck before and, Mike, at first I couldn't understand why you were so good to me—you never struck me or even got mad at me. But after being with you this long, I realize that you are just a very good man, like Mr. Chambers."

"I'd never strike you, Kabuta; I'd never strike any man, except in self-defense."

As they lay there underneath the shade of the trees, just relaxing, they didn't care if the fish were biting or not. They lazed the day away and then went home, where Kabuta prepared their evening meal while Michael took care of the stock.

As they ate, Mike said, "Kabuta, the last time I saw Captain Alcott I gave him a Power of Attorney and asked him to have my assets transferred to the Stockman's Bank and Investment firm in Richmond. He said he'd be back soon, let's go into town and see if he's returned."

They hitched up and Kabuta took the reins and drove them to Richmond. These young men were over six feet tall. Mike weighed about a hundred and ninety and Kabuta about two ten. One was very black with short, kinky black hair, and small ears that lay close to his head; the other an Irishman with curly auburn hair, and was tanned from working long hours in the hot sun.

Michael had been teaching Kabuta many of the old Irish songs he knew and they sang in harmony as they bounced along on the river road. When they pulled up in front of the bank, Michael gave Kabuta a sack of gold coins and a list of things they needed and said, "Would you go over to the mercantile store and pick up these items? I'll pick up some lunch and meet you in the park later; I have some business to take care of."

Michael went into the bank and asked if Captain Angus Alcott had deposited money there for Michael Ross.

The clerk said, "Yes, quite a bit of money I might add."

"I'm Michael Ross, and I'd like to draw out a thousand dollars and get an accounting."

"Just a moment sir," and he disappeared into a back room.

A few minutes later a very distinguished looking gentleman came to the teller's window and said, "I'm Mr. Butterfield, the president of this investment firm. Young man, do you have any identification to show that you are Michael Ross of County Kerry of Ireland?"

"Only this and my Irish brogue," he pulled out a gold pocket watch with 'To Michael from Mom and Dad' engraved on the back of it.

Mr. Butterfield looked at the scuffed-up boots and faded blue denims Michael wore. "Young man, I'm afraid that isn't enough. Half of our police force is Irishmen with an Irish brogue. You could have stolen that watch and your brogue only means you are Irish."

Captain Alcott and Mr. Chambers walked in just then and Mr. Butterfield left Michael and walked around the counter and greeted them enthusiastically, reaching his hand to Captain Alcott.

"Hello, Mr. Butterfield," said the captain. Then he saw Michael and he swept past Mr. Butterfield and gave Michael a big hug, saying, "You're a sight for sore eyes, son. How has America been treating you?"

"Fine Captain, I like it here." He turned to Mr. Chambers and said, "Kabuta and I want to thank you for the use of your cabin."

Ted took Michael's hand and asked, "How's your place coming, Michael?"

"Well, we've moved into our own cabin and we have a rail fence around the place and twenty acres of corn that's just coming up. We've built a corncrib and a shed big enough for our stock to get in out of the weather. We also built a rock wall around the pool and on both sides of the creek. Did you know that the property line between our places ran down the middle of that creek?"

"No, I didn't. If I had, you'd never have gotten it. You're a lucky young man."

"I know," said Michael.

The captain gripped the muscle of Michael's arm and said, "You're as hard as a rock."

"That comes from picking up tons of them to build that rock wall with, and digging post holes and chopping wood," Michael laughed. "Captain, will you do me a favor and tell these men who I am, I can't get a penny out of this place."

Mr. Butterfield had been watching this exchange and when he was assured that this was truly the right Michael Ross, he was very apologetic.

"There's no need to apologize," Michael said, "I'm grateful that you're diligent and efficient. I can rest assured that you won't be giving my assets away."

"No, indeed, we're very pleased you've entrusted us with so large a sum. I assure you we will guard it well and see that it grows."

Captain Alcott said, "Mike, I took the privilege to have them set up a checking account for you with five thousand dollars in it, and the rest of your funds put to work for you. You can change it if you want."

"That's fine, Captain. Mr. Butterfield, I'd like a thousand in cash now and I'll take the checks in case I need them."

Mike thanked Mr. Butterfield, put the money in his pocket and said, "Captain, Ted, I'm going pick up some lunch and meet Kabuta in the park. I'd like you to join us."

Ted said, "Angus, our business can wait, let's go have a good meal on this country squire."

After Ted and Angus had greeted Kabuta properly and they were eating their lunch, they brought one another up on what had been going in their lives for the past year.

Captain Alcott said, "Michael, I sold my ship and business to Bill Sweeney and transferred all my assets here to Richmond. I'm going to retire, Michael. I have no one back in the old country so I decided I would sit on the banks of a good fishing hole and watch this new country grow."

"Why don't you come and live with Kabuta and me?" Michael said. "We'll build you a room on our cabin. You'll love it out there. The fishing is good, and so is the hunting. You could keep us in meat and it would give Kabuta more time to improve the place."

"I'm afraid I'd be a burden on ye' lad, and I wouldn't want that."

"You could never be anything but a pleasure to me, Captain."

"Well, then I'll buy me a closed-in carriage and hire a driver that loves and knows horses. Then we'll come out and look your place over. Maybe you could spare me a little spot of your land and I could have a place built out there. Maybe even find a widow woman who would like to tie up with an old sea Captain."

Mike said, "Old? Captain! You're not over sixty and you are as strong as one of my horses. We'll give you a corner just across the creek from Ted's place just up from the James River near the clearest spring-fed creek you ever saw. You get Ted to bring you out some weekend to eat one of Kabuta's fine fish dinners."

"We'll do that," Ted said. "In fact, it's time I had a holiday. We can stay in my cabin for a few weeks, Angus. I'll bring Lola out to cook for us. Ellis, my driver's twenty-year-old son is good with horses and he can handle a team as good as anyone. We've been business partners for years, and I'll give Ellis to you, old friend, as a retirement gift, if you promise never to sell him or take him away from the Richmond area. I promised Amos, his father, I'd never sell one of his children.

"His wife, Sarah, is my cook, and his younger boys work in the house and gardens. If you want to endear Ellis to you, let him and Amos go with you to pick out your team and carriage. I'd buy young geldings if I were you... they're more stable. Mares are more flighty and if one comes in heat she's nothing but trouble."

Kabuta laughed and said, "Ain't that the truth?"

"Captain, you only buy mares if you want to raise horses," Michael said. "It's been good talking to you, but Kabuta and I must be getting back."

Ted said, "We'll be seeing you soon, Kabuta, I can't wait to taste your cooking again. Angus, you've got a treat in store, that boy can cook."

Angus and Ted walked back to Ted's office where Ted introduced Angus to Amos and said, "Amos, I'm giving Ellis to my dear friend, Angus, to be his driver, with the understanding that he'll never take him from the Richmond area. You'll be able to see one another often."

Amos said, "Thank ya, Massa."

"You take Captain Alcott out to the house and break the news to Ellis and Sarah, then go to the carriage factory so Angus can pick out a carriage. Then go out to Mr. Whitlock's place to see if he has a suitable team for sale."

"Yassa, Massa."

He brought the carriage around and climbed down and opened the door for Angus. When Angus was seated comfortably, Amos drove home faster than he ever had before to give his family the good news. Amos introduced Ellis to his new master and they went to the wagon master's where Michael had bought his wagons and buckboard, and he had a brand new two-seated carriage with a high driver's seat out in front that was truly a handsome thing.

The captain said, "What do you think of it, Ellis?"

Ellis walked slowly around the carriage and crawled under it and examined the undercarriage and the coupling pole. Then he examined the tongue, doubletree, singletree and the breast choke. Then he said, "It sho' is a fine carriage, Massa, I'd sho' be proud to drive that around town."

The captain said, "That settles it; now let's pick out a set of harness."

Ellis said, "We have to get the team first, Massa, to be sure the collars fit."

"Well, let's go to Mr. Whitlock and buy our horses."

"He sho' does have fine horses," Amos said, "and he should have some young geldings broke for harness. If they're a little wild, Ellis can handle them all right, don't you worry yo'self bout that."

When they told Mr. Whitlock what they were looking for he said, "I've got three teams to sell, and you can't go wrong on any of them. I'd caution you on the two-year-olds though, they're still pretty wild."

Ellis drove all three teams and it was apparent that he could handle any of them.

Captain Alcott said, "Ellis, you're the one who'll be driving and taking care of the horses, so it's only fair that you pick out your own team. What do you say?"

Ellis was pleased beyond belief, and there was excitement in his voice when he said, "Massa, the two older teams are more steady and dependable."

"But you like the younger bays better, don't you?" interjected the Captain.

"Yassa, Massa, I sho' does."

"So do I. The bays are yours, Ellis."

Ellis jumped up and kicked his heels together and said, "Oh boy!"

Mr. Whitlock made out a bill of sale and Angus paid him on the spot.

They led the bays back and hitched them to the carriage with all new harness. Amos said, "Ellis, I wouldn't trade places with you, but I'm a little jealous. You serve the captain well now, you hear?"

"I will, dad, I'll make you proud of me, you just wait and see."

"I'm proud of you now, Ellis, and you keep on the way you are and I'll always be."

Ellis proudly drove the high stepping bays hitched to the fine carriage back to Ted's office so Angus could complete their business.

After Ted paid Angus for his last shipment Angus said, "Ted, I appreciate your kindness in giving Ellis to me. No offense, my friend, but I don't want to be a slave owner. Would you consider giving Ellis his freedom papers and I'll hire him to work for me?"

"Sure, I have the papers here," and he made them out and signed them and Angus signed as witness.

"May I leave my horses in your stable tonight, and I'd like to bunk in your cabin a few days? I'm going to ride out to Michael's place in the morning."

"By all means, old friend, and you tell Kabuta that I'll be out there Saturday afternoon to take him up on that fish supper. I'm going to spend at least three weeks fishing and hunting. Do you own a good shotgun, Angus?"

"No, I've never fired one."

"I'll bring two of mine and I'll teach you how to bring quail down in flight. They're good eating too. Now let's go see your new purchase."

When they walked out to where Ellis was waiting, he was wiping the dust off the wheels of the carriage.

Ellis snapped to attention and opened the carriage door for the captain.

Angus said, "Hold on, Ellis, we have something to discuss before we go. Ted has given you your freedom and you are now your own man and you are free to go anywhere your heart desires. But I'd like to hire you to work for me."

When Ted handed Ellis the papers Ellis said, "Massa, I ain't neva gonna forget yo' kindness fo me." He turned back to the Captain and said, "I's proud to works fo'you, suh."

* * * * *

The next morning Michael and Kabuta were throwing corn in the crib when Ellis drove up to the barn and jumped down and opened the door of the carriage and Angus stepped out.

After they exchanged warm greetings Michael said, "Let me show you around, Captain."

Angus gave Ellis the keys to Ted's cabin and said, "Put our things in the cabin and Kabuta can show you around."

Kabuta said, "Mr. Mike," Michael frowned at him. "Do we have anything pressing us today? If not, I'll take this young man fishing."

Michael and Angus walked all over the property and Angus marveled at the way they had walled up the swimming pool, creek and the wall at the lower end to stop the erosion of the top soil.

Michael took him down to the corner of their property just across the creek from Ted's cabin, and said, "Captain, you can build your place right here. There's plenty of clear, sweet, spring water running the year round."

"Are you sure, Michael? I love this spot. I could grow old and die happy here."

"There's only one catch...you have my Power of Attorney and I would want you to look after my investments while Kabuta and I are gone. We're still going west when we feel the time is right. We have established this place so we'll have a place to come back to."

"Done, Michael," said the Captain as he extended his hand. "You and

Kabuta seem to be hitting it off famously. If you see me make a mistake with Ellis I want you to tell me. I like that young man and I want him to stay with me because he wants to, not out of necessity or because he feels obligated."

"I don't think you have anything to worry about. You have him walking on air already, and letting him pick out his own team was wonderful. He probably never had a white man call him anything but 'boy' in his life, and when you called him 'young man' I saw the pride in his face. Continue to treat him like that and he's yours for life. Just don't let him become too arrogant."

"I guess I've handled enough tough sailors in my lifetime to be able to take care of that, Michael."

Michael slapped him on the back and said, "Let's go help Kabuta and Ellis catch our supper. Kabuta will have a treat for us for supper. That man is the best cook I've ever seen."

When they heard Mike and the Captain coming Ellis held up the fish and said, "Almost enough for supper. I'm going to clean them and Kabuta is going to do the cooking."

With all four of them fishing they had enough in no time. Michael said, "Captain, I wish we could enjoy catching more, but Kabuta and I have agreed we would never catch more than we need. That way we figure we'll have fish any time we want them."

"Makes sense to me," the Captain said.

When Kabuta was about ready to put his masterpiece on the table he said, "Mike, coffee or tea?"

Michael deferred to their guest.

"Coffee, if you please. That's my worst vice," the captain said, "I've developed a taste for it, and now prefer it over tea."

Mike said, "I like it, but I don't think it'll ever replace tea for me."

Angus said, "One of the agreements I made with Bill Sweeney, who bought my ship, was that he was to leave a large shipment for me with Ted every time he sailed into port. You know, I always thought this was a beautiful country, and after I met you, Michael, and you left my ship here, I decided this was where I was going to retire. I know I'm going to be happy here."

"On a clear day you can see all the way to Chesapeake Bay, and you can see the ships sailing up the James River," Michael said.

"I'm going to miss sailing, Mike, I surely will."

When they sat down to the table Ellis was surprised that he and Kabuta sat at the same table with Mike and the Captain. He was further surprised when Mike bowed his head and said grace and thanked God for the two guests at their table. He watched Kabuta closely and did everything like he did.

The following morning Michael set up some targets while Kabuta and Ellis took care of the stock and prepared breakfast. When breakfast was over Michael and the Captain began to teach Kabuta and Ellis how to use the crossbow, sword, broadsword and the staff.

With their natural rhythm, intelligence and keen eye, they were able to master these weapons quickly.

Mike said, "Captain, you and Ellis watch Kabuta and me do some shooting. We've been practicing for a year and I think we're getting the hang of it. Then we'll teach you how."

The captain and Ellis stood to one side and watched Michael and Kabuta stand and draw their pistols and fire at the targets. Angus went and examined the targets after the third shot and said, "God pity anyone drawing against either of you. You're both fast and pretty accurate, and you'll get better. I've been told and I've read also that where you're going you're apt to need those skills. After you're satisfied with your accuracy, you should practice the speed of your draw, using ammunition. And, Michael, if you do go west, take plenty of it with you. It probably won't be replaceable if you go too far west."

"When we go west", Michael corrected. "And we'll only use our guns when the bow isn't practical, that way we save our ammunition."

"I'm going to hire a contractor to build my house and stables so Ellis and I can get in it before winter."

He had the barn and stables built first and while they were building the two-story house Ellis borrowed Michael's four-man team and one of his big wagons and filled the cribs full of wheat and corn.

Mike and Kabuta turned water from the creek into all of their corrals, including Ted's place, for him allowing them to use his cabin. Kabuta said, "I'd like to keep this a secret from Massa Ted until he gets out here. Pressing business must be keeping him in town, but I know he'll get out here as soon as he can. He's overdue for one of his vacations out here."

They had just finished the water trough in Ted's corral Saturday afternoon when Ellis walked up with a string of bass and said, "I saw Massa Ted top over a hill about a mile away."

Kabuta said, "Ellis, you clean those fish, times a wastin.' You remember the bunch of poke salad I showed you; go bring that to me as quickly as you can. Then I don't want anybody to bother me until supper is ready. Mike, I'm sure glad you talked me in to baking apple pies yesterday."

Kabuta and Ellis got busy preparing a meal for these three men that they admired so much.

When Amos and Ted drove up and Ted saw the water running through stone watering troughs in each of his corrals and back into the creek, he was deeply moved.

Kabuta and Ellis had killed a mess of young, fat squirrels early that morning, and Ellis had dug young potatoes from the garden and picked their first roasting ears of corn that day. There were still fresh radishes, little green onions, lettuce and English peas in the garden, and mushrooms covered the riverbank.

When Kabuta called them to supper he set a feast of squirrel dumplings and fish, with all the trimmings, before them.

Mike asked the Captain to say grace, and they ate with relish.

When they had put most of it away Kabuta said, "Coffee and apple pie coming up."

Ted said, "Kabuta, I've been dreaming about this meal for weeks, but I never dreamed it would be this good. Could we wait for that for an hour or so, I couldn't eat another bite right now?"

Kabuta smiled with pleasure at those words and said, "Anything you say, Massa Ted."

* * * * *

Soon they put the finishing touches to the Captain's house. The Captain's quarters was on the ground floor, because he didn't want to climb the stairs except to go up on the deck that ran completely around the house, to watch the ships sail up the river or to read a good book.

Angus and Ellis had been slipping away to the Chambers' every Saturday night for the last six months so Ellis could go walking with Lola, and Angus had been sitting on the verandah sipping mint juleps with Ted's widowed sister.

They had brought the ladies out to see the house, and they had added the feminine touch in furnishing it. A week after they finished the house, Angus invited Michael to go with him to Ted's house to be his best man when he married Christine Chambers Olson. And Ellis asked Kabuta to be his best man when he married Lola. The Presbyterian minister married both couples in a double ceremony on the verandah of Ted's home.

Ellis took his bride back to the house where they would live upstairs. But Angus took his bride into Richmond and they spent a week in the best hotel in town. Right after the weddings, when Mike and Kabuta were going home, Mike said, "My friend, maybe we should look for some brides before we go west."

"It's liable to get might lonely out there, Mike," Kabuta remarked. "Ellis told me that Lola was second cook in Ted's house. He said, 'Man, can she cook! You're a good cook, but you just wait until you bite into one of her cakes or pies. The Captain agreed that you two would eat at our table from now on for giving him this land and for all the things you've done for us.'

"Kabuta said, 'you mean she'll do all the cooking? I won't have to cook anymore?'

"She and I will if the captain and his bride will allow it, and I'm sure they will. I won't have enough to keep me busy so I'll help in the house as well as doing the outside chores. The Captain said he intended to take care of the garden and I happen to know that Mrs. Christine was always planting and weeding at Massa Ted's place for the pure pleasure of it.'"

Mike said, "That's great, Kabuta, it'll give us more time together to finish the place."

CHAPTER THIRTEEN

It would be a couple of months before they could gather the corn and Mike and Kabuta had some time for leisure for the first time since they'd come here. They spent their morning hours removing all the dead trees on the place and cutting them into firewood. Afternoons they would saddle their horses, strap on their side arms and ride up and down both sides of the river, sometimes exploring the mountain behind their property. They practiced drawing and firing their guns as they rode or walked on the ground until they were sure they had reached their full capability. And they were fast and accurate.

One day Mike said, "Kabuta, let's fix a lunch and take enough supplies to last us a few days, and follow the road west of our place and see how far it goes. That's the way we'll be traveling with heavily loaded wagons when we go west."

Kabuta said, "I'll get everything ready if you'll go tell Ellis where we're going and get him to take care of our stock."

They had been here over two years and the only wagons they had seen go by were those of woodcutters.

They rode all day and just before dusk came upon a small spring bubbling up from underneath a large rock, forming a small pool. They had been ducking under low branches for the last hour and Kabuta remarked, "I'll bet there hasn't been a wagon up this far in years. As late as it is, we might not find water again before dark. Maybe we'd better camp right here. There isn't anything for the horses to eat. I know we trained them to stay close to us and come at our whistle, but we haven't ridden them very much for a long time. They might start remembering the good yellow dent corn they've been eating and leave us up here high and dry. We'd better tie them firmly to trees tonight."

"You're probably right. But let's ride back to that little stream we crossed a ways back. There's a small meadow there we can stake the horses where they can reach the water, and still fill up on good grass. There was also a large live oak with a thick layer of leaves where we can lay our beds and we'll sleep better there than we would on this rocky hillside. I saw some squirrel nests in the oak. We need more meat, I could eat the two we have and want more."

They turned back and killed four more squirrels on the way. Kabuta skinned them and built a fire while Mike was taking care of the horses.

It was well after dark when Michael crawled in his bed. Kabuta walked a little ways away and Michael heard him as he prayed, "Dear Heavenly Father, let me find Swanna before we go west. In Jesus' name, Amen."

Mike whispered, "And a wife for me to love, dear Lord."

When Kabuta came to bed they talked a while before they went to sleep.

They woke the next morning with the hounds snarling and barking. They sat up and not fifty feet from them was a huge black bear standing on his hind feet, sniffing the air right under the rabbit that Michael had hung high in a tree the night before.

The dogs became more frantic, now they were growling and snarling, waiting for Michael's command to attack, which never came. Kabuta drew his pistol and started to shoot, but Michael hollered, "No, Kabuta, there's no way that pea shooter would kill that big bruiser, it would just make him mad, and he might charge. Let's just pick up our boots and slowly drag our bedrolls and let him have our breakfast. That's what he's after."

They slowly moved to where their horses were tied, saddled up, called the dogs off and rode away.

They had ridden only a short ways when Kabuta said, "Mike, we left our coffee pot and frying pan."

"Leave them. We'll be coming back this way some time and we'll pick them up, if they're still there."

They rode on to the top of the mountain and camped. They had selected a number of places they could camp on their way west.

The following day they camped where they had encountered the bear and used their coffee pot and frying pan that night. The next morning they headed for home.

When they arrived at their place late in the afternoon they saw Ellis drive up to the Captain's house. They saw him open the carriage door, and Angus helped his bride out. They walked to the door of the house and Angus swung the door wide open and swept his bride up in his strong arms and carried her across the threshold as she nestled her head against his shoulder.

Ellis was feeding the team when they reached him.

Kabuta said, "Ellis, do you think Lola could feed a couple of hungry men? We haven't had a bite to eat since last night and we've been riding all day."

"Yeah," said Mike, "We learned a good lesson. We'll never go for an overnight stay in the woods again without plenty of beef jerky." He told him about their experience with the bear.

Ellis said, "Lola knew that the Captain was bringing his bride home today and she said you two would probably be riding in here half starved."

Kabuta turned and headed for the pool to take a bath, with Michael right behind him.

When they returned to the Captain's house, decked out in the best they had, Ellis saw them coming and met them at the door. "Come on in and go right to the dining room."

When they were seated Ellis, went to the Captain and Christine's bedroom and knocked gently on the door and said, "Dinner is served."

When they came into the dining room Angus pulled out Christine's chair and seated her at one end of the table and went around and seated himself on the other end.

Lola brought a dish of hot biscuits and placed them on the table and Ellis poured the coffee. Then he pulled out a chair for his wife and seated her across the table from Mike and sat down beside her. Angus asked them to all hold hands and he bowed his head and said grace.

Later that night as Christine lay beside Angus she rolled over and kissed him and said, "I never dreamed that I'd ever sit at a table and eat with Blacks, but it didn't bother me at all. Actually, I found them delightful."

Angus said, "Why should it bother you? It never bothered you to eat their cooking, did it?"

"No, not at all."

"I never could understand why white people thought they were too good for Blacks to come in their front door or eat at their table, but they were good enough to raise their children when they were traveling or at parties," Angus murmured as he dozed off.

One day in the late afternoon, Mike and Kabuta were fishing downriver and had crossed over to fish near the far bank. Kabuta walked around the bend of the river just as a pretty young black girl pulled in about a half-pound bass, throwing it back over her head. She was squealing with delight and Kabuta startled her when he laughed in his deep, booming voice.

He said, "If you get that excited when you catch a little fish like that, pretty lady, I'd sure like to be there when you catch a big one."

"Little!" she retorted, as she held up her bass, " I'll bet this is more than you could eat, you smarty pants."

"Girl, you didn't take a good look at me, did you? I'm six feet three inches tall and weigh two hundred ten pounds. I could eat a half-dozen fish the size of that little thing."

She stood looking at Kabuta, smiling prettily.

Kabuta said, "Mike and I have a pretty good string back up the river where we're going to camp tonight. We'd be delighted if you'd dine with us tonight. I'm a good cook and all you'd have to do is sit on a log and look as pretty as you do right now."

Mike came around the bend of the river and saw them standing, smiling at one another. Kabuta said, "Mike I've invited this pretty lady to dine with us...what is your name, pretty lady?"

"P-P-P-Peg," she stammered, flustered because she had never been called a pretty lady before.

"That's great, Kabuta," Mike replied. "I'm about ready for it, aren't you?"

Peg said, "I'd love to dine with you gentlemen, but I'd have to ask my Mistress if it's okay."

At that moment a girl dressed in men's pants and a loosely fitting man's shirt walked up. She had flaming red hair tied back in a ponytail, and her eyes were as blue as a clear morning sky. She was tall; five eight, Mike thought.

She said, "I thought I heard voices and I came to see if you were all right, Peg."

Michael doffed his hat, bowed low and said, "Howdy, ma'am. I'm Michael Ross from County Kerry, Ireland, and this is Kabuta. What might your name be?"

Mischief started dancing in her sparkling blue eyes and a little smile played around her shapely lips. "My name might be anything, but it happens to be Katy O'Flannery."

"Miss O'Flannery, Kabuta has just asked Miss Peg to dine with us, would you care to join us?"

"That would be nice," she said, "But we'll have to go home and tell our parents. Whose fish are we eating, yours or ours?"

Michael said, "Take yours to your folks, we have plenty."

Kabuta said, "You had better luck than I did, then, I only have a few little ones."

"Give them to Miss Peg. I've a good string back at camp."

Katy said, "It'll take us until almost sundown to get back here."

Peg had run and brought up their horses when she saw that Katy was as eager as she was to get to know these two handsome men better.

Michael said, "Our camp is just up the river near a large spring underneath a large cottonwood."

"We know the place," Katy said, and she mounted her big gray with ease. Peg was already mounted on a twin gray and they took out of there in a hurry.

Kabuta said, "Mike, those gals can ride."

"I hope their parents let them come back," Mike said.

"They'll be back, Mike...they have to. I may be wrong, but I believe Peg is the little girl I befriended on the boat...the one that clung to my leg at the auction and screamed as they dragged her away."

"That would be quite a coincidence, Kabuta."

"Well, Mike, we read in our devotions the other day that we have not because we ask not. I asked God to let me find Swanna before we go west. I believe He has answered my prayer."

"I asked God to send me a wife before we go. Maybe Katy could be the answer to my prayer," Mike said.

* * * * *

Peg went right to work when they reached the plantation, getting their bedrolls together with a couple of tin plates and cups, forks and knives. She even talked the cook into letting her take a freshly baked apple pie. She knew Katy would tell her parents they were going to sleep out on the riverbank and she would neglect to tell them that there were two men waiting for them.

She also knew that Katy's dad would fuss and fume and refuse to let them go three or four times. Then Mrs. O'Flannery would say, "Oh, Will!" Then he would give in; he never could refuse her anything.

When the girls rode up to their camp just before dark, the men noticed that they had taken time to slip into flattering riding habits. Mike took their horses to tie them up and he was surprised to find bedrolls tied behind their saddles. He removed their saddles and threw them over a log, just behind theirs. He had just finished this little chore when Kabuta said, "Come and get it."

Kabuta had outdone himself with dinner and when they were seated Kabuta said grace. As they ate, not much was said. But Peg and Kabuta keep glancing at each other and smiling shyly.

Katy began to wonder if she had done the right thing. They didn't know these men and yet she had committed herself and Peg to sleep out here and she noticed the chemistry between Peg and the big jovial Kabuta. This worried her, and Michael noticed.

Michael put her anxious heart at ease when he said, "You ladies put your bedrolls in our tent, and Kabuta and I will sleep out under the stars."

A sigh of relief escaped from Katy.

Michael noticed. He said, "Beautiful Katy, you and Peg have nothing to fear from us. We're honorable men, and we are your neighbors...we live across the river up about ten miles and we hope we'll become good friends. Please trust us."

Peg and Katy put their bedrolls in the tent while Mike and Kabuta cleaned up the camp. They built the fire up rather high and Peg and Kabuta sat on one side of it speaking quietly, while Mike and Katy sat on the other side just staring into the fire. Suddenly, Michael's two big wolfhounds came bounding into camp. Katy gave out a little cry and jumped right into Michael's arms.

Realizing what she had done, she pulled away from Michael. "Michael Ross, don't you get any ideas, I'm spoken for."

Peg whispered to Kabuta, "But she doesn't love him."

Mike replied, "Did you accept his proposal, Katy?"

"Not yet, but papa wants me to."

"Don't do it, Katy, until you know you want to spend the rest of your life with him."

"Well, George is a nice man. He's a handsome brute and he says he loves me, but he doesn't excite me. I haven't made up my mind yet whether I love him enough to marry him."

"Katy, you don't make up your mind to fall in love, it just happens. And when it does, you'll know it."

"Michael Ross, how do you know so much about it? Are you in love?"

"I wasn't, until I saw you walk around that clump of bushes and I looked deep into those beautiful pools of blue eyes and saw your impish smile. I'd like to have time to explore this feeling that's caused my heart to beat faster since I first saw you, Katy O'Flannery."

Peg said, "Kabuta, I've never eaten a better meal. You must teach me to cook like that."

"I'd love to, my pretty lady. Though I'm sure there's much you could teach me."

Katy was surprised when Mike told Kabuta he would do the dishes. She said, "You don't act as though Kabuta is your slave."

"He's not, Kabuta's a free man and he has become my best friend. More like a brother, really," Michael said, and he told her how they had met and why he came to America. "His former owners taught him how to read and write, and I've started teaching him how to do his sums. If I should die or get killed, he gets all I have."

"Peg and I are sorta like that...I taught her to read and write and do her sums. In fact, she's better at her sums than I am. She's a smart lady. If my father knew I taught her all these things we'd both be in deep trouble."

Michael said, "Kabuta and I are going over the mountains come spring to explore the far western lands. We have fifty acres with a good house on it, and our good friend, Captain Angus Alcott, has built a house next door, and he'll look after our place until we get back, if we get back."

Katy's heart sank. She already knew that this young man excited her far more than George ever had. She didn't know if it was love, but she sure wanted to find out. She was sure now that she would never marry George.

Peg sat on a log and watched fascinated as two men waited on her for the first time in her life.

After they were through eating and Mike had cleaned up the camp while Kabuta removed his and Mike's bedrolls out of the tent and laid them out, she and Kabuta sat on the log side-by-side. Kabuta told her the same story about how they met as Michael had told Katy, adding that his time with Mike had been the happiest days of his life, but that something was missing."

"What's missing, Mr. Kabuta?"

"I didn't know until today, but what has been missing, I think, is you."

"Why, Mr. Kabuta, we've just met, how could you think such a thing?"

"Little girl, have I changed so much you don't recognize me or even remember my name? Your name was Swanna, and now they call you Peg. I'm Kabuta, the twelve- year-old boy who helped you all those years ago on the slave ship. We were separated when we were sold in Richmond. I've been haunted in my dreams by the tears in your eyes and you screaming 'Kabuta!' as they tore you from my legs and took you away."

Peg put her arms around Kabuta's neck and said, "Oh! Dear, Kabuta, I'm so sorry I didn't remember you, but you've grown so big and strong. I've tried to forget all those horrible men that took so many of our young girls to their beds. And now I remember how you used to hide me when they came into the hold."

She looked around as if to assure herself that no one but Kabuta heard. Then she said, "My Master would be furious if he knew we were out here with you right now. He wants Katy to marry that dull, plodding George and he wants to breed me to a strong slave so I'll produce strong slaves to help on the plantation. The only thing that's stopped him is Katy and her mother, and I don't think they can hold him off much longer."

They sat around the fire and talked until well after midnight, and when Katy and Peg finally got up to go to the tent Mike said, "Katy, we'll be here every evening for a week before we'll have to gather our corn. Will you come, please?"

"We'll be here if my father doesn't find out we spent the night out here with you. He would think the worst no matter what we said."

The sun filtering through the trees woke Michael the next morning and he saw that Kabuta was already building a fire. Mike woke the girls and when they saw how high the sun was Katy said, "We must go at once, before daddy comes looking for us"

Mike and Kabuta saddled their horses and Katy leaned down out of the saddle and kissed Michael on the lips and whispered, "I'll never marry George." And before Michael could respond she kicked her mount in the ribs and sped away.

Peg said, "Kabuta, if the Master starts to send me to the stud man, I'll try to run away. May I come to you?"

"Of course; and we'll head west before the snow falls."

She gave him an adoring smile and sped after her Mistress.

Mike and Kabuta left the tent in place, but decided to go home and start gathering the corn. As they worked side-by-side Kabuta said, "Mike, Peg is Swanna," and he told him what Peg said about being sent to the stud man. "Mike, if her master tells her to go to his bed she's going to run away and I'm going with her. I love her, and I can't let her become a breeder."

"Don't worry, my friend, we'll figure out something."

They worked hard and quit early, took a bath in the spring and headed for the tent, hoping the girls would be there. They were, and there was a pot of beef stew boiling on the fire. Peg ran and kissed Kabuta and said, "Our cook's stew may not be as good as yours, but supper's ready."

After they ate, Kabuta took Peg's hand and led her up the river while Michael and Katy went the opposite direction.

Kabuta said, "Little darling, don't you worry. Mike said we would work something out. He has something in mind. And I've come to believe that Mike can do anything he sets his mind to."

They met like this for four nights and by that time Kabuta and Peg had definitely decided that they would run away together if Mike failed and she was to be sent to the stud man.

By Friday night, Mike and Kabuta had finished gathering the corn and their cribs were full.

They washed up at the spring and went to the meeting place early. Kabuta cooked a good dinner. They waited, but the girls never came.

Kabuta's heart sank and a feeling of doom spread over him like a cloud. What if Peg had been taken to the stud, and she couldn't get away? The more he thought about it, the more agitated he became. Just as he started for his horse the girls thundered in to camp. Peg jumped from her horse and rushed into Kabuta's arms with the tears streaming down her pretty face.

He held her close until she quit shaking and crying.

When Katy leaped from her horse her auburn hair looked redder than it really was and she was so angry she could hardly speak. Mike tried to put his arms around her, but she pushed him away. "Men! I'm so mad at my daddy I could cuss and cry at the same time. He told me this morning he was taking Peg away from me and replacing her with a younger girl. He's going to send her to the big breeder's bed and she has to sleep with him until she becomes pregnant! I had a hard time persuading him to give us this last weekend together.

"My job has always been to help milk the cows, feed the chickens, and gather the eggs. I was permitted to sell all the extra butter and eggs and keep the money for myself. When I was given money to go to the hairdresser or to buy clothes, Peg would do my hair and I bought yardage and made my own clothes. I had to hoard all the money I could get my hands on. I hate to say it, but my daddy's a penny-pinching, insensitive old goat.

"When I asked him to sign the papers for Peg over to me he said he would do it as soon as I could pay him six hundred dollars. Yesterday I begged thirty dollars from mom, which gave me the six hundred. When I took it into dad's office where he was working on accounts and laid it down on his desk, he looked at me and said, 'What's this for?'

" 'Peg, of course,' I told him. 'You promised you would sell her to me for six hundred dollars. Count it, it's all there.' Oh! It felt good to see him squirm in his seat. But then he told me the price had gone up to eight hundred.

"I lost my temper and said things that I shouldn't have said, and he got really angry. He said Joe, our stud man, had been trying to get him to let him sleep with Peg, and he told him he would send her to him tonight. He said he couldn't go back on his word."

"I screamed, 'What about your word to me?'"

He finally said, 'Eight hundred dollars and I'll give you until Monday morning to come up with it. And if you don't, Peg goes to the stud.'

"I went to mother and she tried to get him to honor our previous agreement, but this is one of the few times he wouldn't give in to her. Mother had already given me all she had and there isn't anywhere else I can get the money by Monday night. Peg has never known a man that way and she's scared to death of that big brute."

"Would your father honor his word if you came up with the other two hundred dollars?"

"Yes, mother and I would make his life a living hell if he didn't, and he knows it. In fact, mother has already kicked him out of her bedroom and said he could never come back if he went through with this."

"If you buy her, will he let her stay in the house this winter?"

"He wouldn't dare not to if he wants any peace at all."

"Then there's no problem. I'll go back to my place and get the money you need and we'll go to your place and make the deal. Besides, I think it's time your parents met the man you're going to marry."

She gasped, "Aren't you the bold one! You see a girl four or five times and you make an announcement like that. You may come courting, Michael Ross, but whether I marry you remains to be seen. What do you expect...that I'll just ride off into the sunset with you, never knowing where we will lay our head? You must be out of your mind, Michael Ross!"

Suddenly, what he said about the two hundred dollars registered with her. "Wait! You have two hundred dollars? And you'd give it to me?"

"Yes, Katy, I have two hundred dollars. And I'd give you the moon and the stars if I could gather them for you. And yes, you would go with me if you loved me, Katy O'Flannery."

Katy said, "I'm not telling daddy anything until I have papers for Peg. If he suspected anything at all he might try to force me to marry George before giving me Peg."

Kabuta and Peg were having a conversation of their own and they decided if Katy couldn't buy Peg before Monday afternoon Peg would slip out of the house at night and she and Kabuta would ride west as fast as they could.

Katy said, "We must go. I think daddy saw us come here. I saw him walk out the back door and head for the stable. He could be here any minute."

Mike said, "I'll see you in church Sunday morning and I'll have the money."

CHAPTER FOURTEEN

Sunday morning Michael walked into the church right behind Katy and her mother. Katy made sure her mother entered the pew first, and then as they sat down Michael eased in beside Katy. As they were singing the first song Michael slipped a leather bag into Katy's hand and whispered, "Guard that well. There's two hundred dollars in gold coins in that pouch."

Katy slipped the pouch into the drawstring purse she was carrying.

After the services, Katy said, "Mother, I'd like to introduce you to Michael Ross from County Kerry, Ireland."

Mrs. O'Flannery said, "I know it well, Mr. Ross. I was born and raised on a sheep farm over in County Cork. We used to go to the lakes for vacations. My daughter tells me that you are in love with her, and that you want her to become your wife. And then you intend to ride off into the sunset with her and we may never see her again. That may be romantic, but not very practical, do you think?"

"Maybe not, but I've had my heart set on it for a long time, and I don't see how Kabuta and I can live our lives the way we want to here. Kabuta is a free man and my best friend, and we share everything equally. I have already had to kill one man who tried to take him and sell him into slavery again. I hope I never have to kill again, but I will to protect Kabuta and anything else I hold dear. If Katy falls in love with me as I have her, yes, I hope to go west with her, Kabuta and Peg as our wives, with your blessing, of course. We hope to come back some day. We're leaving a home and fifty acres across and just up the river from you"

"If Katy loves you, you have my blessings; after all, I left the old country and came to America to face the unknown with the love of my life when I was just a slip of a girl, and I've never been back to see my parents. Yes, if Katy loves you enough to go, you will have my blessings, but you may not get Ralph's so easy. By the way, what did you slip my daughter? We don't have any secrets from one another, do we, Katy?"

"Not many. You had better be careful what you say Michael, I tell mother everything; well, almost everything She's not only my mother, she's also my best friend."

Mrs. O'Flannery winked at Michael and smiled sweetly, and said, "Well, she didn't tell me that she stayed all night on the banks of the James River with you until yesterday. She said that she and Peg slept in your tent and you and your friend slept outside, and I know it's true if my Katy said so. She also told me that she knew now that she would never marry that pompous, conceited bore, George, that Ralph has been trying to push her off on. That, and his going back on his word to sell Peg to Katy, has driven a wedge between my husband and me and that makes me very unhappy. I'm sure you slipped her the money she needs to turn the tables on him and that endears you to me. He'll let her have Peg and that will remove the wedge, and I'm glad. You see, I love my husband and I want our relationship to be the way it used to be. Right now he's forbidden to come into my bedroom and I want to unlock that door...I miss him."

Michael liked this lady and he was beginning to get a different picture. Ralph O'Flannery must have many redeeming qualities or he never would have landed this beautiful, levelheaded Irish lass.

"Mike, may I call you Mike?

"Sure, everyone else does."

"You're coming to dinner with us. It's time Ralph meets a real man that a woman can look up to, especially the one that's going to make our Katy happy."

"Wait up, mother, he hasn't asked me yet, and I'm not sure I'd say yes if he did."

Mary said, "Yes dear," with a knowing smile on her face. Her heart was aching, because she was sure Katy would ride away with this tall Irishman, and she knew that they might never come back, and she had no intention of ever leaving the plantation.

When they reached the plantation Ralph O'Flannery met the coach, as he did every Sunday, to help his wife and daughter as they stepped out. After helping Katy out, Ralph turned to follow her into the house as Michael stepped out. Mary O'Flannery said, "Ralph, meet Michael Ross from County Kerry, the young man that says he's going to marry our Katy. Michael, my husband, Ralph."

Michael expected Katy's dad to explode. Instead, the man looked at him intently for several moments. Then apparently approved by what he saw, he said, "I'm pleased to meet you, Michael Ross from Kerry County."

Katy came back just in time to hear him say, "Especially if you're going to take Katy off our hands. I've been trying to get George Burke to take her, but he's isn't sure he wants to try to tame this fiery little redhead of ours. If you'd take her, Michael, I'd be eternally grateful. But there's one thing you have to promise me, and that's to take Peg with her. Peg wouldn't be any good to us at all without Katy. Let's go up on the verandah so we can get out of this blazing sun."

The women went into the house and the men seated themselves in comfortable chairs in the shade. In moments Katy and her mother returned and offered the men cool drinks.

Ralph said, "Michael, can you support our Katy? We wouldn't want her to go without the comforts of life. That's why I was in hopes she could love George. He's rather dull, I guess, but he's well fixed and she would want for nothing."

"Except some excitement in her life," Mary interjected.

Mike said, "I don't want to leave the wrong impression, but I can support Katy in the fashion she is accustomed to. But that doesn't mean that Katy won't face many hardships, because my best friend, Kabuta, and I are traveling by horse and wagon to the far-off western lands. Our lives may be short or they may be long, whatever God wills, but I promise you this, they'll be hard and miserable sometimes, but they will be exciting. Katy, I hope you're as adventurous as I am. If you are, and you love me, I want you to be my wife and come with me come spring."

Katy said, "As I said at the river, you may come courting, Michael Ross, and I'll let you know by spring. I'll only give myself to the man that I'm sure I want to spend the rest of my life with."

"I know, Katy, and I respect you for that, and I respect your wishes. I've waited this long for the girl of my dreams and I can wait a little longer."

She kissed him hard on the lips and ran up the stairs to break the good news to Peg.

Peg was weeping when Katy burst into her room and cried, "Peg, your mine! Daddy gave you to me...he didn't even take the money!"

Slowly, what Katy had said registered on Peg's mind and she wiped her tears away and a smile spread across her beautiful face, showing her even, white teeth. "Katy, does that mean I'll be free to marry Kabuta?" she asked.

"Yes, I'll give you your freedom papers, and since Kabuta is free too, that means that you two can get married any time you want to. But I think we should wait until spring."

Peg said, "I don't want to wait, I want my Kabuta to keep me warm through the long winter months."

Katy said, "I told Mike he could come courting but that he'd have to wait. Oh heck! I guess he's waited long enough. Let's put on our best dresses and go down and tell him and my parents that we want to get married now."

When they came down Mike and the O'Flannery's were still sitting on the verandah. Mike said, "Will you two come and sit with us for a while? I have a story to tell you, and I hope I'll never have to tell it again."

Then he told them the whole story about the loss of his family and the acquisition of his wealth.

"I couldn't stay there, haunted with reminders everywhere I went, so I came to America."

Before he finished his story the three women were weeping, and when he finished Katy, wrapped her arms around him and ran her fingers through his beautiful auburn hair.

Then she kissed him tender and long. She said, "Mike, I do love you, and Peg is head-over-heels in love with Kabuta. When we talked upstairs we decided that we want to get married as soon as we can. Why wait? We know we love you and wherever you want to go, we want to go. We'll be happy wherever we are, as long as we're together. After all, Mike, how could a true-blooded

Irish lass resist the thrill of facing the unknown, especially if she's married to the handsomest man she's ever seen. I'll marry you tomorrow if you want."

The O'Flannery's were happy to hear Mike say, "No, Katy, I want you to have time to give this plenty of thought. You must be sure. Kabuta and I want to teach you girls how to shoot all kinds of guns and the bow; you may have to use them to defend us all out there."

Ralph and Mary laughed at that.

Ralph said, "Mike, I'll bet you a ten-dollar gold piece that Katy and Peg can beat you and Kabuta with the rifle and pistol. They haven't used the bow. Virginia wasn't exactly tame when we first came here. Mary and these girls can shoot, Mike, believe me. Katy and Peg have loaded derringers that they carry in those drawstring bags you see them carry. These girls can take care of themselves. You don't think I'd have let two girls spend the night on the river with two strange men if I didn't trust them, do you?"

Katy said, "Mother, you promised you wouldn't tell daddy."

"Katy, lass, your mother didn't have to tell me anything. Every time you and Peg camped out on the river I would slip up to your camp to make sure you were safe. You can bet I lay out in the brush a lot longer that night you were with Mike and Kabuta. I almost left when I saw Kabuta bow his head and say grace before you ate. I hung around until I saw you two enter the tent and Mike and Kabuta were asleep in their bedrolls quite a distance from you. Isn't this true, mother?'

"That's what you told me. Now you can see that your daddy and I were partners in our little deception. But I do think he went too far with that breeder stud business."

Ralph said, "I regret that part of it, can you girls forgive a stupid old man?"

They both replied in unison, "You're not," and they showered him with kisses in forgiveness.

Mike went back to the cabin walking on air...he was a happy man! He found Kabuta just putting a saddle on the filly he was breaking for Peg. When he told Kabuta the good news he grabbed Mike and they danced around the corral like crazy men. Mike said, "They won't meet us on the river tonight, we can go to the house now and sit on the verandah in comfortable chairs."

Mike caught the filly he was breaking for Katy and saddled her. Both horses trembled in every muscle when they tightened up the cinches, but they didn't buck. They led them down in the freshly plowed cornfield where the horses couldn't pitch as well and if they did fall off it wouldn't hurt as much. Kabuta said, "Let me ride mine first." When he tried to mount her she shied away and tried to kick him. He said, "What's the matter with her? She's never tried to kick me before."

"You've never tried to mount her before. Let me blind her with this burlap sack and hold her head until you get on her."

"All right, but she won't buck with me. She loves me too much."

Mike grinned as he released the filly and slapped her on the flanks with the burlap sack before Kabuta had completely settled in the saddle. That big filly let out a squeal and reached for the sky. She twisted and turned one way and then the other. Kabuta was all over her until she sailed even higher and twisted sharply, sending Kabuta high into the air. He came down on his rear in the soft soil. He got up rubbing his rear and said, "Catch her for me, Mike. I didn't even get seated in the saddle, thanks to you."

When Mike brought her back to him Kabuta wouldn't mount her again until Mike was fifty feet away. This time she stood still, blowing heavily, until Kabuta was firmly seated in the saddle. He touched her in the ribs and she reached for the sky again, but Kabuta was ready for her and he anticipated every twist and turn. She finally realized she had met her master and soon she was cantering around the field, obeying Kabuta's command. He rode her up to the corral, rubbed her down and turned her loose in the pasture. He went back to the field and watched Mike get thrown a couple of times before he could get his horse to canter.

Mike admitted to himself that he wasn't the rider Kabuta was but he soothed his pride with the thought that his horse fought harder...whether it was true or not.

They worked the fillies for a month until they obeyed every command of the reins or knees. If they dropped the reins on the ground the horses would stand in that spot until they were called. If they removed the bits from their mouths they would graze nearby until they were called with a whistle command. It was time to give them to the girls.

When they left the girls after courting Friday night they asked them to walk down to the river to meet in the morning for a day of fishing.

Katy said, "Why can't we ride our horses?"

Peg said, "Yeah, it sure beats walking."

Kabuta said, "Humor us, Sugar."

Mike and Kabuta were at the fishing hole before the girls were and the fish were feeding like crazy.

The girls came up just as Kabuta pulled in a three- pound catfish. They were disappointed when they ran forward and kissed their men and they both gave them a quick peck and Mike said, "Get your lines in the water."

"Yeah," Kabuta said, "The way they're biting we can catch enough to feed the whole plantation and enough for Captain Alcott's table as well."

They caught catfish and bass until they had enough for both households. It was almost noon when Katy said, "Mike, if you'll let me ride your horse, I'll take these fish to the kitchen help and I'll fix a lunch basket so we can have a picnic at the spring."

Mike said, "You girls wait here for a little while, we have a surprise for you." He and Kabuta walked back up the river and returned with Mike leading a long-legged, barrel chested bay mare with a beautiful long flowing tail, brushed to a glistening glow in the bright sunlight. She was wearing a new bridle and saddle with "Katy" carved in them.

Kabuta was leading a sorrel mare that was just as beautiful as the bay and her new bridle and saddle had "Peg" carved in them also.

It was two happy maidens that rode up to the plantation to show Katy's parents the fine gifts their intendeds had given them.

Ralph said, "There's no Indian pony on earth can catch you on those fine mounts."

After the girls left, Kabuta said, "I'll just run these fish over to the Captain's."

"I'll tag along, there's a little matter I want to discuss with him."

When they rode up to the Captain's house, Ellis met them and exclaimed, "Look at those beauties! Are they for us?" He stretched his hand to take them from Kabuta.

"Sure enough," Kabuta said.

"I'll just go clean these. You'll find the Captain and his bride sitting up on the afterdeck enjoying this Indian summer weather."

"They won't be able to sit out there much longer, winter is right on us." Kabuta remarked.

Mike said, "Kabuta, we've been spending too much time with our girls, we'd better be lying in our winter wood tomorrow."

"Mike, you go ahead and do your business with the Captain, and I'll keep Ellis company while he cleans the fish. Don't take too long, the girls will be waiting."

Just then Lola stepped out on the deck and said, "Hello, Kabuta, when are you going to bring Peg over to meet us? I'm just dying to meet her."

"Right soon, name the day."

"Next Saturday for dinner at one o'clock; Dinner will be ready in an hour, Ellis. Should I make enough for you, Kabuta?"

"No, thank you, we're meeting the girls down at the spring for a picnic in about an hour."

Mike walked around the deck to where Angus and Christine were snoozing in the warm sun. He said, "Hello folks," softly, he didn't want to startle them.

They both greeted Mike warmly and he said, "Kabuta and I brought you a mess of catfish."

Christine clapped her hands and said, "Thanks, Mike, they're my favorite. Pull up a chair and sit with us a while."

Mike said, "Captain, as you know, I'll be marrying Katy O'Flannery, and Kabuta is marrying her maid, in the spring, and shortly afterwards we'll be heading west. I'm going to have Ted witness legal papers giving you the authority to use our place any way you see fit while we're gone, and if we never return, it's yours. Kabuta and I have talked this over, and this what we want to do."

"Mike, if it meets your approval, Christine has a son down in North Carolina with a wife and a small son. We just heard from him and he wants to sell his place and move up here close to us so his son can get to know his grandmother. His wife's parents were killed in an Indian raid and they've been taking care of her old maid aunt. She died recently, and his wife has no other relatives. We'll see that they take good care of the place."

"That'd be fine. I'm taking my plow and planter with me, and all of the stock. The field is ready for planting in the spring, but we'll leave before planting time. I'll bring the papers by next week."

Christine came over and hugged him and kissed his cheek and said, "We're going to miss you and Kabuta terribly, but thank you so much. It'll be wonderful to have my only child near me again. I've missed Jim and his wife, Misty, so much. I've never even seen my little grandson, Johnny. I'll write them right away and tell them they can come as soon as they sell their place." She turned to her husband and said, "If they get here before Mike leaves they can stay here with us, can't they dear?"

"Of course, it might be nice to hear the patter of little feet on our deck"

"We'll be hearing that pretty soon any way, dear, haven't you noticed that Lola is with child?"

"I thought she was just getting fat."

"Not the way that girl works around here."

Mike rose to leave and Christine said, "Aren't you and Kabuta dining with us?"

"No, thank you, the girls are preparing a picnic down by the spring. We'd better get going....we don't want to be late."

Just then Ellis and Kabuta walked around the end of the deck and Ellis had catfish fillets lying on a platter. "Look what Kabuta and Mike brought us for supper."

"I can't wait to sink my teeth into one of those," Christine said.

For the next week Mike, Kabuta, Ellis and Angus cut firewood every afternoon until they were sure they had enough to last both houses through the winter. They also stacked a good supply at Ted's cabin.

Mike and Kabuta had kept the girls' horses at their place to continue their training. They wanted to teach the girls how to ride straddle and how to guide their horses with knee commands as well as reins. After the soreness wore off the girls decided they would never ride sidesaddle again.

The four of them put their heads together and figured out what they would take with them. Mike informed the girls that the only containers they would have in which to carry their clothing, and coverings for their beds, would be two large trunks and two smaller ones.

Katy said, "Mike, will we be able to take a couple sets of china and silverware?"

"Yes, we'll bury the china in large barrels of flour to prevent breakage, and that's one thing we won't unload until our final destination. We'll take tin plates and cups for everyday use."

They spent the last month of winter purchasing all the things they would be taking with them, going over their list many times until they were sure they had everything. When they were sure they had everything ready to go, Mike went to Angus and said, "I want you and Ted to go over the list with me and give me your input; can you go into town with me tomorrow to see Ted?"

"Sure, I need to go into town on business anyway, and I'll enjoy your company." He slapped Mike on the knee and said, "I'm going to miss you, son."

The next day as they went over the list in Ted's office, Ted said, "I would advise you to take another cook stove and two pot-bellied heaters with you. You and Kabuta will sure have families and you won't be living in the same house. Looks like you've thought of everything else you'll need."

Angus said, "A good sea captain couldn't imagine going on a journey like that without a couple of good blocks and tackle, with plenty of new rope, and I'd like to purchase those things as a going-away present."

Mike said, "Great, we'll pick them up today, and I must draw out a good sum of cash to take with us. Ted, we plan to leave the first of next month, why don't you come out for a few days and we'll all take off and go hunting."

"How about this Monday morning? I can get away for a week."

Mike said, "Fine, and Angus, while you're conducting your business I'll go get the stoves and the cash money I need."

"Good, and when you get back here I'll have the rope and blocks and tackle waiting."

When they got home Mike put headboards in two of the wagons, put his plow and planter and the stoves in the back of his wagon, and poured shelled seed corn all around them and put two tents on top of the corn. In the front of the wagon he put their bed.

In back of Kabuta's wagon they bolted down one of the cook stoves in a sandbox, put in the wagon bed all the kitchen utensils and most of the food items they would need on the trail. The stovepipe would be braced and curved so the smoke would shoot out the back of the wagon. This way they could cook a pot of beans and ham hock or a stew as they traveled. Kabuta and Peg's bed would be in the front of this wagon.

Mike had ordered another wagon and in it would be the heavy barrels of flour, cornmeal and beans of all kinds, as well as other furnishing for their cabins. All the wagons were covered with heavy canvas that would keep out the rain and hot sunshine. On both of the wagons they would be sleeping in, the covering could be rolled up on both sides so they could open them up to get a cross breeze on hot summer nights, and for shade if they had a layover out on the plains where there were no trees to get their wagons under.

When spring came they had everything ready to go.

Two weeks before they left Mike and Katy and Kabuta and Peg were married on the verandah of the O'Flannery's plantation home, with all their relatives and friends around them. There were many white folks, and every slave on the place was there.

Katy wanted to be married in the church, but when the all-white congregation refused to allow Kabuta and Peg to be married there she decided on the verandah.

After a feast out under the trees, Kabuta took his bride back to their home near the waterfalls, where they had two glorious weeks to get to know one another as man and wife.

Ellis had told them his wedding gift was to take care of their stock until they left, and Lola's gift was to fix all their evening meals. Peg wanted to cook their breakfast. They slept so late every morning they ate only two meals a day. The Captain and Christine had given each of them a sharp two-edged knife and a leather belt and sheath to carry it in.

Mike had taken Katy into Richmond for a two-week honeymoon in the best hotel in town. Here they indulged themselves with the best cuisine Richmond had to offer and attended the theater twice.

The went shopping and bought new boots and wide brimmed Stetson hats, plenty of blue jeans, socks and shirts for all of them, along with a warm sheepskin lined leather jacket and cap with flaps they could tie down to keep their ears warm. Mike said, "Sweetheart, this is the last purchase we'll make this side of the mountains."

When they rode back to the homestead they were both aglow with the mutual satisfaction they had discovered in marriage.

Just before the adventurers mounted their wagons Mike said, "Angus, I was going to give this to you, but I didn't think you would ever need it, so I'm giving it to my father-in-law." He unwrapped the jewel-encrusted sword that Gabriel and Esther had given their lives for, and gave it to Ralph. "Keep it safe, and if you ever need any money, it's worth a fortune to an antique dealer."

Ralph said, "It'll be hanging over our fireplace when you return. Thanks, Mike, I'll treasure it always."

Ralph and Mary, Angus and Christine, Ellis and Lola stood and watched them as they rolled out of sight, headed west into the unknown. The hearts of all six were heavy and Ralph tried to console Mary as she wept, saying, "They're in God's hands, my darling."

CHAPTER FIFTEEN

Mike and Katy were sitting on the spring seat of the lead wagon trailing the buckboard, with four fine horses tied to the back. Kabuta and Peg followed, trailing the other wagon with four horses tied to the back of it. Katy's heart was aching as she tried desperately to hold back the tears.

Mike hung the reins on the hook and put his arms around her and said, "Let them go, sweetheart, cry it all out."

Peg was crying too, as Kabuta tried to comfort her.

After the girls had controlled their emotions, they hugged the arms of their young husbands, thrilled to their very core as they started off for the adventure of their lives. They both determined to never let their husbands see anything in them but love and devotion.

They made pretty good time the first day out because woodcutters had used the road along the James for years and they had removed all the big rocks that might break a wheel or axle. Mike and Kabuta had ridden to the top of the Blue Ridge Mountains and they knew where they would camp for the first four days.

They reached the glade with the bubbling spring about five o'clock and staked the stock on good grass. They would stake all the stock for the first two weeks because they didn't want to wake up one morning and find that all the stock had gone back to their home range. The mules would surely go back where they had been fed so well, and the horses might, though they were better trained.

As soon as the animals were staked out, Kabuta made a 'U' out of rocks and Mike took kindling and some wood he had thrown up on the corn and built a fire. He had thrown up enough kindling and wood on the corn to last them a couple of weeks to give them a little more traveling time each day. He wanted to get a good distance away from home so the girls wouldn't get discouraged right off.

Mike knew that after they passed the settlement down in the Shenandoah Valley they might not find any road after they crossed the valley and headed up in the Alleghenies. These mountains would slow them down considerably.

Peg heated a pot of beef stew that Lola had sent along so they wouldn't have to cook their first night out.

They were through eating and the fire was out before dark, but the moon was bright and it had been an easy day. Mike got his violin out and played a few tunes and they lifted their voices in song.

When they started to bed Mike put two of the hounds to watch Kabuta and Peg's wagon and two of them to watch Katy's and his. This would be their nightly assignment until the end of the trail.

Brother and Sister were out of Daisy's first litter, and that was what Mike called them from the first time he'd seen them. Sister had only one litter of four pups. He kept two of them and left two with Angus. Mike named the younger dogs Wolf and Lassie.

They slept soundly and when Mike started dressing in their cramped quarters, Katy stretched and yawned and murmured, "Good morning, my love, do we have to get up? It's not daylight yet and this is such a good bed."

Mike said, "Good morning. Kabuta and I made sure we had good beds, we didn't want you girls to turn back the first morning after we started."

"Michael, you've got a lot to learn about the girl you married. I'm not frail nor am I a quitter. And neither is Peg."

"That's good to know," Mike said, "because we intend to travel from dawn to an hour before the sun goes down.

"We'll stop early enough to cook before dark and gather enough wood for the morning fire. We'll put the coffee pot on and you girls will cook breakfast by firelight while we get ready to roll, and we'll be moving before the sun rises."

When Katy looked out over the wagon seat she could see that Kabuta had the fire going and she could barely see Peg as she dipped the coffee pot in the spring. Mike was getting the big frying pan ready to place on the fire. He had sliced sides of bacon before they left and rewrapped it.

By the time she had washed up at the spring she could hear the coffee boiling and smell the bacon frying. Her stomach started to growl when the smell of that bacon wafted over and hit her nostrils. In no time at all they were eating bacon and eggs and sheepherder's bread.

Mike said, "We'd better enjoy these eggs and butter. We've only enough for about a week and you may not taste more for a mighty long time. I noticed a lot of tree squirrels in the woods. We'll try to pick enough off with our bows as we travel for fried squirrel and cream gravy for supper. The milk will only stay fresh a few days and it will be water gravy from then on."

Katy said, "Mike, why are we cooking on an open fire when we have the cook stove?"

"We need the light from the fire. We'll use our candles only when we have to. We brought cases of them but we won't be able to get any more, and the ones we make won't be nearly as good."

Mike and Katy were on their wagon seat headed into the trees just as the sun started to glow in the east. The dogs had already headed into the woods to catch their breakfast when Peg said, "Kabuta, we forgot to feed the dogs."

"Honey, we don't have to feed the dogs, they'll find their own food. Mike said there'd be times they'd bring us our meat."

Peg said, "They sure are a comfort to me when we're sleeping."

They traveled over one hogback after another, but there weren't any long steep pulls. They made good time and they reached their second stop earlier than they had the previous day. They had time to chop wood for the fire tonight and Mike did that after they had staked the animals.

Kabuta joined Mike and said, "This dead live oak makes good fire wood, I suggest we cut all we can and stack it on top of the corn. There may be times we can't find a place to stop before dark." So they cut wood until Peg said, "Come and get it."

"Katy, I'll cook the squirrels and bread if you'll do the gravy, I'm not very good at gravy," Peg said sheepishly.

When they had their plates filled Mike said grace and thanked the Lord for the first meal their wives had cooked for them.

The men ate the food without a word and the girls cleaned up and Mike and Kabuta took the crosscut saw and cut some more oak wood, just the right length for their cooking fires. They were both strangely silent until Kabuta said, "Mike, that was the worst squirrel meat I ever did eat."

Mike snickered and whispered, "And that lumpy gravy was a waste of milk."

The girls went down to where the small branch ran into the river and took a bath. When they were bathing in a shallow pool Peg said, "I felt sorry for our men tonight. That was the most awful meal."

Katy said, "How well I know. We've just got to tell them that we've been spoiled brats that were never taught how to cook, and they're just going to have to teach us."

When the girls walked into camp the men had just finished loading the wood and there was a neat pile lying by the fire pit, ready for morning.

Katy said, "Peg and I have something to tell you. We don't know how to cook."

Mike and Kabuta laughed until their sides ached. Then Mike said, "Honey, you sure didn't have to tell us that after that meal. I'll cook breakfast and Kabuta will cook supper until we can teach you how it's done."

Mike climbed into the spare wagon and went to the box of books he brought along. He handed a cookbook to Katy. "This is how I learned to cook. I studied this book until I knew it by heart. Kabuta's had training and he's a great cook, and before many days we'll have you cooking as good as we can."

Kabuta said, "That's a fact. After that meal, oh! My aching stomach." And he and Mike burst into laughter.

Peg started to cry. She said, "I want to learn to cook for you, Kabuta, don't you want to learn how for Mike, Katy?"

"Of course. But we can't help it if we've been pampered and spoiled."

Mike said, "We'll pamper you all we can, but it won't be easy where we're going."

Kabuta said, "You know, Mike, I feel a little sad about leaving our home that we worked so hard on to get it the way we wanted. I wonder if we'll ever see it again."

"God only knows, Kabuta. But I know what you mean."

When they started out the next morning after a good breakfast, the girls were riding their horses and Mike noticed that Katy had taken the cookbook. He also saw Peg slip something into her saddlebags.

The road got much rougher and started winding back and forth up the mountainside. One o'clock came and the men hadn't seen their wives since they had ridden out in front of the wagons.

Katy and Peg didn't stop until they reached the meadow with the small lake, nestled down in a narrow canyon with a little creek running out of it. They dismounted and watered their horses. Then they tied them in the shade of a small grove of live oaks.

Katy got the cookbook out of her saddlebag and said, "Peg, we have to learn how to cook."

"I know, but can't it wait? Look at those rainbow trout jumping out of the water into that swarm of flies!"

They spent an hour catching enough fish for supper and then they unsaddled their horses and sat on the saddles and did some serious studying. By five o'clock they still heard no sound of the wagons coming. They were getting concerned when they heard Kabuta's booming voice shouting, "Get up there, you lazy mules!"

The girls ran to the creek and started cleaning fish. When the men pulled their teams to a stop on level ground, Peg ran to the wagon and got wood and put it between the rocks she had put in place just like she had seen Kabuta do, and she soon had a good fire going.

Katy filled the coffee pot and put it on to boil and ran and got the frying pan. She brought the nice clean fillets of trout to the fire just as Kabuta walked up and saw the meat. He said, "That's enough, girls. I'm thankful you caught the meat for our supper, but, well, I'll do the cooking."

Mike walked up and heard what Kabuta said and added, "Amen to that." Then he and Katy went to take care of the animals.

Peg took a small book of poems from her saddlebag and began reading aloud as Kabuta prepared the meal.

Mike threw a dead log under the wagon tongue and put the girls' saddle blankets over it to dry, hung their saddles on the side of the wagon, then he and Katy sat on camp stools and waited for dinner.

Kabuta said, "Mike, why don't you dig out some beef jerky for us to chew on in the middle of the day. I'm so hungry my belly button's making love to my backbone."

Mike said, "I was thinking about that, but I'm so tired I'm not getting off this stool until you call us to dinner. I'll get the jerky after we eat."

When Kabuta had everything ready, the other three were standing in line with their plates and coffee cups in their hand. Kabuta filled them, including his own, filled the coffee cups and they attacked the dinner.

When they finished Peg hugged and kissed Kabuta and said, "Sweetheart, I hope I can learn to cook like that. I know I will, but in the meantime I'm truly thankful for your cooking." Then she put her lips to his ear and whispered; "I'll show you how grateful I am tonight. You've already taught me how to do that real good."

Katy got up and put a bucket of water on the fire, and when it was hot enough, she and Peg washed the dishes and put them away. They had already taken their baths, so each of them gave their husbands a bar of soap, washcloth and a towel. Katy said, "There's the lake. The water isn't too cold to bathe in."

"Are you trying to tell us something?" Michael said.

"You just hurry up and come to bed, I'm going to crawl under the covers and heat it up."

The next morning Kabuta and Mike were up early. Mike built the fire, put the coffee on and started breakfast, and Kabuta started harnessing mules and tying horses to the buckboard and wagon. Peg hollered, "Honey, would you be so kind as to saddle our horses, we're going to ride on ahead today."

By the time the women were dressed and at the campfire Mike was filling their plates with pancakes, bacon and eggs. After they had finished a hearty breakfast Peg took the frying pan to the creek and began to clean it. As she was scrubbing it she glanced up at the cliff above her. Staring down at her was a large mountain lion, switching his long tail back and forth. She had opened her mouth to scream when she heard Kabuta say, "Quiet! Don't move!"

Peg's eyes were locked onto the cat and she sat paralyzed with fear as the cat sprang from the rocky ledge he had been perched on. Peg closed her eyes, waiting to die. When the cold water splashed all over her she opened them to see the cat laying in the creek just a few feet away from her, an arrow from Kabuta's crossbow sticking into its chest. Peg let out a blood-curdling scream.

This brought Mike running with his rifle in his hand, and Katy with her pistols drawn. Kabuta had his arms around Peg trying to console her as she shook like the aspen leaves in a stiff breeze. When she finally calmed down,

Kabuta said, "Honey, you disobeyed a cardinal rule by leaving camp without your side arms. From now on, the first thing you do after you dress in the morning is to put your guns on."

Mike said, "That's become automatic for Kabuta and me, and I want you to do the same, Katy."

Kabuta led his frightened wife back to the wagon while Mike quickly skinned the cat and whistled for the dogs. They came running and he gave them each a chunk of the meat from the legs of the cat. While the dogs were gorging themselves Mike cleaned his knife and headed back to his wagon, leaving the rest of the cat for the wild wolves and the buzzards.

Peg mounted her horse as she and Katy prepared to leave. Michael said, "I'm not so sure I want you riding on ahead today after Peg's scare."

Peg said, "Don't you fear. I learned a valuable lesson today. Our rifles are loaded and in our saddle boots and we're wearing our side arms, we'll be fine."

"That's right," Katy said, "we've taken some jerky with us and a canteen of water each. We'll go on to the little creek on top of the mountain you told us about and try to catch some fish for supper."

Michael said, "You might not find anything in that little creek but some crawfish and a few perch. It's just not big enough. But you might put some rocks across it and create a small pool deep enough we can dip our pots in for water."

Peg said, "Hand me the coffeepot and some coffee, Kabuta, and we'll have the coffee hot for you when you come in."

Kabuta said, "This is going to be our most difficult pull so far because the road is steeper and rougher. It's a much shorter haul though, and we should pull in about four o'clock, but don't worry if we're a little later than that."

With that the women said goodbye and took off up the mountainside.

This was a tough day for Kabuta and Michael. There hadn't been anybody this far up for a long time and the rains had washed the dirt from around some big rocks they had to roll out of the way or break up with their sledgehammers. There was one ditch they had to fill in and a large pine tree they had to cut out of their way that had blown down across the road. They could see where their wives had tied a rope to the tree and tried to pull it out of their way, but had given up on it.

Kabuta said, "Mike, our girls are going to be all right, they're trying hard."

"They're shaping up fine" Mike replied.

The haul that day was tough, but it was much shorter than they remembered it and when Mike drove up into the meadow on top of the mountain about a quarter to four, he saw Katy and Peg studying the cookbook.

Mike and Kabuta pulled their wagons across the creek and parked them side-by-side on a level place. They had decided that when they came to a creek or river at the end of the day they would cross over in case it rained in the night and flooded it. The only exception to this rule would be if it was too dark or if their teams were worn out.

When the men climbed down off the wagons their wives ran and hugged and kissed them and Peg blurted out, "Katy and I are going to fix breakfast in the morning."

"There'll only be bacon and pancakes," Michael said, "There are only two eggs left."

Katy said, "There'll be a little more than that, you just wait and see."

Kabuta said, "Mike, if you'll take care of the animals I'm going to rest for a spell before I start supper, it's going to take me a little longer tonight."

The grass in this mountain meadow was the best they had seen since they left home and there was plenty of it. The animals would get a good rest and feed. They needed it.

The trees and brush were very dense around the meadow. Mike took Katy's horse and rode around it and he found only two small openings where a mule might squeeze through but a horse wouldn't. He tied ropes across these two openings and across the trail leading back down the mountain. Then he pushed the buckboard across the trail going down the other side. For the first time he turned the animals loose to run free. It was good to see them roll in the tall grass to scratch their itching backs and then to bury their muzzles in the deep green grass.

When Mike came into camp for a much-needed rest, he saw Kabuta sitting on a campstool, drinking coffee, and he joined him and Katy handed him a cup. Mike said, "Well, we won't have to lead the animals to water or stake them tonight. I think we'll let them run free from now on. That is, if we aren't afraid Indians might steal them. We might run into some after we cross that valley down there. We've trained the dogs well and they won't let them stray too far."

Kabuta said, "That'll ease our load some, and I'm all for that. Well, I'd better get our supper on."

When Mike saw Kabuta piling a large stack of wood on the fire he couldn't resist asking him what in the world he was doing.

"My secret, Mike, don't ask any questions, just rest, you've had a hard day."

While the wood burned down to a bed of coals Kabuta joined the others for a cup of coffee and a bit of fellowship.

* * * * *

Earlier they'd passed a small bay tree and Mike hadn't noticed that Kabuta stopped and gathered enough leaves to fill his pockets.

When Peg nestled up to him, she said, "What's that smell, Kabuta?"

"You're mashing my bay leaves," he said, and he took one out of his pocket and touched it to her nose.

"Phew, what do you want with those?" she asked.

"Never you mind, pretty lady, just you wait and see." Mike got up and walked into the brush, with Wolf and Lassie following him.

Katy said, "Peg, let's take a walk," and they walked away in another direction with Brother and Sister following them.

Peg said, "It's weird the way those two dogs follow us everywhere we go."

"Yes, but it's comforting," Katy said. "After that cat sprang at you I feel more at ease when they're near."

Kabuta didn't go along because he wanted everyone out of camp. Taking a shovel he shoveled the coals aside and buried four potatoes in the ashes. Then he wrapped tenderloin he had carved out of the big cat and laid in on a burlap sack. He sprinkled it with dried onions, salt and pepper with a little sage, and placed a number of the bay leaves on it and rolled it in the burlap and tied it with string. He buried this in the ash and covered it with hot coals.

Then he used the last of their milk and made biscuits and three apple pies. He baked the pies first in the oven of the cook stove, and he slipped the biscuits in the oven just as Mike came into camp with a half-dozen squirrels, cleaned and ready to cook. A few minutes later Katy and Peg came into camp laughing.

Kabuta had a pot of hot water on top of the stove. He had some of the biscuit dough left so he seasoned the water and put the squirrels in it and when the meat was almost done he put cubed potatoes and dried onions in the pot and spread strips of dough over the top of it and placed it on the back of the stove to simmer.

Peg said, "Oh boy! Chicken and dumplings, boy do I like chicken and dumplings."

Mike said, "Better, squirrel and dumplings."

Katy said, "I'm not sure whether I want to eat squirrel again or not, I'll admit I like them fried, but I can't keep from thinking about a big rat."

Peg said, "Katy, don't you know they only eat nuts, seeds and buds, they don't eat dead things like rats do."

Kabuta said, "Get your plates ready," and he went and uncovered his masterpiece. When he sliced tender pieces of tenderloin onto their plates, with a baked potato and fluffy brown biscuits, with the last butter they had, they forgot all about the dumplings.

When they gathered close to eat Mike asked Katy to say the blessing. She hesitated for a moment, she had never done it before, but she had heard her father, mother and Michael do it. She said, "Dear heavenly Father, we thank you for this food and this wonderful man that has prepared it. Bless it to the nourishment of our bodies. In Christ's name, amen."

Everyone ate with oohs and ahhs and when they were all stuffed, Katy said, "Where in the world did you get a pork tenderloin? That's the best I've ever tasted."

Kabuta said, "Mike, didn't you noticed that I hung back this morning when you pulled out?"

"No, I was too busy steering the team out up that narrow gorge. You pulled up right behind me when I stopped to move that first rock out of the way."

"Well, you didn't get very far ahead of me. It didn't take me very long to trim those tenderloins out of that big cat."

Katy said, "Oh my! Peg, we've been eating rats, and now cat. What else will we eat on this trip?"

"Oh, I remember eating cat when I was a little girl in Africa," Peg said. "But I'd forgotten how good it was."

"I've seasoned another tenderloin and wrapped it in burlap that we can cook in a few days, this cold weather up here in the mountains will keep it fresh for a few days," Kabuta said. "There's enough of this one left to make biscuit sandwiches for lunch tomorrow, so we won't have to chew on jerky, and the squirrel dumplings will be tomorrow's supper. Mike, I wish we had brought our cows along. They wouldn't have slowed us down, and we could have had milk and butter all the time. I just used the last of them both. We're going to really miss that."

"I thought about it, but ruled it out because I thought the young bull would give us trouble."

"Not if we'd put a ring in his nose to lead him by. Believe you me, he would only hang back once with that ring in his tender nose."

"I'm learning, Kabuta, maybe we can buy a couple of cows and a young bull in the settlement down there."

Kabuta had made another pot of coffee, and he brought out one of the apple pies. They ate and talked for a while longer; Then Kabuta buried the big glowing coals with ashes and crawled into bed beside Peg. Mike and Katy went to bed soon after.

The girls were up long before the men and they woke to the sound of the coffee perking and the smell of fresh rabbit frying in the pan. After they all enjoyed a good breakfast the men got busy getting ready to leave. From here on the trail was strange to them and Mike said, "We'll camp the first place we find where we can level the wagons, and that has some grass and water for the animals."

Peg and Katy decided they would ride on to see if they could find a place. About mid-morning they found a small stream where they could boil tea and eat their lunch. They knew they were far out in front of the men, so they rode on.

They came to small stream running between two rather steep hills. The hill on the west side of the branch was covered with trees, but the hill on the east side was bare of trees, but it was covered with tall enough grass for the animals, scattered in clumps among large boulders. Peg said, "It might be hard for the men to level the wagons, but this will have to be it. They can't make it any further today."

They rode back to the little stream, where they decided to have lunch, and made a pot of hot tea. It wasn't long before Mike and Kabuta arrived.

Katy said, "Mike, you have a few rough, steep inclines ahead and where we figured we should stop for the night will be the worst camp we've had. It'll be difficult to level the wagons, but there's water and grass for the animals. We rode about five miles further on and found nothing better. We didn't go any further because we're sure you couldn't make it that far. We'll ride further on after lunch and try to find a suitable place for tomorrow night."

"Good," Michael said. "Now let me at that tea. I smelled it a hundred yards back. I for one would like to have it more often."

Katy never forgot that, and from that time on she made sure they had tea as often as they did coffee.

Peg said, "It might be dark before you get there, but the moon will be almost full tonight and the trail is straight downhill until you cross the creek. I don't think you'll have any trouble."

Kabuta said, "I'd like to rest a while, but Mike, I think we had better water the animals and get these wagons rolling. You girls make sure the fire is completely out before you leave."

When Katy and Peg caught up with Kabuta they had to ride along behind a ways until he pulled up at a place where they could get by single file. Peg stopped just long enough to brush Kabuta's lips with hers before she rode on.

Kabuta sent a shrill whistle down the trail to let Mike know that the girls were coming so he would stop at the first place they could pass him. Mike pulled up on a ridge where it was level enough to stop to give the mules a short rest and the girls could squeeze by. After the girls rode on Mike set his brake and climbed down to stretch his legs and to relieve himself. Kabuta pulled up behind him and did the same.

When Kabuta caught up with him Mike said, "That turn down at the bottom of this incline looks rather sharp. Let's chock our wheels and walk down and take a look before we go any further."

When they reached the bottom of the incline they discovered that the trail turned to run along the bank of a dry gully about seven or eight feet deep.

Mike said, "If we lose a brake and the mules aren't able to hold back the load we could lose a wagon and team here."

"Well, you have the heavier load and if it starts to go, you be sure you don't go with it."

Michael and Kabuta removed a dozen or more rocks from the trail that a mule's foot might slip on or might roll under a wheel that would catapult a wagon into the gully.

The mules got a twenty-minute rest before they eased into their collars to move on.

By keeping his foot on the foot brake and hand on the hand brake, Mike was able to ease around the curve and ascend the hill that ran along the gully. When he came to a level place he stopped to wait for Kabuta, just to make sure he made it all right. When Kabuta made it to the top, Mike breathed a sigh of relief that eased the tension that had held his chest tight. Kabuta had no trouble at all.

They had a stretch for about a mile that was small inclines up and down. Mike let his mules trot here to make up lost time, because he didn't see any large rocks along this stretch.

At the end of this stretch was a hogback they had to climb that was the steepest one yet. The mules really had to dig in and when they reached the top they were blowing hard. The other side was even steeper so Mike stopped to let his team rest until he heard Kabuta coming up behind him. When he eased the team down the hill, Mike was holding them back the best he could with his foot pressing the foot brake so hard it was hurting his hip. He was almost down when his foot slipped off the brake and the mules couldn't hold the load back, so Mike whipped them into the fastest gait they could run to keep the wagon straight on the trail. He was thankful that there wasn't a creek at the bottom. When they hit the bottom the mules were running all out to keep the wagon from running over them. They were halfway up the next hill before the mules had to pull.

Mike kept them going until they reached the brow of the hill, where he pulled out his bandana to wipe the sweat from his brow. He was at a loss as to why his foot slipped from the brake until he examined the brake carefully. He'd hung his water-soaked canteen on the sideboard and it had been leaking on the brake, making it slick, and he hadn't noticed it. He wouldn't make that mistake again.

Kabuta pulled up behind him and walked alongside and said, "Mike, what happened?"

Mike showed him the slippery brake and said, "My canteen has been leaking water on the brake and my foot slipped off and the team couldn't hold the load."

Kabuta said, "That's a flaw in the design of these wagons. Mine is hanging in the same place. I'll change those hooks to the other side when we get in tonight."

Mike said, "I've dried the brake, we'd better get moving, that sun is getting low."

Kabuta said, "Wait, you've been riding that brake all afternoon, your leg must be exhausted. Want me to switch with you?"

"I am weary; I appreciate your taking over. I might just let you stay there the rest of the way down this mountain. You've had more experience than I have with a four-mule team. We never needed them in Ireland."

"Why don't we make it permanent then, I love driving a four-mule team?"

"You have a deal. But you have to promise me you'll tell me if you get tired."

"You betcha my life I will. I don't want to kill my self or lose our load."

Kabuta mounted the seat, released the brake, and said, "Yaaah," and the mules lunged into their collars. Mike was right behind him when he pulled to just around a bend. Mike set his brake and walked around Kabuta's wagon and Kabuta said, "Climb up here and sit a spell." When Mike was seated, Kabuta pointed at a glowing firelight.

"Man, I'm glad to see that," Michael said.

"Me too, it's too dark for us to judge how steep this grade is. Let's just sit here until the moon clears the tree tops so we can see better."

"Good idea." Kabuta put two fingers in his mouth and sent a piercing whistle down the slope. Two whistles came back, one right after the other, letting them know that their wives had heard them.

They sat there talking for an hour. When they finally reached the little stream Kabuta pulled his front wheels across it until his wagon felt level. Michael had just enough room to pull along beside him.

Mike said, "Now if we don't get a cloudburst in the night we'll be all right.

The girls had the food ready so they ate heartily. Peg and Katy cleaned the dishes and banked the fire. When they went to bed they found their tired husbands sound asleep. It had been a grueling day.

Kabuta and Michael slept like dead men through the night—even the smell of coffee boiling and of frying bacon didn't wake them the next morning and the girls let them sleep. They knew that the next day would be shorter and not as difficult.

The sun was well up when they finished breakfast.

Mike said, "Kabuta, let's give the mules corn this morning. They deserve a treat after what they went through yesterday." Katy asked, "Don't our horses get corn too?"

"No, they've had it pretty easy. And we want to save our corn for the long haul and save enough to plant a crop when we settle somewhere. Then we can have cornmeal if we run out of flour. We won't feed them any of the wheat we have, because we only brought enough to plant a crop."

CHAPTER SIXTEEN

Three days later they saw a farm complex when they were about a mile out. Mike said, "Katy, you take the reins, I'm going to saddle Blackie and ride on and see if I can buy a couple of cows and a young bull. We won't have to lead the horses any more. They'll follow along, Wolf and Lassie will see to that. Then we can lead the cows and the bull. I just don't want us to have to do without milk and butter if I can help it."

When Mike rode up to the farm a man and two strapping young boys were just leaving the house with buckets in their hands. Mike noticed that they moved the buckets from their right hand to their left, leaving their hand free to reach the pistols they wore, and a lady stepped out the back door with an apron on that didn't quite conceal the shotgun she was trying to hide.

The three stood side-by-side until Michael approached them. Michael stopped about twenty paces from them and said, "I'm Michael Ross, and my wife, my best friend and his wife are coming on in wagons. I rode on ahead to see if it would be all right if we spent a couple of nights nearby. And I would like to buy a couple of fresh cows and a young bull, if possible."

"I'm Bob Ferguson, my boys, Jim and Dennis. Thee are welcome to camp across the road under the oak trees if thee be friendly. We don't get many visitors in Hope. Where are thee from?"

"We just came over the mountain from Richmond, and we're going west until we find a place that fits our fancy."

"I can sell thee some milk, butter, and eggs, but the only place thee might find a cow is about a mile further on at Bill Robertson's farm. He's been talking about leaving Hope, but I wouldn't put much stock in it. He's been saying he was leaving for the past two years."

Mike said, "I'll take three dozen eggs now and three gallons of milk and all the butter you can spare if you can wait until our wagons get in. All our milk buckets are empty."

"That will cost thee two dollars."

"If you have some empty syrup cans with lids on them you can spare, it's worth five dollars to me."

"Dennis, thee go tell mother to clean enough syrup cans to hold the milk, butter and eggs. Mister Ross, you get your camp set up and we'll deliver thy order after we finishing milking and have gathered the eggs. That way everything will be as fresh as it can be. Tomorrow I'll take thee to see Bill."

"Thank you, sir." Mike rode back to guide the others to the campsite.

The following morning Mr. Ferguson took Mike to see Mr. Robertson. After introductions they got down to business. When Mike saw the cows and the young bull that wouldn't be able to breed for about seven months, he made an offer that he knew was too much, but he desperately wanted these cows. One would go dry about the right time and the other one had just had her first calf and would become a good producer.

Mr. Robertson said, "If thee will take the other cow that will be coming fresh somewhere down the trail, at the same price, thee has bought thyself some fine milkers. Then the wife and I can get back to Richmond."

Mike paid him on the spot and said, "We'll pick them up on our way out in the morning."

The next day they crossed the narrow valley and camped at a spring at the foot of the Allegheny Mountains.

Kabuta knew he had to cook the other tenderloin, because if he didn't it would spoil. He knew from his childhood in Africa they could boil spoiled meat and kill all the germs, but he also knew that Mike and Katy would have to be half starved to eat it. So he duplicated the meal he had cooked before. Katy and Peg hovered over him and watched his every move, and Katy wrote down the amount of seasoning he used. She said, "Peg and I are determined to become as good a cook as you are."

"That'll make Mike and me very happy."

They had the fire roaring when they sat down to eat, well after dark. Michael said grace and when he said, "amen", a voice out of the darkness said, "amen."

All four of them leaped out of the circle of light and drew their pistols and Kabuta reached into his wagon to get his loaded double-barreled shotgun.

Then the man said, "May I come into the light of your fire to show you I mean you no harm? I could smell that coffee for the last half mile and I haven't had a cup in over a week. I would dearly love to have one."

Mike said, "Come in with your hands held high."

As he drew near to camp Mike said, "Halt where you are. It sounds like there is more than one of you."

"That's just Jenny, my pack mule."

"Come on in."

When the man came in to the edge of the fire two young men and two young women walked out of the brush from four different directions.

Mike realized he'd made a serious mistake by sending the dogs out to hunt for their food instead of having them on guard. It was careless of him and he vowed he wouldn't make that mistake again. They were getting too close to Indian hunting grounds. Kabuta said, "Get your plate, there's plenty of food."

"I don't have one. I walked away from my camp to take a bath night before last and Indians stole my horse and everything I had. I guess Jenny was off in the brush somewhere and they didn't find her. They searched for me but I heard them in camp, so I waded down the middle of the creek and I've been walking every since. Jenny just caught up with me a ways back. By then I could see the glow of thy fire."

Kabuta filled his own plate and cup and said, "Man, you must be starved, take mine," then he sat back and watched him devour the food. Then he washed the plate and served himself.

"I'm Dan Boone, and mister, it was kind of thee to give me thy plate. I'm sorry I was too hungry to refuse it until after thee ate. I wish I had the where-with-all to pay thee for thy kindness and this fine meal, but the Indians got all I had. My cash was in my saddlebags."

Mike introduced everyone and said, "Maybe you can pay us by giving us some sound advice. Did you come over the Alleghenies from Charleston?"

"I sure did."

"Can we get these wagons through to Charleston?"

"It'll take thee some time and thee will have to go slow or thee will break a wheel, an axle, coupling pole, tongue or maybe a rocking arm. Thee better have sledgehammers to break up a few boulders. That's one thing about a mule, or burro, they don't break down easy.

"There's one incline that thee will need every mule thee have to pull these wagons up and over, and if one of them slips and falls thee will never make it. If thee make it up that rocky incline it's not bad from there on through the mountains, and once thee reach the valley it's smooth sailing from there."

"How big is the village?"

"It's not much. There's a saloon that serves pretty good meat, but the whiskey will kill you. There's a small store, but most of the time he's out of most things. There are a few houses, and there are some good farms about.

"Be careful around the saloon, there are a couple of tough's that hang around there and they'd cut thy throat for a quarter."

"They won't find that an easy matter," Kabuta said.

"Watch your women folks too; they get scarce from here on. I just came from Saint Louis and I'd bet I didn't see a dozen decent women. There are quite a few of the other kind, if thee know what I mean."

"We understand," Mike said.

"How many days to Charleston?" Katy asked.

"Depends on thee and thy mules; If thee go by horseback it will take thee ten days. With the wagons, ten weeks I'd guess; if thee are lucky."

"We're taking them, all right," Mike said. "We may have to abandon them in the canyon somewhere, but we're going to do our best to take them through."

"I admire thy guts, young people, and my bet is on thee, but thee have a chore ahead of thee, thee surely do. Grease those wheels in the morning before you head out." He'd noticed the six big hounds that took up their place under each wagon. He said, "Keep thy dogs close—those mountains are full of mountain lions, bear of all kinds, timber wolves, bob cats, wolverines and Indians. Rattler snakes, too. They're beginning to move about. I killed a big one on the trail this morning."

Kabuta saw Peg shiver. He slipped his arm around her and said, "The dogs will keep them away, Sugar." She shivered again, but said nothing.

Dan said, "One other thing, if thee don't mind me saying so, if thee are careless again as thee were this evening when I approached thy camp, thee will never make it. I wasn't trying to be quiet. Indians would have slit thy two men's throats before thee knew they were in thy camp, and I'm sure thee know what they would do with thy wives."

Katy's Irish temper flared a bit when she said, "If you're trying to scare us, you're doing a dammed good job of it."

"I was just trying to make thee aware of the dangers of thy fiasco so thee will take proper precaution, that's all."

When Katy and Peg started to do the dishes, Boone said, "Could I have a small pan of hot water and a little soap, and borrow a razor. I'd like to shave this miserable beard. I have a sweet wife and two young sons in yonder village. I was supposed to come home loaded with gold, but I'm coming home with less than I left with. I just hope they will be as glad to see me as I'll be them." When he finished shaving, he thanked them for their hospitality and walked into the night.

Mike said, "Let's get a good night's sleep and we'll hit it hard in the morning."

Katy whispered to Peg, "I'm not looking forward to this."

Peg got up rather stiffly and said, "I'm hurting in every muscle now, Katy. Does it ever get any easier?"

"If I didn't think so, I'd ask Mike to take us home right now."

* * * * *

Four weeks later they were camped on a rugged hillside at the base of the steep incline Dan had told them about. The wagons were two hundred yards apart because they couldn't find a level spot big enough for both wagons. They were grateful for the kindling and wood they had on the wagon. The men were too tired to think about chopping wood tonight. There was one good consolation, Peg and Katy had become hardened travelers now and they didn't hurt in every joint and muscle any more. They had only leftover cold meat and biscuits and cold water that night, and they were in their beds early with the six dogs surrounding them a hundred yards out on guard. All of their guns were kept cleaned and fully loaded now and always close at hand.

Early the next morning Mike said to Katy and Peg, "While you're getting breakfast Kabuta and I are going to walk to the top of that grade and try to figure out how to get our wagons up there."

They saddled their horses and rode up the incline. Up on top they discovered that the trail ran along a shelf of almost solid rock as far as they could see. They rode west and about a quarter of a mile further on it turned sharply to the left, but not so sharp that they couldn't get around it. Kabuta said, "Mike, this shelf might run down to nothing and there's a sheer drop twelve to fifteen feet. You go back and eat your breakfast and I'll ride to the end of this thing to make sure we can get off of it somewhere if we have to."

"That's a good idea, and in the meantime I'll try to figure how to get the wagon up that solid rock incline. There is no way the mules could pull that heavy load up that slick rock. They just can't get enough footing to make that climb."

When Mike got back to the slope he noticed the shelf narrowed about three feet, twenty feet west of the top of the hill. Right after, it turned slightly to the left. A large pine tree was rooted down in the canyon at the base of the shelf and grew way above it. If he could tie a rope around that tree by the time he got it back to the brow of the hill it would lay directly in the middle of the trail.

He went and ate and hitched just two mules to the wagon and drug it to the bottom of the hill and set the brakes and unhitched the team. He was afraid that the coupling pole wouldn't stand the strain so he ran a three-eighth-inch rope to the back axle and stretched it tightly between the back and front axle. Then he ran it through the end of the tongue to keep the wagon straight. Next, he tied the block and tackle to the tree, measured the length of the rope and determined that by pulling the block and tackle completely together the wagon would be on level ground up on top.

He took the team of mules up top and tied them to the pine tree. He ran the block and tackle rope back down the hill underneath the wagon and hitched the four-man team to the end of the rope and waited for Kabuta.

Kabuta rode for about ten miles and found where the shelf ran down to the canyon floor. There were a few rocks they would have to remove and a tree or two they would have to cut down, but they could get off the shelf. Mike was getting impatient when he heard the clippity clop of Kabuta's mount. Mike said, "Get his food ready, I can't wait to see if this idea works or if we lose our wagon."

Kabuta ground-hitched his horse up on top and walked along Mike's engineering job and inspected it as he followed it down the hill to where the team was hitched to the end of the rope. He went under the wagon. When he came out from under the wagon he said, "That'll work. Let's do it."

Peg said, "Not until you eat."

Kabuta ate hurriedly. This was a job he wanted behind them as badly as Mike did.

Mike said, "Kabuta, when I get back up on top of the hill and whistle, you lead this team back down the trail and they'll draw the wagon up on top. When I whistle the second time, stop and hold the team there. Then when I whistle the third time, untie the rope."

When he whistled the second time for Kabuta to stop, the wagon was sitting with the back wheels about two feet on level ground. Mike climbed up on the wagon and set both brakes, removed the rope, hitched the team on top, and drove the wagon about a hundred yards further on and set the brakes. It didn't take nearly as long to get the other two wagons and the buckboard. By noon they were rolling along the shelf and except for a few small rocks, it was almost as smooth as the streets of Richmond.

The sun was dropping fast when Kabuta pulled his team to a halt about a mile before the shelf slanted down to the canyon floor. "Mike, we'll have to camp up here tonight, there are some rocks we're going to have to move, and a couple of small trees we've got to cut down where we go down the slope into the trees in the canyon. You and I could take the animals down and tie them to trees where they can reach water and eat a little grass, but I don't think we should, I saw a number of unshod horse tracks near that stream and I would swear they were carrying riders, by the depth of those tracks. The dung looked like it wasn't more than a day old. We are definitely in Indian country.

"There's a good place there to camp under large trees that will hide our wagons pretty good. I would suggest that after we get off of this place we spend a day there and grease our wagons and give our mules a rest."

Early the next morning Mike and Kabuta were rolling rocks out of the way and filling holes. The trees turned out to be no problem and by nine o'clock they had the wagons hidden under the trees and the girls were getting breakfast, using the stove. They had the back of the wagon under a large pine where the smoke would drift up through the foliage and dissipate quickly. While they were eating Kabuta said, "Mike, there's plenty of grass here in a meadow at the base of that shelf back a ways. What do you say about us holing up here a few days for some fun and relaxation? The squirrels are hopping all over these hickory nut trees and the stream is teaming with fish."

Mike said, "Sounds like a plan to me. I noticed that the ground is covered with last year's crop of nuts too. I cracked one and it was good. We could crack up a bunch and take them with us."

Peg said, "Katy, let's go fishing."

"Let me see if Mike will catch some grasshoppers for us." So Mike started catching grasshoppers and Katy and Peg went to the creek. But Peg couldn't wait, so she caught a hopper and pulled in a good trout just as Mike walked up and set a jar of hoppers down between them.

Peg and Katy were having fun pulling sleek, fat trout out of the stream, discussing how they were going to seduce their husbands that night.

Katy said, "Peg, all you have to do is smile sweetly and wink your eye."

"Truer words were never spoken," Peg giggled, as she pulled in another fighting trout.

Katy said, "Here come the men, and it looks like they were as successful as we were. Let's go fix supper and maybe we can get Kabuta to fix us a chocolate cake tomorrow. I have a half dozen eggs hidden away, wrapped in a wet towel to keep them from spoiling. I checked them this morning and they're still fresh."

The dogs had disappeared into the woods and Kabuta took his bow and walked down the creek. He hadn't gone very far when he met Daisy, dragging a young doe, with Wolf walking slowly behind her. He said, "Bless you, Daisy," and he bent down and scratched her sides and behind the ears, cooing to her all the while. Wolf waited until Kabuta called him to scratch and coo to him as well.

Kabuta took a small coil of rope from around his neck and tied one end around the deer's hind feet and drew her up in a tree, where she hung over the center of the creek. He took the sharp knife that Angus had given him, cut her throat and pierced her heart so she would bleed good. He skinned her quickly and gutted her just as Shep, Lassie Brother and Sister showed up. He let the dogs gorge themselves on the organ meat. Kabuta had gutted the deer over the swiftly running water so the blood and what organ meat the dogs and fish didn't eat would be carried far from camp and be scattered so if any Indians happened to come near they wouldn't see that an animal had been butchered up stream.

He heard Peg's voice echo back from the hills when she hollered, "Come and get it."

He whistled just low enough that she could hear to let her know he got the message. His supper would have to wait. He carved out the pieces he wanted and kept the other parts for the dogs, wrapped it in the hide, threw it over his shoulder and took it to camp.

Mike had eaten and was just getting ready to go looking for him when he heard him coming, singing softly an old Irish lullaby he had taught him.

Kabuta greeted him with, "Deer tenderloin steaks tomorrow, Mike."

"You must have used your bow; we never heard the sound of your rifle."

"Daisy brought her and laid her at my feet."

"Remember, I told you they would bring food to us at times. I've always been proud of my hounds, and they haven't disappointed me yet. We can rest at night pretty secure because of them."

"Mike, have you forgotten that we are in Indian country, and should be making as little sound as possible? They could have heard Peg's voice for a mile, drifting on this cold mountain air. If they did they'd be all over us."

When Peg heard them coming she got up and had Kabuta's food ready for him by the time he washed the blood from his hands. He kissed her gently and said softly, "Honey, if an Indian heard your call, you might become an Indian's squaw. Mike is spacing the dogs around camp now to warn us if any show up. We must move through their hunting grounds as quietly as possible."

Peg didn't say anything, but she went to her wagon and made sure all of the extra guns were loaded as the tears slipped slowly down her cheek. She prayed, "Dear Lord, please don't let anybody be killed because of my thoughtlessness, we don't want to kill an Indian, so please, dear God."

Katy had heard Kabuta's remarks and she had gone to her wagon and checked their extra guns also, and then she went to Peg. She knew she would be hurting. She climbed up in Peg's wagon and just opened her arms and Peg fell into them, weeping softly.

When Mike returned he started to hang the deer meat high up in a tree.

Kabuta said, "You'd better take that down the creek a ways. We've camped in the domain of a large bear of some kind. I saw his markings high up on a pine tree about three hundred yards down the creek. And there are signs of timber wolves everywhere; we could very well have visitors tonight."

Mike did as Kabuta suggested and came back and said, "Kabuta, I've seen the evidence of the wolves and some unshod pony tracks also, but I didn't want to alarm the girls. But they have a right to know what could happen. So we're going to have all our fires out before dark and move out every morning and eat somewhere further down the trail every morning, and it's time to reiterate to the girls the danger we face."

"Mike, you don't have to, Katy just heard me mildly rebuke Peg for hollering too loud. And I told them what you were doing with the dogs. They both went to their wagons, and you can bet they checked all the extra guns to make sure they were loaded. Then Katy went to our wagon. They're probably having a good cry right now."

"You know, Kabuta, I've done my share of crying. It cleanses the soul. Don't ever be ashamed of crying."

Mike and Kabuta went to the meadow where the animals were grazing contentedly and milked the cows. They made sure they were all there. When they went to put the milk in the creek to cool Mike said, "I think one of us should stand watch tonight and if nothing happens we'll lay over one more day to grease the wagon wheels and rocking bolsters on all our rolling stock and pull out early the next morning."

"That suits me, I've been uneasy ever since I heard Peg's voice echoing back from the hills."

Mike said, "I'll go tell Katy and I'll take the first watch."

When Kabuta crawled in bed Peg cuddled up to him and said, "Baby, I'm sorry, will you forgive me?"

"Oh! Baby, the thought of losing you scares me to death. And of course I forgive you." He started to kiss her gently, but her kisses became more demanding and she started unbuttoning his long johns and running her hands all over his manly chest. He had been thinking along the same vein all day. Their lovemaking was fast and furious and mutually satisfying.

Several yards away Mike was a little slower and more tender—he was still a little afraid of hurting this beautiful creature that had become his wife.

She hit him on the shoulder and said, "Mike, I won't break." And she showed him how tough she really was.

As Mike was dressing he told her that he was going to stand watch until one a.m. and that Kabuta would the rest of the night.

When Katy crawled out of bed, making sure she didn't wake Mike, she saw that Peg was already up and Kabuta was making biscuits. Peg said, "After breakfast Kabuta is going to make us a couple of cakes and a half dozen fruit pies to take with us. We're leaving this beautiful place in the morning."

Mike crawled out of the wagon when he smelled the bacon frying. He said, "I was looking forward to deer steaks this morning."

Kabuta said, "No such luck, my friend. Mister Bruin paid us a visit last night and helped himself to our deer, and he didn't even leave us a thank you note, unless not disturbing us was enough."

Mike said, "That had to be a mighty big bear. That meat was at least ten feet from the ground."

Kabuta said, "We should be thankful that we had that meat hanging that far from camp. If we hadn't, he'd have come into camp or got one of our mules."

Mike said, "Katy, let's saddle our horses and ride on down the trail and see what our next stretch is like, and locate our next campsite. We'll take our bows and maybe we can replace our meat supply."

Mike and Katy hadn't gone far when they spotted a young elk grazing in a small glade. Mike said, "You stay here," and he took his bow and crept forward. Mike froze and stood as still as a statue when the elk raised his head and looked right at him. After a while the elk lowered his head for another mouthful of grass and Mike sauntered forward and hid behind a big pine.

He looked around the tree just enough to see the elk looking around. Something had disturbed him and it wasn't Mike. The elk was looking the other way. He definitely got a whiff of something and he started walking toward the thick brush, still looking away from where Mike stood. Just as he started to bolt, Mike shot an arrow right behind his right shoulder into his heart. Then Wolf and Daisy came charging out of the woods. Mike said, "Wolf, Daisy, I'm sure glad it was you disturbing this elk instead of an Indian. I'm afraid my desire for a good steak made me a bit careless." He cut the tongue out of the elk and fed it to the dogs, and then commanded them to stay while he and Katy went back to camp to get the buckboard to carry it to camp.

Kabuta was sleeping when they returned and Peg was reading the cookbook.

Mike said, "Girls, we've seen no sign of Indians. Now that we have all this tender meat we'll stay here a few days and make jerky out of most of it, if it meets with Kabuta's approval."

Peg said, "Just before he went to bed Kabuta said he would sleep in the daytime and keep watch all night if you would stay in this lovely spot a few days longer."

Mike hung the elk in the same tree Kabuta had dressed the deer in, for the same reason. He laid the skin in the buckboard with the hair against the floorboard. He was loading the last piece of meat when Kabuta walked up and said, "We have the stove hot and a pit fire going. Peg told me you wanted to spend the next day or two making jerky. While you're cutting up the meat I promised the girls I'd bake a couple of cakes and half a dozen fruit pies with the last of the eggs."

Mike said, "Sounds good, but I'd rather have these," and he handed Kabuta four thick filets from the tenderloin.

Kabuta said, "Ho, ho, ho, I'll cook those first! Lunch will be ready in an hour."

They spent three more days here, the men making jerky. Kabuta got the anvil out and handed a hammer each to Katy and Peg and a bag of hickory nuts. He gave each of them an empty syrup can and said, "See who can fill their bucket first."

They kept the best cuts of the meat for steaks and roasts and they would eat elk meat every day until it spoiled and then they would boil the rest of it for the dogs. Katy said, "This is the best meat I've ever eaten."

Peg said, "I was getting tired of squirrel and fish, and this is a wonderful change, I don't think I'd ever get tired of this meat."

The morning they were leaving Katy said, "I sure hate to leave this beautiful spot."

Mike said, "I do too, sweetheart, but we have to go, the animals have just about depleted their food supply. Look how they're kicking up their heels.

They're well rested now and ready to go."

When everything was loaded and the wagons were ready to roll, Kabuta said, "Let's all hold hands and thank the good Lord for our stay here.

Mike said, "It was your idea, my friend, so you get the privilege."

Kabuta prayed, "Dear Heavenly Father, we thank you from the bottom of our hearts for this beautiful place you have created for our wonderful stay here. We thank you for supplying all our needs and now we ask you to prepare the way before us and keep our minds on Thee so we'll not sin against Thee. We ask these things in the name of Jesus. Amen." He gave Peg a big hug and lifted her up on in the saddle. Then he climbed up over the wagon wheel, took the reins and led off, with Mike not far behind.

Peg said, "Katy, I'm sure glad that this riding straddle doesn't hurt any more."

"Yeah, this is the only way to ride a horse. I wonder what mother would think if she could see us now."

Peg said, "Knowing her, I'd bet she'd approve. She probably wishes she was going with us."

"She'll miss us, all alright, and we'll miss them in time. But right now I'm having so much fun I haven't thought of much besides my husband and how happy I am," Katy replied.

Peg felt a thrill fill her when she heard Kabuta's deep voice when he said, "Yaah—fill those traces, you beautiful mules, we have miles to travel."

The four mules eased into their collars and the big wagon started rolling westward, with Mike right behind.

Brother and Sister had become so attached to Katy and Peg that they were never far from them except when they were sent out hunting. Now they were loping along in the shadows of their horses.

* * * * *

It had been eight weeks since they'd left the little settlement of Hope. They were well down the western slope of the mountains now, but they still had to go around some large boulders that had come rolling down the mountain-sides, and once in a while there were large clusters of rocks that looked as if they were pushed up out of the depth of the earth by an ancient cataclysmic eruption of some kind.

The trees were sparser, but they were much bigger and the travelers had to weave their way through them. Once in a while they would have to cut down a small tree to get through. There were low bushes and ferns that they just rolled over, but this slowed them down considerably because the mules had to pick their way through this maze, and often one of the mules would stumble when he caught his hoof on a stiff shrub. When they got through this they stopped and examined all the animals' legs. One of Kabuta's mules had blood running down his right front leg.

It wasn't a serious cut, so Kabuta applied pine tar to it to keep blow flies off so the mule wouldn't get screwworms in the cut. About four o'clock Mike and Kabuta crossed a creek where there was a good camping place. But their wives were nowhere in sight.

Mike said, "We camp here," and he sent a shrill whistle over the airways, but no response came. Normally, by this time of the day the girls would have turned back to check on the men's progress, but they hadn't seen them all day.

Mike realized he hadn't seen any evidence of the girls' passing all afternoon. "Kabuta have you seen any sign of the girls today?"

"No, none at all, and I'm getting worried. It's not like the girls not to check on us. I was so busy weaving our way through that maze today I haven't thought much about it, but now I'm really worried."

"Me too, let's saddle our horses and go look for them. I'll send the dogs out; they're more apt to find Brother and Sister, than we are the girls. There's where we'll find the girls."

"That can't be soon enough for me."

They had about two hours before nightfall, and they were just mounting up when Brother and Sister came into camp. Sister had an Indian's arrow through the loose skin just above her neck. Mike leaped from his horse and cut the shaft and pulled it out. She hadn't bled much, fortunately, because the arrow went in just under the tough skin. Mike said, "Take us to them, Sister, old girl."

She ran off with Brother, Shep and Daisy, with Mike and Kabuta staying as close behind as possible.

Mike commanded Wolf and Lassie to guard the camp.

The dogs could slip through the brush faster than the horses could, but they knew not to leave Mike and Kabuta too far behind. It was almost sundown when the four dogs came back and sat on their haunches, looking up at Mike and Kabuta. Kabuta said, "We had better walk in from here, they must be camped for the night somewhere close. They're not in a village. If they were, we would have seen the smoke from their cooking fires by now. If we go pounding in there on our horses they may get away to their village, and we might never get our wives back."

Mike leaped from his horse with his rifle in his hand. They ground-hitched their horses, checked their guns to make sure they were loaded, took their bows and started out. Kabuta had learned in Africa as a boy how to slip through the brush quietly, as Mike had in Ireland. They saw the dogs go around a point of rocks up ahead, creeping slowly forward. They were keeping low to the ground and when Mike saw Kabuta go down on his stomach and wiggle forward he did the same. When they went around the rocks they heard laughter, men's laughter. And just as Mike stood slowly up they heard Peg scream, "Ka-bu-ta!"

There were six big, red, stalwart Indians and they were all stark naked. One of them had ripped Peg's Levis off and had her on the ground, trying to pull her underwear off. She was fighting him like a tiger. Katy was fighting another and she clawed him across the face, ripping deep gashes with her sharp fingernails. He screamed and struck her a mighty blow on the side of her head and she fell limp on the ground. The Indian grabbed his face and kicked her on the thigh as Mike shot him through the heart with his bow.

Kabuta was as cold as ice when he sent an arrow through the other brave's temple with such a force it went through his head and out the other temple.

The other four stood in shock for just a moment, and that was time enough for the dogs to get in action. As the dogs came sailing through the air the Indians tried to fight them off, but they had no weapons and no chance. They were bowled over by the charge of these big fierce dogs and Wolf, Daisy, and Brother got their victims by the throat, and three more Indians went to their happy hunting ground. Sister hit the Indian she had attacked high on the forehead, knocking him to the ground and he rolled over and sprang to his feet and started to run, but she leaped and caught him on the back of his neck and crushed his cervical spine. The fight was over.

Peg flew into Kabuta's arms, weeping uncontrollably. When she finally controlled herself she said, "Kabuta, my shirt and pants." Mike was too busy with Katy to notice when Kabuta dressed Peg.

Mike was down on his knees examining Katy. She had a bad bruise along the side of her head where the Indian had struck her. She moaned and slowly opened her eyes and they were filled with fear. Then she sprang up, reaching for her knife, but it wasn't there. Screaming and clawing she flew at Michael. He folded his arms over his face saying, "Katy, Katy." His calm voice finally penetrated her fear-crazed brain and she wrapped her arms around him sobbing, "Oh Michael!"

* * * * *

He picked her up and took her to a little stream where he washed her face and hands. He removed the Indian's torn flesh out from under her fingernails as she sobbed.

Peg had controlled herself as Kabuta held and consoled her, and she and Kabuta retrieved the girls' knives, and Kabuta removed the arrows and pushed Indian arrows into the same place. They left everything the Indians had and left their bodies where they lay for the vultures and wild animals.

When Mike saw what Kabuta had done with the arrows, he said, "That's a good trick: If wolves get to these bodies before their people find them, they might figure four of them killed the two with the arrows and wolves killed the others.

Peg was trying to console Katy, but she was still whimpering when Mike picked her up and started back toward the horses. By the time they met Kabuta coming with her and Peg's horses, she had made Mike put her down, but she was still clinging to his hand. Katy climbed up on her horse. Mike whistled for his and Kabuta's horses and as soon as Mike was mounted, Katy moved as close to him as she could and stayed there until they reached camp, well into the night.

When they finally reached the wagons Katy went to bed with a throbbing headache. She realized how foolish she and Peg had been the last few days by ignoring Mike and Kabuta's warning not to ride their horses too far out ahead of them. They had grown careless, and she would never do so again.

Kabuta was cross with Peg and gave her a direct order for the first time in their brief marriage. "When you ride your horse again you will ride behind us."

Peg meekly said, "I'm sorry, Kabuta, that you had to shed blood to save me. I'll do my best never to cause you to have to do that again."

"It's not easy to kill someone, it weighs on the soul."

Kabuta prepared a quick meal, but they all ate sparingly. It was too soon after a tragedy none of them would ever forget.

Kabuta said, "Mike, why don't we let the women drive the teams and we scout out ahead from now on?"

"I don't think so, Kabuta, I think one of us should drive the heavy wagon with the four-mule team and let the girls drive the lighter wagon. I want one of us with them from now on."

"That suits me better," Kabuta replied.

"You or I will take Wolf and Lassie and scout out ahead every day and leave one of us, with Brother and Sister, with our wives and I'll have Shep and Daisy guard our rear."

The women slept fitfully and the men even less. Kabuta fixed a quick breakfast and Katy and Peg came down and ate a little, and Katy went back to bed, and Peg started to, but Kabuta called her back. "Honey, I wish you could go back to bed, but Mike and I decided last night that from now on he or I would scout out ahead of us each day and you or Katy will have to drive the lighter wagon. Mike said this morning that Katy was still suffering with a bad headache. Do you mind driving today?"

"Being perfectly honest, I'd rather be sleeping, but I'll drive."

By daylight Mike rode out carrying his rifle, shotgun, two pistols and his knife in his belt, and his saddlebags were stuffed with ammunition. When he moved out he called Wolf and Lassie to go with him. Kabuta and Peg were sitting on the wagon seats waiting for it to get light enough for them to weave their way through the forest. They drove all day, eating only a piece of jerky as they rolled along. Mike wore his horse out doubling back to see if everything was all right. He only took time about noon to change his saddle to Katy's mare.

They had put about twenty miles behind them that day when Mike guided them to a live oak grove. He had taken his rope and pulled a branch aside so they could drive into the middle of the grove. When he removed the rope the branch sprang back in place, hiding them so well that the only way an Indian would find them there was to run across their tracks and follow them in. And Mike knew there had better be a number of them for their own good. One or two would never get by the dogs. What a comfort they were, but Mike or Kabuta would stand watch through the night also.

When they all got down off the wagons and were stretching their tired muscles, Mike rode in and dismounted. He said, "No fires tonight, and we'll have to use the water from the barrels for ourselves. The animals won't suffer because they drank their fill at the creek we crossed a ways back. Kabuta, we'll feed corn to the mules and the two horses I rode today and the two you will be riding tomorrow."

Kabuta had anticipated they would not be building fires that night and the next morning, so he had brought a container of cold coffee. He brought out the last cake he baked and they dined on cold coffee and cake.

Kabuta said, "Mike, the girls are really scared for the first time, I think you should stay here with them while I take Brother and Sister and scout around a bit, and I'll stand the first watch. I know you're worn out from being in the saddle all day."

Mike just stretched out his hand and said, "Thanks," as Kabuta took it.

Kabuta scouted completely around their camp and went at least a mile back down the trail, and the only thing he saw was a lone coyote. When he reported that all was well they all went to bed, and when Kabuta didn't come, Peg came back and said, "Honey, why aren't you coming to bed?"

"I'm going to stand the first watch, but never fear, I'll be close to you until Mike relieves me about one in the morning"

She said, "Katy said she'd drive tomorrow. I can sleep in late in the morning. May I stay up with you?"

"For a little while, we all need to sleep every chance we get. You never know when we may have to keep moving all through the night."

Later in bed, Katy slipped into Mike's arms and said, "I feel safe when you're near; I'll be my old self in a few days." Then she drifted off to sleep.

A week later they rolled into the little village of Charleston, but it was tiny and there wasn't anything there they needed, so they drove on through.

There were four men just tying their horses to the hitching rail of the saloon as Mike and Katy approached, riding their fine horses. The men turned and leaned against the saloon wall and watched them. Mike heard one of them make some remark he couldn't understand and the others laughed. Katy didn't look at the men at all but when Mike spoke to them politely he noticed that they were a dirty bunch, with long hair and straggly beards, and their clothing looked like they had been worn for weeks without touching a scrub board.

Michael spoke to Katy and said, "Let's ride back and join Kabuta and Peg." They were a quarter of a mile behind them and they felt safe, now that they had reached Charleston, but after seeing those men Mike felt more protective of the girls than he had before. When they met the wagons Mike called a meeting. He told Kabuta and Peg about the men. He said, "One of them made a remark when we rode by them and the others roared with laughter. I can imagine what he said, though I didn't understand it. Kabuta, if they make some insulting remarks about us, keep your head and I'll keep mine, and maybe we won't get into a shooting war. But keep your rifle and shotgun handy in case they start something.

"Peg, I'll take over your wagon and you ride with Kabuta. Keep back under the canvas of your wagon with your shotgun in your hand. Katy, you do the same in our wagon. I figure if they don't see you again and they see our horses tied behind Kabuta's wagon they'll figure that there are at least two guns trained on them and they won't make a move against us."

When they drove by the saloon there was only one man leaning against the wall. He had a bottle in his hand and a cigarette hanging from his lips. He just nodded his head as they went through. Mike said, "Katy, you can join me now, but I don't think we've seen the last of those ruffians."

The man waited until they were out of sight before he mounted his horse and followed them, keeping out of sight. He held back in the brush until he was sure they were spending the night at the Moon's farm. Then he rode back and joined his companions and they drank themselves into a stupor.

About five miles out of the village Mike's group came to a well-kept farm and they pulled up.

A buxom woman walked out on the porch and shook the dust from a throw rug. She stood looking at them as Mike and Katy walked toward her. Mike said, "I'm Michael Ross, From County Kerry, Ireland, and this is my wife, Katy, from Richmond. We wondered if it would be all right if we camped somewhere nearby tonight. We'll keep our animals tied to our wagons and move on in the morning."

"I'm Martha Moon. My man, Charley, will be here shortly. He's never late for supper, and he makes all the decisions in this family. With a little nudging from me," she added.

She put two fingers in her mouth and sent a call over the fields and six boys wearing straw hats, and four girls wearing sunbonnets came toward the house with hoes over their shoulders. Then a man came around the corner of the barn driving a wagon loaded with pole wood.

The man saw the wagons at once, so he pulled his wagon alongside of a woodpile and got down and joined his wife on the porch. She said, "Charley, meet Mr. Michael Ross and his lovely wife, Katy. They want to camp somewhere on our place. They seem like mighty fine folks, I say let them camp in the shade of the oaks across the road."

"That's fine with me, love," Charley said.

Katy had gone to the wagons and said, "Kabuta, Peg, come meet Mr. and Mrs. Charley Moon."

When they were approaching the house Charley said, "All you folks come up on the porch out of that hot sun and sit a spell."

As the children started around the house Martha said, "You youngins come meet our guests." She introduced the boys and girls and said, "Mr. Ross, why don't you introduce your group?"

Michael said, "Well, I'm Michael, but everyone calls me Mike, and this is my wife, Katy, and these are my best friends, Bob Kabuta and his wife, Peg."

After they exchanged pleasantries Martha said, "You folks are going to have dinner with us tonight. Charley, you take care of these folks while I put another pan of cornpone in the oven." As she went in the door she threw back over her shoulder, "Supper in an hour."

Charley said, "Park your wagons and turn your stock in that big corral over there and the boys will feed them corn."

Mike said, "Thanks, but you must have a mare in heat, Midnight has been going crazy ever since I tied him to that tree."

"Yes, both of the mares I just drove in here are in heat. I have a small corral in back of the barn, I'd be beholding to you if you'd let him spend the night with them."

"That's fine, and there isn't a better stud anywhere. By the way, I have my hounds tied up because I was afraid they might get in a fight with your dogs and kill them, but I've seen no evidence that you have any. I've never seen a farm without dogs before."

"We had four full-breed golden collies, but they were stolen a month ago.

Nearly broke our hearts. The only one that's come back is our younger one, Lassie. She's in heat also and Martha locked her up in the cottonseed bin. She doesn't want her to breed with just any old dog."

"I've got a full-blooded Irish Wolfhound. They're big gentle dogs, but they're fierce fighters. They were bred in Ireland to kill the timber wolves. If your collie were pure bred you would get some great pups from that combination. If we put Wolf in the crib with her she'd be bred by morning."

Charley said, "This is our lucky day. Wolves are one of our biggest problems around here. They pulled down one of my young heifers a few days ago, and we didn't even get a roast out of her."

After they got all the animals where they wanted them, Mike, Kabuta, Katy, and Peg went to the wagons and changed into their best clothes. They tried to get the wrinkles out of them, without much success. Charley came out, and said, "Supper's ready, folks."

When they got to the house Kabuta and Peg started around the house and Charley said, "Where are you going, folks?"

Kabuta said, "To the back door, sir."

"Not in my house, Mr. Kabuta. We came here from Pennsylvania. We're Mennonites and don't hold with slavery. You and your pretty wife come right in the front door. You are as welcome at my table as any man."

Kabuta said, "The further we get from Richmond, the better I like it. Thank you, Mr. Moon, my wife and I would be honored to sit at your table."

Mike reached into the wagon and pulled out a hindquarter of an elk and said, "Charley, could you use this elk meat? Kabuta shot him yesterday. We have more than we can use before it spoils."

"We sure could, we haven't had anything but hog meat for a while now. That'll taste mighty good for a change."

He took the meat and put it in the smoke house where it would be safe from the dogs. Mike had untied them and they were away chasing rabbits for their supper.

When they gathered around the table Charley reached for the hand of a child on each side of him and as they held hands around the table he said grace and they ate.

When they all gathered on the front porch to enjoy the summer breeze Martha started satisfying what she knew was all of her family's curiosity.

"Mike, tell us what part of Ireland you came from. And what made you come to America."

Once more Mike told his story, leaving out the part about his wealth. When he finished, many of them were wiping tears from their eyes.

Then it was Kabuta's turn. He told how the neighboring tribe killed all of the elderly and babies in their village and sold others to slave traders; And how happy he'd been since Mike bought him and set him free.

"Good for you, Mike," Charley said.

Then Peg told how Kabuta had hidden her on the ship to keep the sailors from taking her to their bed, and how broken hearted she was when she was torn from him and sold to different masters. She told how happy she had been as Katy's companion and how quickly she fell in love with Kabuta when they met again. "And now, Katy has set me free."

Katy told them how she had been pampered all her life as the only girl in a household of three boys. "I never knew what a hard day's work was until we started on this trip. I'd never even cooked a meal until Mike gave me a cookbook, and with that and Kabuta's teaching, I think I'm getting better."

Mike said, "Pretty soon you'll be as good as Kabuta."

She brushed his cheek with a kiss, and said, "Those are kind words, my darling," and the Moon girls on the porch sighed wistfully.

Then Martha told how she and Charley met and how they came here looking for a warmer climate.

Mike said, "We can't thank you enough for your hospitality. We have a long ways to go before winter, so we'll be moving on in the morning."

Charley said, "Mike, we need good neighbors around here, and there is some fine land adjoining our place just west of us. All you have to do is clear the land, build your houses and dig a well. The boys and I would help you get that done. We would count it a real joy to have you and the Kabuta's as neighbors. We've fought off a number of Indian raids, and we expect more."

Mike told them of killing the six Indians that had taken Katy and Peg, just in time. And then he said, "Charley, what you say has merit, and it's appealing, but we would still be in a slave state. We want to get as far away from that as we can."

"I can't argue against that, go with God, my friends."

They sat up late that night visiting and they didn't wake up the next morning until the roosters started to crow. When Mike and Kabuta rolled out they saw all their animals lined up at a long trough, eating corn, and one of the girls leaving a chicken house with a basket stacked high with eggs, and four of the boys leaving the cow shed with two buckets of milk each. Mike and Kabuta went back to their wagons and said to their respective wives, "You lazy bones had better get out of those beds, the Moons have been up for hours."

When they gathered around the table it was stacked high with ham and eggs, buttermilk biscuits, jam, honey and ribbon cane syrup, and two of the biggest bowls of butter Mike had ever seen. There were large goblets of sweet milk, but no hot drink of any kind.

Mike thought maybe Mennonites didn't believe in drinking coffee or tea, but he didn't question them about it. He said, "Martha, I noticed that one of the girls had a large basket of eggs this morning. We'd like to buy as many as you can spare."

"Oh Mike, you couldn't possibly use that many eggs, half of them would spoil."

Mike said, "We can eat two dozen a day, and we can boil the rest of them and pickle them in vinegar, they'll keep a long time that way. We cook a number of cakes and dried fruit pies also. They keep a few days."

"I was saving eggs for setting in the springhouse, but we have plenty of laying hens. I could spare you about ten dozen and I could let you have a bag of dried apples, apricots, peaches and plums." Martha was the business one in this family. She said, "That would cost you, say...five dollars."

Mike said, "Now, Charley, what do we owe you for all the corn my stock ate and the ten sacks of wheat I saw your boys stack in the back of our buckboard and the extra corn they threw up on my wagon?"

"You didn't ask for those things. Mike. We can spare it, and you might need it before you get to wherever you're going. Besides, you're going to find night catching you where there's no feed for your stock. By the way, there was a man through here a few weeks ago and he said there was a wagon road from here all the way to Saint Louis on the Mississippi. At least you won't have to cut down any trees from here to there. But you must be leery of highwaymen and Indians. The highwaymen are more dangerous than the Indians are."

It was after nine o'clock when they regretfully pulled away from these new friends. Mike had given Katy two twenty-dollar gold pieces and said, "When you hug Martha good bye, drop these in her apron pocket."

Martha was hugging Kitty so tightly she didn't feel the weight of the coins when she slipped them in her pocket.

* * * * *

The leader of the foursome that was at the saloon said to his men, "I want those wagons and everything in them, and those mules and horses. I've never seen better." When they rode by the Moon farm they saw that the wagons had gone westward. They followed them slowly because they didn't want to catch up with them until they were in camp. When they rode out of the trees into a meadow they saw the wagons parked under a large cottonwood on the south bank of the Kanawha River.

Kabuta and Peg had ridden on ahead and when they saw this lovely spot Peg said, "Let's stay here tonight and you and I go fishing until Mike and Katy get here."

They had caught two nice blue cats when they heard the rumbling wagons. Kabuta went to direct Mike to where he wanted them to park their wagons while Peg took the stringer with the two fish. She held them up for Mike and Katy to see when they drove in. Kabuta said, "Peg wanted to stay here tonight."

They had traveled only about ten miles though, and Mike was reluctant to stop so early in the day, but he gave in when Peg said, "Please, Mike, I want to cook these fish for an early supper tonight."

They turned the stock loose in the meadow and Kabuta and Peg took their shotguns and went to the river to clean the fish, while Mike got a fire started and Katy got the utensils together.

Wolf got up from where he was dozing in the shade of the wagon and began to growl, looking back the way they had come.

Katy walked alongside of Mike when he turned to face four men. All of them were wearing two waist guns and their hands never strayed far from them.

Their spokesman said, "Folks, we're trappers going west for the winter. If you're traveling far it would benefit all of us to travel together. There are a lot of hostile Indians out there."

Mike said, "Where are your packs, you seem to be traveling light if you're going far?"

"Oh, we left them in town; we wanted to ride out to see if you wanted to join up with us."

Mike said, "Men, before you go for those guns, I suggest you look behind you."

The man said, "We've heard that one before. How stupid do you think we are?"

Kabuta spoke in a spine tingling, cold voice. "You'd better be smart enough to take my friend's advice."

Two of the men turned to look down the barrels of two double-barreled shotguns.

Mike and Katy pointed their hands at the other two and the men were surprised to see a pistol in each hand of both Mike and Katy. They were so fast they couldn't believe it.

Kabuta and Peg worked themselves around until they were standing beside Mike and Katy. Mike said, "We don't want to kill you, so just ride on back to town. If you're thinking about sneaking back in here tonight—or any other nigh— I warn you: these Irish wolfhounds would have you by the throats before you knew they were near you. They've been trained to kill."

"We're going, but you'll see us again," the leader said.

Kabuta said, "Let me take him now, Mr. Mike," and he cocked both barrels of his shotgun.

The men whirled their horses and bolted back toward town.

Mike said, "We won't see any more of those pickled brains."

Kabuta said, "Mike weren't you proud of our wives?"

"I sure was." He picked Katy up and danced round and round with her.

They broke camp early the next morning and were on the road before the sun began to spread it's life-giving rays across the land. They traveled twenty-five miles that day and camped in a bend of the river where it turned north.

Mike and the girls went to sleep right after they ate. Though Mike was sure the four men wouldn't bother them again, Kabuta remained uneasy.

There was a pale moon and he could barely see to get around, but he wasn't about to go to bed as long as this uneasy feeling possessed him. He took his bow, a quiver of arrows and a throw line and some pieces of fresh rabbit he'd shot that day, baited the hooks, threw the line into the river, tied the string around his boot top, and sat down with his back to a tree.

He had two good catfish on a string when he decided to go get a cup of cold coffee from the pot. He tied the line to the tree and went for the coffee, and just as he reached for it Wolf growled low in his throat. He, Lassie Brother and Sister faded into the woods, but Daisy and Shep stayed with the wagons.

Kabuta placed an arrow in his bow and slipped quietly into the trees in the direction he saw the dogs disappear. He hadn't gone a hundred yards when he heard one of the dogs attack. The man screamed a bloodcurdling scream that awakened Mike and the girls.

When Kabuta reached the commotion he saw the dogs wrestling with three of the men. The forth one had a pistol in his hand, dancing around trying to get a shot at Wolf as he shook a big man furiously. Kabuta hollered and the man turned and fired. Kabuta heard the hum of the ball as it passed his ear. The arrow that Kabuta released from his bow went through the man's heart.

Mike came running up behind Kabuta, calling his name, and Peg and Katy weren't far behind. They were holding a pistol in each hand. They were dressed only in their red long johns and boots, but it was over. The dogs had released the three men at Kabuta's command.

Two of the men were dead, and the other one was badly mauled.

Kabuta said, "On your feet," and the man got up unsteadily and leaned against a tree. Kabuta gave him a minute and said, "Now examine the others."

"They're all dead," he said.

Kabuta took the sharp two-edged tinker knife that Angus had given him and removed the arrow from the man's chest.

Mike retrieved all the weapons and ammunition the men had and put them in one of the wagons and then he and Kabuta loaded the dead men on their horses. Mike said to their compadre, "Do whatever you want with them. We should have let Sister finish you off like the rest of them and tie you and them on your horses and let them take you back to town. If you ever bother us again, that's what we'll do. Now get out of here before we change our minds and do it right now."

Mike and Kabuta patted and hugged the dogs, saying over and over, "Good dogs."

Peg hugged Kabuta and said, "I love you dearly, and I love those wonderful dogs. This is the second time they've saved Katy and me from a terrible fate."

Katy, Peg and Mike were able to go back to sleep eventually, but Kabuta was too pumped up to sleep. As he walked along the riverbank with the ever-watchful Brother walking tall by his side, remorse set in. He'd killed two men in the last few days and it didn't set well with him. This time it was a white man. It kept running through his mind what the white men in Charleston would do when the man reported what took place here tonight. Would they come after him? He finally went to bed, but he couldn't sleep.

Long before daylight he slipped quietly out of bed and went and shook Mike and whispered, "Come."

Mike reached for his boots and climbed out of the wagon without waking Katy.

Kabuta led Mike away far enough from the wagons so they wouldn't disturb the girls. He said, "Mike, I just killed a white man and by this time they must be back in town. There might be a posse of white men headed this way right now to hang me high in one of these trees. And there's no telling what they would do to my Peg."

"What have I been thinking?" Mike said, "Let's get out of here."

Camp became a beehive of activity as they prepared to leave. As soon as they got the wagons on the road, Mike said, "Kabuta, tie my wagon team behind your wagon and let's saddle all the horses and put all our guns and a bag of jerky, and two canteens of water on each horse. That will give us better mobility if we have to run."

Kabuta said, "Mike, would you leave everything to save Peg and me?"

Mike gave him a quick hug. "Kabuta, these are just things. I only have one best friend, and Peg is my wife's best friend. Go along with me in what I want you to do, my friend."

"Anything, Mike."

They took the guns they had taken from the bandits and made sure they were loaded and Mike put them in the front of the lead wagon he would be driving, and then he called them all together. "Kabuta, you take Katy and Peg and ride on down the trail for at least ten miles at a gallop, and then walk your horses. I'll come on as fast as I can get these mules to move. If a posse overtakes me and I get in trouble, if I can, I'll send Wolf and Daisy to you and I'll fire my shotgun and you run. If everything is all right, I'll fire my rifle and you can come back and help me with these wagons."

Kabuta protested vigorously, but Mike stood firm. Kabuta and Peg galloped away, but Katy firmly refused to leave Michael to face the posse alone.

Mike got the wagons rolling an hour before sunup and they were miles down the road when Katy said, "Mike, I don't believe they're coming."

"I hope not, Katy, but with the lies that man will tell them back in town I'm sure we'll be questioned."

Just then they heard the faint pounding of the hooves of a number of horses. Mike pulled up under the shade of a tree and he and Katy walked back behind all of their belongings and stood in the middle of the road and waited for the posse.

There were a dozen men coming fast, but when they saw a man and a woman standing in the road they slowed and came up to them with their horses walking. Mike and Katy were relieved to see that Charley Moon was with them. One of the men was wearing a star on his leather vest, and the bandit was with them.

Charley Moon moved forward and said, "Sheriff, this is Michael Ross and his wife, Katy that I told you about. They are mighty fine folks."

The sheriff said, "Mr. Ross, this man tells us that they came to your camp to see if you would let them join you for the journey to Saint Louis, and a Black man set your dogs on them and they killed his boss."

Katy, with her blue eyes flashing said, "Sheriff, that's a pack of dirty lies."

Mike gripped Katy's arm and said, "That's the gospel truth, Sheriff. These men attacked us in the middle of the night. These are my dogs and I turned them loose on them and when I hollered, his boss fired at me and I shot him through the heart with this," and he held up the arrow that Kabuta shot the man with.

The bandit said, "The Black shot him."

A man in the back of the posse said, "We can't let a Black man get away with shooting a white man." Some of the others agreed with him. Another said, "What are we waiting for, let's go after him."

Charley Moon said, "Hold on, men, think about what you're saying. Those Blacks are free, and they sat at my table. They are educated, fine Christian people, as are Mr. and Mrs. Ross. Are you going to take the word of a bandit against people like this? I say they did us a favor. Let them go and invite this bandit to leave our community, headed east.

The sheriff said, "That's my thinking. This riffraff was no asset to our community. You may be on your way, Mr. Ross." He tipped his hat to Katy and turned to his men and said, "Thank you, men, for doing your duty. Now let's go home."

As they rode away Charley tarried long enough to say, "Mother insisted I go with the posse and use my influence to get you out of this mess."

Katy hugged him and kissed his cheek and said, "Thank you, and give Martha and the family our love."

Mike shook his hand and Charley mounted his horse and Mike and Katy watched him ride out of their lives. When they were alone Mike bowed his head against the tailboard of the wagon and thanked God for delivering them. Katy said, "Mike, untie the team from your wagon and I'll drive them and we can make better time."

Mike stood in the middle of the road and watched the posse until he was sure they were sincere and were returning to Charleston.

"No, Katy, I need your loving strength beside me right now. Maybe it's relief from the dread I had in meeting this crises, but I feel as weak as a kitten."

Mike decided not to waste a shot, so he tucked a note in Daisy's collar and sent her to Kabuta. In an hour Kabuta and Peg joined them.

Mike said, "We have nothing to worry about. There was a posse of twelve men, led by a sheriff. The bandit that we let go was with them and the sheriff said that the bandit said they came to our camp to ask us if they could join us for the trip to Saint Louis and that you set the dogs on them and killed his boss. Charley Moon was with them also, and he spoke highly of you and Peg, Kabuta, and the sheriff believed my story. I lied a little; I told the sheriff I fired the arrow that killed the leader of the gang.

"The sheriff said it made no difference and that those men were no asset to their community, and we were free to go."

Kabuta said, "That's a load off my mind. I don't mind telling you, Peg and I were scared we could both wind up dead or back in slavery."

Mike said, "You and Peg go ahead and find us a camp site and let's stop early. We all need some rest, you most of all."

This was one time Kabuta didn't need any urging. He and Peg mounted their horses and set a fast pace to find their next stopping place as soon as possible, Kabuta was all in.

When Mike and Katy rolled to a stop about three o'clock, Kabuta and Peg had a fire going with a pot of hot coffee ready. He cut the last apple pie that he had baked. Kabuta ate a piece of it and went to bed as soon as he unhitched the team and turned them loose to graze.

They had been traveling on flat ground all day and as soon as Kabuta and Peg had left them Mike built a fire in the cook stove and put ham hocks and pinto beans on to boil. The pot held enough to last them at least three days.

When Kabuta climbed up in the wagon Peg said, "He's worn out, the poor dear."

Mike turned all the stock loose in the meadow and commanded the dogs to watch them. Then he milked the cows. Katy started churning butter and Peg got what she needed to make biscuits.

Mike thought he heard a turkey gobble somewhere up the river. He got his bow and headed that way. As he drew near he was sure there was a flock of turkeys feeding just ahead of him. He slipped quietly forward and parted the brush and looked out on a large flock. He killed two young hens, and as they took to the air he brought down a young tom.

He walked into camp with the birds and said, "Beans and ham hock can keep; we eat turkey for a few days."

He put water on to boil, and then he said to Katy and Peg, "Why don't you two get a nap while I clean these birds, and I'll grab one while you cook supper."

Mike scalded the birds so he could remove the feathers, dressed them and cut the smaller hens in pieces for frying and the bigger tom he hung high in a tree. They would roast it in the oven as they traveled in the morning. Then he routed out the girls and went for his nap.

An hour later they awakened their husbands to a good turkey dinner.

CHAPTER SEVENTEEN

A week later they were following a small creek that ran east and west through a narrow valley on a hard packed road. To their left was a low range of mountains that seemed to go straight up. The side of the cliff was almost as smooth as a man-made wall, and it was covered with vines. The road was wide and well used. They saw many pony tracks and tracks from travois's.

Kabuta said, "We must be near a large Indian village."

Mike said, "There's not much doubt about it, but we can't turn back now. Keep a sharp eye out for a place we can camp where we can defend ourselves or we can slip away on our horses."

They came to a large overhang and Mike said, "Katy, Peg, you stay on the wagons, Kabuta and I will investigate this place to see if we should spend the night here."

In the back of the overhead was a wide-mouth cave with a low flat ceiling that ran as far back as they could see. They walked back a hundred feet and saw another smaller cave running southeast. Mike said, "This looks like two ancient underground rivers that came together just before they emptied out on the valley."

There was a large stack of wood underneath the overhang that almost touched the roof, and the walls and the roof were black from many fires.

Kabuta said, "Mike, this must be a meeting place for neighboring tribes where they hold great parties or religious meetings of some kind. And they're preparing for a meeting soon. This place gives me the creeps; let's get out of here. If we got bottled up in here we could never get out."

Mike said, "There are moccasin tracks and Indian pony tracks everywhere. It looks like they're preparing for a meeting soon."

Their shod mules and horses and the vehicle wheels could not be hidden from a sharp eye, but Mike was hoping that the Indians would be so intent in getting to the meeting place they wouldn't notice them.

They drove another three hundred yards or so and turned right, off the road, onto a rocky hog back and dropped down in a sheltered cove near the creek. They didn't unhitch the teams, but removed the bits from their mouths and fed them corn. Mike said, "Hitch another team on your wagon and I'll hitch another on mine, that'll give you six mules and me four. We may have to run for it. We'll saddle our four fastest horses and put a bedroll behind each saddle and hang a sack of jerky and two canteens of water on each saddle horn. Put the backpack on two of the horses and distribute our ammunition between them and as much food as we dare. We might have to leave the wagons."

After they got that all done they ate a cold supper. Mike said, "You three try to get some rest, sleep if you can. I'm going to scout around."

He commanded Daisy, Wolf, Lassie, Sister and Brother to stay with the wagons, and he took Shep and walked back toward the cave and settled down in the brush, where he had a clear view of the road both east and west of the cave. He leaned his back against a tree and dozed, trusting Shep to alert him. He knew that twenty minutes of sleep was sufficient to carry him all night and day, if it became necessary.

He wasn't sure how long he slept before Shep woke him growling very low. He patted him on the head and said, "Quiet. Good dog." He didn't get up, but sat there studying the trail. It wasn't quite dark yet and he could make out that there were horses pulling travois's loaded with something, going east toward the cave. And there were many women and children with the men. Then he noticed another procession, just as large, traveling west along the road they had traveled. He hoped they didn't notice their wagon tracks.

Flames licked up the side of the pile of wood in the cave, enabling Mike to see more clearly. The cave was full of Indians, and the children were chasing one another in and out of the cave. Mike watched the roads from both directions for an hour to make sure there were no latecomers to this party.

He woke the others, urgently whispering, "Come! We're getting out of here. I think every Indian that lives miles around here are at this meeting. When we get to the hard surface of the wide trail we were on, you girls ride your horses on ahead, leading the packhorses. Kabuta, you'll be next and I'll bring up the rear with Wolf and Daisy. Kabuta, when we hit the hard trail, let the mules trot as long as the trail is level. Thank God it's a dark night. We're going put as much distance as we can between this place and ourselves. I'm in hopes their celebration, or whatever it is, will go on all night and they'll be so tired when they return to their village they won't see our tracks. Let's move!"

Katy and Peg had gone only a mile when the creek turned across the trail, and back up in the canyon, just up from the trail, was a large Indian village. They turned back and informed the men of this. "But it seems to be deserted," Peg said.

Mike said, "Don't you girls get very far in front of us. Be very quiet as you cross the creek. Let the horses drink. And don't go near the village and keep your guns handy."

They trotted on and kept a sharp eye on the village as they let the stock drink at the crossing.

The village was definitely empty. They pressed on and the pull up the incline from the creek was keeping them at a slow walk, though they wanted desperately to run.

When they topped the hill the trail dropped noticeably and the mules broke into a ground-eating trot; the wagons were almost rolling down the slope on their own. Hours later, about an hour before sunup, Mike figured they had put at least thirty miles between themselves and the village.

Kabuta pulled up in a wide creek and let his mules drink and Mike did the same. The other stock drank as well. Katy and Peg rejoined them there and Peg said, "Could we start a fire in the stove and heat up the beans and ham hock and make coffee while we roll along?"

Mike said, "I don't see why not, but I want that fire out before daylight."

He started a fire in the stove and put the beans and coffee on and said, "Kabuta, we'd better let the mules walk from now until our food is ready.

Then we'll stop. We won't unhitch, but we'll feed the mules plenty of shelled corn from feed bags; they need it if we're going to drive them all day."

Ten minutes later they were moving out at a steady walk. Peg and Katy had tied their horses behind the wagons and Peg took the reins of Kabuta's team and Katy took Mike's, and the men hit their beds and were sound asleep in minutes. An hour later as the sun was turning the night to day, the girls pulled to a halt under some trees that hung out over the trail.

They spent thirty minutes here to eat and rest. Then Kabuta and Mike took the reins while their wives slept.

The dogs had dropped down in spots of sunlight to sleep in the warmth of the sun for the thirty minutes, but they sprang up when the wagons started to move. Mike fully intended to put another thirty miles behind them before they stopped again.

They had been traveling all day on the rocky slopes of the foothills, and about an hour before dark Mike led his little group off the trail onto a rocky ledge behind a thick grove of juniper trees that was just high enough to hide the wagons and stock. They tied the stock to trees that night so they wouldn't wander away looking for feed, and fed them out of their precious stock of corn. There was no water in this camp, the stock would have to wait, but they could use the water from the barrels.

Kabuta built a fire out of dead wood underneath a juniper with thick foliage so the smoke would sift up through the foliage and dissipate so it couldn't be seen very far. He prepared a meager meal and they ate and climbed wearily into bed exhausted, trusting the dogs to warn them if danger came near. They had been traveling almost non-stop for two days; Just before they went to bed Mike said, "Kabuta, set your mental time clock for four hours and we'll move out."

About five hours later Mike woke up at the gentle shaking of Kabuta. When he dressed he found the teams hitched and the horses saddled. He said, "Why didn't you wake me?"

"I've had more sleep than you have for the last two days. You needed the rest."

When Kabuta got up on the wagon seat Peg asked wearily, "Aren't you coming back to bed?"

"No, pretty lady, sleep if you can, we're moving out."

When Mike eased his wagon down the rocky slope behind Kabuta, Katy rose up and said, "It's still dark, and I'm so tired."

Mike said, "I know, my sweet, go back to sleep. We'll be off this rocky slope soon and it won't be so rough."

"It's all right dear, nothing will keep me awake." And she was sleeping soundly in minutes. The mules and horses were young and five hour's rest with a good feeding of corn was all they needed to move on.

The moon was getting bigger each night and soon it would be full, so they traveled nights and lay over in the daytime, as long as the trail was good enough to do so. Mike had read that Indians wouldn't travel at night unless it was absolutely necessary.

They did lay over the next day, hidden in the deep woods. But there was no grass for the stock, so again they tied them up so they wouldn't stray. They didn't know if they would be able to buy any more corn, so they fed the mules only. Five day later, it was about noon when they reached the Wabash River just below where the White River entered into it. The river was very wide here.

Mike said, "Kabuta, hold them here until I take Midnight across."

Mike went only halfway and turned back and said, "The bottom is very muddy, and we could bog down. Wait here until I get back, I'm going to look for a safer crossing of both rivers further up. The water won't be as swift, either."

Mike rode about a quarter of a mile up the Wabash, where he crossed over on solid rock bottom. The water was pretty deep, but he was sure they could cross here all right. He rode across a meadow to the White River. It was wider, but shallower and the bottom was firm. He rode back and led the wagons to the place. He tied a rope to the lead team and tied it to the saddle horn. "Katy, Peg, you ride your horses over, and Kabuta, don't enter the river until you see me get this rope around that big tree over there. When I raise my hand, come on."

The girls went across ahead of Mike and turned to watch Kabuta ease his team into the water and Mike took up the slack on the rope as they crossed. When they reached the deepest part of the river the lead team had to swim about three feet before they could dig in again, but they pulled the big wagon up on high ground and Kabuta said, "Mike, I'm going have to take the lead team back to bring the other wagon across. And we've got to move, that river is rising. While I'm going back across you pull this wagon up on the top of that little rise. Then come back and tie your rope the way you had it before."

Kabuta lost no time getting the team back and hitched to the other wagon, and Mike was just behind him. Kabuta entered the river and was almost to the deep water when Mike got his rope taut. When they hit the deep water the wagon swung around, miraculously it didn't turn over. Mike was pulling for all he was worth and the big mules got footing and dug in, and when the wagon wheels touched bottom the wagon straighten out and they pulled it to safety just as a headwater came rushing down the river, overflowing its banks, almost reaching the top of the rises where the wagons were sitting.

Kabuta said, "We'll never be able to cross the White River until these rivers subside."

Mike said, "Maybe, according to my map the White swings off to the west. You know how these summer storms are, it might not be raining upriver on the White."

When they got to the White River it was calm and they crossed it without any trouble, but when Kabuta pulled the last wagon alongside the other one, the mules' sides were heaving. They had a trying crossing the Wabash and they deserved a good rest, and Mike resolved they would get it right here.

They had left the cows, calves and four horses between the two rivers, so he sent the dogs after them. The cows were reluctant to enter the river, but when these big dogs started nipping at their hocks they plunged in. Mike said, "Look, the Wabash has overflowed the meadow between the rivers and is now flowing into the White. We got across just in time. We might have been stuck over there for a week or more. Kabuta, we'd better get these wagons to higher ground. If that storm is coming this way, the White might overflow its banks before morning. That grove of live oaks up on that hill looks like the highest place around here. Let's get them under that massive oak."

Kabuta got busy cutting down some small oaks that blocked their way, as Mike brought the wagons up. The girls started a fire in the cook stove and Mike and Kabuta erected a tarp over the wagons. A dark cloud was rolling over them and rain was imminent.

Just then Wolf and Daisy each laid a turkey at Kabuta's feet. Kabuta said, "Thanks, Wolf and Daisy, for bringing us our meat for supper."

Mike went to the river and dressed the turkeys and put the larger one in the oven to bake and the other smaller one was tender enough to fry. He would be their supper and tomorrow it would be a roasted turkey.

The mules and horses had a good roll in the grass and the air that was sweeping across the meadow refreshed them immensely. Katy said, "Peg, look at those horses and mules romping and jumping as they kick up their heels."

Peg said, "Yeah, my spirits are rising too. I heard Mike tell Kabuta we were going to stay her until the mules got a good feed and a few days rest."

Mike cut down three slender trees and tied the top of one to each end of the other to make a ridge pole for the tarp he and Kabuta erected over the back of the wagon with the stove in it. This would act as their kitchen for their stay here. When they had it up and secure they dug a deep trench around it so the water would run down the slope so the floor wouldn't get wet. They stretched another smaller tarp on the ground as a floor that they could sweep and keep clean.

Katy said, "You boys are setting this camp as though you meant to stay a while."

Mike said, "Well, it's beginning to rain, and the way that storm looks we just might be here a week or two. This ground will get so muddy we might not be able to move these wagons for a while."

They had a good meal, thanks to the dogs.

It was a tired bunch of travelers that went to bed that night, and they slept so soundly that they never heard the rain pelting down on the tarps all night.

They slept late the next morning, a luxury they hadn't had since they left home.

After breakfast Mike said, "Kabuta and I are going for a ride this morning. Do you girls want to go?"

They spoke in unison, "Yes!" So while the women did the dishes, the men saddled their horses. The clouds had passed over, but the way the clouds were gathering in the west it wouldn't be long before the next downpour.

They rode downriver past where the White ran into the Wabash to where the water rushed through a narrow gorge. They were sitting on their horses watching the water when they saw a large tree tumbling down the river. When it entered the narrow gorge it stuck momentarily, causing the swift water to fly high up into the air, creating a mist. Hundreds of small rainbows appeared and with the sun reflecting on the mist, it looked like millions of stars were twinkling around the rainbows.

Katy gasped, "Have you ever seen anything so beautiful in your life?"

Mike said, "You, my love."

She smiled and slapped him playfully on the shoulder.

Peg and Kabuta sat their horses in awe.

Then the river rocked the tree back and forth, ripping away the roots and branches that were holding it in place and it went rolling on down the river and the awesome scene disappeared.

Peg said, "Katy, my girl; that was worth this trip in it's self."

They left the river and rode a mile out, circling their camp, and when they came back to the river they saw a fat, one-point buck deer. Mike held up his hand and said, "He's young enough to be very tender."

He was over two hundred yards away, but Kabuta already had his Hawking long rifle trained right behind the deer's shoulder and when he squeezed the trigger the deer leaped high into the air and lay where he fell.

Mike remarked, "Good shot. Our meat supply is secured for a few days. This ground is soaked so deep that the mules would have a difficult time pulling the wagons. There's plenty of feed for the stock, what do you say we spend a week or so here?"

They all thought that was a fine idea. There was no sign that anyone else had ever been here, and they were all ready for some much needed rest.

The rivers were too muddy for fishing but on the sixth day Kabuta and Peg went fishing.

Mike said, "Have fun, Katy and I are going to ride west to locate our camp site for day after tomorrow. We might be gone all day; I want to look over this country a little better."

Mike saddled up and they rode for twenty miles on the wagon trail west to locate where they would camp next.

Their horses were rested and they wanted to run and Katy said, "I'll race you," and she kicked her gray in the side and dashed away, but there was no way the gray could outrun Midnight. When Midnight passed the gray, Mike hollered, "Come on, you slow poke."

They passed the day riding through the hills and meadows. At lunchtime as they lay on a blanket Mike said, "This is good ranching country. If we decided to stay here I know Kabuta and Peg would agree, but Kabuta's heart wouldn't be in it, and neither would mine. Something is driving us to our destiny. I feel it in my spirit."

Katy rolled over and kissed him and said, "This would be a good place to settle, and when you were studying your maps yesterday you said we weren't far from Saint Louis and that this country was growing so fast that this land would be covered with farms in years to come. But Mike, go where you'll be happy. If you're happy, I'll be happy." They spent a quiet two hours here under the shade of a maple tree.

When they returned to camp Peg and Kabuta were already in bed.

They had spent ten days here and the animals were getting fat on the semi-green grass, and the cows were pouring milk. The ground had dried out with the help of a hot dry wind that had been blowing without ceasing since it quit raining. When they pulled the wagons back on the trail the wheels didn't sink. They were in hill country now, headed for the bustling town of Saint Louis.

CHAPTER EIGHTEEN

As they rolled along Mike began to think that perhaps they should turn back and set their roots down right there in the forks of the Wabash and White rivers. There was a beautiful building site on a high hill, far above any floodwaters. The soil was a deep loam that would grow just about anything and they would never want for water. He knew wherever he decided to put down roots, the others would not object. But he pushed these thoughts onto the back road of his mind; he was going on to his destiny.

Eight days later they pulled up on a hill overlooking the mighty Mississippi River. They saw the little town of Saint Louis sitting on a high bank on the west side of the river. As they stood there side by side, they were all remembering how close they came to losing one of their wagons when they crossed the Wabash, and it was just a creek along side of this river.

Peg said, "Oh! My, do we have to cross that?"

"No, we can't do it." Katy said.

"There, look," Mike said, and he pointed to a ferry slowly crossing the river toward them. "That's how we get across. Let's get down there!"

They mounted their spring seats and rolled down the hill to the river, and the ferry was there waiting for them. It took three trips to get all their belongings across, but the price was fair, and Mike was happy to pay it.

The ferryman said, "Where did you come from?"

Mike said, "County Kerry, Ireland."

"No," The man said, "I mean where did you start from with these wagons?"

"Richmond, Virginia," Mike replied.

"Where're you going?"

"West, until we come to the place we think the Lord wants us to put down roots."

"Good luck, all you'll find west of here is a few mountain men and a lot of Indians; some friendly, and some not so friendly. You could lose your hair out there."

"Well, we've managed to dodge them so far."

"You won't dodge all of them out there," the man said, simply.

When everything was over the river they took their stock to a stable and the man assured them that their stock and wagons would be safe with him.

They found a hotel that would rent them rooms and Peg and Kabuta's color didn't seem to matter when they knew they had money to spend.

They enjoyed the beds and someone else's cooking for seven days while their animals put back on most of the fat they had lost.

Mike and Kabuta went into the saloon and questioned everybody they could about the western lands. They were talking to a tall man, dressed in buckskins from his knee-high moccasins to his coonskin hat. He had just come into Saint Louis with his partner on a raft loaded with pelts. He said, "We've been trapping in the Rocky Mountains and we floated down the Missouri to the Mississippi to Saint Louis to sell our furs. Mr. Ross, what are you looking for?"

"We're looking for a fertile valley where there's plenty of game and a river to fish in, and trees big enough to build cabins."

"There are some beautiful valleys out there with beautiful rivers running through them. And there's more game and fish than you ever dreamed of. And the pine, spruce and cedar trees abound. But there are some fierce Indians living in those valleys. You could get killed out there, and nobody would ever know it."

When they left the saloon an elderly Indian followed them and when they were well away from the saloon he called after them in broken English. He said to Kabuta, "I know of a place where there is a beautiful waterfall on a river that runs through a valley into a lake. But there are many smokes that come up out of the ground. It is a river that runs into the Big Muddy."

Kabuta said, "That's what they call the Missouri."

Mike flipped the Indian a twenty-dollar gold piece and said," We'll follow the Missouri and see what we'll see."

The old man said, "Take needles and threads of different colors and iron hatchets and axes to trade to my people and they will help you."

Mike said, "Guide us to this valley and I'll give you…" and held up his hands with two fingers held wide, "more of the gold pieces I just gave you."

The old man shook his head vigorously. "No, I'm an outcast. I can never return to my people." He turned to walk away, but Mike called him back, and gave him another coin.

The next day Mike bought all the sewing kits he could find, with many spools of thread, as well as many axes, hatchets, and knives. He bought two cast-iron pot-bellied heaters and another cook stove. He bought windowpanes and wrapped them tightly and buried them in a large barrel of flour, in hopes he could get them to the valley without breaking them.

He purchased all the salt pork and side bacon and ham hocks he could find, along with sacks of beans, peas, rice, tea, coffee, sugar, salt and pepper. Mike paid for the goods and loaded them onto their wagons.

The morning he started to pay his stable bill the man said, "Mister, you won't get far with those young calves you have there."

"Why not?"

"Wolves, bear, cougar and all kind of Indians; I don't give you much chance of making it yourselves, especially with your pretty wives. There are white scum out there, as well as Indians, who'd kill you men for them as well as for your goods."

Peg shuddered, and Katy said, "Mister, if you're trying to scare us, it won't work; we've come too far to turn back now."

"Mister Ross, you have a young heifer there that if I'm any judge, is carrying a calf, and a younger heifer and a young bull calf. If you let me have them it will save you a lot of trouble and your bill is paid."

Mike said, "You're right, she should drop her calf in a month or so. It will be months before that bull calf can produce. I'll let you have him and the older heifer, but we'll take our chances getting the younger heifer through. We hope to build a herd with her and the two cows and our bull."

"Deal and good luck."

Four days later they were camped on the south bank of the Missouri River about a mile west of the Mississippi.

Katy and Peg walked up the river looking for a secluded spot to take a bath. They found a good spot and when they had finished bathing and were on their way back to camp, Peg reached for Katy's arm, held her fingers to her lips and said, "Shhhh, listen. Do you hear crying?"

"It sounds like it's coming from over there," Katy said.

They slipped quietly forward and came upon a young Indian girl who was hiding in the bushes, weeping softly. When the Indian girl saw Peg and Katy she cowered further back in the bushes.

The women held their hands out to her and motioned for her to come with them.

"Oh, Katy, it's so frustrating not being able to speak to her in her language," Peg said.

"I know, Peg, we need desperately to learn their language."

The girl surprised them by saying, "Peg, Katy." She pointed to herself, "Running Springs."

"You speak our language," Katy said.

"Little, no much," she replied. "Know, more than talk."

Peg said, "Don't be afraid, and come with us." She took her by the hand and Katy took the other and they walked into camp that way, to where Mike and Kabuta were busy greasing the wagon wheels. Peg said, "Running Springs, this is my man, Kabuta."

Running Springs said, "Kabuta."

Katy said, "And this is my man, Mike."

"Mike," she repeated.

The beans and ham hock were simmering on the stove, an apple pie was cooling and the biscuits were baking in the oven.

They all sat around in a circle on the ground sheet to eat, with Running Springs sitting between Peg and Katy. Kabuta said grace and Katy filled their plates.

Running Springs ate as if she was starving. When Kabuta brought out the apple pie and poured sweet milk in her cup, she ate this more slowly. When she finished, a shy smile broke across her pretty young face and she rubbed her tummy and said, "Much good."

After the utensils and dishes had been cleaned and put away, they sat in the pale moonlight and Running Springs told them how she happened to be here, far from her home in the Valley of the Smokes.

With her broken English they finally pieced together her story. Her father was the Chief in her village and there were two braves who wanted to take her for their squaw. She had persuaded her father to let her go with the suitor of her choice, which was the younger of the two. She would be his first, and she hoped only, squaw. Her father wouldn't let her marry until her sixteenth winter and this winter would be her sixteenth.

She went on to say that the other brave was bigger and ugly, and he said he wanted many squaws, but she would be the first and head squaw. When he was rejected and her father told him that this winter he would give her to her chosen one, he became very angry.

"One night my suitor and I were standing in the moonlight, rubbing noses, when he came up behind us and laid my lover's head wide open with a club. Then he hit me on the chin with his fist and knocked me unconscious. When I woke up he had me tied on a horse and was taking me away from my village. He said he knew of a hidden valley where no one would ever find us.

"We rode for five days, stopping only to relieve ourselves or to water the horses; we ate as we rode. I tried to run away, but he caught me and started beating me. I screamed and screamed.

"Suddenly he stopped beating me and reached for a knife and tried to throw it at a man riding down on us on horseback. The rider shot the brave and left him where he fell. After assuring me he meant me no harm, he took me back to where he and his partner were camping."

"He was a kind man and he said he would take me back to my father, but first he had to go to Saint Louis to sell his furs and buy trade goods to take back to the Indians. It took us three weeks to get back to Saint Louis.

"During those three weeks the man that saved me told me his name was Frank Lee, and his partner's name was Sam Crowley, and they started teaching me some words. Mr. Lee said he had a wife and little boy and girl and I could stay with them for two months until he was ready to take me back to my father. They were good people and taught me a lot.

"I didn't see Mr. Crowley again until he joined us for the journey to my home. Mister Lee never touched me at all, he was a good man, but his partner, Crowley, was always touching me and smiling at me in such away it made me afraid.

"Frank Lee told Crowley to leave me alone, but three nights earlier he left camp to hunt for fresh meat. As soon as he left Mr. Crowley started touching me here," she placed her hands on her breast. "When I tried to push him away he grabbed me and put his lips to mine. He smelled bad and I fought to get away, but he was too strong. He threw me on the ground and tried to take my clothes off. He was sitting on me when Mr. Lee hit him with a stick.

"Mr. Crowley laid there for a long time. Mr. Lee said we had to get away from him, so he started loading his goods on his pack mules and I rolled up our bedrolls.

"Mr. Crowley got up and I saw him start to stab Mr. Lee in the back. When I screamed, he turned in time to duck and the knife stuck in the pack of goods Mr. Lee was tying on the mule.

"They fought with knives, they both cut real bad, then Mr. Lee fall down dead. Mr. Crowley reached for me, but he was cut bad and I run away and hide in the brush. Later, I crawled back to see if Mr. Lee really dead. When I knew he was I went to Mr. Crowley's bedroll and he was groaning and there was much blood. He opened his eyes and saw me. He said, 'Help me,' but I ran away much fast and hide in bushes; soon after, you find me."

Mike said, "Can you lead us back to your camp?"

She said she could. They went immediately to the camp and found both men dead.

Mike said, "Greater love has no man than this; that a man lay down his life for a friend. This is what Mr. Lee did for you, Running Springs."

Mike and Kabuta buried them there and put crosses at the head of the graves with their names carved in the cross stick. The horses and mules were tied to trees. They went through Crowley's things and found nothing on him to indicate where they could send what little money he had on him or his goods, but they did find an itemized statement of the cost of the goods. They put Crowley's goods on his pack mule and took everything with them.

That night as they sat around the campfire, Mike said, "This is a good camp with plenty of grass for the stock. I'll ride back to Saint Louis in the morning and see Mrs. Lee and give her these personal things and pay her for the goods."

Katy said, "I'm going with you."

"No, Katy, I'll take your horse so I can change mounts often and I'll ride all the way to Saint Louis tomorrow. I might have to stay in the hotel overnight. I'll ride all the way back in one day. It'll be a grueling ride. I'll feel better if you stay here."

"All right," she said, "you get in bed and I'll fix a food pack for you to take with you."

Mike agreed and as he headed for the wagon he said, "Kabuta, would you feed the horses a good feed of corn? I'll be riding them hard tomorrow."

Kabuta went to do his bidding.

When Mike was dressing the next morning Katy said, "I wish you'd let me go, I'll miss you, and pray for you to have a safe trip."

Mike said, "Don't worry. I leave you in good hands and I'll be back as soon as I can." He kissed her good by and stepped out of his wagon to find Kabuta waiting for him with both horses saddled and ready to go. He said, "I fed them corn and took them to water an hour ago. They're ready to ride."

Mike gave him a quick hug and said, "Thanks," mounted Midnight and walked the horses softly out of camp.

Kabuta leaned his head against a tree and whispered, "Dear God, bring him safely back to us. In Jesus' name, Amen."

Katy couldn't go back to sleep. She cried a little. She wasn't worried about those he left in camp, but she couldn't keep from worrying about her husband.

Mike rode into Saint Louis well after dark and went straight to the stables. He told the stable man to feed the horses the best grain he had and to put fresh hay in their stalls, and then he went to the hotel and ordered a hot bath.

He ate an early breakfast the next day and was standing in front of the trading post before it opened.

He was sitting on the hitching post in front of the store when two men walked up. He said, "Good morning, I'm Michael Ross, and I'm looking for Mrs. Lee."

"I'm Sam Allsup and this is Charley Brewer. Mrs. Lee works for me, but this is her day off. Come into my office."

When they were seated Sam said, "Mister Ross, Amy Lee not only works for me, she and Frank are among my best friends, and Frank has asked me to look after her while he's away. He's been very successful in trapping furs and this is his last trip into the wilds."

"Mr. Allsup, I have some bad news. Crowley tried to take advantage of Running Springs and Lee tried to defend her and they killed one another with knives. We buried them and marked their graves and I've drawn a crude map so you can find their graves, if you desire to do so. I've brought all of Mr. Lee's weapons and personal things with me, but the animals and trade goods are back in my camp. You can go with me to pick them up or I am prepared to give Mrs. Lee a fair market price for all of it, including Crowley's things."

"Frank and Crowley bought all their trade goods here and I have a copy of the invoice on file. It's upstairs. Give me a minute to get them and I'll go with you to see Amy. She'll need a friend there when she hears this news."

He returned shortly and his wife was with him. He said, "This is my wife, Annie. Annie, meet Mr. Michael Ross. She'll go with us in case Amy needs her. Let's go."

Michael followed the couple down the street to a small house with a freshly painted white picket fence around it, with roses around the door. Amy Lee opened the door at their knock and said, "Please come in." She took their hats and said, "Sit down, I'll get coffee. I just made a fresh pot."

Sam said, "Amy, meet Mr. Michael Ross, he has some business to discuss with you."

"Howdy do, Mr. Ross, good to meet you, but let's discuss our business after we enjoy our treat," and she disappeared into the kitchen and returned with four cups of coffee and four freshly-baked cinnamon rolls and invited them to sit around the table. They chitchatted around the table as they enjoyed the treat.

Amy said, "I can't imagine what kind of business we might have to discuss, but let's get it done."

Sam said, "Amy, I'd like you to look over these invoices and see if this is all the trade goods Frank and Sam bought before they left."

She scanned the pages for a few minutes and nodded her head and said, "Yes, Sam, that's all of it."

"Okay, Amy, get a grip, girl."

"What's wrong, Sam?"

"Amy, Frank and Sam killed one another over that Indian girl that was staying with you."

Amy bowed her head and gripped her hands together in a hard knot in her lap. Tears slipped down her cheeks and it was several minutes before she could speak. Finally she said, "I can accept that they killed one another, but if it was over that girl it was because Frank was protecting her. Frank would never—" she began sobbing and ran into her bedroom.

Annie went in to console her.

As Sam and Mike sat waiting in silence with bowed heads, Mike prayed silently that God would give her the strength that she would need now.

When the women returned Sam said, "Michael, will you tell Amy what happened and what you would like to do?"

Mike said, "Mrs. Lee, you're absolutely right. Sam started touching and fondling Running Springs and Frank told him to leave her alone. Frank went into the woods to hunt for meat, and when he returned Sam had Running Springs down on the ground, trying to take advantage of her, and your husband knocked him off of her and they fought, and you know the results. When Running Springs knew your husband was dead she ran away and hid in the brush, where my wife and her friend found her and brought her to our camp. We're going to take her back to her father, as your husband was going to do.

"We buried your husband and Crowley in such a way that the wild animals will never be able to disturb their bodies. Sam has a map showing the way to the graves. I have all the goods they had in our camp. They're safe and you can come with me and pick them up and I can show you where the graves are, or I'll pay you for the trade goods and all the animals, if you wish."

"Whatever you and Sam agree on is alright with me. Thank you, Mr. Ross, for your kindness. Now, will you all excuse me? I must get ready to tell my children that their father is in heaven."

Annie said, "Amy, dear, would you like me to stay with you?"

"No, my friend; Just pray I have the strength to get through this."

There was nothing more to say, so Mike and Sam tipped their hats politely and the three of them left.

After they were gone, Amy went to her bedroom and buried her head in her pillow so she wouldn't wake the sleeping children. She thanked God that her children were young and that when they grew older they would have only vague memories of their father.

When they got back to the store Sam figured out the worth of the animals and gear and handed Mike a bill. Mike looked it over and said, "Fair enough," and he paid the man.

Sam signed Amy's name to the Bill of Sale and initialed it. He said, "You're a good man, Michael Ross. My wife and I love Amy and those two children like they were our own. I padded your bill a little bit."

"I knew, but I'm glad you did. It eased my mind about how that young lady would get along with two babies."

Annie said, "Don't you worry about Amy, Mr. Ross. Amy is a good book-keeper and Sam pays her well. Frank was a good man but he was always running to the wilderness, leaving her alone with those two babies. Well, she deserved better. She'll wear black for a while, but when she quits grieving she'll get on with her life. She'll have every available bachelor in town running after her, and there are some good ones among the bad here."

Mike went to the cafe and ate a good lunch and had the cook make sand-wiches for his supper and went for his horses. By eleven a.m. he was in the saddle. He rode the horses hard until nightfall. He would never abuse a horse, but he knew these horses were in good condition and they would have many days to rest, so he rode on through the darkness.

He slowed them down to a steady walk when it got dark and he dozed in the saddle. He woke up when Midnight bent his head to drink from a stream. He dismounted, laid a night sheet on the ground, and removed the bits from the horses' mouths so they could graze. He ate his supper and slept for twenty minutes, and he was back in the saddle.

He rode into camp just as they were sitting down for breakfast.

Katy flung her arms around him and kissed him as if she hadn't seen him for a month.

As they ate Mike said, "I paid Mrs. Lee for all of the things we kept here, including Crowley's things. She's a beautiful young lady with two babies, a boy and a girl, but the man she works for said she would be all right."

When Peg started to get up, Mike said, "Wait, Peg, I have something for you girls." He went to his horse and returned with three boxes wrapped in gold colored paper, and handed one to each of the girls. Peg and Katy started unwrapping theirs carefully to save the pretty paper, but Running Springs just stared at the one Mike had placed in front of her. He said, "Katy, Peg, wait. I want all three of you to open them at the same time, they're just alike.

Running Springs open yours. And remember, girls, these are from Kabuta and me. Peg, Kabuta asked me to pick something up for your birthday and I thought it was time for me to get something for Katy, and I couldn't leave Running Springs out."

When the girls opened the packages they saw they contained a silver-backed brush, comb, and mirror set, and two dress combs of bone and mother-of-pearl. The women laughed with delight as they looked in the mirror and started brushing their hair. Running Springs watched as Katy and Peg placed the mother-of-pearl combs in their hair and looked in the mirror to admire them, and she did the same.

After the girls showed Mike and Kabuta their appreciation Mike said, "Katy, if you'll drive my wagon today, as soon as we can get things loaded and ready to travel, I'm going to bed."

Kabuta said, "You go on to bed, man, you look all in."

Mike said, "Thanks," and he went to the river and took a quick bath and crawled into bed, and in a few minutes he was so sound asleep that the noise of hitching the teams to the wagons didn't wake him.

The first thing Kabuta did was to unsaddle the horses and Katy set a bucket of corn under their noses. She said, "You beauties have earned a good treat."

An hour after Mike went to bed Kabuta strung them out along the Missouri River, headed west.

That night Mike and Kabuta went and sat on the riverbank and discussed what they would do from here on.

Mike said, "We'll be as quiet as we can, which means we'll use only our bows for hunting. We'll use our guns only to defend ourselves."

Kabuta said, "I hope I'll never have to kill another human being again. It makes me sick deep down in my soul."

"That goes for me too, my brother, we never have, except when we had to, and we'll do it again if we have to, to save our party."

Katy and Peg had been trading off driving the wagons so one of the men could scout on ahead, and sometimes both of them. They were surprised that they liked doing it almost as much as riding their high-spirited horses.

They wouldn't leave camp from now on until one of the men scouted way out in front first, which meant they wouldn't get as early a start as they would like, but they were getting deep into Indian domain and had to be far more alert and cautious. They'd stop earlier each day so they could have their fires out before dark. They were cooking on top of the stove more as they traveled so their food would be ready each day when they stopped.

They traveled for three days up the old muddy Missouri without seeing anyone at all. They were able to kill enough deer and catch enough fish on their throw lines at night so they could save what ham hocks they had to cook with their beans when they wanted a change of diet.

Mike came into camp one morning after scouting, to pancakes, the first they'd had in days. He said, "Katy, where'd you get eggs to make pancakes?"

She said, "Running Springs and Peg found a pheasant nest full of them and two prairie chicken nests with several each. We want to stop early today so we can make a couple of cakes and some fruit pies."

"Sounds mighty good to me, I hope you save all the eggs for that and pancakes and maybe some biscuits. "

Running Springs said, "I can't drive the wagons, but I can hunt eggs and there should be plenty of them this time of the moon."

Running Springs had never eaten any kind of pork until she got to Saint Louis and she dearly liked it, and eggs made it like icing on a cake. So she hunted eggs every day. She had an inquisitive mind and was learning English quickly with Katy and Peg teaching her. Running Springs was teaching them Sioux, also. Mike and Kabuta were picking it up almost as fast as the girls were.

The fact that Running Springs was guiding them and they now had a destination, and her bubbling laughter and constant striving to do all she could to show her new friends her appreciation for all they were doing for her, made the trip more enjoyable for them all.

One day Mike was scouting way out ahead when he heard the hounds bark. The tone and pitch of their bark told him that they had run something aground or up a tree.

He galloped to where the dogs were and all four of them were sitting around a salt cedar tree with thick foliage and branches close to the ground. The dogs could have easily climbed to their prey, but they showed no inclination to do so.

Mike got off of his horse, drew his guns and peered up in the tree. He saw three little Indian girls as high up in the tree as they could get, and the little one was crying.

Mike said, using the Sioux language, "Come down, little sisters, the dogs or I won't hurt you. Come to our camp and we'll feed you."

No matter how hard he tried, he couldn't coax them to come down. He said, "I'll be back."

They showed no indication that they understood anything he said. He commanded the dogs to stay and they flopped on the ground. Mike rode quickly back to the wagons and told Kabuta, "There's a good camping place just ahead, if you and Peg will set up camp there, Katy, Running Springs and I will bring three young ladies to dine with us tonight. Do you think you and Peg could make about four apple pies for supper?"

"You won't believe it, but I was just thinking about making apple pies and a cake. Running Springs found a dozen eggs today."

"You said it, I believe it."

Mike said, "Katy and Running Springs, get on your horses and come with me," explaining about the girls. "I couldn't get them to come down, but I think you can."

When they reached the trees the dogs rose to meet them. The girls had managed to get in a more comfortable position, but fear was still evident in their eyes. When Running Springs said in Sioux, "Little sisters come down and we will feed you," the girls came scrambling down out of the tree and the two oldest ones ran and held onto Running Springs and she put her arms around them to comfort them. The smallest ran to Katy. Katy picked her up and held her close, and when this frightened child wrapped her arms around Katy's neck a thrill ran through her that was shocking.

Running Springs was crouched down with her arms around the other two girls, comforting them, when Mike came forward and handed them each a sugar cookie laced with hickory nutmeat. He ate one to show them they were all right to eat. When they bit into those cookies their little eyes popped wide open and they wanted more.

Running Springs said, "Come to our camp and we will feed you yummy food," and she rubbed her tummy and smacked her lips.

When they got to camp Kabuta had apple pies in the oven, and he was preparing prairie chicken to fry. Peg was churning butter.

Katy got her milk pails and went to milk the cows and Mike took care of the horses. As soon as Peg finished churning, Kabuta removed the pies from the oven and made biscuits with the buttermilk and Peg started frying the chicken.

It wasn't long before the girls had a plate of fried chicken, buttered biscuits and cream gravy, with a cup of sweet milk sitting before them. Peg had cut the meat off the bones and gave them a fork and showed them how to use it. They started to eat too fast and Running Springs took great pride when she slowed them down by saying, "Don't eat so fast or you will make yourselves sick. Watch Peg and Katy and eat like they do."

When they finished eating the smallest girl ran and climbed up in Katy's lap and laid her head on her shoulder. Katy kissed her on the cheek and she thought her heart would burst with the love that flooded it.

After they cleaned up Kabuta noticed the girls' eyes turning toward the pies. He also noticed that one of them was shifting from one foot to the other and squeezing her legs tightly together. He said, "Peg, if you ladies will take the girls to the bushes for a while, I'll cut the pies and have the milk ready when you get back."

He spoke the best he could in Sioux, and one of the girls broke for the bushes and the other two followed her.

When Peg started to follow them, Running Springs laid a hand on her arm and shook her head. "They won't run away, and they need their privacy. They told me their camp isn't far away, and we can expect their fathers any time. They'll be out looking for them by now. Kabuta, I would suggest you save some pie and have a pot of coffee ready and offer them a piece of pie and a cup of coffee with lots of honey in it. They've probably never tasted apple pie or coffee, but I know they love sweet things."

"I've two more ready for the oven," and he went and slipped them in and put coffee on to boil.

It was an hour before dark when he took them out of the oven to cool, and twenty minutes later three men rode in.

The girls ran to their fathers, jabbering away, telling them how the great dogs scared them and how these people saved them and fed them, and the chief's little daughter ran back and reached up to Katy, and when she picked her up she threw her arms around Katy's neck and kissed her on the cheek, like Katy had kissed her. One of the others ran and held Peg's hand and the other held Running Springs'.

Kabuta had seen them far before they reached their camp and when he and Mike started to go out to meet them Running Springs said, "Let's all stand behind the girls, and when these braves ride in we will hold our hands out, palms up. That shows them that we are peaceful."

The Indians held out their hands in peace and the chief spoke, but none of them understood him.

Mike said, "Great chief, do you understand Sioux?"

"Yes."

"Would you come and join us for pie and coffee?"

When they dismounted Running Springs ran and took their horses and tied them a good distance downwind from camp.

Katy started pouring coffee as Peg cut the pies in four pieces. Mike invited their guests to sit in a circle on a night sheet that they had placed on the ground. Katy and Peg placed a piece of pie and a cup of coffee in front of each man and brought their own and joined the circle, as well as Running Springs.

Mike said, "Chief, it's our custom that before we eat we bow our heads and thank our God for supplying our food." They all bowed their heads and Mike prayed, "Dear Heavenly Father, we thank you for sending these three men to be our guests, and we thank you for the food, bless it to the good of our bodies. In Jesus' name, amen."

The Chief and his sub-chiefs sat and waited until they saw Running Springs and the rest of them take their forks and put a bite of the pie in their mouths. Running Springs smiled sweetly at the Chief and said, "Much good."

The Chief nodded at Katy and Peg and they took a bite of the pie and so did Kabuta and Mike. They blew on the hot coffee and took a sip of it.

The chief took a bite of the pie and his sub-chiefs followed suit. After the second bite and sips of coffee, a broad smile broke across the chief's face and he nodded his head at Running Springs and said, "Yes, much good."

When they finished eating Mike said, "If the three of you will come back in the morning we have some thing to trade."

It was almost dark and the chief rose and said, "We will return when the sun is here," and he pointed to the east, indicating about one hour after sunrise. "Come, daughter."

The little daughter ran toward her father, but halfway to him she ran back and jumped into Katy's lap, hugged her, then ran back to her father.

Kabuta and Running Springs went for the chief's horses. When they rode away the chief turned and raised his hand in a friendly salute.

Running Springs said, "Mike, you won't have to stand guard tonight. The chief will inform his people we are not to be disturbed."

That night as Katy lay in Mike's arms she whispered in his ear, "Honey, I want a little girl of our own."

"Katy, I'd rather not." Her heart dropped, then leaped back in place when he went on to say, "Until we get a cabin built somewhere. Then I'll do everything in my power to give you what you want."

"I guess I can wait that long, but Kabuta and Peg will be ahead of us. She missed her monthly last time and she thinks she may already be with child."

Just then she heard Kabuta and Peg getting out of their wagon and she heard Peg say, "I'm sorry, Kabuta, I thought I was ready to give you a son."

Kabuta said, "That's all right my love, it's best it doesn't happen until we get settled somewhere."

Katy said, "Did you hear that, Mike?"

"Hear what?"

"Peg's not in the family way, after all. I'm sorry for her. I know how badly she wants to give Kabuta a son, but I'm kind of glad. I want us to be that way together."

When the three chief's came into camp the next morning Peg had donuts and coffee ready, and Mike had three axes, three fine double-edged knives, three sharpening stones, and three sewing kits with all sizes and shapes of needles, and a number of spools of thread in a variety of colors lain out on a night sheet.

After greetings were exchanged they sat down to donuts and coffee. When the chiefs examined the things Mike had to trade they were extremely impressed.

The Chief looked at Mike and asked, "What can we trade you for these?"

Mike said, "We will give these to you if you will give us free passage across your land and one brave to guide us as far as you think is fair."

The chief said, "This will please our squaws, but we each have two squaws and they would fight over them. We will give each of you a pair of knee-high moccasins and you can rest in the safety of our village as long as you like, and I will escort you to the edge of our hunting grounds when you decide to leave us, if you give us three more sewing kits."

"Fair enough, but could we stay here?"

"As you wish, and you can be sure none of our people will disturb you, unless our three daughters slip away to see you. They can talk about nothing else since you treated them so kindly."

Katy said, "Mike, Peg and I would like to trade something. May we?"

"Sure."

Both women ran to their wagons and returned with their old combs, brushes and hand mirrors. They were as good as the ones Mike had given them, but not as beautiful. They handed them to the Chief and Katy said, "These are the only ones we can spare, but you could use them as a family. We will trade these for a jacket for each of us, like the one you are wearing."

The Chief reached and took Peg and Katy's hands and said, "We will all be very happy to have them. You must come to our village. After our daughters told the women how beautiful the black lady and the red-haired lady are they can't wait to see you. They have seen white men before, but never a black one, and all the white men were bearded and you have no beards.

"You are invited to our village tomorrow for a big gathering in honor of the people that have captured the hearts of our daughters."

"What time?" Mike asked.

"When the sun is here," he pointed to the sky that indicated between twelve and one p.m."

"We'll be there, and thank you."

The Indians took their goods and rode back to make their squaws happy. They were sure that they got the best of this trade. After they left Mike realized that he hadn't seen Daisy all morning and Shep only once.

"Kabuta, have you seen Daisy today?"

"No, I haven't seen her since early yesterday morning. I'll bet she's gone off to hide somewhere to have her pups."

"I'll bet that's it, we'd better go find her to make sure they're all right, I'd hate to lose her." They started calling the dogs and they all showed up except Daisy.

They took their bows and arrows and went looking for her, hoping that at the same time they might run into an elk or maybe a buffalo. They had been told that they could run into buffalo out this way, but they didn't think they had reached their range yet.

They were about a half-mile down the river when they saw Daisy drinking from it. It was obvious she had given birth to her litter. They hung back and when they saw her crawl under some low-growing thick brush, they went and parted the branches. There she lay with seven puppies sucking away, and another one running and nudging a pup from a tit and latching on to find the milk all gone. He nudged pups from tit to tit, trying to satisfy his hunger. Kabuta laughed and said, "Looks like he came late for dinner."

Mike reached in and patted her head and said, "Daisy, old girl, you did yourself proud. Kabuta, Shep will feed her, so we'll leave them right here until Daisy brings them to us."

When Mike and his little group reached the village the next day, the tribe was assembled in a natural, crescent-shaped amphitheater along a slightly rising hill. The chief and his counsel were out in front of the people. He called Mike and his group to him and he shook their hands and turned to his people and said, "My people, I want you to meet Chief Michael Ross and his sub-chief, Kabuta, and their pretty squaws and their friend, Running Springs.

"You are to treat them like brothers and sisters while they are in our hunting grounds. They are to move freely and safely among us. Now let's go to our feast."

The chief's little daughter went and latched onto Katy and the other two girls latched on to Peg and Running Springs, and stayed near them until they left the village.

They all thoroughly enjoyed the barbecued meat that was placed before them.

When the meal was over Katy said to the Chief's head squaw, "I don't believe I've ever eaten better meat. What kind is it?"

She and Peg almost lost their dinner when she answered, "Young dog."

Mike and Kabuta didn't fare much better.

On their way back to camp Katy couldn't get the fact that she had eaten dog meat out of her mind, and all of a sudden she leaped from her horse and it all came up. When Peg saw that, she did the same. Neither one of them ate a bite until late the next day.

CHAPTER NINETEEN

They stayed among the friendly Indians for the rest of the winter. Mike and Kabuta had unloaded the supply wagon and erected a large tarp over it so it would remain dry and handy.

After winter set in Kabuta had ridden out on the plains and discovered a small herd of buffalo grazing on tall nutritious grass in a long secluded valley, with a clear creek running through it. He was sure the herd was there for the winter.

He went back and told Mike about it and they took the wagon out there and with their strong bows and iron-tipped arrows they shot ten young cows. They had a hard time loading two of the smaller ones on the wagon. They drove into the Indian village with the buffalo and Mike said to the chief, "Kabuta found a small buffalo herd and we killed ten young ones. We thought you could use the meat. We only need one. If you will give us some men to load them on the wagon, we will haul them to your village."

The chief was overjoyed for this good fortune; this would be enough meat to carry his people through the rest of the winter and give them ten prime buffalo robes. He said, "What can we trade you for this meat, Chief Mike?"

Mike said, "Chief, you have been so kind to help us through the winter, all we want is our arrows back when your butchers can remove them from the carcasses."

Kabuta said, "It isn't necessary, but a jacket for Mike and me like the ones your squaws gave our wives would be nice."

The chief said, "You will have them, along with two fine buffalo robes."

The snow melted and spring was bursting out all over and the ground had dried well enough to travel. They loaded their wagons and were ready to hit the trail when the chief rode in with the jackets he had promised them earlier in the winter, and in addition there were buckskin pants, new knee-high moccasins, and coonskin hats for everyone.

Mike said, "We were coming into the village to tell you all goodbye, and Katy and Peg have a gift for you and your sub-chiefs daughters, and Kabuta and I have a gift for you and your son."

When they reached the village many of the village people gathered to see them off.

Daisy's pups were getting big and Mike and Kabuta had decided they only wanted two of them and they had picked out the two they wanted.

When the girls came to Katy, Peg, and Running springs, they were thrilled when they gave them each a pup.

The chief said, "Will these dogs get as big as their mother?"

Mike said, "Yes, and Chief, they will protect your daughters from all harm. If the girls will be kind to them they would die protecting them from anything, man or beast. The other three you can do with as you like. But if I were you, I'd never let anyone eat these dogs or their offspring; they will serve you well. You have seen them bring down deer and elk and wild turkey."

"They will never be eaten, Mike, unless my people are starving.

Mike and Kabuta had discussed the advisability of giving the chief and his twenty-year-old son the two rifles they had taken from Lee and Sam, and all the ammunition that fit them.

Kabuta had said, "We won't need them and the ammo will run out soon enough."

When they started to leave Mike said, "Chief, Kabuta and I would like for you and your son to ride out a ways with us."

The chief sent his son to get their horses and they rode alongside of the wagons for about a mile when Mike pulled his team to a halt near a clay bank.

Kabuta went and got the rifles and said, "Chief, because you gave us more buckskin clothing than we asked for, and the beautiful robes, we want to give these to you and your son. We will show you how to use them."

He took two sticks and stuck them in the ground near the clay bank. He took one rifle and gave Mike the other. They aimed and fired, and splinters flew from each stick.

Then they showed the chief and his son how to aim at the target. They did this for an hour, showing them how to squeeze the trigger instead of jerking it.

Kabuta said, "If you jerk your finger on the trigger it will pull the end of the barrel off target and you waste your ammunition. You take a deep breath and let it out slowly as you gently squeeze the trigger."

The wise old chief was patient, but his young son thought Mike would never let them fire. Mike took the gun and loaded it and handed it to the chief and stepped back saying, "Fire!"

The chief took his stand, fired and missed, but not by much.

Mike reloaded and said, "You were a little too high, and I think you shot over the stake."

This time the chief split a splinter off the side near the top of the stake. Mike slapped him on the shoulder and said, "That's great!"

A large grin spread across the chief's weather-beaten face, then he said, "Let my son, Rising Star, see what he can do."

Kabuta handed Rising Star the loaded gun and he missed twice.

The Chief said, "One more load, Kabuta."

When Kabuta handed the loaded gun to the Chief the Chief said "Like this, son," and he took his stance and aimed down the barrel. Then he handed the gun to Rising Star.

Rising Star took his position and fired quickly, splitting the stick dead center.

The Chief beamed with pride and said, "I'm glad you are my son."

They practiced a while longer until Mike said, "You both can shoot well, but you should save the ammunition, because when it is gone you might never be able to get more. These rifles and ammunition are yours if you give us your solemn word that you will never use them against us."

"None of my people will ever harm you or Kabuta and yours, unless you come against us."

Mike said, "If you run out of ammunition the guns will be of no further use to you, but if you take care of these pups and their offspring they will serve you well for many years.

The Chief said, "My brother, stay three more moons. I've sent runners to all our kindred tribes to the Valley of the Smokes, advising them to give you safe passage. If you go further over the big mountains to the great waters where the big ball of fire sets, we can't protect you. But you should be safe to the valley where our little sister, Running Springs lives."

Mike agreed to delay their departure time. The day they were to leave Rising Star took Mike and Kabuta to one side and said, "You have nothing to fear from my Chief and me, but be ever alert. You have beautiful horses and mules and your squaws, as well as Running Springs, are as beautiful as the flowers in spring. The temptation may be too great for some of our young braves to obey our chief. If they hurt you and we find out about it, they will pay with their lives."

"Thank you, brother," Mike said.

That evening they were invited to join the tribe in a farewell feast. Katy and Peg were delighted to learn that the meat would be young buffalo, roasted as it turned slowly on a spit over an open fire. They sure didn't want to eat any more dogs.

The next morning just before their departure, the Chief asked all five of them to stand before him, and when they complied then his and his sub-chiefs' wives came forward and gave Katy, Peg and Running Springs beautiful beaded buckskin riding habits, with knee-high moccasins. They gave Mike and Kabuta buckskin jackets, pants and moccasins.

The chief requested them to go into teepees and don their gifts so the squaws could see if they fit well. They did, and the squaws were very pleased with their handiwork. Katy, Peg and Running Springs hugged them and thanked them with tears in their eyes.

Mike said, "I don't have words to fully express our appreciation to you and your people for the gifts and the hospitality you've shown us."

As they started to leave the chief's little daughter clung to Katy until her mother gently took her arms from around Katy's neck; the other two girls were hugging Peg and Running Springs

Peg and Katy were weeping as they rode away. Running Springs didn't weep, but her heart was aching.

CHAPTER TWENTY

Kabuta said, "Mike, we've learned a lot from our friends here. The squaws have taught Peg and Katy all the different kind of berries and leaves of different plants they season their food with, as well as what roots and leaves of plants to eat, like wild onions and squaw cabbage, among other things. The most important foods they taught them are the many kinds of tree fungi and mushrooms, there are far more than I know about. They also taught them the plants they use for medicines.

"We've learned that if we're fair in trade and treat their children with love and kindness, they'll respond in kind. If we remain strong and show no fear, and continue to treat them the way we want to be treated, we're going to be all right out here."

"Yes, Kabuta, and we don't want to ever forget the promises of God either, where He says, 'I will keep him in perfect peace whose mind is stayed on Me.'"

"Amen."

Their first night out it began to rain, so they parked their wagons side-by-side and stretched a tarp between them to shelter Running Springs as she slept. Mike tied one pup to the front wheel of his wagon and one to the back wheel of Kabuta's wagon. They would only have to be tied there a few nights until they would automatically sleep there as long as they were on the trail.

Mike told everyone, "This is the way we'll camp most nights from here on. I pity the Indian that tries to slip by those dogs at night."

The dogs they had with them now were Shep, Daisy, Brother and Sister from Daisy's first litter born in America, and Wolf and Lassie from her second litter, and now Rover and Browser.

When the dogs weren't posted on guard at night, or hunting in the daytime, Shep would be near Mike, Daisy near Katy, Sister near Peg, Brother near Kabuta, and Wolf and Lassie, had become Running Springs' shadows. Rover and Browser would learn from the other dogs.

Mike said to Katy one day, "I don't quite understand these dogs, they all used to come flying at me, but now they've all left me except good old Shep."

"Mike, sometimes I think these dogs are smarter than we are. They've separated themselves from one another to guard all of us at all times. If we ever do part ways, God forbid, these dogs would all go with you. You always have been and you always will be their master, and they know it."

"You might be right. But I sure hope I never have to find out."

Katy said, "I couldn't bear the thought of being separated from Peg and Kabuta, especially my dear, dear Peg. We've been inseparable since we were nine years old and she's more like a sister to me than she ever was a maid. It would rip our hearts out to be separated now."

Mike said, "I feel the same way about Kabuta. I promise you that I'll never be the one to separate us, and I know Kabuta is as happy as he can be. He told me a few days ago that he and Peg agreed that they would always remember their parents and regret the way they died, but they're glad they were brought to America and they'd never want to go back to Africa. 'We're happy that you and Katy gave us our freedom,' he said, 'but we're really still slaves because we could never leave you.'"

"Still," Katy said, "there's something missing...." she saw the frown on his face, but went on anyway... "Our little boy or girl."

Give it time, my sweet. They'll come, if the Lord is willing."

She brushed her lips to his and said, "Stop the wagon. I want to get the girls to ride our horses with me. Mike, I feel completely safe. Let us take our dogs and ride on ahead and have a camp site ready when you come in."

"Well, we haven't seen any sign of Indians. Go ahead, but if you see anyone, Indians or mountain men, you come back to us as fast as you can, don't try to converse with them. Promise me."

"I promise, worry wart."

"Not worried," Mike retorted, "I just don't want you making eyes at another man."

She tousled his hair and climbed down saying, "That'll be the day!"

When the men came into camp that night the women had two pheasants roasting over an open fire and fresh fish cleaned and waiting for the frying pan.

When they were getting ready for bed Mike said, "Katy, you said today that you thought Peg was as happy as you are. I think she has more to be happy about. She was a slave and thought she was going to be turned over to a stud that she despised and was afraid of. Now she's free and married to a handsome man that she adores. All you got was me."

She winked at him. "Do you think our bed is too close to the others, or should we take a blanket and go for a walk in the woods?"

"Kabuta and Peg don't seem to think we're too close, but let's do take a blanket and a towel and walk down to the river for a swim."

Later they made passionate love on the thin blanket spread over the green grass along the riverbank, oblivious to everything except one another. Afterwards they lay there for a long time, talking about many things.

Mike said, "Katy, thank you for giving me back my life. Less than four years ago I almost threw myself in the lake. I never dreamed I could be as happy as I am tonight. You know, making love to you has always been wonderful, but tonight it was better than it has ever been. I just know we've conceived a child."

Katy said, "I know, Mike, I felt it too."

* * * * *

At noon the next day they crossed the Platte River where it ran into the Missouri. They camped here in the fork of the rivers, where Indians had camped many times before. There were fire circles everywhere, with blacken stones from many fires. This evidently had been a large village at one time, but it had been deserted for a long time because the grass was tall and lush.

They knew they could let the animals run free because they wouldn't stray far and the dogs would guard them.

Mike's stallion, Midnight, hadn't been neglecting his small harem of mares.

They were all carrying foals and three of them were ready to drop them any day, and this was a good place for it to happen.

Kabuta didn't know horses as well as Mike did, but he was learning fast. He had a way with them and though he had become a superb rider, he knew little about birthing foals.

Mike showed him the physical change in the mares that indicated they were about ready. He said, "I know these three were bred within a few days of one another. We're going to have foals very soon and I propose we stay right here until it happens. The Platte's water is a lot cleaner than the muddy old Missouri and the animals will get fat on this good grass."

Running Springs came to Mike and asked to use his spear.

He said, "It's hanging on the side of our wagon. Help yourself."

She got the spear and they all watched her wade out in the middle of the river near some large stones, and she stood there, stone still. She held the spear just above the surface of the water. Suddenly, she plunged the spear downward and brought up a nice brown trout, which she put in a sack hanging from her shoulder. They watched in amazement, as she got another and another.

Katy said, "Fish tonight! Mike, if you men will gather wood for the cook stove we'll have a feast tonight. Peg said she'd bake biscuits and fruit pies, and I'll cook everything else. I'm glad we stopped early today, I have cream to churn."

Mike said, "You must have been saving the cream for a few days. We aren't getting much milk these days. With all this traveling the Jersey isn't giving much milk, and the other two are dry.

Kabuta said, "The old Jersey won't be very long. I saw our young bull breed her a long time ago, and you can see she's heavy with calf." The Guernsey can't be far behind her. We'll have more milk than we can use pretty soon."

Running Springs joined them and showed them the fish she had caught.

Mike said, "I can almost taste them now. Kabuta and I think we should lie over here a few days to let our mares have their foals and let all the stock fatten up a little on this good grass, and the cow will start producing better too."

Peg, said, "That sounds good to me," and Katy said, "Then we can all enjoy hot biscuits and pies for a few days, and maybe a chocolate cake."

Kabuta said, "Girl, will you hush your mouth and let my little sugar plum start baking."

They all laughed, and then got busy preparing the camp for a long layover. The women went to the wagons and Kabuta unhitched the teams as Mike started cutting wood for the stove.

When Running Springs came up out of the water she had enough trout for a couple of meals and a pot of fish chowder. She walked out to where the men were cutting and splitting wood for the cook stove and said, "Mister Kabuta, this is good firewood and if there is room to haul it, you should take as much as you can with us. We are going across the plains where there is very little wood."

They loaded as much split wood on top of the wagons as they could carry and swung as much pole wood underneath the wagons as they felt it was safe to haul.

The week they were there the old cow strayed off and had her calf and hid it in a thicket. In the middle of the night everyone in camp was awaken by the growling and snarling of fighting dogs. The hounds had been alerted by the sound of the cow bawling and when they reached her they found her in the middle of a pack of snarling wolves. She was swinging her horns back and forth, kicking with her back feet at her attackers, trying to protect her newborn calf.

One big wolf leaped on her back and was just getting ready to clamp his powerful jaws down on the back of her neck when Shep went sailing through the air and knocked him off the cow. Now it was a furious fight, with four big wolfhounds and two half-grown pups that were out numbered about two to one.

By the time Mike and Kabuta got there with their shotguns a big wolf had broken Lassie's front leg. She had put up a good fight for a half-grown pup, but she was no match for the old wolf. Only Kabuta and Mike's timely arrival had kept him from killing her.

Mike shot the wolf before he could do any further damage; then he and Kabuta each shot once more. Brother and Sister had killed one wolf and Shep another, but when the shotguns started roaring the wolves broke off the fight and headed for the thickets. The four big hounds went right after them, with a half-grown pup that had just had his first taste of battle and wanted more. But when the dogs heard Mike's shrill whistle calling them in, they broke off the chase and returned to the men.

When they got back to camp they heated water and cleaned the wounds on the dogs and Kabuta cleaned the cut on Lassie's leg and set the bone and laid her on a night sheet. When Mike examined all the dogs he discovered that all their cuts were located where they could lick their wound and he knew they would heal themselves better than the ointment he had and they would lick the ointment off anyway.

Mike and Kabuta got ropes and took Shep and Daisy and went after the cow. They had no difficulty finding her; she was bawling as she searched for her calf. They came up to her just as she found where the wolves had devoured the calf. They had carried off its bones but they found the hide, but it was so full of holes it was of no use to them. They roped the half-crazy cow and half dragged her back to camp and tied her to a tree and started milking her. The milk wouldn't be fit for human consumption for a few days, but she had to be milked to save her udders.

As they were eating their breakfast the next morning Mike said, "We'll let the dogs run loose in the daytime, and tie them up at night for the next thirty days. When the dogs are running loose, nobody is to go near them, or pet them, and you are to carry your guns at all times. If one of them bares his teeth, or growls at you, don't hesitate a second—shoot him on the spot!

"One or more of those wolves could have been infected with rabies, and if they were, our dogs are sure to become infected. If a rabid dog bites one of us, we'd more than likely die. I can't impress this on you enough. I repeat, don't think for a second about how much you love them. Shoot them immediately, before they kill you."

For the next thirty days everyone stayed away from the dogs. It nearly broke the girls' hearts to see the mournful look in their eyes, and to hear the pitiful pleading of the pups for attention. On the thirty-first night they weren't tied up, and all the humans hugged and scratched them and romped with them, and the dogs were frantic with ecstasy. They leaped and ran in circles, begging for affection, and their masters were happy to give it to them.

Peg said, "Thank goodness that mournful look has left their eyes."

Mike said, "It's a shame we had to tie them up like that, but we had no choice."

Three of the mares dropped foals while they were here, two fillies, and a stud from one of the black mares. He would be as black as Midnight, and

Katy named him Midnight Jr.

Peg said, "Mike, won't the colts slow us down?"

"Not at all," he replied. "You'll be surprised how well they'll do."

As they sat around eating breakfast, discussing the way they would go from there, Mike said, "Running Springs, do you know the best way to go?"

She said, "When Mister Lee took me from the brave that had stolen me away, we were on the Big Muddy and we followed it down all the way. But it twists and turns and it's so muddy in places you can't use the water. It's also farther that way. If we go west from here and follow this river the water is cleaner and the fish are better. It goes almost dry sometimes, but we have had many storms this year and the water will be good all the way.

"Mr. Mike, my parents have grieved long enough for me. I want to get home to let them know I'm all right. I know my father will still be looking for me. Can we please go the quickest way?"

Mike said, "Folks, we go west, goodbye Big Muddy."

CHAPTER TWENTY-ONE

Five days later they were traveling across the flat plains along the Platte River and they were hounded with small flies that were unbearable to both man and beast.

In the late afternoon they pulled under some cottonwoods where there were a lot of dead branches scattered about. Running Springs said, "Mr. Kabuta, if you'll pile that dead wood upwind of us and set it on fire, it will keep these flies off of us. The smoke will burn our eyes a little, but it's better than these flies.

"For the next three or four days we should eat before sunrise and after sunset. The flies won't bother us at night, and not as bad when we're moving."

Katy said, "These flies are driving me mad."

Running Springs said, "Three or four more days, two if we are lucky, we will be out of this misery."

When they entered the sand hills the wagons sank into the sand making the teams labor and their progress became much slower. They hitched two of the horses to each of the wagons to make it easier for the mules. The wagons were much heavier from all the firewood they were carrying.

It took them three and a half miserable days to clear the sand hills. When they hit the prairie the wagons were rolling smoothly and Mike wanted desperately to travel through the night, but he knew the animals needed their rest after the hard pulling through the sand hills, and he stopped as soon as it was dark.

The next morning they left two hours before daylight and when the sun came up they discovered they were traveling alongside of a large herd of buffalo that were grazing as they moved slowly westward. All of a sudden they started to run, and it looked like there were a thousand of them. Running Springs said, "They will run miles and slow down for a stretch, and run again, then walk on until dark. Then they will lie down and rest in the early hours of the night. Then graze until sunrise, and then run again. They will repeat this until they are across the area where these flies swarm.

"They will beat the ground down smooth with their sharp hooves. As soon as the dust settles, turn your wagons where you can follow in their footsteps and you can move easier."

At noon they crossed a small stream and stopped just long enough for the animals to drink, then moved on and didn't stop until after dark.

Mike and Kabuta removed the bits from the teams' mouths and fed them corn and let them stand in their traces for an hour, while they rested on their beds.

The moon came up and it was almost full, so they moved on through the night. Katy and Peg were handling the teams and Mike and Kabuta mounted their horses and rode on ahead. About midnight they came up on the herd that was just getting up from where they were sleeping and started grazing slowly along. Mike said, "I'm so tired I could sleep right here on this hard ground."

Kabuta said, "If you can stand the smell and find a spot big enough to lie down without lying in a pile of dung, go ahead. And I'll ride back and let Katy and Peg sleep, and Running Springs and I will drive on."

Mike said, "I'll ride toward the river and sleep there for a while, and when you reach this place drive toward the river and if I can find any wood, I'll have a fire going when you get there. Then we'll feed the stock, and ourselves, and sleep until sunrise."

They got about four hours sleep before the swarming flies prevented them from sleeping any longer, and they were so eager to get moving they didn't even take time to boil coffee.

Mike and Katy were driving the wagons and Kabuta, Peg and Running Springs were riding horses out in front. Katy had insisted it was her turn to eat the dust in the trailing wagon and Mike couldn't talk her out of it. They had only driven a few miles when Running Springs brought Katy her horse and said, "Katy, let me drive the wagon."

Katy said, "I could kiss you, little sister," and she traded places with her and rode out in front to find Kabuta and Peg.

At about noon Mike pulled the team to a halt for a brief rest, and Running Springs pulled alongside of him, and said, "Mr. Mike, the flies are thinning out, we should be out of them by nightfall."

"I sure hope so," Mike replied. "You take the lead and let me eat dust for a while. And by the way, my name is Mike."

"Thank you, Mike, the dust is pretty bad back there."

The buffalo herd had left the river where it made a half-moon bend and they hadn't seen water for most of two days now and their water barrels were getting low. Just as Mike pulled up to make camp for the night, Peg and Katy rode into camp with a couple of pheasants. Katy held them up and said, "We'll have chicken and dumplings for supper. Kabuta will be coming in late. He rode toward the river to see how far we are from water. He said the barrels are almost empty."

Mike said, "They are that, and if we don't find a stream soon we'll have to drive to the river no matter how far it is. But you can bet we'll use enough of what we have for chicken and dumplings. We haven't had a decent meal for days."

Kabuta rode in just in time for supper and said, "I must have ridden fifteen miles toward the river and I still didn't see any sign of it."

Mike said, "Well, if we don't find water by tomorrow noon we'll turn toward the river anyway."

Before they filled their plates they all stood, holding hands and bowed their heads and Mike thanked the Lord that they were rid of the flies, and for the bounty He had supplied for the best meal they'd had for days.

That night they had a good rest and the next morning Kabuta said, "Mike, the going is easy now, you take the girls and go find water and I'll tie one team behind my wagon and come on, and if you don't find water by noon you'd better come back and meet me and let's head for the river, we haven't enough water left for two more days."

Mike said, "We couldn't beat that offer with a stick, let's go girls."

Peg resisted, but Kabuta insisted, saying, "Honey, we all need a bath and if you find water you can all bathe, and when I get there I don't intend to do a blessed thing but soak in water for an hour or two."

She brushed his lips with hers and said, "If you insist, a bath does sound mighty appealing."

Kabuta was glad to see them go. He couldn't stand himself and the two of them just made it worse.

About ten a.m. Mike and the girls entered some low-lying sand hills and he called a halt. He said, "We just get rid of the flies, and now these sand hills are going to really slow us down. We don't dare enter these hills without water. I think I saw some treetops off to our left a few miles back, let's go investigate to see if there's water near there. If there isn't, we have to go back and meet Kabuta and head for the river."

They retraced their steps and turned off toward the trees. Their hearts leaped with joy when they rode over a low hill and saw a clear lake of water, almost perfectly round, about two hundred yards across, and surrounded with cottonwood and willow trees. And surrounding the lake was the first green grass they had seen in days. They let the horses drink and turned them loose on the green grass. Mike took off his hat and bowed his head and said, "Thank you, Lord, that the buffalo passed this lake by and for providing us water and food for our stock."

Mike had walked around to the other side of the lake where he would be out of sight of the girls as he bathed. He could already hear the girls squealing with pleasure as the cool fresh water soaked days of grime and dust from their aching bodies.

Mike didn't stay in nearly as long as he would have liked to, he couldn't keep from thinking about Kabuta back there all alone. As he walked along the fringe of the trees back to where the girls were he hollered, "You'd better get down in the water. We haven't seen another living soul for days, so I think you girls will be safe here. I'm going to go give Kabuta a hand and guide him in here. I just saw a couple of prairie chickens drinking near a small stream that runs out the other side of this lake. If you get tired of swimming you might be able to find some fresh eggs. If you do, we'll lie over here a few days and have some fun. You might clear out a space for the wagons under those two big cottonwoods; they're big enough to give us shade most of the day."

Katy said, "Give us an hour."

"It will probably take us three hours to get here. You be careful of snakes now."

After Mike left Peg shivered and Katy said, "Are you cold, Peg?"

"No, I was thinking about snakes, Mike could have talked all day without mentioning snakes."

When Mike got back to where the buffalo had left their trail he took his glass and looked back down the trail and he could barely make out the wagons, about five miles back he figured. He kicked Midnight in the ribs and let him run for a mile before he pulled him into a comfortable gait. When he reached Kabuta he said, "Kabuta, five miles further on and about a half-mile off the trail is the prettiest little lake you ever saw and the buffalo passed it by. The girls and I figured we would spend a few days there and have some fun."

"Sounds good to me, time's a wasting, let's move. I'll untie the other team and you can lead me to this paradise. Anywhere I can get a bath would be paradise. I can't stand myself much longer."

When Mike pulled under the cottonwood tree he was glad to see the girls had cleared the debris away as best they could, but they were gone and it worried him until he heard Katy laughing. Kabuta pulled his team underneath the other tree and said, "Mike, you're going to have to care for the stock tonight. I'm going to soak in that water for at least two hours," and he went hopping on one foot, removing a boot as he ran, and he plunged into the water with all his clothes on. It had been a hot day, but down in the deeper part of the lake it was very cold because this lake was fed by deep springs.

The girls had discovered that a small spring-fed creek ran out of the south end of the lake and ran about three hundred yards and disappeared into the side of a sand hill, but there was about four acres of green grass that seemed to be watered with seepage all over the acreage. They had found a number of prairie chicken nests and a couple of pheasant nests where they gathered a few dozen fresh eggs. They had plenty of fresh eggs the four days they stayed here and Kabuta baked cakes and pies to take with them when they left.

Mike and Kabuta cleaned out the water barrels and discovered that there were hundreds of dead flies in the water. They let the barrels soak in the lake for a couple of days and the last full day they stayed here they filled them with the fresh spring water.

It was with real regret they left this beautiful little oasis, but the stock had depleted their food supply and they moved on.

"It's so peaceful here I hate to leave it," Peg said.

Katy said, "Me too, Peg, we really had some fun the four days we were here, didn't we, Mike?"

"Yes, and I hate to leave here as badly as you do, but we still have miles to go and we need to get there before winter sets in."

Mike was crawling up on the wagon when Kabuta came walking up from the tall course grass that grew out of the sand hill where the little creek disappeared. He had his shirttail out, holding it out in front of him and he said, "Look what I found! They're all fresh too; I tested them in the water. I thought you ladies found all the eggs around here. I've been enjoying eggs, cake and pie so much I had to go looking for myself. Now we can have all the eggs we want for breakfast tomorrow."

When Peg counted the eggs and put them in a bucket she said, "There are forty eggs here."

Mike said, "We've been hoarding our bacon, but we'll have bacon and eggs and pancakes for breakfast until the eggs run out."

The men were disappointed the next morning when the ladies gave them only two eggs.

Kabuta said, "Two eggs? I figured on eight eggs this morning."

Katy said, "If we only eat two eggs each we can have eggs for four mornings."

Kabuta said, "I have to admit that's good planning, but I could have enjoyed my eight this morning."

Peg said, "My big ebony lover, I believe you're hollow right down to the tip of your toes, the way you eat."

"I do love to eat," he said.

Mike said, "Would you look at those animals. They look like they've put on weight in just four days."

Kabuta said, "They were awfully gaunt when we got here. Rising Star said that this grass is so nutritious the buffalo get fat just looking at it. And the cow is pouring milk after feasting on that green grass."

The animals' backs had been itching fiercely from all the fly bites they had sustained. They had rolled over many times the past four days in the long grass to scratch their backs. Their bellies were full and they had a good rest and were ready for another long haul.

The humans bathed every day in the clear, cool water and had dined on fresh fish, pheasant and prairie chickens. They had fared well here, but it was time to move on.

For the next two days the going was slow and they had to stop often to let the teams blow, but on the morning of the third day they started climbing up out of the sand flats and were soon up on the plateau of the western plains. The ground became hard and the wagons rolled much easier.

About three o'clock the next day Katy, Running Springs and Peg were riding their horses side-by-side. They crossed a seep about fifty feet across. It ran from the river way out onto the plains. It would take too much time to go around it. The wagon wheels sank deep in the mud. Kabuta and Mike got off their wagons and hitched all the teams to the heavier wagon. Katy drove it across while Kabuta and Mike waded through the mud, pushing with all their might. They didn't stop until they had the wagon on hard ground because they were afraid it would sink so deep that they could never get it rolling again. The lighter wagon wasn't much of a problem.

Katy said, "You know, Peg, when Mike said there would be many hardships on our journey I didn't think much about it. But now, after the Alleghenies, crossing flooded rivers, days of those miserable flies, those sand hills and now this mud, I know what he meant. I'm so tired I feel like I could sleep for a week."

"I don't know what's gotten into me, Katy, but I feel invigorated." Peg laughed and kicked her horse in the ribs to catch up with her man. She got off her horse and tied him to the wagon and climbed up on the wagon seat with Kabuta. She slipped her arms around him and snuggled up to him.

Katy caught up with Mike and she too tied her horse in back and climbed up with Mike, but she didn't encourage him. She whispered a prayer, "Please, dear Lord, not tonight."

Mike said. "It'll be easy sailing tomorrow, honey."

She said, "Running Springs has been telling me that things would get easier soon. I sure hope she knows what she's talking about."

A few minutes later Mike pulled his team to a standstill underneath one lonely large cottonwood and Kabuta pulled his wagon on the other side where the huge trunk would be between their beds and no sound could reach the other wagon.

It wasn't long until the camp was silent, save for the sound of sleep.

Just as they were beginning to start breakfast the next morning, a little Indian boy came into camp. He was wearing only a dirty buckskin loincloth that barely hid his privates and rear. He was scared and shaking like an aspen leaf from the cold morning air, but he was so hungry that his need for food overcame his fear.

He stood looking at the two big covered wagons and a white man down in the flat catching some mules. A white woman was putting something on an open fire.

He watched her put bacon in a pan and he smelled coffee boiling. When the smell of the bacon hit his nostrils his little stomach started to growl. Just as he started to walk forward Kabuta walked from behind the wagon facing him. He froze. He had never seen people like this before, a redheaded white woman and a big black man. Then a black woman walked up beside the man and slipped her arm through his.

The boy started to bolt back the way he had come. Oh how he wished he were back in the Valley of the Smokes—there wasn't even one bush he could hide under here. He was surprised again when the Black man spoke to him in his own language and held both arms out toward him, palms up, and said, "Come, little brother, and we will give you food."

His fear kept him glued to his spot until he saw Running Springs coming up from the river with a pail of water in her hand. He heard the man say, "Running Springs, will you come and try to convince our little brother we're friendly?"

It reassured him somewhat when the big man kept smiling at him and speaking in his own tongue.

Running Springs set down her pail of water and came around the wagon.

He squealed, "Running Springs!" and ran and leaped into her arms.

She said, "Rising Star! What are you doing way out here on the prairie so far from home all alone?"

"Our enemy slipped into our village one night when the Chief and most of our braves were out looking for you, and toted off all of our food. The young enemy chief saw me leave the teepee to pee. He slipped up behind me, put his hand over my mouth and took me away. He said that a grizzly bear killed his little boy about my size and he was taking me to his squaw so that she might quit wailing.

"I sneaked away from their camp in the middle of the night three suns ago. They almost found me the next day, but I saw them first and slipped into the river and hid near the bank under the roots of a willow tree.

"They sat their horses just above me and looked all around. I heard one of them say, 'He wouldn't come downriver; he would go upriver to try to get back to his valley.'

"It was almost dark when they turned back upriver to where there were a few small trees. I saw their campfire and I was so cold and hungry I almost went to them, but I knew my father would be coming after them so I kept coming downriver."

Mike came up and Running Springs said, "Chief Mike, this is Rising Star, a boy from our village." Then she told Mike his story.

Mike said, "Rising star, I'm glad to meet you. You stay with us and we'll take you home."

Katy was still frying bacon. Running Springs picked up a piece of bacon laying on a tin plate to cool and gave it to Rising Star and he gobbled it up. Then she took him to the river and gave him a good bath and washed his dirty loincloth.

She wrapped him in a towel and took him back to the fire. Katy handed Running Springs a plate of pancakes and bacon. She buttered the pancakes and poured honey over them and cut them up, and then she took a fork and showed him how to use it. She said, "Now eat slowly and you will like the food better." As he was eating she poured him a cup of sweet milk that had been cooling in the river all night.

He was starving, but he remembered to slow down after a few bites and he thoroughly enjoyed the food. When he'd cleaned his plate he rubbed his little belly and threw his arms around Running Springs' neck and said, "Much good."

* * * * *

The sound of the mules hooves on the hard prairie soil and the clicking of the wheels were strange music to Rising Star's ears as he slowly came awake about eight hours later. He rose up when he heard Mike say, "Darling, there are some small willow trees up about a mile near a clear hole of water with some good sized fish in it. We'll camp there, and maybe we can get Kabuta to fix us his famous fish dinner tonight."

Katy said, "Gee! I hope so. Peg and I have watched him fashion that meal a dozen times and we've written everything down. We've tried and tried, but we just can't get it to come out as good as he does, and it makes us both so mad."

"Neither can I," Mike said. "Fish has to be cooked just right, and Kabuta seems to have the knack for it."

As Rising Star climbed over the back of the seat and sat down beside Katy he noticed she was eating a cookie. She slipped her arm around him and squeezed him tightly to her. She could hardly wait to see the little life she knew was living in her. She released him and passed the reins from her left hand to the right and reached in a box and handed him a cookie.

He ate it and held his hand up for another. She said, "One more, and that's all you get until you get some of Kabuta's famous fish. That is, if we catch any."

Rising Star said, "Much good," and he put his arm through Katy's like he had seen Peg do to Kabuta.

The prairie was alive with grasshoppers and the fish were fat from eating so many of them, but they weren't feeding. They wouldn't take a hook, so Peg and Running Springs took spears and speared enough for supper.

Kabuta started a fire in the cook stove with the last of the split wood they had brought.

Mike took care of the stock and Katy was churning butter. Rising Star was eating another cookie and drinking a cup of milk that Katy gave him. She whispered to herself, "After all, he slept through lunch."

Mike removed all the pole wood they had swung under the wagons and started cutting it to stove length and after supper he and Kabuta finished splitting it and loaded it onto the wagon.

The next morning broke bright and clear, but everyone was still lying in bed because the day before had been a grueling one. They were all awake and had just finished dressing when they heard the dogs growling.

When Mike and Kabuta came out of their wagons they both had two waist guns strapped around them and a shotgun in their hands. Peg and Katy were hidden in the wagons, each holding a rifle. All six of the dogs were lined up in a row facing a dozing Indians wearing war paint.

The dogs were baring their teeth and growling. Mike gave them a command and they quieted and lined up behind Mike and Kabuta.

The young chief held his hand out, palm up and said, "We come in peace."

Running Springs and Rising Star were at the river washing their hands and face, and when they walked around the wagon holding hands, Running Springs recognized these men as being from her village, and Crazy Horse, one of her father's young sub-chiefs, was among them. Rising Star broke from her grasp and cried, "Father!" and ran forward. The young chief leaped from his horse as the boy ran into his arms. They held one another for a long time. Then Rising Star started chattering excitedly, relating his story of kidnap and how Chief Mike and his people had taken care of him.

The Chief walked up to Mike, again with his palms up. Mike held his hands up the same way and the man stepped forward quickly and crushed Mike to him, then stepped back and grasped Mike's hand and said, "You have my unfailing devotion for taking care of my son."

Then he turned to Running Springs and said, "The tribe has grieved for you for a long time and the Chief and his men are out looking for you and the brave that took you."

Running Springs said, "When I get home I will tell my story to the tribe. I knew that father would never stop looking for me."

"We will take you and Rising Star to your mothers, they have grieved long enough."

"No," she said, "I can't leave my friends. You go ahead and tell them that a fine white trapper killed the ugly one who stole me away, before he could harm me. His partner tried to take my clothes off and they fought with knives. The good man said, 'Run and hide,' and I did.

"These kind people found me hiding in the brush and they have fed me and are taking me home. I must stay with them and guide them to our village."

When the Indians started to leave Rising Star ran to hug his new friends goodbye, but he hugged Running Springs longer.

The Indians were riding good horses and could be in their village weeks before Mike and his group could with the heavily loaded wagons. Mike said, "Chief, may I ask a favor?"

"Anything, Chief."

"Could you lead our extra horses and turn them loose with yours when you get to your valley? That would help us a lot."

The chief was happy to do so and Mike sent all their extra stock with them, except for the two mares that were broke to harness, and Midnight, his stallion, and Katy's Goldie. He figured two riding horses were all they needed and if they needed more they could ride the two mares that they used for the extra team.

The Indians left them in the dust as they galloped away to take the news to their great chief that his darling Running Springs was healthy and well, and to assure him she would be home in a couple of months.

The wagons rolled along easily all day, and late in the afternoon they reached a large, rough, sandstone rock formation that seemed to rise up out of the prairie about three hundred feet. They pitched camp some distance from it on the banks of the river.

After supper and the camp chores were finished, they had some time before dark so they hiked to the formation.

Peg started running on ahead and she didn't see the big old prairie rattler spring back into a coil to strike until she was right on it, but Kabuta running just to her left and back a ways, did. He wasn't even conscious of the draw, but the pistol slipped smoothly from the holster and spit flame. His first shot caught the snake near the middle of its body, causing it to miss Peg's leg by inches. He jerked her away from the snake and shot it through the head.

Peg fell into Kabuta's arms, shaking violently.

Kabuta looked upward and said, "Thank you, Father God."

When Peg could get her voice, she said, "Running Springs warned us about snakes. I forgot, but you can bet I won't forget again."

Running Springs said, "It makes good soup."

"No, thank you," was Peg's reply and they proceeded more carefully.

When they reached the rock they found two names carved deep in the sandstone: "Pierre and Paul Mallet—1798."

They carved their names just above these names:

"Michael Ross, County Kerry, Ireland, 1803; Katy O'Flannery Ross, Tipperary County, Ireland, 1803. Kabuta and Peg from Africa, 1803;

The river was running through some low, rolling hills here, with scrub pine and salt cedar trees growing sparsely on the hills. This was a welcome change after days of swamps, sand hills and dusty flat prairie.

Their barrels of side pork and ham hocks were about half gone and they had been hoarding them. They hadn't had anything to eat but a few pheasant and sage hens and fish for days. They had eaten so much fish they hated the sight of it.

They had six buffalo hides stretched over their wagons, but the meat had spoiled rather quickly and Mike and Katy couldn't bring themselves to eat spoiled meat after their first try. They discovered that Kabuta, Peg, and Running Springs knew what they were talking about when they said, "It won't hurt you if you boil it long enough." It didn't make them sick but the smell of it was enough that they never wanted to try it again.

Mike said, "Kabuta, that tasted palatable and I would eat it again if I had to, to stay alive, but until then, no thank you!"

Katy said, "That's my sentiment exactly."

Kabuta and Peg wouldn't cook it if Mike and Katy wouldn't eat it so they never cooked it again.

Their first morning there Running Springs said, "Mike, I know these trees aren't very big and the grove is small, but it's the last you will see until we reach the mountains, days from now; we should replenish our wood supply before we leave here."

The stock were doing well on the nutritious prairie grass so they spent three days here making repairs and setting in a good supply of wood for the cook stove. It was late in the afternoon when Kabuta stacked the last armful of wood on the wagon. He said, "Mike, I stink so bad I can't stand myself. Let's get a cake of soap and hit the river."

"Sounds good to me."

As they sat down to a fish dinner and Kabuta said grace, Peg said, "It's kinda hard to be thankful for fish these days. Mike, how about breaking down and letting me cook a big pot of ham hock and beans tomorrow?"

"I'm as tired of this fish as you are, and I'm all for that. Maybe Kabuta will make us a chocolate cake and a few fruit pies to take along. I need to repair some harness tomorrow and we'll make tomorrow an easy day and leave the following morning."

When they finished supper Katy asked Mike to put a pot of water on the stove to boil. "Peg and I want to take a bath, and that river water is just too cold anymore. And would you take care of the dishes? When we finish our baths we want to crawl into our warm beds."

"Your wish is my command," he said.

The next morning as the men were doing their thing, Katy, Peg and Running Springs hiked around the monument looking for other names, but they found none. They sat down on a rock in the shade of a small pine tree and Katy said, "Peg, have you and Running Springs told Mike or Kabuta that you are expecting?"

Peg said, "No, I wanted to be absolutely sure before I told Kabuta."

Running Springs said, "Katy, there is no way I would steal Peg's thunder. I can just hear Chief Kabuta holler as loud as thunder when she tells him."

Peg said, "Yeah, or be so dumbfounded he can't say a word."

Katy said, "Well, I wanted to get you two behind this rock before I told you that I'm sure I'm carrying Mike's child, too. And I'm going to tell Mike tomorrow night after we're in bed."

Peg hugged Katy and said, "Hooray! I wonder how far apart we are."

Katy said, "I'm a little ahead of you, but it can't be more than a month, I'm sure."

After supper that night and the camp chores were done, Mike and Kabuta took their bows and walked up the river in hopes they could kill a deer. Katy took a sponge bath and went to bed early, but Peg and Running Springs decided they would take a swim in the river one more time before it got too cold. When they asked Katy if she would like to join them she shivered and said, "No, thank you."

The men came back just at sunset, empty-handed and Katy was glad when she noticed it. The girls had rested for three days and Katy wasn't tired at all and she wanted Mike to come to bed.

They hadn't made love for a week now, and she couldn't wait to get him in bed, but she was hoping he would make the first move. She had seen Peg with a bedroll in her hand and she and Kabuta were walking down the river. She knew they wanted their privacy where Running Springs couldn't hear what was going on. She got a bedroll ready and looked out the back of the wagon and saw Mike going toward where Midnight and Goldie were grazing and he went and patted Midnight on the neck and then did the same to her mare. She thought he would never come to her.

When he finally started to climb up over the wagon wheel she shoved the bedroll at him and said, "Didn't you see Kabuta and Peg going down the river with their bedroll?"

"I was just coming to invite you for a stroll up the river, but I see you had the same idea."

Katy already had on her moccasins and a robe and she climbed down and took his hand and led him up the river.

When Mike rolled out the bedroll in a secluded spot Katy dropped her robe and laid down and said, "Come to me, my love."

He started caressing her body with his hands and kissed her passionately.

After, they were mutually satisfied they lay side-by-side, talking.

Katy said, "Mike, now that I'm expecting, it just gets better and better.

Mike rose up so quickly that he threw the covers off of them. "When? How? Are you sure? How long have you been keeping this from me?"

She said, "Lay back down Mike, I'm cold. I've been pretty sure some time now, but when my time passed for the second time, and my passion got so strong, I knew. Mother told me it gets that way for some women."

"Well, you won't find me complaining. And Katy, I couldn't be more pleased. I hope it'll be a little girl just like you."

"It will be a boy," she said. "Mike, it's getting mighty cold at night and we've been on this prairie it seems forever. Are we going to get to where there are trees big enough to build a cabin before winter sets in?"

"I don't know, Katy. But we still have the buffalo robes. We may have to spend the winter in a teepee, but I'm sure we'll reach the forest before the snow falls, and with the little stoves we brought we'll keep warm. Don't worry, darling, we're going to be fine."

She nestled in his arms, feeling safe and secure.

When Mike walked up to Kabuta the next morning with his chest sticking out, strutting like a peacock, Kabuta said, "What's got into you this fine morning?"

Mike said, "It is a fine morning, isn't it? Katy just informed me last night that I'm going to be a father."

Kabuta slapped him on the shoulder and said, "Congratulations, old friend. Now it's your turn to congratulate me. Peg just told me I'm going to be a father."

The men shook hands and hugged, and then Kabuta said, "I'd better get busy. I promised Peg breakfast in bed this morning."

"I promised Katy the same," Mike laughed. "Running Springs will think we're crazy." They headed for the cook stove; laughing and cutting up like a couple of kids.

They headed west later than usual that morning, but it would be the last time they would. Now that they knew that their wives were each carrying a little one they were anxious to reach the valley. They'd decided that from now on they would travel from dawn to dusk and they wouldn't take a noon break unless it became absolutely necessary.

When Mike told Running Springs about Katy and Peg she didn't let him know she was the first to know of the girls' condition and their desire to find a place where they could build a cabin in which to spend the winter. She said, "I'm sure we will reach the Valley before the snow falls. My father, Chief Big Thunder, will have teepees in place, with plenty of bear rugs on the floor, when we get there."

One day Peg and Running Springs were driving the wagons, and Kabuta was riding one of the mares up one side of the river and Mike and Katy rode up the other side. About noon Mike and Katy went back to relieve Peg and Running Springs and let them ride the horses, but Kabuta went on.

An hour before dark they rolled over a hill and saw Kabuta down in a valley where a small lake nestled in a circle of low hills. A grove of trees circled the lake. Kabuta had a half-grown buffalo heifer drawn up under a sturdy branch. He'd already gutted her and taken the waste meat away, and the dogs were gorging themselves.

Kabuta had the skin almost off when they drew to a stop in a level place. Katy got a fire started in the stove and Running Springs went to the lake for water. Peg went and milked the cows. Old bossy had dropped her calf a few days ago and they were getting more milk and butter now than they could use. Mike took care of the stock and came into camp just as Kabuta slipped a pan of biscuits in the oven. Katy was cooking tenderloin steaks on the grill. He said, "Steak and gravy over buttermilk biscuits, man, I can't wait."

This was the first fresh meat they'd had in days and they really relished it.

Mike said, "I'm sure glad we were able to refill our barrels with flour and buy two more, we can enjoy pastries for a long time yet."

Kabuta said, "If you'll clean up here I'll make four or five peach, and an apricot cobbler, we're about out of dried apples."

"I knew we didn't bring enough dried fruits with us," Mike said.

"We'll miss that more than anything," Katy added.

"If not coffee." Peg remarked, "I've sure come to prefer it over tea."

Mike said, "We've enough coffee and tea to last a long time. I've been saving our old coffee grounds and letting them dry out. It won't be near as good the next time around, but it's better than none at all."

Katy said, "Are we ever going to get back to forested land? I'm getting so sick of these plains."

Running Springs said, "It won't be long now before you're in the most beautiful mountains you've ever seen. And you're going to a valley where hot water shoots up out of the ground night and day, there a beautiful waterfall cascades off the mountain that causes a mist. When the sun hits that mist there are millions of little rainbows and bright glistening spots all around.

"There is a clear river that runs into a blue lake and out the other side of it, to cascade down through a steep gorge. The meadows are rich with wild hay and there are buffalo, elk, deer, big horn sheep and goats. There are many bears and mountain lions in the mountains, and there are honeybees everywhere. The river and lake are full of fish. My people do well.

"What you have that the men will want most are the things you cut wood with and those beautiful hunting knives, and the women will fight over the sewing kits you can trade them. It is very hard for us to gather enough wood to cook with and keep our teepees warm in the wintertime when the ground is covered with snow."

Mike said, "With the axes we brought and the ones that were in Lee and Slim's packs, we have two and a half dozen. We'll give your father two dozen to distribute to whom he pleases, and I think we have enough sewing kits to give the Chief's squaws each one for the teepees he's preparing for us."

"That will please him as much as bringing me home."

"Not on your life, little sister," Katy quipped.

Mike's small party had traveled along the North Platte River to where it turned southwest, and here Chief Big Thunder met them with a group of his best warriors. When Running Springs saw her father she ran forward and threw her arms around him and laid her cheek against his rugged face. Neither of them spoke, but their embrace said volumes.

After Chief Big Thunder expressed his appreciation for their care of his daughter, he convinced Mike and Kabuta to let him take the girls on to his village. He said, "I'll leave five men with Chief Crazy Horse to guide you, and help you through the mountains to the village."

Early the next morning Mike and Kabuta had a hard time getting their wives to leave them. They were all aware that they might not see one another for a month or so. The ladies finally conceded when Running Springs said, "It will be freezing at high altitude this time of year. You could be sleeping in a warm teepee in no time if you went with us, and I assure you, you will be safe. My father and the whole tribe will protect you as well as they would me."

When Kabuta kissed Peg good-bye he whispered in her ear, "Now don't you get sweet on one of these handsome braves before I get there."

She hugged him tightly and said, "I can't see any man other than you." They rode away, but the girls turned a number of times and waved at their husbands who stood there until they were out of sight.

Mike said, "Kabuta, "We're going to be two lonely men before we see them again."

Kabuta said, "Let's get these wagons rolling."

CHAPTER TWENTY-TWO

The group on horses would cover the journey to the village in eight days of hard riding, where it would take the wagon party six weeks or more to cover the same distance. There would be snow flurries in the mountains before Mike and Kabuta would see their wives again.

Crazy Horse changed their directions and cut cross-country northwest to the south fork of the Powder River. They spent one night there after they crossed the river, and hastened to the north fork of the Powder.

They followed the north fork to its head and crossed to Nowood Creek, and followed it until it spilled into the Bighorn River. They crossed the Bighorn and traveled northwest to the Raybull River. After they crossed over they filled all their empty containers with water because Crazy Horse said, "We will find no more until we reach the Shoshone River, a number of days further on."

Five days later they crossed the south fork of the Shoshone Rive and camped for the night. Then they crossed to the north fork of the Shoshone and followed it into the Valley of the Smokes.

Crazy Horse said, "Chief Mike, you won't be able to take the wagons through the mountains. You will have to leave them when we reach the end of a box canyon. We can pack everything in them by pack mules, but the wagons will have to stay."

When they left the wagons Running Springs had said, "Girls, we will sleep in warm teepees in nine days, or ten days at the most."

Five days had passed when the Chief sent two men on ahead with four horses so they could change mounts often. He said, "Ride night and day and tell the tribe to roast a young elk and have a feast ready by high noon three days from now to welcome my daughter and our new friend's home."

When the Chief and the rest of his party finally rode into the village the whole tribe was out to meet them. The reunion of Running Springs' family was a touching one. After her mother and sister greeted her, her eighteen-year-old brother folded her in his arms and tears of joy were running down his cheeks in small streams. Little Rising Star flew into Katy's arms when he saw her.

Five weeks later when Mike, Kabuta, Crazy Horse and the rest of his braves came in, leading the mules and horses loaded down with goods, there was a feast waiting for them just as good as there was for the girls.

Rising Star ran to tell Peg and Katy that Mike and Kabuta were coming. He was hopping up and down and jabbering so fast they had to slow him down to understand him. When he said again, "Kabuta and Mike are here," they flashed out of the teepee and rushed across the compound to fling themselves into their husbands' eager arms.

The Chief was standing by; ready to greet them, when the girls flew by him. When they finally let their husbands go, they turned to face the Chief, a little embarrassed. He smiled and said, "Kabuta, Mike, I believe your squaws are happy to see you."

"No happier than we are to see them," they both blurted out at the same time.

The Chief said, "My people and I welcome you to our village, and we hope you will spend the rest of your lives with us. It will take us a lifetime to show our appreciation for your bringing our son and daughter safely back to us."

Mike and Kabuta assured him that Running Springs and Crazy Horse had more than paid them for guiding them to this beautiful valley.

The Chief said, "Now, ladies, take your tired husbands to your teepees and pamper them. Tomorrow there will be a feast in their honor, but the rest of the day the tribe has been instructed to respect your privacy."

Katy whispered in Mike's ear, "What a wise and kind man he is."

When the teepee flap was tied securely, Katy said, "Are you exhausted, my love?"

"Not at all," he said, I slept well last night and we didn't walk far today."

She said, "You will be when I get through with you," and she started to unbutton his faded flannel shirt."

Mike, Kabuta, Peg and Katy were conversing later about how spacious their teepees were. Katy said, "Maybe the chief intends to give Mike and Kabuta more wives, I understand he has three and another is being groomed for him."

"Over my dead body," Peg remarked, "I'm not sharing this big ebony lover of mine with any woman, and I don't care what the Chief says."

"Never you fear, my little dove, you're all the woman I can handle or want," Kabuta said.

"That's my sentiment exactly," Mike said. "If that time ever comes we'll just explain that isn't our custom. Unless Kabuta and I get used to their customs and change our minds."

Kabuta said, "Yeah."

Peg knocked him halfway across the teepee, and Mike dodged Katy's punch at his shoulder. It was just a love punch and Kabuta was putting on when he staggered across the teepee.

Katy said, "Well, Peg, you'd still be head squaw."

Peg said, "It wouldn't be fair to the other squaws. They'd never get to sleep with him. It's all he can do to take care of me, anyway."

Katy said, "If Mike ever entertains such a thought he's going to find out that this old redheaded Irish girl has a temper he'll never forget. If you think Indians are the only ones that go on the war path, you just wait until you see me if something like that happens!"

"No thanks," Peg said, "If that ever happens I want to be way up river, with Kabuta sitting safely by my side, fishing."

About one o'clock the chief called all the tribe together for a great homecoming feast to honor their brothers, Mike and Kabuta. They had been expecting them for days and everything was ready. The tender young buffalo had been turning slowly on the spit over the open fire since early morning. Its juices were soaking back into it as it rolled around and around, making it tender and juicy all the way through.

The Chief got up on his podium, which was a buffalo hide stretched over a huge stump. He gave an impressive speech. He said, "My people, listen well and understand what I say." He called Mike, Kabuta, Peg, Katy and Running Springs forward and said, "Now my daughter will tell you her story."

And she told them how she had been kidnapped and how the trapper saved her from the brave and also from the bad white man, and how Katy and Peg found her and brought her and Rising Star safely home.

Then the Chief said, "Now, my people, you are to treat them like brothers and sisters and they are to enjoy all the benefits that the tribe enjoys. They are subject to me only."

Then he held his hands high, palm down, as though they would protect all of them, and he prayed to the Great Spirit, saying, "Thank you, Great Spirit, for bringing Running Springs and Rising Star safely back to us, and thank you for the feast we are about to partake of. Now eat, everyone, and when the camp is cleaned you may do as you please until tomorrow, and then we will take up our respective duties."

When the Chief stepped out of his teepee the next morning to stretch himself in the early morning sun, Kabuta approached him and said, "Good morning, Chief Big Thunder. I have something to show you. Take me to the largest tree you'd like to have cut down."

The Chief took him out into the field where they would plant their corn in the spring and showed him the biggest pine tree he'd ever seen. The tree was half dead. Kabuta had his axe sharp enough to shave with and the Chief was amazed when he saw the large chips start flying from the tree. By the time Kabuta got the carp the way he wanted, a crowd had gathered and Mike had walked out with another axe.

Kabuta made sure that everyone was back far enough that they weren't in any danger of being hit by a flying branch when the huge tree came crashing down. He and Mike took turns making the back cut, and in less than an hour the giant tree came crashing to the ground, sending dead branches flying in all directions.

Mike started cutting the branches from the trunk and Kabuta dragged them away and started cutting them into sizes they needed for the small heaters and the cook stoves they brought with them. After all the branches were removed Mike went and got a crosscut saw and showed the braves how to use it, and they cut the trunk into pieces just the right length to be used for tables, if anyone needed them.

Mike and Kabuta started splitting wood. It took them two days to split all of it.

Kabuta said, "Chief, we have more of these axes, and if you will give me twenty men I'll teach them how to use them and we'll go into the forest and cut down all the dead trees. We can easily supply the whole tribe with all they need to carry them through the winter, in a few days. Then we can remove all the trees from the fields you want to plant."

Mike said, "And I need four good men to help me break down the wagons. We can pack them in here on the mules and re-assemble them. It may take us two weeks to get all our supplies and the wagons here, and the wagons will make life easier for everyone."

The Chief said, "Mike, we have horses that can carry packs. Why not take more men and many horses? The gorge could be packed in snow in two weeks."

"Then we'd better go tomorrow."

Mike went to the teepee to talk to Katy and Peg.

"Can you make sacks out of the ducking tent that we haven't used so we can put the flour, cornmeal, sugar and our side pork and bacon in them? We can't pack those heavy barrels through those rugged mountains on pack mules very well."

Katy said, "I'll get Running Springs to get some of the Indian ladies to help us and we'll get it done as quickly as possible."

Mike said, "You have three days at most. The Chief said that the gorge could be snowed in any time now."

Peg said, "I want that flour and sugar, we'll get it done."

Mike and ten men riding strong horses, leading twenty pack mules and horses, went for the wagons. The morning after they reached the wagons they unloaded them. Mike thanked God that no animals had disturbed their precious supplies.

The side gates and the floorboards of the wagon beds were held together with bolts, and Mike started removing the bolts carefully so as not to lose any of the bolts, nuts and washers. As soon as they had enough boards to pack a horse they did so and sent two men back to the village with them.

When they got the wagons torn down they packed their animals, left two men to guard the supplies that were in the barrels, and Mike led the pack-horses and the rest of the men to the village. They reached the village well into the night and Kabuta and some other men relieved Mike and his men so they could get in bed for needed rest.

Mike dropped into bed exhausted. He stayed in the teepee most of the next day, and the next morning he and Kabuta took some men and went after the rest of their supplies.

It took them three days to bring in all of their supplies. They had just loaded the last mule when a light snow started to fall. They made it through the gorge and hit the valley floor just as the sun set. Mike said, "Thank God we made it out of those mountains before dark."

They had just got the supplies into their waterproof supply teepee when it started pouring rain. Mike was wringing wet when he entered his teepee. Katy said, "Step into this wash tub and strip off," and she toweled him down.

She slipped a flannel nightshirt over his head and he crawled into the warm bed that she had just left. She crawled in and wrapped him in her arms and held her warm body against him until he quit shivering and fell asleep.

As Katy lay beside her sleeping husband she silently prayed that he would never have to leave her again.

Mike woke Katy in the middle of the night, shaking like a leaf. He was chilled to the bone and no amount of covering stopped his shivering.

Katy heated milk as hot as he could stand it and he drank a quart of it. Then he asked her to get him a shot of whiskey. "My throat is sore and I think I've got a fever."

Katy hovered over him all night. By morning he was on fire. His lungs were filling with liquid and he could barely breathe. Katy went to Kabuta and Peg, asking for advice.

Kabuta said, "I'll go talk to the Chief, he'll probably know of an Indian remedy that might help."

The Chief sent the tribe Shaman, who placed a pot of boiling water with dried root bark of the sassafras tree near Mike and place a small skin tunnel to direct the hot steam directly onto Mike's face so he could breathe the steam. Then he coaxed him to drink the bitter tea made from the root. Next, he placed hot prickly pear poultices on his chest and back to try to draw the infection from his lungs.

Mike grew steadily worse for the next several days until one night Katy came into Peg and Kabuta's teepee, haggard and worn.

Peg folded her in her arms and she cried out, "I'm going to lose him, what am I going to do?"

Kabuta slipped on his shoes and coat and said, "You stay here and drink some hot milk and try to get some sleep. You look like you haven't slept for a week."

"I haven't much, I'm afraid," Katy said through her tears.

"I'll sit with him the rest of the night," Kabuta said.

When Kabuta came near his bed, Mikes eyes fluttered open, and he said weakly, "Kabuta, my friend, I'm dying. I'll be with Gabe, Esther, Mom and Dad before morning. I'm not afraid to die, because I know where I'm going, but leaving my Katy is more than I can bear. I trust you and Peg to take care of her and the child I'll never see. Good bye, my friend." He closed his eyes.

Kabuta had known fear: When the neighboring tribe killed his mother and father and sold him into slavery: when the two men were going to sell him back into slavery after he had his freedom and Mike saved him; but that was nothing to the fear that gripped him now. He threw back the covers, stripped the poultices from Mike's body and lay down beside him. He put his strong arms around his dearest friend and held him tight against his chest as he began to pray. "Father God, I can't let him go. Please forgive me of my sins, in Jesus' name I ask it. Now, Father God, my brother Mike told me that you said that we have not because we ask not. But you said if we ask anything in Jesus' name, you would give it to us. Now Father, I'm asking you for Mike's life to be spared. If you must take someone, Lord, let it be me. I give you my life for Mike's."

Kabuta held Mike close as the hot tears streamed down the side of his face, wetting the pillow where his head lay. He had been lying that way for two hours when he realized that the sweat was pouring out of every pore of Mike's body. He was still hot, but it wasn't from fever, but from the warm covers and Kabuta's own hot body.

He slipped out of the bed and knelt beside it and poured out his heart to God, who had heard his plea. Mike would never know what Kabuta did that night, and neither would anyone else. This was between him and his Heavenly Father.

When Kabuta entered his own teepee he found Peg putting the coffee pot on to boil and Katy was sleeping the sleep of the truly exhausted. He took

Peg in his arms and kissed her and said, "My little dove, he's going to live, his fever has broken and he has saturated his bed with sweat. Could you come and help me strip him and get him in dry clothes and change his bed while I hold him?"

Peg had just finished making his bed and Kabuta laid Mike's head on his pillow when he opened his eyes. A wan smile crept across his pale face he said, "Peg, could you bring me a bowl of hot soup?" Crying, she said, "Yes, praise the Lord," and she went to fill his request.

Kabuta didn't leave Mike's side until Katy came in, hours later.

Mike ate the soup and went back to sleep just before Katy came in. Kabuta jumped up and hugged her and said, "Katy, he's going to be all right. His fever is gone. He coughed up a quart of corruption and now he's breathing easy. Peg fed him a bowl of soup and he's sleeping peaceably now."

Katy had kept her emotions pretty well in check when she was taking care of Mike, but now she let herself go, and she sobbed out her fear and anxiety.

Kabuta held her while she sobbed and when she extracted herself she said, "Thank you, you go get some sleep. I'll be fine now."

After a couple of weeks of rest and nourishment Mike was back on his feet, though still somewhat weak.

Kabuta hadn't strayed far from Mike during his ordeal, but now that he was sure Mike would be all right, and he himself had rested, he gathered his twenty-four woodcutters around him. He said, "Men, these axes are very sharp and if you miss what you swing at you might cut your leg or foot very badly. I want all of you to gather around and watch me cut down the first two trees and trim off the branches.

He quickly fell a tree and removed all the branches, keeping the trunk between him and the head of the axe. He said, "You see how I kept the trunk of the tree between me and the axe? That's so I won't cut myself. Never let the sharp blade hit the ground, so it will not dull or chip the sharp edge."

After he had spread the men out through the woods to remove all the dead trees, he went from man to man, giving them pointers and correcting their mistakes until he was satisfied that twenty of them would become good woodsmen. But there were four men who couldn't seem to get the hang of it, so he took their axes away and put them to stacking brush in large piles.

When Mike had reassembled the wagons he and four men started hauling the wood to the individual teepees and stacking a neat cord at each one, starting with the Chief and sub-chiefs. Mike didn't completely supply his until every teepee in the village was supplied. The Chief noticed and said, "Mike, why didn't you supply your teepee first?"

"Chief, Kabuta, our wives and I want to be accepted by all of your people, and we figured if they saw that we expect no special privileges they'll learn to trust us quicker."

Mike had just stacked the last stick on his cord when it started to snow. There were still a lot of piles of cut and split wood scattered around the forest yet to be hauled.

Kabuta said, "Men, you've done a great job and I'm sure we have enough wood to carry us through the winter. What do you say we take a couple of days off to do anything we want to do? I'm going to take Peg fishing. And after that maybe the Chief will let us start hunting. I'll ask him if we can do that. He'll know if it's safe to hang the meat for winter."

The respect for this big Black man that the Chief had put over these men was building by leaps and bounds. They sure liked the sound of two days just to do anything they pleased.

The snow fell gently and it was warmer than it had been before, and Mike and his crew continued to haul wood until it was all brought in. They stacked it in cords in the middle of the village and if a family ran out of wood they were welcome to go to the community woodpile for more.

When they had hauled the last load there was enough wood to last them all winter, even if it proved to be a long one.

The Chief sent word for Mike and Kabuta to come to his teepee. When they entered, the chief invited them to join the family in the circle around the fire. He said, "My family and I wanted to thank you for the wood you have stacked at the door of our teepees. This is a chore that keeps us busy summer and winter. Your tools and teaching our men how to use them has done in three weeks what it would take the whole tribe much of our time throughout the year to do. Now we can spend more time enjoying one another these cold winter days."

Day after day, Big Thunder saw Mike and Kabuta put everyone ahead of themselves, and he could see that they were happy men. He started to speak to his people more and his face became softer and he smiled more like he saw Mike and Kabuta did.

Crazy Horse said to one of the other sub-chiefs, "Our Chief is getting soft", and Big Thunder overheard it. Big Thunder was forty years old, lithe and strong. He was chosen to be Chief over this Sioux tribe because of his strength, bravery and wisdom. He called a meeting of all the tribe for the next day when the sun was halfway to midmorning. When the Chief called a meeting of the tribe it was usually for something of great importance. The people were pleasantly surprised when he said, "I overheard Chief Crazy Horse say I'm getting soft. I've called this meeting to give him the rare chance to prove this to you."

He called Crazy Horse out of the crowd and said, "Strip to the waist," and he did the same.

Crazy Horse was filled with glee—this was the break he'd been waiting for, a chance to show the people how powerful his medicine was. In his conceit he was sure he could beat the Chief at anything, but he thought he would never get the chance to prove it. And here it was.

The chief said, "The best two out of three falls is the winner."

They circled around and around and Crazy Horse darted in and tripped the Chief and he fell on his back and Crazy Horse pinned his shoulder to the ground quickly. He was thrilled when he heard the crowd gasp in disbelief.

The Chief leaped up and came to the mark quickly.

They circled around and around and when Crazy Horse tried the same trick he found his chin plowing up the ground.

Big Thunder toyed with him so he would look good to the people and not lose face. And when he pinned Crazy Horse's shoulders to the ground, he made it look harder than it was, but he had tightened his strong muscles around Crazy Horse's neck just tight enough that Crazy Horse believed him when he whispered in his ear, "I could snap it like a reed." Big Thunder made short work out of the third and final round.

The people cheered their Chief and no one cheered louder than Crazy Horse. All the people knew their Chief was not getting softer, just kinder, and they liked that.

CHAPTER TWENTY-THREE

Mike had been neglecting his hounds lately and he wanted to take them on a wolf hunt. He said, "My Chief, do you know where I might find a pack of wolves? My hounds haven't had a challenge since we've been here."

Big Thunder said, "We can take you where you can find wolves, but they'll kill your dogs."

"No wolf has seen the day it could kill one of my beauties," Mike bragged. "If you'd like to see a dog kill a wolf or two, come with us."

This was something the chief wanted to see, he had seen many dogs killed and eaten by wolves, but he had never seen a dog kill a wolf.

They were in luck, they heard a wolf pack not far from camp that night and as they listened to them howling, they realized they were coming closer.

The hound's rose and their hackles rose, and they were whining with eagerness, but they would wait for either Kabuta or Mike to give the command that they longed to hear.

Mike commanded them to stay and they dropped on their haunches.

Big Thunder said, "Mike, those wolves will get one of your calves tonight, if not both of them. And if that pack is as big as it sounds to be, you might lose a cow. I'd hate to see you lose them. I've become rather fond of milk and butter."

"I'll have the dogs circle our stock all night."

The Chief just laughed.

Mike said, "Shep, Daisy, Brother Sister, Wolf, Lassie, go guard the animals."

The dogs were off in a flash. Mike held back the two younger dogs, Rover and Bowser. He wanted them full grown before they engaged; some wise old lobo might kill one of them at this young age.

The Chief said, "There's a full moon tonight and it will be almost as light as day with the moon and stars reflecting off this snow. Those wolves are coming down, and they will get your calves, Mike."

Mike said, "Kabuta, let's get our shotguns and some extra shells. We might need them if there are too many in that pack."

Then he said to the Chief, "We don't want a lot of men out there, but your sub-chiefs might want to see this."

When they gathered Mike said, "Please don't try to shoot the wolves with your arrows, you might kill one of our dogs. If there is any need to shoot, Kabuta and I will use these shotguns."

They all walked out to where the stock was grazing on the grass that stuck up stubbornly above the snow. They saw the six big wolfhounds trotting slowly around the animals in a wide circle. Once in a while, almost on cue, they sat on their haunches and rested for a few minutes before continuing their circling of the herd.

The Chief pointed to the top of a small rise. "Twelve, I would judge," he said, pointing to the wolves.

Mike commanded the dogs to get them.

The chiefs watched in amazement as the hounds bounded forward and challenged the wolves, then backed up and formed a tight circle, their rumps almost touching.

The leader of the wolf pack bounded down the rise with his pack right behind him. When they drew near, the hounds bared their big teeth and started their guttural growling.

The wolves slowed and started circling the hounds. The circle grew smaller and smaller, but the hounds never broke rank. Suddenly, twelve wolves attacked and leaped at the hounds. The hounds rose off their haunches and threw themselves upward, each grasping a wolf by the throat and shaking until the wolf ceased to move. Then the hounds went after the others.

When it was all over, twelve big timber wolves lay scattered along the ridge, with their blood staining the snow. The hounds came bounding back to Mike and Kabuta, who went down on their knees and the dogs were all over them. They wrestled and rolled with them in the snow, saying over and over, "Good dogs, good dogs." Then Mike gave a sharp command, "Stay!" and the wrestling ceased. When he said, "Go!" the dogs loped back to the village.

As the men were walking back to the village the Chief said, "Mike, hitch up a team and bring those wolves into the butchering block. There's enough meat there to make soup for the whole village for two days and the hides make warm parkas for the papooses."

Mike didn't tell the chief that the thought of eating the wolves made him sick. Instead he said, "Right away, chief. We would wait until morning, but another wolf pack might drag them away and they should be hung up skinned and gutted tonight."

"I'll get our butchers out while you and Kabuta bring them in," said the Chief. "Chief, I'll give you the next litter of these dogs if you give me your word that none of them will go into the stew pot until they get so old they can't feed themselves."

"You have my word. As long as I am Chief they will never be eaten, and if their offspring perform as well as these dogs do, we'll bury them just like we do our children."

This big redheaded Irishman from far across the ocean, and this big red man, whose ancestors had migrated across the frozen Bering Straits from Asia to the North American Continent, gripped hands in a solemn vow, and Mike knew it would never be broken.

Mike said, "Chief, I'll always be your friend. And I hope you won't be offended, but the only time any of my people ate dog it made us very sick. So please forgive us if we refuse to eat dog or wolf meat."

"Of course; But it is as good as any other meat. And if you are out where you can't get anything else, you'll soon change your mind. We have a story that has been handed down through the ages that when our ancient people came across the frozen north, they were starving to death because they ran out of food and all the animals had migrated south to warmer climates.

"They were huddled together in a snow cave and had grown so weak they had decided to die there in the cave together. They prayed to the Great

Spirit to either send them food, or take them to the beautiful hunting grounds quickly.

"They said when they were there in that season there was no day, just night, but finally the whimpering of the children ceased and they went to sleep to die. But a mighty growl came from outside of the cave and woke them. When they raked up the courage to look out, there, lying on the blanket of white snow was a giant bear. He was so white they would have thought it was just another hill of snow if its tongue hadn't been hanging out of its mouth. This huge bear had awakened them, then lay down and died.

"The Chief told his people that the Great Spirit had sent them meat. This was repeated three times until they got far enough south to find their own meat. This is the reason my people still worship the Great Unknown Spirit."

"We worship Him too," Mike said, "but we know him as God, the Creator of all things."

Just then Kabuta drove up in one of the wagons and they went to pick up the wolves.

The next morning the Chief said, "Mike, I know you wouldn't lie to me, but I would not have believed what happened last night if I hadn't seen it with my own eyes. You say they can bring down an elk? I would like to see that, too. One of my braves brought in a report that he saw two big ones up on the mountain near the waterfalls. The water drops from such a height and with such a force it keeps one small area from freezing over. That's where they come to drink. If we took the dogs and watched for a while, we might find them."

Mike said, "I'll get Kabuta and we'll go elk hunting."

When he told Katy they were going hunting, she said, "Would you cut a couple of small holes in the ice on the river so Peg and I can go fishing? We're getting hungry for fish."

"Are you sure you two should be standing out there in the cold in your condition?"

"Mike, these babies aren't due for six months or more, and we're as strong as one of your mules."

"All right, I'll get the axe and cut the holes while Kabuta is hitching the team."

By the time Mike got the second hole open Peg had already pulled two nice trout out of the first one. They were striking the little red ribbon she had tied on her hook almost as fast as it hit the water.

Mike said, "I'm sure glad you girls like to fish. I'll try to get back in time for Kabuta to fix us one of his fish dinners. Do we have any dried fruit left?"

"Some prunes, apricots and peaches, the apples have been gone a long time," Katy said.

If you catch enough fish, let's have the Chief's family over. Running Springs hasn't been around for a while. And Katy, could you make a peach cobbler to top off the meal?"

"Yes, but we won't have enough milk to drink. The cows aren't getting much feed and they aren't giving much milk."

Kabuta brought the wagon around with the Chief's with their bows and spears. Mike put the axe in the wagon and climbed aboard with his crossbow. They rode up into the foothills of Abasarka Mountain as far as they could go and tied the team to a tree and hung a feedbag on each of them with a little corn in it.

The brave that had seen the elk the day before was with them and he said, "I don't think we will find any elk here. There's a den of wolves just ahead with a couple of half-grown pups. There may be a lot of them. It's a pretty big cave. It's behind those big boulders just up ahead."

When they walked around a big boulder they saw a flat ledge running along the face of a bluff, and there were two big timber wolves standing just above Daisy and Shep, and four pups were behind them.

None of the Indians made any move to shoot, they had seen the hounds in action last night, and they couldn't afford to lose an arrow. They hung back to watch the standoff.

Daisy, Shep, Brother and Sister knew Mike was near and they waited for his command to attack.

Suddenly, the big male wolf leaped off the ledge right on top of Daisy. The hound gathered her strength and braced herself and when the wolf landed on her she locked her vice-like jaws onto his throat. He bowled her over and they rolled down the snow-covered slope. The wolf kicked and twisted, but he couldn't shake Daisy loose. His kicks became feeble and then his great body shuddered and he was gone. While this was going on the other dogs kept a sharp eye on the other wolves, but remained still.

Daisy came back to the ledge and looked up at the female wolf and issued a silent challenge. The female sprang from the ledge and in minutes was lying lifeless on the carpet of snow.

The pups broke and ran but the other three dogs were after them. Daisy started after the other one, but Mike said, "Daisy!" sharply, and she came to him. "Good dog," he said, scratching her ears.

A few minutes later the three hounds returned, and each dropped a wolf pup at their feet.

The Chief said, "I can hardly believe what I see."

Mike said, "Didn't I tell you these dogs would feed themselves and help you feed your people?"

They loaded the wolves in the wagon and had driven along the foothills about four miles when they heard Shep up on the mountain give two sharp barks. Kabuta said, "He's found something and is calling the other dogs."

He drove the team up to a tree and Mike leaped down and tied them.

They all started climbing up the mountain, slipping and sliding on the powdery snow. Then they saw Shep and Daisy sitting on their haunches, watching two big elk in an aspen grove far up on the mountainside. Brother and Sister loped up and dropped on their haunches beside Shep and Daisy.

Mike said, "Now watch. Shep and Daisy will work together and so will Brother and Sister." The Indians placed arrows across their bows and Kabuta said, "You won't need those."

The elk had backed into the aspen grove, watching the hounds. Mike gave the command and the dogs paired off just like he said they would, and chose their elk. They teased and tormented the elk until they just couldn't stand it any longer and one of them broke to run. In a small clearing the elk was running all out when Daisy sailed through the air from his side. She caught him on the nose with her powerful teeth and when her hundred and thirty pounds struck, she flipped the elk on his side with his feet fanning the air, as Shep clamped his powerful jaws on his throat. The elk rose to his feet and shook his massive antlers, but he couldn't shake the big dog off and his life slowly seeped out of him. Shep released him and leaped away as the elk pitched forward on the snow, dead.

Brother and Sister weren't as experienced as their mother and father and it took them more time to induce the other elk to bolt. But when he did leap out of the thicket for open ground it was Brother that threw him and Sister choked the life out of him. He fell within twenty feet of the first elk.

There was a ledge about the height of the wagon just below where the elks fell on the side of the hill. Kabuta was able to back the wagon up to the ledge near a large pine. Mike and Kabuta tied ropes to the hind legs of the elk and the seven men had no trouble pulling the elk down the slope and rolling them into the wagon. There were places where ice had formed under the shade of the larger trees and the mules had a difficult time keeping the wagon from rushing down the mountainside. The men solved this problem by tying ropes to the back axle of the wagon and wrapping them around the trees and letting the wagon slide down the steeper slopes slowly, until they reached more level ground.

They got home in plenty of time for Kabuta to cook the fish and Katy had the cobbler made. Peg had gathered some clean snow and with some of their precious cream she made something like ice cream.

When the Chief and his family ate dinner with them, Running Springs said, "You keep surprising me with good things. I've tasted your cobbler before, but the snow cream! It was so good!"

The Chief and his three wives and their children said it was the best meal they had ever eaten. They thanked their host and went to their teepees.

Kabuta and Mike told the girls that they outdid themselves with their ingenuity in whipping up the snow cream.

"Peg gets the credit for that," Katy said, "I only made the cobbler."

They all went to bed that night, pleased with their day.

CHAPTER TWENTY-FOUR

The long winter dragged on into early spring and the feed for the stock was almost gone when the snows began to melt and the green grass started pushing up from the earth. The thick ice on the lake melted and the river was breaking up and floating down the river in great slabs.

The clean white snow had disappeared and the village grounds had turned to deep mud, but no one minded—spring was here and the happy days of summer would soon follow.

The geese flew in and landed on the lake and all the songbirds that brought music to the valley had returned. The spirit in every heart began to sing in tune with nature.

The furs from their winter trap lines were piled high in the storage teepee.

The Jersey had dropped a calf and the Guernsey wouldn't be far behind. The two young heifers would be bred soon and the older two would drop calves in a couple of months.

Mike, Kabuta, Katy and Peg were all praying all the calves would be heifers so their diary herd would grow.

Soon there would be many new lives in the village and they needed all the milk they could get. Peg said, "Katy, can our stomachs stretch any further?"

"They'll have to, I guess. You know as much about this as I do"

The men started removing the trees from the fields where they grew corn and vegetables. Then Mike started breaking the land deep with his walking plow and Kabuta harrowed it down, breaking up the clods with some long logs tied together. One of the Indians took over the harrowing and Kabuta started planting corn with their walking planter. The Indian children didn't have to gather wood any more so they could fish, hunt and play. The hunters were out and there would be a welcome change in the diet. There would be fresh vegetables from the garden, bulbs, mushrooms and squaw cabbage. They were all looking forward to some greenery to eat.

When the travelers first entered the valley it was almost wintertime and they were busy getting wood cut for the winter. Then the snow was so deep they only did what they had to, and now it was planting time. They'd had no time to really explore the valley.

One day the Chief came to Mike and Kabuta and said, "The crops are all planted. Let's take a few days and load the wagons with food and our bedrolls. I want to show you some of the wonders of our valley. I know you have seen the smokes, but you haven't been near them. Another month and your squaws won't want to make the trip. It will take a few days."

Mike and Kabuta bolted the cook stove back on the wagon and filled the sand box. They put their beds in the wagons and put the canvas covers on them.

The Chief took them to all the hot springs; some of them with just hot, moist clay bubbling up out of the ground, with the underground pressure pushing it up and letting it fall again.

There was one spring that shot water a hundred feet into the air every hour on the hour as regular as clockwork. They camped in the trees near this spring for their stay in this part of the valley and rode their horses to all the other springs.

They rode to one spring and the Chief told them to stand back. "Two of our young men were killed because they were too close when it exploded out of the ground."

He moved them to a safe distance and said, "This spring doesn't go off often, but when it does, it's huge. It will scare you and your horses. I'd advise the ladies to dismount."

"It's too hard," Peg said.

"We'll lift you and Katy off and on," Kabuta said. "If you get thrown you could lose the baby."

Peg said, "Get me off this horse, now!"

Mike had already lifted Katy off and tied their horses to some trees.

They had just returned to where the Chief and his family were standing when the geyser went off. When it exploded it staggered their imagination.

Mike said, "That was as big as a three-story house."

Kabuta said, "I'm going to stay right here and see that again."

The Chief said, "No, Kabuta, we were lucky today. It might not go off again for a month or so."

Two days later they moved the wagon near the waterfalls and that night they slept to the music of the water cascading over the rocks. It was late in the day when they had arrived and they had to prepare for the fast approaching darkness, so they saw little of the beauty all around them. But there was always tomorrow.

In no hurry, they laid in bed late the next morning, listening to the roar of the waterfall. Upon arising they washed their hands and face in the cold water from the pool at the face of the falls before they ate the breakfast Kabuta had prepared.

They all walked out from under the trees into a clearing where they could get a better look at the falls.

The Chief said, "This is the best time of the day to see the falls because the sun is just at the right height."

They stood in awe at the beauty of the multicolored rainbows and what looked like millions of huge diamonds dancing on the misty water as it cascaded down.

"Listen," Mike whispered, "Do you hear singing? Do the angels come here to play, too? Katy, it's as beautiful here as it is on the shores of Killarney Lakes in Ireland. I'll take you back some day, to see my beautiful home in County Kerry.

"I'd love it, of course, but could we take Peg and Kabuta with us? I'm afraid they have become like a pair of comfortable shoes—I don't want to go anywhere without them."

"I understand. Kabuta has become my strong right arm and best friend. I couldn't get along without him."

They camped here for the rest of their stay and rode back to every geyser great and small, and every creek. But Kabuta was disappointed that he never saw the big one erupt again, but he never tired of Old Faithful that put on a show every hour.

They hunted, fished or just laid in the shade, enjoying this time of leisure.

On their way back to the village Mike and Kabuta brought down two big bucks with their bows and gave them to the Chief.

Katy and Peg were getting more irritable as they got heavy and awkward with child. A couple of weeks after they returned from exploring the valley, Peg came wobbling into Katy's teepee right after Kabuta and Mike had escaped outside to get away from their complaining. She was holding her stomach with both hands and Katy was doing the same as she went to put water on for tea.

Suddenly Katy screamed, "My water broke!"

Peg stuck her head out the teepee and called Mike, and he and Kabuta came running.

Running Springs heard Katy scream and she went and got her mother. They came over and Running Springs said, "Mike, you and Kabuta go fishing, hunting or something. This is a women thing."

As they lingered, Peg said, "Kabuta, Mike, get! Didn't you hear the woman?"

They got, but they didn't go fishing. Mike wasn't about to get far away and Kabuta stayed with his friend.

Katy was in labor for sixteen hours and it tore Mike apart every time he heard her scream.

Early in the morning, June 4, 1803, Katy gave Mike his son. He was a handsome baby; twenty inches long and weighed about eight pounds, five ounces, indicating that he would be a tall man like his dad.

He had a mop of auburn hair and his eyes were as blue as the clear blue sky. He announced to the world in a robust voice that Gabriel Will Ross had arrived.

It was three weeks later in the middle of the night that Peg woke Kabuta and said, "Go tell Running Springs and her mother, I think its time."

Kabuta, who was always so calm, fell apart. He jumped up and ran out of the teepee barefooted and in his underwear, screaming at the top of his voice,

"Mike, Running Springs, Peg is having a baby!" He woke half the village with his hollering.

Mike came running, and said, "Get a hold of yourself man; you'll wake the whole village."

Running Springs and her mother came and Running Springs said, "Mike, get this wild man out of here and let us do our work."

Mike led Kabuta down by the river and he quieted down, but he was a nervous man.

Peg didn't have as difficult birth as Katy did and ten hours after she went into labor she gave birth to an eight-pound boy, nineteen inches long. Like his parents, he was jet black and his hair was as black as a raven's wing. His eyes were dark brown. They named him Riley Michael, after Mike and his father.

Both mother and baby came through the birth experience with no complications.

Mike and Kabuta were strutting around the village as if they'd had a great deal to do with this ordeal of bringing these two stalwart young men into the world.

But everyone was happy and it was a time of great contentment.

CHAPTER TWENTY-FIVE

Mike and Kabuta stayed close to their families for a month after Riley was born. Then they took their axes and one of the wagons and went up on the mountain and started cutting logs. They hauled them to their teepees, where they built a framework, with a steep ridgepole from the door of Mike and Katy's teepee to the door of Kabuta and Peg's. They stretched buffalo hides over this framework, creating a waterproof passageway between the two teepees. Mike made a swinging door at each teepee.

They placed a swinging door into the passage half- way between the teepees.

Both families could remove their muddy boots here and put on moccasins before they entered the teepees. This would keep the cold air from entering their homes every time they opened the door.

The chiefs came over to inspect this strange contraption.

The Chief saw right away why they had built it. It would help keep the teepees warm and clean. He said, "Mike, when our wives see this they are going to be very hard to get along with unless they can have it too."

Kabuta said. "Mike, we could build them one if we had the buffalo robes. We used the last one we had."

Mike said, "Chief, if you can get us the buffalo hides we'll construct one that will connect all of your teepees. All of your chiefs' teepees are pitched in a circle. It would be an easy thing to do. Give us the men to cut the poles and

Kabuta and I will build the passageway."

"That's good; may we bring our squaws over to see what we are going to do for them?"

The Chief had three sub-chiefs and they each had three squaws

The Chief had three wives and he had three teepees and a storage teepee in the middle, and the sub-chiefs had copied his setup. The Chief put his woodcutters to falling and hauling logs while Mike and Kabuta constructed the framework. They constructed these passageways with plenty of doors so there was an easy escape in case of fire.

When they arrived in the valley they had seven mares and Mike's big black stud and the young black stud that was born on the journey here. All of the mares dropped foals and they were thankful that six of them were fillies. The old mares were carrying again, but the young ones wouldn't be bred until they were eighteen months old.

Mike and Kabuta were looking over the stock one-day and Mike said, "Kabuta, we need more brood mares and more milk cows to build our remuda and dairy herd. It just isn't right that the chiefs and their families and we have milk and butter and the rest of the people have to go without."

Kabuta said, "Peg and I were talking about that, and she said she heard two of the women talking. They are getting jealous."

"What do you think about us going to the Chief and propose that we take ours and the tribe's furs to Saint Louis and trade them for more cows and mares and we'll share all we have with them?" Mike asked.

Kabuta said, "Now that we've decided to make our home here among the villagers and become a permanent part of it, I agree, with the stipulation that we get first choice of any horses we want for our families and give the Chief the privilege to give the others to any of his people he wants to. I would suggest that we keep any of the Indian studs away from our purebreds."

"We'll make that understood," Mike replied.

Kabuta said, "Let's go see the Chief. You do the talking, he expects that."

The chief was coming out of his teepee when they approached. Mike said, "My Chief, may we have a word with you?"

The Chief said, "Sit."

Mike said, "Chief, you can see that we have fine horses and you said you were getting fond of milk and butter. We don't have enough cows to furnish milk and butter for all of the people, and we don't think that is fair. We have many furs stored and your people have many more. In the spring Kabuta and I would like to take some braves and take those furs to Saint Louis and trade them for milk cows and a few more mares. Kabuta and I would like to give you first choice of any horse you want and let us have second choice of any horses we want for our families, and then you can distribute all the other horses to your people as you choose."

The Chief said, "I'll take it up with our counsel and let you know what we decide."

A few days later the Chief came to Mike and said, "The Counsel all agreed that this would make our squaws and children happy, but we would request that you bring back as many sewing kits as you can find, and some colored beads, if you have enough wampum."

Mike said, "Agreed, and we should build a warehouse in which to store all the community furs."

"Take any of the men you need and I'll leave that up to you."

They started building the warehouse right away so they would have it ready for the next winter.

One bright morning the Chief came to Mike and asked him to take a walk with him along the river. They chatted about a number of things when the Chief said nonchalantly, "Mike, I would like to give you Running Springs as your number two squaw."

Mike had seen this coming and he had tried to prepare Katy for it. He told her that he had no intention of letting it happen, saying, "I'm just not sure how to convince him that my faith won't permit me to take two wives; he may ban us from the village."

"Leave that to Peg and me," Katy said.

Katy spoke to Peg about it and Peg let out a low whistle and said, "I could have told you so, but Kabuta said to forget it, that Mike would know what to do."

I hope he does."

"Peg, Mike said the Chief might ban us from the village if he refused to marry her. This is the first time I've ever seen Mike unsure about anything."

Peg said, "Why don't we get Running Springs and her mother over here for coffee and some of your good cookies and just explain that our religion absolutely forbids it?"

"That's what I had in mind, but I wanted to see if you thought it would work."

"Katy, it just has to."

Early the next morning Peg invited the two ladies to Katy's teepee.

They arrived right on time and after they had visited for a while, Katy took a deep, steadying breath and blurted, "Running Springs, did you know that your father wants you to be Mike's number two wife?"

Running Springs gasped, "No! I don't want to marry your husband. I love Mike like a brother and you like a sister. I know you and Mike would never allow such a thing. When I marry, it'll be because I love a man the way you and Mike and Peg and Kabuta love each other. There will not be a number two wife for the man I marry, either, if I can prevent it. Mother doesn't like it either, but she had no choice. It's the way we do things.

"When we tell him that I will not marry anyone I do not choose myself, he'll get wild and cloud up like a great windstorm, but it will blow over. He won't force me to marry someone I don't love. Don't you worry, Katy, we'll take care of our Chief!"

When Mike came in that night with a frown on his face, Katy said, "Don't worry, honey, about the Chief's reaction, everything has been taken care of," as she smiled sweetly and kissed him.

One morning the Chief told them that they were going to move the village out onto the plains along the south side of the Big Horn River for the yearly buffalo hunt. "There will be plenty of them there by the time we get ready for them. The older men and women and a few braves will remain here. Crazy Horse and his warriors will remain here to protect our village. All the rest of the village will move next week."

Shortly after they were established in the village Mike and Kabuta had taken a dozen braves and all the sledgehammers they had and went to the place where they'd been unable to get the wagons through. They worked many days breaking up rock to make a trail so they could get a heavy load through by using two teams to each wagon.

When Mike told the Chief that they could travel this way now with the wagons and travois's he was pleased. This would cut many days off of the time it used to take them to travel around the mountain—now that they could go through.

As soon as they had their temporary village set up, the men started cutting dead wood for the cooking fires. They had killed a couple of elk for fresh meat but the chiefs were worried. The hunters had ridden far and wide, but there were no buffalo. They knew that if the buffalo didn't come they would have to settle for what elk, deer, mountain lion and bear they could find. They could survive on that, but they much preferred buffalo and they needed the hides.

The wise Chief timed the hunt each year as near as he could figure to when the snow would fall so they could hang fresh meat in the trees to freeze and not spoil, and the delay of the buffalo run was causing him great concern.

One morning it was bitterly cold and Mike saw him studying the skies over the mountains. Mike said, "Good morning, Chief. It's cold this morning."

"Yes, Brother Mike. And if the buffalo don't come soon we will have to give up the hunt. It's cold enough for us to preserve our meat, but if a storm comes we could never get it back to our village."

Mike said, "We will pray that God will hold back the storm. He does control everything, and He tells us to ask for the things we need and He will give it to us."

"I have been praying to the Great Spirit, but I don't know this God you talk about. If you know him, pray, my brother that the buffalo will come in time. I would like to know this God of yours."

Mike said, "Kabuta, Peg, Katy and I have been praying and we believe the buffalo will come."

"Sometimes they don't, Mike, and it makes the winters hard when they fail to come."

When Mike told Katy about this conversation with the Chief after they returned to the village, she said, "Did you lead him to Christ?"

"I started to try to, but the Holy Spirit stopped me. We'll pray that it happens, but if it does it will be in God's time."

They had been burning huge bonfires night and day for two weeks because they needed the ashes to tan the hides if the herds came. When they finally came, it looked like a black sea flowing slowly toward them as they came, eating the tall, nutritious prairie grass. When they reached the valley where the tribe usually made their kill, they were fat and healthy.

Mike took the Chief and showed him where to shoot the buffalo and he was surprised when Mike told him to shoot them in the brain. They had always shot them in the heart with their bows and arrows, just behind the front shoulder.

The Chief squeezed the trigger and a young cow dropped in her tracks. And the others didn't seem to notice and the crack of the rifle shot didn't disturb them at all. Mike handed the Chief his rifle and reloaded the Chief's. They continued in this manner until the Chief had killed a dozen and Kabuta got a half dozen.

The braves were disappointed when the Chief had held them back at Mike's request. Mike wanted to be sure of a good kill before the Indians caused the herd to run. The Chief said to the braves, "You can have your fun in two days. These we have now will keep us busy for at least that long."

Kabuta rigged up a tripod and used the block and tackle to lift the buffalo so they could back the wagons under them to be lowered into them. They hauled them to where they had erected long poles between trees and hung them up with their heads toward the ground so it would be easier to skin, gut and bleed them.

The hunt was so successful that they worked in shifts night and day, butchering and cooking until they had enough jerky to last them all winter, and it was cold enough that they would have plenty of fresh meat. As they were traveling through the canyon toward the hard climb where they had broken up the rocks, the Chief rode alongside the wagon Mike was driving and said, "Mike, look at the clouds gathering over the mountains, it's snowing in our village. We are getting through the mountains just in time. Mike, I've got to meet your God."

It was the Indian custom for the men to do the hunting and the women did most of the hard work in butchering and preparing meat and tanning of hides, and making the moccasins and clothing. The young girls spent most of their time helping their mothers or gathering wood. Now that the men had come with axes and wagons the children had more time to play and Mike and Kabuta started doing the butchering and some of the braves helped them. This gave the squaws more time to rest.

One of the things some of the Indian men didn't like about Mike and Kabuta was they did much of what they considered women's work and their squaws had noticed it and started complaining for the first time in their lives. All the chiefs' wives asked Katy and Peg to meet with them for a confab down by the river where none of the men could listen in.

When they were all seated in a circle Running Springs' mother said, "Katy, we want to know why your men help you so much."

Katy said, "Peg; would you like to tell them?"

Peg laughed. "I never thought you were bashful, Katy, but I would be delighted."

Peg said, "Our good friends, our men don't want us to get too tired to be good lovers."

Katy said "Our men know if we're too tired we don't like making love, but if we're rested we enjoy it as well as they do and that makes it better for them too, and we do it more often."

The Chief's head wife told him what Peg and Katy said and the wise old Chief called a meeting of his counsel. The counsel all agreed that they would call a meeting of all the married men and tell them they were going to try this for three months to see if it worked.

Many of the men weren't happy about this because it meant they would have to start doing things they had always considered women's work, but they would not incur the Chief's wrath.

At the end of the experiment the work was going smoother and the women were much happier, and very few of the men wanted to go back to the old ways. When the winter snow had iced over and the lake and the river were frozen over, the work for the men grew harder because they had to cut holes in the ice every day so the stock could get to water, as well as for themselves. But it was a happy time too. There was time for story telling and much more time to love and be loved. Katy and Peg had given sewing kits and scissors to the chief's wives. This made the making of moccasins and clothing much easier and the men started learning to do these things just to break the monotony of the long winter.

The women had already come to love Katy and Peg and the gifts of the sewing kits endeared them to them all the more.

Near the end of January, 1804, Running Springs, Peg and Katy were sitting on the snow covered banks of the river, fishing through holes in the ice, when a young Indian brave staggered out of the brush on the opposite side of the river. He slipped and fell when he hit the ice and he slid halfway across the river, where he finally came to a stop. He lay there, unconscious, with his dark red blood staining the ice.

Running Springs ran and with Herculean strength and effort, she picked the young brave up in her arms, slipping and sliding until she gained the snow covered bank, where she practically flew to her teepee and laid him on her own sleeping pad.

Katy and Peg retrieved their fish and lines and followed her as quickly as they could. Katy cleaned the fish and Peg made fish chowder to feed the young man if he regained consciousness.

Running Springs asked her mother to heat water and she went to find Michael to take care of the man's wounds. She knew this might offend the Shaman, but she had learned to trust Michael's medicine more.

When Mike came into the teepee he found the young man stripped to his waist and Running Springs was cleaning some nasty cuts on his left shoulder and arm and a deep rip across his chest. She stepped back when Mike entered the teepee and said, "Save him for me, Brother Mike."

Kabuta stuck his head in the teepee and said, "Can I be of any help?"

"Go get me a lot of fine hair out of a horse's mane and put it into the boiling water as soon as I remove the scissors," Mike said. Then added, "And a quart of whiskey."

Mike washed his hands thoroughly in hot soapy water and boiled scissors and needles in hot water for twenty minutes. Shortly after he had placed these utensils on a clean rag Kabuta dropped the hair into the water.

Michael was thankful the brave was unconscious because the pain would be intense when he poured the hundred-proof whiskey into the cuts to kill the germs, and he wouldn't feel the needle as he sewed up the cuts. He put a hundred stitches in the young man's cuts, which looked like he had been clawed by some animal. It was obvious that the heavy buffalo coat he wore saved his life, if he lived. Michael imagined he must have fought the animal desperately.

The young man had lost so much blood that he lay on Running Springs' bed, hovering between life and death for a week before he started showing some improvement. They had been able to get enough water and soup in him to sustain him, but when he regained consciousness he ate heartily. He regained his strength quickly and his wounds were healing nicely.

Running Springs came to Mike and said, "Mike, the brave you saved said his name is Running Deer and his wounds are itching at every stitch so badly he can't keep from scratching them."

"Tell him that I'll be over after a while to remove the stitches and pour more whiskey over the wounds to relieve the itching. Just praise God they are itching; it means he's getting well."

Mike removed the stitches and saturated a clean rag with whiskey and gently applied it over the itching wounds as Running Deer gritted his teeth.

Then he told them his story; how he had been viciously clawed by a huge mountain lion. "I spent the night rolled up in my blankets in a narrow gorge underneath an overhanging rock. In the morning I crawled out from under the rock, stood and stretched my cramped muscles just as a large cat sprang at me from a cliff.

"I had just enough time to draw my knife with my right hand and throw my left arm up to protect my face when the big cat knocked me over. We rolled down the slope of the gorge, with the cat screaming and clawing me. It's a mystery to me that he never bit me at all. It might have been because I was stabbing him in the side. When he finally went limp and fell away from me, I realized that my knife blade had finally reached his heart.

"I knew of your village and I tried to get here for help, and I'm thankful to the Great Spirit that Running Springs was the one who brought me to you, white man, and nursed me back to health. I've heard bad things about white men, but you are the only one I've ever seen, and I will be your friend as long as I live. I owe my life to you."

"No, you don't," Mike said, "You owe your life to Running Springs for getting you to me as quickly as she did so I could stop the bleeding. You would not have lived if you lost much more blood. If she had walked from the river instead of running, you would have died.

"Katy and Peg still don't understand how she did it, but she picked you up and ran swiftly with you for a quarter of a mile. No, it was not I that saved your life, Running Deer, Running Springs did."

Running Deer said, "The river is still frozen over and the ground covered with snow. Has it snowed since I came here?"

"No," Mike said.

"Then my trail would be easy to follow. I'd like to go back to see if the wild animals have found that big cat. If they haven't, he will still be frozen and his flesh would be good roasted over the spit. I would love to be able to tan his hide so I could show my children someday the big cat that scarred my body."

The following day Mike, Kabuta and Running Deer were delighted when they found the big cat back underneath a bush, still intact.

Running Deer went straight to bed when they reached the village because he was all in.

Kabuta skinned and dressed the cat for the spit, and Running Springs took the hide to Running Deer and said, "We thought you would want to tan the hide while you are getting well."

He reached for her hand and looked deep into her eyes, and said, "Thank you, my star."

They roasted the cat and after Running Deer ate the plate of food that Running Springs brought him he said, "He was a strong cat, and now I have his strength in me to help me get strong again."

Katy and Peg both commented how much they liked the roast, and Mike said, "Didn't Kabuta and I tell you it was good? Don't you remember the first time you ate it?"

Katy said, "Of course we do, but this is the first we've had since then."

By the time Running Deer had regained his strength, everyone could see the love that had developed between him and Running Springs.

On June 15, 1804, Running Springs married the man of her choice, just as she had said she would.

Before they were married Running Springs saw the love and respect that Mike and Kabuta had for Katy and Peg and she wanted desperately to have that same kind of love and respect from Running Deer. And she wanted to be such a good wife that he would never want another, so she decided to ask Peg and Katy for advice. She asked them many questions, and by the time they were through talking most of her anxiety was eased. She asked the girls to ask Mike and Kabuta if they would have a talk with Running Deer also.

Mike and Kabuta invited Running Deer to go fishing with them and as they sat on the banks of the river they talked the afternoon away. Kabuta said, "Running Deer, have you ever had a woman?"

It took Running Deer completely off guard and he was embarrassed and he hesitated before he stammered, "No."

Then Mike said, "Then you must be nervous about your wedding night?"

"Yes."

Kabuta put his arm across his shoulder and said, "My friend, would you like two old married men to give you a little advice on how you should treat your bride on your wedding night?"

"Yes, I would be very happy."

Then Mike told him every move he should make on their wedding night before he consummated their marriage.

Kabuta said, "If you do as Mike said she will be ready to receive you, and your wedding night will be beautiful, like the Great Spirit intended it to be."

Then Mike said, "If you are too soon and hurt her, your lovemaking might never be as beautiful as it should be. If your first union is as it should be, she will never have any fear; in fact, there may be times that she will come to you and ask for it in subtle ways."

Twelve months later, the union of these two produced a fine son, whom they named Sitting Bull.

CHAPTER TWENTY-SIX

Sitting Bull, Riley, and Gabriel were seldom apart as they grew to manhood. They were very competitive, trying to outdo one another in all kinds of weaponry, horse riding, wrestling and boxing.

Generally, they were equal in everything except wrestling. Riley was a little bigger than Sitting Bull or Gabriel and he was by far the strongest of the three.

Mike and his little group had become an integral part of the village and the Chief expected them to share in everything. They were treated no better and no worse than anyone else in the village. If a fight arose with some other tribe they were expected to fight along with the braves. There had been only one fight since they'd unofficially joined the tribe

One of their hunting parties under the leadership of Running Deer had killed a young buffalo, skinned, gutted and butchered it. They laid the skin on a travois with the hair down, and wrapped it around the meat, tied it together, and started back to the village.

Theirs was a strong village and no one had disturbed them in a long time, so they weren't expecting trouble this close to the village.

They were taken completely by surprise when a dozen Indians hit them from both sides of the trail.

Two of Running Deer's men were hit in the back and they were dead before they hit the ground, and three other were wounded badly, as they scattered for the brush. The attack was swift and effective.

Running Deer and his three wounded companions were separated and had no chance for a counter attack. Running Deer lay low and waited until the Indians disappeared, leading the horse that was trailing the travois with its precious cargo of meat. After he was sure they were gone, he found his wounded companions and helped them on their horses and sent them to the village. He said, "You get to the Shaman as quickly as you can and I will see about our brothers."

When he found their companions both of them had a large hole in their backs and he could see where a muddy moccasin had been placed on their back so the arrows could be jerked out. They were both scalped. "Shoshone Apache," Running Deer whispered. He had some difficulty getting the men on their horses. When he did, he tied their hands to their legs underneath their horses with leather thongs.

The three wounded men were very weak, and were riding slowly, and Running Deer caught up with them just before they entered the village. After they reached the village there was much weeping and wailing over the two dead braves.

Mike and Kabuta couldn't understand why the Chief didn't send men after the culprits right away.

"We must give the people time to mourn," the Chief said.

Mike said, "But if they get away with this, won't they think we are weak and come back with a bigger force?"

The chief said, "Running Deer wants to go after them too, but he said there were twelve or more Shoshone Apache, my brother. They are fierce fighters and I would have to send a large force after them, and if they do attack the village with a large force, I'll need every man to protect our women and children."

Mike said, "Give me Running Deer and three of your best braves and Kabuta, and we'll go after them. One of your wounded men said he knew that their village was far south of us over the mountains. They're pulling a travois with a heavy load of meat, which will slow them down. They'll expect us to take time for mourning, or they'll think we are a bunch of old women with no courage to fight.

"Our guns and hounds are strong medicine. Let us go bring our meat back and avenge our two brothers."

The Chief grasped Mike's hand and said, "It's almost dark. Go with the rising of the sun, my brother."

That night Mike and Kabuta had a hard time convincing their wives that going after the murderers was the thing to do.

"Peg, Katy, if we don't stop them before they reach their village, they may bring a large force and try to drive us out of our valley. This valley is a prize that any tribe would love to have. I, for one, don't want to leave it."

Kabuta said, "Neither do I."

Peg said, "Katy, my friend, we must let them go with our blessing. They're going anyway, can't you see that? And we'll love them for it because they're risking their lives for us."

"You're right, of course."

Early the next morning Katy, Peg, and Running Springs clung to their husbands for a long time before they kissed them good-bye. They bit their lips and refused to cry. But after they were out of sight they hugged one another tightly and cried shamelessly.

The Chief had said, "I wish I could go with you, but my place is here with my people to direct them in case there is an attack on our valley.Other tribes have tried to drive us out before, and failed miserably. So they have left us at peace for a long time. I will die before I let anybody take our Valley of the Smokes. We have been safe here ever since my father brought us here when I was a small papoose. Now go with your God's protection."

"Chief, Our God is the Great Spirit that you pray to."

They had to tie Daisy up for the first time since they arrived here because she had just birthed ten pups and was still too weak for a long run and a fierce fight.

By mid-afternoon they had arrived at the spot where the ambush took place. The trail was easy to follow. The travois was loaded with a good-sized buffalo and the tracks had cut deep into the moist soil.

They had followed the trail for about two hours when they came to a small creek. They staked their horses on the lush spring grass where they could reach the water. Kabuta went to the creek and started feeling under the bank and was soon pitching fish out on the bank. The Indians started cleaning them as Mike got a fire started. Mike was sure the Shoshone wouldn't expect them to be on their trail this soon, they also knew that they'd travel as fast as they could for the first few days to put as much distance between them they could. Building a fire was safe, for now.

They had eaten and had the fire out before dark and were all sound asleep, with dogs standing watch, by the time night shadows stole over the mountain. By daylight they were riding as fast as the terrain would allow, eating cold pemmican and drinking creek water as they rode. They took no time for lunch, but pushed on.

Near the end of the day Mike suggested they camp where they were without a fire. "Running Deer, you and the others get some rest. Kabuta and I are going to scout on ahead."

Kabuta said, "Mike, they can't be far ahead. Look at Shep, he's had a whiff of them or he heard something."

Shep's body was taut with attention, his head was up, and he was staring forward between the travois tracks.

"I think you're right," Mike said. He scratched Shep's ears and said, "Good dog, Shep old boy, you rest now. We'll take it from here."

Shep wandered over to where the grass was thicker and lay down with his head on his paws and closed his eyes.

Mike and Kabuta slipped quietly through the brush and hadn't gone more than a half mile when they heard laughter up ahead. They crawled into a clump of brush and laid low until a faint moon rose over the mountain peak. Trillions of stars sparkled like a sea of diamonds and lit up the small clearing where the Indians had tied up their horses.

The braves didn't seem concerned at all, they had eaten and were lying around a huge bonfire on their blankets, telling stories and laughing as though they didn't have a care in the world.

Mike and Kabuta located and counted twelve braves before they eased back out of the brush, stood up and beat a retreat back to their camp.

Kabuta built a small fire in a sheltered spot and boiled coffee, and Mike gave everyone an elk steak sandwich and a piece of chocolate cake that Katy and Peg had prepared for them. Mike wished he dared to cook bacon to place over the elk steak. He wanted this meal to be the best it could be. They would attack the Apache camp at daybreak and he was aware this could be the last meal for some, possibly all of them.

Mike said grace, and then they ate heartily but quietly.

Kabuta said, "Men, if you have a pipeline to the Great Spirit I would suggest you talk to him tonight, I'm sure going to pray to God that he blesses our endeavor in the morning."

Mike said, "Amen, now let's get some sleep."

When Mike and his small band of men slipped quietly near to the Apache camp, Mike pointed out to the others that one of the blankets was empty. He said, "I hope he returns to his blanket soon. You all stay here; I want to scout around a bit."

He wasn't gone long, and when he returned he said, "He's removing something from one of the horses' hoof, if he comes in after we attack he'll be coming from that direction," and he pointed east.

Mike placed his men around the sleeping Indians, leaving the space where the man attending the horse would come from. Mike said, "Don't shoot until I turn the dogs loose. Pick out the man closest to you and shoot to kill."

The man had not returned when the other Indians started to stir. One man put wood on the fire and two others joined him to warm themselves when Mike gave the dogs the command to attack.

The three men saw these huge dogs leap for them and the big man putting wood on the fire swung a stick at Shep and broke his left front leg, and when Shep hit the ground the Indian started to crush his head with the stick when Mike cut him down with a 44 slug through the back of his neck, shattering his spine. The other two dogs knocked their opponents to the ground and the men fought furiously, but they had no weapons and the dogs finally found their throats and shook the life out of them.

The other eight Indians dashed for their knives and bows, but Running Deer shot one through the heart before he could reach his weapons, and two of Mike's braves shot two more, but they were able to get their knives even though they were wounded. Mike's two men went into them with knives drawn and the four men were locked in mortal conflict.

It was a fierce fight, and Mike's men were cut badly, but they eventually killed their opponents. The other three bolted for the brush. One ran right into where Mike was hiding and Mike shot him through the head with his pistol. The other man ran into the brave, who was the brother of one of the Indians that the Apache's had scalped.

As the Apache approached him, leaping over bushes, the brave's arrow missed, but he stepped in front of the running Apache with his knife drawn. These two Indians were locked in mortal combat, one with a frenzy of fear, and the other with the hot blood of revenge for his brother running through his veins. He took a number of bad cuts before he put his opponent away.

The last brave that was in the camp when the attack started was just a boy, with no weapons, and his only thought was to get away and he ran right into the vice-like grip of Kabuta's arms. He fought valiantly, kicking and clawing, trying to break free. Kabuta keep saying in the boy's ear in every Indian dialect he had learned, "Stop boy, I won't hurt you, I have a son of my own."

Finally the boy realized that Kabuta wasn't going to hurt him and he ceased to struggle, but he had left his mark on Kabuta's face with his sharp finger-nails. The Indian that had been attending the horse came running and when he saw the boy struggling with Kabuta he started toward them with a knife in his hand.

Mike ran toward the charging Indian and raised his pistol to fire, but he caught the toe of his boot on a root and fell forward onto the brave's legs. His shot went into the ground at the Indian's feet, and his pistol was knocked from his hands.

The brave went down, but he came up fast, facing Mike, who had drawn his knife. They each tried to stab the other, and then grabbed each other's wrist. Strong and agile, the brave heeled Mike, sending him down on his back and knocking the breath out of him. As Mike fell, he brought his knee up in the Indian's crotch. It took both of them a few moments to regain their composure and spring back to their feet.

When the young man that Kabuta was holding saw the big man hurling himself at Kabuta he screamed, "Father," and nearly broke free. Kabuta had his hands full and Mike couldn't expect any help from him. And the Indian code wouldn't let them interfere when two great braves were fighting one-on-one.

Mike had dropped his knife when he hit the ground, and when he faced the brave he had no weapon in his hand. The brave lunged at him, but Mike dropped to the ground, rolled sideways and tripped the Indian. They both came up quickly and the brave lunged again, but Mike had time to reach the knife that he wore in a sheath that hung between his shoulder blades. He threw it and it sank deep into his opponent's chest.

When the young brave saw that his father was dead, and noticed the dead all around him, he screamed, "Kill me too!"

The Indian, whose brother had been scalped said, "Kill him."

Mike put his arm across the Indian's shoulder, and said gently, "No, my brother. We want him to go back to his people and tell them what happened and what powerful medicine we have. Believe me, these dogs will be as big as mules and our shotguns will be cannons. Kabuta will be a black giant, and all of us will be ten foot tall by the time he tells this story."

Mike turned to the boy and said, "Young man, is there plenty of meat in your village?"

"Our children cry from hunger," the boy said.

Mike said, "We will load the bodies on their horses and you can take them and the meat to your village. Tell your Chief that I said not to take this bit of kindness as weakness. We are a strong village with strong medicine. Our dogs are fierce fighters and our braves are more so. We want peace, but if any of your people come against any of our people again, we will come to your village and kill you all."

After they had the horses loaded with their gruesome burden, Mike took his shotgun and the boy to an old rotten pine stump and said, "Watch the stump." He loaded both barrels with double ought buckshot and pressed the butt of the gun firmly to his shoulder and let go with both barrels. The old pine stump disintegrated before their eyes. "Now go tell your story to your chief, "Mike said.

As the young man rode away Mike said, "Farewell, brave young warrior."

Mike, Kabuta, Running Deer and the three braves went back to the village in their beloved Valley of the Smokes, satisfied that the Shoshone Apache would never bother them again.

They went and gave their report to the Chief and then the men went to be wrapped in anxious, loving arms.

Mike put a splint on Wolf's leg so it would mend. Wolf would have a slight limp, but he would serve his master for many more years.

CHAPTER TWENTY-SEVEN

The winter catch of pelts was enormous that year and the warehouse was full of prime pelts. Mike was trying to figure the fastest way to get them to market in Saint Louis. They could take them across country in the wagons, now that they had cleared a road through the mountains, but it would take them much of the summer and Mike and Kabuta agreed that they didn't want to be away from their families that long. He knew that they were going to have to break more land for growing wheat and corn to feed the increase of stock through the winter months, and he was in hopes of bringing back two or three more wagons and mules to pull them.

Mike and Kabuta started constructing a large sailboat and by the time they had finished it the ice on the river had broken up and swept away, and the river was running swift and high.

Mike, Kabuta, Running Deer and five young braves had become hunting and fishing buddies. Mike went to the Chief and said, "Good morning, Chief, may Kabuta and I take Running Deer and five braves of our choosing to take the furs to market? We want to leave as soon as we can load the boat."

The Chief granted Mike his wish and said, "Oh! How I wish I could go with you, but I don't dare. The Shoshone Apache might try to seek revenge this spring and I must be here to defend our valley.

Mike went to where Running Deer and the five braves were putting the last coat of pine pitch on the boat and said, "That's enough, men. Now go get cleaned up and tell your families we'll be leaving for Saint Louis in three days."

Mike and his party kissed their wives and children good-bye and sailed down the Yellowstone, headed for the Big Muddy.

Everyone in the village was strung out along the riverbank to see them off.

Katy, Peg and Running Springs stood watching until the boat sailed around a bend in the river, out of sight, before they turned and started for their teepees.

As they walked toward the village Peg's voice broke when she said, "I'm lonely already."

Katy broke into a run and Peg and Running Springs were right behind her and they all ran into Katy's place crying hard. Running Springs' mother came over and tried to comfort them, but she was largely unsuccessful.

The river was flowing swiftly after the ice had melted, and the snow pack in the higher elevations in the mountains was melting fast by a warm spring rain. Mike didn't have to raise their sails at all; in fact, he was having some difficulty keeping the boat in the middle of the river. More than once he had to dodge around some large trees that were floating downstream slower than they were.

One time the boat hung up on the branches of a tree that was stuck in the middle of the river under water. The men had a hard time getting the boat free and they were soaking wet when they climbed back into the boat.

It was late in the afternoon and they were making such good time. Mike decided they would stop for the night as soon as they could find a place to tie up. When he saw a small stream flowing into the Yellowstone near a large bay tree, he eased the boat into the mouth of the little stream and Kabuta jumped out and tied the bow to the tree. The water swung the boat around and they tied the stern to another tree and drew the boat tightly against the bank.

Mike got a fire going so the men could get dry, they were all shivering from the cold, and as the men stood around the fire to get dry Running Deer took his bow and faded into the forest to find their supper.

There was a dead oak tree nearby, so Mike cut enough firewood to stack on the boat to last them all the way to Saint Louis. By the time he finished cutting up the wood Kabuta had the fire roaring and most of the men were dry.

Kabuta was preparing sheepherder bread when Running Deer came into camp with the best cuts of a deer. They dined on sheepherder bread and steaks that each man roasted over the fire.

This had been a hard day. They were tired and they banked the fire and rolled into their bedrolls very early.

Mike said, "We'll stop each day after we see a good place to tie up after mid-afternoon from here on, but we will be floating down the river at daybreak each day."

The next morning when Mike hollered, "Rise and shine!" the men were glad to see that Mike had the fire going, water boiling and deer steaks cooking on an iron grill. They would drink hot water tea. They had run out of coffee, tea and sugar weeks ago. That was the main reason that Mike set out when he did. He knew it would have been much safer if he had waited until this wild river settled down a little, but they were all missing their two favorite hot drinks, as well as the sugar to sweeten them with. They only ate two meals a day because they would only tie up at night.

That night as they lay in their bedrolls, Mike said, "Kabuta, this old river is flowing fast. We must have floated two hundred or more miles today."

Kabuta said, "It sure beats looking at the rear end of mules all day too, doesn't it"

"You can say that again," Mike laughed. He added, "We'll be doing that many days on the way back."

"Yeah, I'm dreading that long haul, especially without Peg to keep me warm at night."

"We won't have our comfortable beds, either," Mike said, "Now let's get some sleep."

The following night when they tied up and got their meal prepared, Mike called a conference. "We didn't see a log in the river all day and the moon is almost full," he said. "We can sleep on the furs on the boat. Let's float downriver all night."

By doing this for the rest of the way they were tying up at the dock in Saint Louis early in the morning of the seventh day after leaving the valley along the Yellowstone.

Mike took them to a cafe and they ate the first bacon and eggs Mike and Kabuta have had for a long time, and it was the first time any of the Indians had ever tasted bacon.

Mike said, "Running Deer, you and the rest of the men stay with the boat and Kabuta and I will go and see if we can purchase a couple of wagons and some mules."

When they reached the trading post there were a dozen mules in a corral and a number of wagons all in a row. Mike said, "Kabuta, would you check these wagons and see if any of them would serve our purpose? I'll go in the stables and see if I can get someone out here to do business with."

Mike went into a large salesroom attached to the stables and a man was waiting on a customer. When the man started to leave Mike said to the proprietor, "I'm Michael Ross and I'm looking for a dozen good mules and harness for them, and two good wagons."

"Mr. Ross, I'm Jim Butler, pleased to meet you. I have eight young mules in the corral that are about half broke for the wagons, and two slightly older that are as steady as a rock. I have some used wagons for sale at various prices. But I have only eight sets of harness."

"Let's look them over," Mike said.

Mike had noticed that the man leaving the store paused for a moment when he told Mr. Butler he was looking for mules and wagons.

When he and Mr. Butler went out to where the wagons were parked he saw the man talking to Kabuta.

When Mike and Mr. Butler walked up Mike said, "Mr. Jim Butler, meet my partner, Mr. Kabuta." The men shook hands and Mike said, "What do you think of the wagons, Kabuta?"

"One of them is a good wagon, but I don't think the others would make it through the mountains with the loads we'll be hauling. I've had a good look at the mules too. They are mighty skittish, but they look like they'll whip into shape, and they're what we're looking for."

Mr. Butler said, "Eight of them are about half broke to harness, but the other two are steady."

"We can handle them," Kabuta said, "but Mike, we're going to have our hands full driving the extra horses and cows with two of us driving wagons. Mister Timmins here said he has a good wagon and four good mules and six sets of good harness for sale. He said this was the end of the road for him and his missus."

Mike said, "Mister Butler, we'll take your mules and harness, and the one wagon and eight of the best saddles you have. Kabuta, why don't you go with Mr. Timmins and if you like those mules and his wagon, bring them back to the dock and we'll buy them also, and thank God we've been so fortunate as to find them."

When Kabuta and Mr. Timmins drove up to the dock Mike could see that the wagon was a sturdy one and those big Missouri mules were fine looking. You could tell right away that Mr. Timmins was a man that took good care of his belongings.

Kabuta said, "Mike, if you'll take care of Mr. Timmins, we'll start loading furs."

He pulled in on the dock and Running Deer came and joined him in the wagon and the other men started tossing bundles of furs to them.

When Kabuta pulled up in front of the trading post with the wagon piled high with furs, Mr. Butler let out a low whistle and said, "I've never seen this many furs come in at one time before." When he had examined and graded the furs, he said, "Mr. Ross, these furs are top grade. I can use all you can bring in and I pay top dollar. I'll take all the buffalo, deer, elk, bear, and cow hides, and mountain lion, beaver and any other kind of fur you can bring me"

Mike and Kabuta were flabbergasted at how much they got for the furs. They looked all over the store and decided that just about everything they needed was right here. Mike purchased every cook stove and cast iron heater he had in the place. He bought twenty good rifles and cases of ammunition, as well as the following: every barrel of flour, sugar, coffee, tea, salt, pepper, dried beans, and dried fruits of every kind; every sewing kit and all the thread and buttons with beads of every color in the rainbow. Twenty good skinning knives, twenty more axes and a turning plow, and a walking corn planter.

They loaded the stoves, planter and plow in one wagon and poured wheat all around them. When they loaded up all the barrels of foodstuffs the other wagon was nearly full.

Kabuta said, "We've forgotten bacon, side meat, and cured hams, if you have them."

Mr. Butler said, "I've got two barrels of bacon, two of ham hocks, one of side meat, and one of hams."

Mike said, "We'll take them, and we've got to buy another wagon. We've got to have a wagonload of seed corn."

"I have the corn," Mr. Butler said.

Kabuta said, "Mr. Timmins has another wagon for sale as good as this one."

"Go get it," Mike said. "Mr. Butler, if you can tell me where I can buy some chickens, cows, mares and a couple of sows and one boar, I'd like to leave the mules and supplies with you until I can purchase them, and we'll be on our way. We have a long way to go and our wives are going to be worried until we get back."

Mr. Butler said, "Your things will be safe with me. Leave them as long as you like and I'll see that your mules are fed plenty of corn so they'll be fit for the long haul. Where are you folks from?"

Mike said, "Many miles from here." He had no intention of telling anyone where his valley was.

Mr. Butler said, "Men, will you have furs like this next year?"

Kabuta said, "Every other year; we won't make this trip every year. If you have any bear traps we could bring you a load of bear robes next time."

"I have twenty bear traps and about a hundred beaver traps back in the storehouse. Your furs and three hundred seventy-five dollars will cover your purchases, and if you promise to bring all your furs and hides to me, I'll throw in the traps."

Mike said, "We have a fine sailboat we need to sell. It just happens to be three hundred and seventy-five dollars," Mike laughed. "Do you think that's fair, Kabuta?"

"That's a mighty fine boat, Mike, and if we don't break it down and take it back with us we'll just have to build another one two years from now," Kabuta replied.

Mr. Butler was surprised that Mike asked a Black man his opinion, but he just said, "Let's go take a look at it."

He went over the boat, bow to stern. "I'll give you two hundred for it and if you bring me your furs two years from now on another boat like this, we may be able to take it off your hands, if it's as good as this one."

Mike said, "Anything Kabuta makes is the best."

Kabuta said, "Mike, if he'll throw in two each of those crosscut and ripsaws I saw hanging on the wall of the warehouse, with a dozen files to sharpen them with, I'd say it's a fair deal."

Mike said, "What about it, Mr. Butler?"

"Go get the saws, Kabuta, and I'll get the files for you."

Mike said, "Now tell me, where I can buy the horses?"

"The stable should have them. There's a poultry farm west of town and a dairy next door to it. They might sell you a few of what you want, but I doubt it, they're both doing a good business selling to the town folks."

Mike and Kabuta went to the stable and they had only four mares Kabuta would have.

Mike said, "We'll have to settle for them. If you agree, I'd like to get out of here tomorrow morning."

They paid for the horses with the understanding they would pick them up early the next morning.

Mike took all the men to the cafe for a good steak dinner. He asked the owner if they could get a good breakfast before sunrise the following morning, and he was assured they could.

The sun was just coming up when they pulled out of town, headed west.

When they came to the dairy, Mike went to see the owner. After introductions, Mike said, "I'm looking for two dozen young milk cows."

I can't sell you any of my milk cows, but I have that many young heifers that will be dropping their first calf in a few months. They'll run you fifty dollars each."

Mike said, I'll take them, and I'll give you another hundred for four of those young sows and one young boar, if you have crates I can put them in so I can throw them up on a load of corn."

"Mister, I have the crates and you have a deal."

They went next door to the chicken ranch, where Mike bought three-dozen white leghorn pullets and four young roosters in a wooden crate. The dairyman let Mike put his stock in a corral and feed them corn night and morning for a price, and they all slept under a grove of trees that night.

Early the next morning, Kabuta and their Indian friends headed west on their long journey back to the Valley of the Smokes. They were leading twenty-four young heifers that were fighting the ropes, making it more difficult until they realized it was better to follow along. Mike had gone back to St. Louis with the two ranchers to get the money to pay them for his purchases. He invited them to have lunch with him, and as they sat enjoying a good steak,

Mike said, "I wish I'd brought three or four more men with me. I sure could use them to drive those heifers."

About then four young men came into the cafe and ordered a meager meal. They were wearing old derby hats and spoke in a thick Irish brogue.

Mike heard one of them say, "Did you hear about the load of furs those men floated down the river?"

One of the others said, "If we had enough money to buy some traps and supplies we could go furring'."

Mike said, "Excuse me, gentlemen, I want to speak to my countrymen." He went over and introduced himself as Michael Ross from County Kerry. "It's good to meet some fellow Irishmen way out here."

The oldest of the four introduced himself as John O'Rourke, "And these are my brothers, Joseph, David and Peter. We went back home after a stretch in The Spanish Brigades to see our folks before coming to the new land. Our folks said there was a family near Killarney that were all killed in two separate tragedies, but one son, and he just disappeared and no one knows where he is."

Mike said, "Well, you've just found him, and I've a proposition for you. If you'll help me and my friends drive a small herd of cattle and take four heavily loaded wagons across the prairie and through some of the most rugged, but most beautiful, mountains you've ever seen, I'll outfit you with what you need. When you reach the valley, you're on your own.

"If you decide to stay, I'll give you a couple dozen traps. The winters are long and cold and you'll have to build a cabin this summer and cut enough wood to last you through the winter. You'll be required to hunt and plant to help supply food for a large Indian village, if the Chief will allow you to stay. We take care of one another out there. Shirkers will be driven from the village to shift for themselves, and one man alone wouldn't last long out there.

"You must consider this carefully because life is hard, especially for a man who doesn't have a woman to help keep his bed warm at night. There are some beautiful Indian maidens, but the Chief won't tolerate any fooling around with them. He'll allow a white man to marry one if he thinks he'll treat her right. But the man that doesn't will be severely punished.

"If you have good horses, weapons and plenty of ammunition, and good warm clothing, you can ride out with me this afternoon to catch up with the rest of my party. Oh, and one other thing—my partner and best friend is a big black man, and you may be told to do something by him. I'll expect you to do it without question. If you have tempers, I'd advise you to curb them. If you're drinkers, forget the whole deal. Those are my terms."

John said, "We have all those things and a pack horse, but we're short on food supplies. We'll have no problem obeying orders. We left the Spanish Brigades only a year ago, remember--- we're used to taking orders. We're good with guns, bow and arrow or blades of all kinds. If there is a fight, you'll find us handy. We've worked hard all our lives and we're not shirkers.

"We've done our share of drinking and fighting, but we've had so little money for the last six months we haven't bought a drink in a long time. And we haven't been in a scrap since we left the army. I think we can fit in all right, and we're happy to tie up with a fellow Irishman that knows his way around. Mister Ross, we have very little money left."

"It's Mike, John, and you won't need any money after we leave St. Louis, and that will be in thirty minutes if you're going with me. Don't worry about food, we have plenty."

Mike had mailed letters to the O'Casey's, Captain Alcott, the Fullers and Ted Chambers. He'd also written his banker in Richmond advising him to transfer all his assets to their branch in St. Louis. He had mailed letters from Katy and Peg to Katy's parents, and one to Ellis and Lola from Kabuta.

By one o'clock Mike and four other rugged Irishmen were riding fast to overtake the wagons. The trail was easy to follow, but dark caught them out on the prairie and they strayed off the trail, and when Mike realized it he called a halt. He fired his pistol in the air three times. Two shots rode faintly over the sound waves back to them. Mike kicked his horse into an easy gait and the brothers followed. When the five men rode to where they could barely make out the wagons and the animals scattered around them staked out on the grass, Mike hollered, "Hello, the camp. We're coming in."

Kabuta stepped out from behind a wagon with a rifle in his hand and two pistols strapped around his waist, and said, "Come on in, the coffee's hot."

Not until Mike had introduced the O'Rourke's to Kabuta and they saw them shake hands, did the six Indians come into the light of the campfire. And it didn't escape the O'Rourke's attention that they came in from six different directions.

The dogs charged Mike and he rolled on the prairie grass with them.

Joseph said, "Begorra', Mike, seeing those hounds make me think of home."

The grass was lush and green and the game was fat and tender. They ate well on the way home.

Running Deer said, "Mike, because we had a heavy snow fall this winter and the spring rains have been heavy, all the little streams will be running. We can go across country instead of following the rivers. We can cut off eight or ten days going that way. We won't have to go through the mud flats and sand hills where the flies eat you alive, either."

Mike said, "Kabuta and I were dreading those mud flats and sand hills, but we were especially dreading the flies."

Running Deer said, "The pheasants and prairie chickens will have plenty of fresh eggs in them. When we scare one up we should be able to find all the fresh eggs we can use and we can net fish out of the small creeks with ease."

Kabuta said, "Praise the Lord, doesn't that sound good, Mike? And I've been away from my Peg too long already."

"Isn't that the truth?" Mike said.

It took them fifty days to haul the heavy loads and drive the cattle to the village.

Mike and Kabuta were thrilled to be home to take their children on their laps while their loving wives placed food on the table.

John, Joseph, David and Peter O'Rourke were introduced to Katy and Peg, and Peg invited them to have supper with them.

After they ate Mike said, "Ladies, I'd do the dishes, but Kabuta and I must introduce our friends to the Chief and see if he'll allow them to join us."

When Mike and Kabuta took the four brothers to the Chief he welcomed them warmly. When Mike said, "My chief, I'd like you to meet my friends, John, Joseph, David, and Peter O'Rourke. They came from Ireland, near where I was born and raised. I think they are good men and would be an asset to your village, and they are here to ask you to allow them to join your people."

The Chief's smile faded as he studied the faces of these strangers for a long time, it seemed, before he said, "Kabuta, what do you think of these men?"

"They proved to me on our trip here that they are hard workers and men you can depend on. They have been soldiers in a foreign army and they know how to defend the village if we were ever attacked, and they assured us that they would serve you in any way you see fit."

"You must understand that my counsel and I are the law that governs our people. Before you do anything that affects the people, you must consult me. Is that understood?"

They quickly assured him that it was.

"Then if you contribute to the village as Mike and Kabuta have, you are welcome. I'm sure Mike has advised you how you must conduct yourselves among us. We will not allow our women to be disrespected. If you and one of our maidens become interested in one another, you may marry, but there is to be no foolishness beforehand. That keeps our village pure and it pleases the Great Spirit. Our people will watch you closely before they will accept you. If they see you are trustworthy, they will accept you in time, but you must be patient."

John said, "As the oldest, I promise you we won't do anything to cause you to regret your generosity. We have come from far across the ocean and our bodies carry scars from fighting many battles, and we will help you defend your people. But we desire a peaceful life. We're overjoyed to be here in your beautiful valley."

The Chief took the four brothers to a large teepee that they used for storage. It was empty now. "You may use this teepee until you can build your cabin, or a teepee of your own."

Peg, Katy and Running Springs had arranged to have Gabriel, Riley and Sitting Bull sleep over with some of their friends for their husband's homecoming.

When Mike came into their teepee he found Katy in bed waiting for him. She stretched out her arms and said, "Come to me, love." He crawled in beside her and was where he belonged, wrapped in her arms.

When Kabuta went in to his teepee Peg dropped her doeskin robe and he pulled her roughly to him and claimed her lips and that kiss had all the emotion and longing that had been building up in them for days. Peg pushed him from her and started undressing him so they could rejoice in one another's love.

The next morning Kabuta and Mike stretched a large tarp on the ground and placed a sewing kit with needles of all sizes, curved ones as well as straight ones, and spools of thread of every color, along with small piles of glass beads of every color they could find. When the ladies saw these they were ecstatic.

Kabuta said, "Ladies, there is a sewing kit for every married lady in the village, and a small pile of beads of each color."

The Chief said, "You and Mike are wise men. There will be no dissension over the sewing kits and beads."

When the Chief saw the rifles he said, "Mike, I want you and Kabuta to teach our warriors how to use these weapons and to keep them in perfect order. These are different from the ones you gave my sub-chiefs and me."

"We'll be pleased to teach them, but I would suggest that we keep these rifles stored in a safe, dry place and use them only for defense and the buffalo hunt."

Then Mike took the chiefs and showed them the cook stoves and said, "We couldn't find enough stoves for every family in the village, so you will have to decide who gets these. We ordered enough for everyone and they will be waiting for us when we go back to St. Louis two years from now."

When the Chief saw all the new axes he said, gleefully, "Now it will be easier for us to supply our village with firewood."

It was decided they would drill the men on the first day of the week for about an hour each morning until they were satisfied they could handle the rifles as well as they could.

Mike had told the Chief that it was their custom to work six days a week but that on Sunday they worshipped their God in special ways and rested. So on Sunday they only did what was necessary.

The first thing they built was a warm chicken house with a safe pen to keep the animals from killing the chickens. The chickens and hogs had been the most difficult to transport and they were tempted to eat them on the trail, but when the chickens started laying eggs they were glad they hadn't. It wasn't long until they had a number of hens setting on a dozen eggs each, and it wasn't long after the eggs hatched before they were eating fried chicken.

Next, were the pigpens, and then a barn to store their grains in. Then they built a large milk shed with a corral to keep the milk cows in at night. They didn't want to lose a cow or calf to an animal. These were fast becoming the tribe's prize possessions. This would make it more comfortable for the men, because they would be under a roof as they did the milking in bad weather.

After the O'Rourkes saw how Katy and Peg had their teepees arranged they decided teepees were good enough for them, so Mike and Kabuta told them if they would help them build their cabins they could have their teepees, if the Chief would permit it.

The next morning Mike, Kabuta and the four brothers took two of the heavier wagons, with four-mule teams, and headed for a mountainside that was covered with tall, straight pines the size they wanted, and started felling trees.

It was soon apparent that the O'Rourke brothers had no experience with an axe. Peter said, "Mike, when it comes to cutting peat from a bog, we're the best. But we're not much good at cutting wood."

Mike said, "Well, Kabuta's the best teacher I've ever seen in the use of an axe. He'll soon have you cutting wood along with the best of us."

At the end of the day when they brought the wagons in, loaded high, Mike went to the Chief and said, "My Chief, Kabuta and I would like to build our houses on that hill overlooking the river, and if you like our houses we will build one big enough that each of your wives can have their own bedroom, anywhere you want it."

"Build wherever you like, my brother. I have lived in a teepee all my life and it suits me fine, but we will see your house. And then we will let my wives decide."

The next day John said to Mike, "I'm a cabinet and furniture maker and Joseph, Peter and David could rip logs for furniture and flooring."

"Good thinking," Mike said, "John, you can get your brothers started on that tomorrow."

It was decided that Mike and Running Deer would notch the logs and with the help of some strong braves to lift the logs, they would frame the houses.

Kabuta recruited some braves to help him cut and haul logs and with all this help the houses rose quickly.

By mid-summer Mike and Kabuta's houses were finished and John had made all the furniture for them.

Katy said, "John, I could kiss you for all the beautiful things you've made for us."

Peg said, 'I'm going to,' and she did, and so did Katy, and John blushed like a rose as he stammered, "Thank you, ladies," and he rushed from the house.

Mike took the Chief and his three wives through the houses after they were completed and filled with furniture. The women were so impressed that the chief squaw looked longingly at Big Thunder and said, "Could we have a house like this?

Big Thunder turned to Mike and said, "Could you start building our house at once?"

"Kabuta and I would be delighted," Mike said.

The Chief's massive house was finished, as well as a meeting house forty feet wide and eighty feet long, where the whole tribe could come in for all kinds of meetings.

When the meeting hall was finished John had made a sign that said, "Meeting Hall," with a hole in each end and matching holes in the log just over the door, to mount it.

Mike asked the Chief to have all the people there for the dedication of the hall to the people.

When they were gathered, Mike said, "Chief, you get the privilege of driving the last peg," and he handed him the hammer and showed him where to drive the peg to erect the sign over the door.

The Chief held the sign high over his head so all the people could see it, saying, "The white men, Kabuta and our braves have given us this magnificent meeting hall. I command that you all treat it with respect. Now, let us all bow our heads and give thanks to our Great Spirit." And he drove in the two pegs that would hold the sign over the door.

That spring the Indians built rail fences around a large field where they planted wheat and corn, along with beans and other vegetables of all kinds, as well as Irish potatoes. They had also fenced another field where they planted oats. When winter came the barn was filled with corn, wheat and oats and there were large stacks of dried oat and wheat straw for the stock to eat through the winter months.

All the heifers had dropped calves and Mike said, "Katy, in a couple of years we will have enough milk and butter for all the people." As it was now, they rationed it out so everyone could have a little once in a while.

Christmas day, 1804, they had a feast for all the people in the meeting hall and the Chief said, "Kabuta, would you ask the Great Spirit to bless the food and our time together."

When Kabuta prayed, everyone in the great hall could hear his booming voice. He ended his prayer with, "Thank you, Father God, in the name of your son, Jesus Christ our Lord."

Kabuta had been so thankful for all God had done for him he didn't realize what questions he may have put in the minds of the people as he prayed the only way he knew how.

After the feast was over, they removed the tables to make room for dancing and merrymaking.

The Chief called the people to attention and said, "I have an announcement to make. Running Springs and Running Deer are going to give us another grandchild in a few months."

A cheer rose from the crowd, and then they started dancing.

* * * * *

John built a boxing ring that could be erected and removed easily in the middle of the great hall. Michael had bought the only pair of boxing gloves he could find in St. Louis, with the thought in mind to teach the young men of the village the fine art of fisticuffs. It would be good entertainment for the older folks and a good way to blow off steam in the winter months when they had too much time on their hands.

Mike had been hoarding the soft down from the breast of the geese they shot for food when they landed on the river. He said to Running Springs one day, "Will you pick out a soft doeskin and make it as soft and pliable as you can?" He showed her the boxing gloves. "I want to try to make three pair of these. I have plenty of goose down."

Running springs said, "Give those to me. My mother can duplicate anything, especially after you gave her the sewing kit."

The buildings were all finished when Gabriel and Riley were a little over two years old. On September the fifth, 1806, Peg gave birth to a little girl she named Katharine.

When Kabuta held Katharine in his arms he said, "My little dove, you have made me proud. This tiny little princess is as cute as a bug's ear, and I predict she'll be almost as beautiful as her mother."

When Katy was rocking Katharine and singing to her, she couldn't help but wonder if she would be so lucky. She wanted a daughter so badly it hurt.

She bowed her head and prayed, "Dear Heavenly Father, let it be so." Peg and Katy had always done things together and they had planned to have their babies close together, but this time it wasn't to be. Katy's Peggy Kathleen wasn't born until March 4, 1807. She was a healthy baby and Katy had some difficulty with her birth and it was weeks before she was her old self again. Mike worried himself sick over her until she was completely well again. He said to Katy one morning, "I thank God he gave you your beautiful daughter, but I don't want you to ever go through this again."

Katy said, as she held Mike's head against her breast, "Darling, you worry too much, I'm as good as new. And it's up to the good Lord how many babies we have, and we'll love every one of them."

CHAPTER TWENTY-EIGHT

The meeting hall had been up two years and every Saturday night Kabuta would light the large candles placed on the wall all around the room to light up the boxing ring in the middle of the room. The older folks would gather to watch their young ones box. Mike and Kabuta had taught them well and there were some great matches.

When Mike first taught Kabuta how to wrestle he could pin him, but after Kabuta learned the gist of it, no more. And none had ever pinned Kabuta after he pinned Mike for the first time. Mike could still out-box Kabuta, but Kabuta had decked him a few times.

In the fall of 1806, the tribe had gathered in the great hall one Saturday afternoon to watch a boxing match between a number of the younger children, when a brave came in and whispered in the Chief's ear. The Chief got up quickly and left with the brave.

An hour later they returned and the Chief commanded all his braves to get their weapons and assemble at the river's edge. Then he said to Mike and Kabuta, "Get the guns and your trained men, there are a number of longboats coming up the river and there are soldiers carrying muskets."

Then the Chief commanded the women and children to go to the place he had chosen as a place of safety for them in case of an attack on the village. Mike and Kabuta's men gathered around them. The braves that had bows and arrows were strategically placed behind trees scattered up and down the river, and Mike and Kabuta placed their men in a straight line, with Mike on one end and Kabuta on the other, with the Chief standing by Mike's side in plain sight. The chief was wearing his headdress that indicated he was the headman of the tribe.

The longboats came on and tied up at the dock. A young Indian woman stepped out of the lead boat and approached the Chief and said, "I'm Sacagawea, and these white men come in peace."

The Chief said, "With drawn guns?"

"They are to be used for hunting food and to defend ourselves if we are attacked," Sacagawea said.

"Who is in command?" the Chief asked.

Sacagawea motioned two men forward and introduced them as Captain Louis and Captain Clark.

"The Chief said, "Command your men to stay here and you come into my lodge. Kabuta you are in command here, if these soldiers raise their guns, shoot them. Mike, you come with us."

Kabuta stepped forward and said, "Yes, my Chief."

The Chief had moved his counsel to one end of the great hall and John had built him a large round table. He, Mike and his four sub-chiefs, sat on one side of the table, and Louis, Clark and Sacagawea sat across from them.

The Chief said, "Now, tell us how many are in your party and why have you come to our valley."

Captain Louis said, "We have twenty-three enlisted men, one civilian, three Indian guides, and Sacagawea is our interpreter. We have been commanded by the United States of America to find and map a route to the great waters in the west, called the Pacific Ocean. Winter will soon be closing in and we were looking for a valley where we might spend the winter. We would deem it a rare privilege to be able to spend the winter here near your village."

The Chief said, "You may rejoin your men and Mike will let you know our decision after I've discussed the matter with my counsel."

It was an hour later when the three were summoned to come back for the counsel's decision. When they were seated the Chief said, "Here are our terms, you may camp three miles down the river from our village, and your men are not to come into our village. If one of your men defiles one of our women, that man must die, and the rest of you will be escorted from our village, and if any of you return you will be put to death. If you want to winter over here under these circumstances, we will help you in any way we can. We are a peaceful people, but we have strong medicine and brave warriors, and we'll fight to preserve our way of life. What is your decision?"

Captain Louis said, "We accept with grateful hearts."

"Now, my brother, Mike, will guide you to where you may pitch your camp."

As Mike and their visitors left the counsel, Mike said, "I'll get my horse and ride down the river. You get your people and take your boats back down the river and you will see me on the bank near some large trees where you may tie up your boats, and in the shelter of those trees you may build your camp for the winter, but the Chief will expect you to move on in the spring."

The next morning Lewis and Clark got their men busy setting up winter quarters and they were delighted for the loan of wagons and mules to haul wood from the mountains. This was a luxury they didn't expect.

The next evening Louis and Clark were sitting in Kabuta's home, drinking coffee and eating cookies, and Mike and Katy were there.

Captain Clark said, "Can you imagine what a shock it was to see all those stone-faced Indians and this big Black man, and you with rifles far better than ours, facing us, and Indians with bows behind every tree? When we came up the river and saw this beautiful valley we didn't know there was an Indian village here. And we sure didn't expect to find a white and black family here."

Kabuta laughed and said, "We could see the surprise on your faces. Our Chief is a kind man, but if one of you had made a false move, you would all be dead now."

Captain Louis said, "We are well aware of that, and here we are enjoying the hospitality of two fine families. We've met many Indians, but we've not seen any tribe as well equipped."

"Thanks to Mike," Kabuta said.

"To us," Mike corrected.

"How did you come to be here?" Captain Clark asked.

Mike said, "Kabuta and I and our young brides were coming west looking for a valley to settle in. A young Indian maiden, sixteen years old, was stolen away from her family, it's a long story that I won't go into, but Katy and Peg heard her crying as she was hiding in some bushes. They brought her to camp and she told us her story and we offered to take her home. She guided us here and she was the Chief's daughter. He was so grateful to get his daughter back he invited us to become a part of his people. We're so happy to be here, we've done everything we could to show our appreciation."

The expedition spent a long, restful winter in the Valley of the Smokes, and left in the early spring with deep regrets. They had a long, rugged haul in front of them through range after range of high mountains and across the Great American Desert before they floated down the mighty Columbia River to stand on the shore and gaze out across the dancing waters of the mighty Pacific and watch the giant waves crash against the rocky shoreline.

CHAPTER TWENTY-NINE

For the next twelve years Mike, Kabuta and Running Deer made the trip to St. Louis every other year to sell their furs and boats and get supplies, and the last year Gabriel, Riley and Sitting Bull went with them. They were superb horsemen at this young age and they could handle their weapons just as well as they rode. The four Irish O'Rourke lads had married Indian maidens and cast their lot for the rest of their lives with the tribe here in the beautiful Valley of the Smokes.

Mike and Katy were lying in bed Christmas morning, 1818, when Mike said, "Katy, I'd like to take you back to see your folks and then go on to show you my beautiful home in Ireland."

"Oh! Mike, I would love to go, but could we take Peg and Kabuta and their family? Our kids would be miserable without Riley and Katharine. And I'd be lost without Peg."

"I wouldn't think of going without them. Kabuta has become so much a part of me; it would be like losing my right arm without him. Let's go talk it over with them."

When Mike broached the subject to them, Kabuta and Peg weren't terribly enthusiastic about it. Mike showed his surprise, Kabuta had always been eager for any new adventure before.

Kabuta said, "Well, Mike, our experience on a sailing ship was down in a black hole with a lot of sick people starving and scared to death. We've found peace, respect and happiness here, and we have no idea what to expect in Ireland."

Mike said, "Kabuta, I promise you that if you and Peg aren't happy there, we'll come right home."

Peg said, "I can't imagine being separated from Katy. Can we go, Kabuta?"

"If Mike and Katy go, we go," he said. But Mike knew his heart wasn't in it.

When Mike and Kabuta finished the sailboat they planned to sail to New Orleans and sell it there.

Mike went to the Chief and said, "When Joseph and the men take the furs to market this year we're going to sail down the Mississippi River to New Orleans and catch a ship for Ireland, and we may not be coming back. I'm taking Kabuta's and my family back to my homeland."

The Chief had a hard time hiding his disappointment, but he said, "Mike, when you tire of Ireland, your homes will be waiting for you. They will not be occupied by anyone until you return, but they will be kept cleaned and aired out. You will return, my children—the Great Spirit has told me so."

Mike was deeply touched; the Chief had never called them his children before.

"My Chief, your generosity overwhelms me. I have promised Kabuta, Peg, Katy and the children that I'll bring them home if they are not happy in Ireland."

Mike assured the Chief that the four Irish lads and the four braves he sent to St. Louis with the furs would return with the supplies they needed. "We'll get there before they do and I'll stop at the Trading Post and let them know that Joseph will be handling that part of our business until we return."

The night before they were to leave the Chief gave them a going away feast in the lodge.

Running Springs, with tears running down her cheeks, gave Katy, Peg and the girls beautiful white doeskin riding habits, with beaded knee-high moccasins to match. And tears were blinding the eyes of Katy and Peg as they hugged this Indian woman that had become like a sister to them.

The Chief gave Mike, Kabuta and the boy's buckskin pants and jackets, with knee-length moccasins, as well. The air was fraught with emotion as they went to their beds.

CHAPTER THIRTY

There were few dry eyes as the tribe stood on the bank of the Yellowstone River and watched them sail away the next morning. Even the Chief was seen wiping away a tear, and Mike could hardly see to guide the boat out into the center of the river. But it wasn't long before the swift current swept them around the bend out of sight.

When they reached St. Louis late in the afternoon they went and rented rooms in the hotel then went to a Chinese restaurant for supper.

Mike and his entourage spent three days purchasing new clothing and Mike went to the bank and got some cash and enough bank drafts to take care of their needs.

Mike had sent the wagons on ahead weeks ago and he decided they would wait until they came in so he could introduce Joseph to the proprietor of the trading posts and sign papers giving Joseph authority to draw on Mike's account if it became necessary, and to conduct their business while he was gone. Joseph never had to draw on that account. Their furs and hides were sufficient. Mike was pleasantly surprised to see the wagons pull up at the trading post just four days after they got there. When Joseph climbed down off his wagon and extended his hand to him, Mike said, "You made better time than I thought you would."

"Things went smoothly all the way and the grass was good. We came the short way and there was plenty of water, but we want to start back as soon as possible because some of the watering holes are getting low."

As soon as the wagons were unloaded Joseph gave the merchant the list of supplies they needed and said, "We'll load those out in the morning and hit the trail."

The merchant said, "Fair enough, and you men can turn your stock into the corral and feed them from the corncrib. You may sleep in the hay loft, if you wish."

Joseph said, "Thank you, we'll do that."

John came up to Mike and handed him a package of letters and said, "Mike, will you post these in Ireland for us?"

Mike took the letters, shook hands with all of the men, and bade them good-bye. He said, "We may be floating down the river for New Orleans before you crawl out of the hay in the morning."

Joseph said, "Not if we can load out tonight. If we can, we'll be rolling by daylight."

The merchant heard him and said, "That's no problem, and we can start loading now."

Mike said, "Not until I take these men for a good Chinese dinner."

Mike and Kabuta came down and saw them off the next morning and went back and got their families ready to leave.

When they were floating down the Mississippi at a good clip early that morning, Katy said, "I can't get over how big this river is and how fast we're moving."

She wasn't prepared for the great, wide expanse of water where the mighty Ohio River entered the Mississippi. After they passed the Ohio, the Mississippi narrowed and when the boat hit this narrow stretch, it shot forward, and when she expressed her concern excitedly Mike said, "Don't fret, John, Kabuta and I built this boat and she will take anything this old River wants to throw at her."

He would have sailed closer to shore to calm Katy's nerves, but now that they had started on their journey he couldn't wait to sail across the lakes of Killarney to old Fort Ross, to stand over the graves of his beloved family once more.

The river got bigger as other rivers and creeks flowed into it, but it flowed much slower where it widened out. The children and Peg and Katy started fishing with lines trailing behind the boat. The further south they went the commercial barges and ships got thicker, so they started tying up at night.

One day they passed a couple of plantations where the fields came right down to the river's edge and there were black slaves in the fields, and that night they tied up at a dock in Natchez, Mississippi, and Mike said, "Kabuta, let's go into town and pick up some supplies."

Kabuta and Peg were becoming concerned for their family's safety and he said, "No, Mike, Peg and I want to have a talk with your family. We have already told Riley and Katharine that as long as we are in the south they are to call Gabriel and Peggy 'Miss Peggy' and 'Massa Gabriel,' and Peg and I will address you, 'yassa boss,' and 'nossa boss,' and 'yassa, misses Katy' and 'nossa, missus Katy.' If we do that, we might not have any trouble."

Mike flatly refused, saying, "You are my partner and best friend, and I will treat you as my equal, as you surely are."

When Peg pleaded with Mike and Katy to do as Kabuta had requested, Mike and Katy finally agreed. But Katy said, "I don't like it."

"Neither do I," Mike said, "But I can see the wisdom in it. So just to please you, we'll do it, but it's going to be very hard not to slip once in a while. "

Kabuta said, "That's why it's best we not be seen together any more than we have to."

Mike said, "Then maybe you should lay low here and I'll take Katy, Gabriel and Peggy to the store with me.

They had to lay over in New Orleans until a ship came into harbor on which they could book passage to Richmond, Virginia.

Mike and Katy were rankled that Kabuta and his family couldn't eat in the nice cafes with them, but had to stay in their rooms and have their meals brought to them.

Their third day in New Orleans Mike and Katy were sitting at a corner table in a French cafe on the waterfront, just getting ready to order, when Bill Sweeney and another sailor walked in the door. Bill was the First Mate on Captain Alcott's ship when Mike boarded her in Dublin, Ireland, when he was nineteen years old. Mike knew that Captain Alcott had sold his ship and his shipping business to Bill when he retired. Bill was almost gray now, but he was still straight and agile. Mike recognized him at once and he rose and said, "Bill Sweeney! Gee! It's great to see you. You and your friend join Katy and my family for lunch as our guest."

It had been seventeen years since they sailed across the ocean together, and fought together when Mike had killed his first man. It was Bill who had comforted Mike when he felt so badly about killing another human being. Bill had changed little, but he didn't recognize this big, broad shouldered man dressed in buckskins that came forward with his hand stretched out to him.

"I'm Bill Sweeney alright, but I'm sorry, I can't place you."

"How could you forget me? I acted like a baby when I cut one man's hand off and killed another on Captain Alcott's ship that day."

"Michael Ross! How could I forget the man that saved the life of the best Captain I ever had? I'm sorry I didn't recognize you; I should have remembered that mop of curly red hair. I'm Captain Bill Sweeney now, and this is my First Mate, Peter Callahan."

They made introductions all around and ordered lunch.

While they were eating Mike said, "We're waiting for a ship to go to Richmond, Virginia, and from there, on to Dublin, Ireland."

"I bought Captain Alcott's ship, and she's still a great ship, we just dropped anchor a few hours ago. It will take us about four days to unload our cargo and load the ship with goods for Richmond. Can you be ready?"

"Sure. But there are eight of us; my best friend and his wife and two children are going with us and Bill, they are Black; will that be a problem?"

"As long as they have the fare, there's no problem. We only have four cabins, and they're very small, with two single beds in each cabin."

Mike said, "I know those cabins well, I came over in one of them, remember?"

"We lay over in Richmond for two weeks. We have a full cargo to unload there and a full cargo to load for London, where we'll lay over another two weeks before going on to Dublin to pick up a cargo of wool."

Katy said, "Two weeks in Richmond to spend with mom and dad will be great."

Mike said, "We'll take all four cabins, if they're available."

"They're yours."

"My friend, Kabuta, and his family are cooped up in a hotel and would love to get out of there. Could we board tomorrow morning? With the understanding our fare starts then, of course."

"Any time you like," Bill said, and Bill and Peter tipped their hats to Katy and Peggy and said, "We'll see you on board."

When Mike took supper to Kabuta and his family he said, "We board ship in the morning, but we won't sail for four or five days."

Kabuta looked up at the ceiling and said, "Praise You, Lord! These walls are beginning to close in on us."

Peg said, "You can say that again, and if we don't get out of here soon Riley and Katharine are going to kill one another, if I don't kill them first. They're running us crazy, cooped up in this room. They just can't understand why we can't get out of here and walk around town, but we're afraid if we do they'll say or do something that'll get us all killed."

Mike hugged Peg and said, "I'm sorry I put you through this. We can go on board at five in the morning and eat breakfast on the ship. And the kids can walk on the deck. The captain said they could have the run of the ship as long as they don't get in the way of the men when they're working."

The Gulf of Mexico was rough enough, but when they sailed around the tip of Florida and headed up the eastern seaboard, the ocean was tossing high. Peggy and Kathleen got seasick and Riley and Gabriel were making fun of them, until it hit them and they went running for the rail to lose their breakfast. Captain Sweeney saw this and he told Katy to take her sick ones to the galley and see the cook. "They need to eat every time they empty their stomachs. You kids eat whatever the cook gives you, no matter how hard it is to do, and you'll get well quickly and you won't get seasick again."

"Yes, Captain Bill," they said in unison.

Katy and Peg rushed the children to the cook and he fed them some kind of heavy gruel. He said, "Eat until you think you can't eat another bite, and then take two more, and you'll be well. But don't lie down. When you get through eating go up on deck and walk around it five times. Don't look at the edge of the ship, look way out to sea."

Katharine said, "Mama, I'm going to die. I can't eat that much. I just want to go to bed."

"Sit, eat, young lady, or I'll tan your little black bottom until it turns blue!"

She ate, and Peg and Katy walked the deck with them to make sure they went around it five times. They were all surprised that when lunchtime came they were looking forward to it.

By the time they reached Richmond the children were sure that Captain Bill was the smartest man in the world.

When they started sailing up the James River, Katy and Peg were beside themselves—they could hardly wait to see Katy's family.

As soon as they docked Mike went and rented a large carriage and they went and bought gifts for everyone and drove out to the plantation as soon as they could.

When they drove through the fields they saw they were clean of weeds and the crops were good. The house had just been repainted and it shown like new money in the early afternoon sun. The trees were trimmed, the lawn was manicured, and the flowers were in full bloom. They could smell the honeysuckle that grew on trellises across the front of the verandah. A new croquet court was in place.

A boy came to take care of the horses and as they walked toward the house along the path that was lined with beautiful tree roses, Katy's younger brother, Patrick, walked out on the verandah. When he saw them he flew down the steps and Katy rushed into his open arms. He held her a long time, and then extended his arm to grip Mike's hand.

Then Peg threw herself at him and hugged him good, and stepped back and held his hands wide, and said, "Look at you! You were no bigger than our Riley when we left, and now you're a handsome man."

"Thank you, Peg." He reached for Kabuta's hand and said, "Hello, Kabuta, I never did quite forgive you for taking Peg away from us. This must be Riley and Katharine."

"And Gabriel and Peggy," Peg interjected.

Patrick asked them to wait on the verandah until he could break the news to their parents. "The shock of seeing you all might be too much for dad's heart. He's been having some problems."

He went into the parlor where his dad was dozing in his easy chair and his mother was reading.

"Wake up, dad,'" he said, shaking him gently. "Mom, dad, if you could have one wish come true, what would it be?"

Mary didn't hesitate when she said, "To see Katy and Peg and their families come through that door right now."

Ralph said, "Amen to that."

Katy and Peg were listening at the door and Katy could wait no longer, she burst through the door, with Peg right behind her.

Her mother and dad sat for a moment in shock, then rose slowly from their chairs and went for Katy and Peg.

Mary threw her arms around Katy and showered her with kisses as Peg was doing the same thing to Katy's dad.

Katy held her mother until Mike said, "Mother, aren't you going to save a little of that loving for me and your grandchildren?"

She released Katy and hugged Mike. Gabriel and Peggy were a little shy, but they soon warmed up to their grandparents and Riley and Katharine did too.

They talked the day away and soon after supper they all went to bed.

The next morning they saddled horses and took the children down to the river and showed them where they met and fell in love.

Katy and Peg went back to the house to spend as much time as they could with their family, while Mike and Kabuta took their children to see their place up and across the river.

When they rode up to the boathouse Ellis and Lola were sitting on the deck. They were excited to see them and welcomed them warmly. Kabuta and Mike introduced their children to them and Lola got up and walked along the deck to the rail on the west side. Her voice drifted down the creek to the river as it danced over the heat waves to reach the ears of their two sons, Sterling and Arthur. She said just one word, "Come!" Ten minutes later a ten and a twelve-year-old came riding two beautiful pinto horses out of the river bottom, carrying a string of fish and two cane poles.

When the boys came up on the deck Lola introduced them to these strangers, here with their parents and then she said, "Folks, the tall one is Sterling and the young one is Arthur."

Mike and Kabuta spent a few hours with their friends, catching up on what had taken place over the years. The children got acquainted, and soon were fast friends.

Ellis said, "The Captain and Christine never gave up hope you would return, but when Mrs. Christine died, the light just seemed to go out in the Captain.

He tried to hang on, but his spirit just seemed to die in him. He entered into his rest two weeks ago and we buried him beside his darling Christine.

"Mr. Mike, he deeded this place to us and set up what they call a trust so we would have an income the rest of our lives. Your and Kabuta's house is empty, but Lola keeps it cleaned and aired out. If you need it, you'll find it always ready. That was the Captain's wish.

"Mr. Chambers sold his import, export business and moved in next door. He eats with us most nights. He's all alone now. He went into Richmond to tie up some loose ends, he said, but he'll be back early in the morning."

Kabuta said, "Ellis, could I get in his place?"

"He never locks it. Leaves it open so his friends can use it when he's not there. He'll be here about seven in the morning though. He asked Lola if she would make breakfast for him. He said he'd rather eat her cooking than at the best cafe in town."

"Lola, could you give me the fixings I used to cook for him and his friends when they would come out here hunting and fishing. I'd like to be in there fixing his breakfast when he walks in the door."

"I'll have everything ready for you in the morning."

Early the next morning Kabuta had the stove hot and the biscuits ready to slip into the oven when Mike said, "He's coming, and should be walking in that door in ten minutes."

Kabuta slipped the biscuits in the oven and started the bacon frying and put the coffee on to boil. Mr. Chambers saw the smoke curling up from the chimney and he could smell the bacon frying when he drove up to where Ellis waited to care for his team, like he always did. Ellis noticed that Ted looked tired.

After greetings were exchanged, Ted said, "Ellis, for the first time I can remember, I was hoping none of my friends would be out here. I just wanted to eat a good breakfast and go to bed. Who is it this time?"

"I don't rightly know, Massa Ted," he lied.

"Thanks, Ellis, I suppose I should go in and greet them before I go to your house for breakfast."

When he walked in the door Kabuta boomed in that deep voice of his, "How would you like your eggs this morning, Mr. Ted?"

Mr. Chambers stood there for a moment with his mouth wide open, and then said weakly, "Scrambled, if you please, Kabuta, the way you know I like them." And then he rushed across the room and hugged Kabuta like he would if he had been a long-lost son come home.

He heard Mike get up from his chair and he turned, "Michael, boy, how good it is to see you, too! I wish Angus could be here. He left us just two weeks ago."

Mike said, "We know, Ellis told us all about it."

Kabuta pulled a pan of fluffy brown biscuits out of the oven and set them on the table and said, "Butter them while they're hot, and Mike, will you pour the coffee?" He was already scrambling eggs. Ted went to a cupboard and brought a jar of apricot jam and set it on the table. They sat down and did justice to Kabuta's masterpiece.

Ted said, "It's like old times, I've never forgotten what a good cook you are, Kabuta. I've missed you."

With a second cup of coffee in front of them they reminisced of bygone days, and when Mike and Kabuta described their valley, Ted wished he were young again.

He said, "Mike, have you checked on your assets yet?"

"Yes, I had all my assets transferred to St. Louis and I checked on them on the way through. I've dug into them deeply and there's little left, but we have our valley the way we want it and there's little need for money out there anymore.

"Angus told me you saved his life, and he never forgot it. He deeded his place over to Ellis and Lola and left them a good income the rest of their lives, but son, he left you a tidy sum. He made me Trustee of his estate and if you will give me a couple of days to rest, I'll go into town with you and get it transferred to you and you can transfer it to your account in St. Louis."

"Bless him, that's good news. I'm taking my family and Kabuta's to Ireland to see the Emerald Isle and where I grew up, and I figured that trip would just about wipe me out. I first thought we might stay there, but I'm already getting homesick for our green, green Valley of the Smokes."

Kabuta let out a big sigh of relief, and Mike heard it. When he glanced at him Kabuta said, "That news is going to make two beautiful women and four children as happy as it did me."

"Katy has hidden it well, but I was beginning to catch on to how she really felt, and Riley and Peggy have made no bones about how they felt about leaving, in the first place."

They talked the morning away and were a little surprised when Ellis knocked on the door and walked in and said, "Lola said lunch will be on the table in twenty minutes."

By the time they washed up and walked across the footbridge to the boathouse, lunch was on the table.

They bowed their heads and Ellis asked Kabuta to say grace.

When they finished eating Ted said. "Mike, I know I look ancient, but I'm only fifty-two years old. Do you think I could make it out there?"

"I don't know why not. Be ready when we get back from Ireland and we'll take you with us. But you'd better ride a horse every day and get your butt toughened up, and the soreness out of your muscles, because we're going to ride horses all the way, and we're going to make time. You'll need two good riding geldings, three-year-olds, if you can get them, and two big pack horses with pack saddles. Get yourself a double-barrel shotgun, a rifle and two forty- four pistols. And get Ellis to show you how to use them. He's good with guns, and he can teach you how to draw those pistols from the holster as fast as your talent will permit. I almost forgot; you'll need a good crossbow and plenty of arrows, too.

"When we get back I'll go into town with you and help you pick out the other things you'll need, we'll help you load your pack horses the first ten days on the trail and after that you pack your own; fair enough?"

"I'll be ready! Mike, you'll never use this place, and I'll never use mine after we leave for your valley. Neither one of us needs more money. Sterling and Arthur are going to need a place to bring their brides to some day. They're good young men, Mike. I'll deed my place to Sterling, and how about you deed your place to Arthur?"

Mike said, "That's fine, if that's all right with Kabuta, its half his, you know."

Kabuta said, "Do it, I don't ever want to leave our valley again."

"Good, we'll go into town in a couple of days and make it legal, with Ellis as their guardian. The boys will get the property when they bring a bride home."

Ellis sat with his mouth agape and Lola ran from the room, crying tears of joy.

Their two weeks here was too short, but they would stay longer on their way back, if they came back. Mike knew that a little piece of him would always be in County Kerry. And if Katy and the others liked it, he would build a beautiful house there near where the cottage stood.

The children had so much fun riding horses and fishing with Sterling and Arthur that they hated it when they were on the rocking ship watching the green shores of Virginia fade away.

Katherine turned to her mother, Peg, and cried, "Mother, I love Sterling and I might never see him again."

Peg said, "Katharine, you hush your mouth. You're only nine years old and Sterling is only twelve. You're too young to love a boy."

"Well, I love Sterling!" She broke from her mother and ran to her cabin.

Katy gave Peg a big hug and said, "We've truly been blessed to be able to remain together and stay such good friends. Mike told me that he and Kabuta made a vow that they would never separate us."

"Kabuta told me the same thing, and if I know these men of ours as well as I think I do, we're going to grow old together, girl."

By the time they docked in Dublin Mike was so eager to get off the ship he was nearly impossible to be around. This was the first time Katy could remember when Mike didn't see to everything, and make sure that she and the children were happy and taken care of. He just said, "Katy, take care of the luggage," and he rushed down the gangplank.

Katy's Irish temper started to flare, but she regained her composure quickly. She realized this wasn't like him, and she didn't like this side of her husband. Was this Ireland? Or was he just anxious to see his birthplace and where he grew up? All kinds of crazy questions started creeping into the recesses of her mind, and then leaped to the forefront, to send her into despair.

Maybe there's a girl he promised to send for, or come back to. She knew how the Irish could be; she thought what if Mike had asked a girl to wait, and she had remained an old maid and he never came back. She also knew that if there was a girl who waited all these years, and he showed up with a wife and two children, there'd be hell to pay.

Katy got downright angry with herself; her Mike wouldn't do a thing like that! She told herself, if I'd made a promise like that, I would have broken it when I fell so madly in love with Mike. She would have married Mike, no matter who it hurt. These things were racing through her mind when Peg and Kabuta joined her on deck with their belongings.

"Why so quiet?" Peg asked her.

"Oh! Peg, I've had the craziest things flooding my mind. Mike's been so preoccupied he hasn't been himself for days. What if there's a girl waiting for him? There could be you know. I…"

Peg and Kabuta laughed so hard their sides hurt. When Kabuta could stop laughing, he said. "Katy, if Mike had left a girl behind, I'd have known about it. Don't worry about it, Katy," and they all went into another fit of laughter.

Just then Mike drove up in a fine closed-in carriage with a pair of high-stepping horses, jumped out and picked Katy up and danced around like a crazy man and said, "Mrs. Ross, may I help you into your carriage? Mr. Kabuta, won't you and your lovely wife join us?"

Gabriel popped up and said, "How about us, are you going to leave us standing here on the dock?"

"Not on your life, hop in," Mike said.

When they had loaded their luggage, Mike drove to the best inn in Dublin and rented four rooms.

When Kabuta expressed his surprise at his renting four rooms, Mike said, "I don't know about you, but there was very little lovemaking on that ship and I want some privacy tonight. I intend to make Katy's first night in Ireland one she will never forget."

"That's for me," Kabuta replied. "Mike, I'm sure glad we met. You've taught me an awful lot."

"No more than you've taught me, old friend. We make a pretty good team."

Mike took the kids out to eat and picked up some guidebooks for them to study, and while they were gone the women took hot baths and stretched out on the comfortable beds and took a nap. When the men got back to their rooms they told their wives that they were going to take a bath and they should get ready for a night out on the town.

The girls had missed the lovemaking too. And though they'd planned to go out early, it was a couple of hours before they left their expensive rooms.

What a time they had that night. They dressed and went out for a delightful supper, with champagne. It was the first Kabuta and Peg had ever tasted. It made them feel just good enough to relax and enjoy the evening. It also made them forget that they were the only Blacks in a sea of white faces, and it kept the curious glances of the people from offending them. After a superb meal they lingered over coffee and pastries.

As they were leaving Kabuta said, "I think I could get used to this kind of life."

Peg said, "It's great for a change, but I'll take our life back home any time."

Katy said, "I agree, Peg, but I'd sure love to take a lot of that sweet-smelling toilet water back with us, and a bathtub to use it in."

Mike tucked that bit of information into a crevice of his mind.

They went to a dance and danced well into the night, and as they were walking back to their inn, two burly fellows stepped out of an alley in front of them with knives drawn. One of them said, "Give us your purse, mates, and you can be on your way."

Mike whispered, "Kabuta, make like your reaching in your inside coat pocket for your purse. Then let's take them."

They stepped toward the two men and two hard fists contacted their chins, backed by two strong arms, and in seconds the two men lay on the sidewalk, unconscious, but not badly hurt.

Mike and Kabuta took their wives' hands and walked calmly to the inn.

As they walked down the dark street, Katy said, "Michael Ross, I'll never again be afraid when I'm with you."

"That's good, Katy. Too much fear cripples one, but a little fear is a good thing. I felt a little fear run up my spine when I saw those knives shining in the pale moonlight." He held up a sharp two-edged knife, ten inches long, and Kabuta held up the other one.

Neither Peg nor Katy remembered them picking up the knives.

Kabuta said, "We'll keep these to remember our welcome to Dublin."

They broke into a run for the inn when it began to pour rain. They weren't a hundred yards from the inn, but they were drenched to the skin when they reached their rooms.

They didn't wake up the next morning until the children came knocking on their doors, saying they were hungry. They spent four days here riding around the town, seeing the sights. They rode up and down the coast and marveled how green everything was. The rains came and went. The sun peaked through once in a while. Peg said, "Now I understand why Mike rented a closed carriage."

The constant changing of shadows reaching across the land made the sunsets breathtakingly beautiful. Katy said, "Mike, how could you leave this beautiful country?"

"You haven't seen anything yet, my Katy. Our place on the shore of Lake Killarney is far more beautiful."

"Oh! Michael, I can't wait to see it. Can we go tomorrow?"

"Tomorrow," he replied.

He took them back to the inn for their last night there, and then took the carriage back to where he rented it.

The next morning he settled their bill and they caught a boat that took them down the Grand Canal to the River Shannon to Limerick, where they found lodging for two nights.

After breakfast the next morning Peg and Katy took the children down on the banks of the river and sat on a bench and chatted while the children skipped rocks on the water.

Mike and Kabuta went to the horse auction. They saw many fine horses auctioned off and a number of carriages and teams. Mike had his eye on a fine closed carriage that was big enough for them, but he didn't know if it was for sale.

He said, "Kabuta, I want that rig and team." The highest anyone had paid for a carriage and team was five hundred pounds, and it was almost as good as the one Mike wanted. Nearby, a big fat man spoke to a lad that looked as though he might be his son, and the lad hopped up on the seat and swung the team in on the auction block.

The auctioneer hollered, "Folks, this is Pat Donahue's coach and it is a fine one, with the finest pair of matching mares I've ever seen. The bidding will start at five hundred pounds."

Mike saw the fat man shake his head as if he couldn't believe it would start so cheap. Mike couldn't recognize this man as the man he whipped soundly seventeen years ago, but the twelve-year-old lad looked like Pat did when he was that age. Mike was sure now that this was really Pat. He said softly, "If that is enjoying your money, I'm glad I haven't enjoyed mine."

Kabuta said, "What did you say?"

"Tell you later. The bidding has started and I want that coach and team. Kabuta, you move away from me about twenty feet and bid on it and don't lose it. I don't want to draw attention to myself yet."

He worked himself through the crowd until he was standing right behind Pat's right shoulder. He heard, "Five hundred."

"Five seventy-five," boomed Kabuta.

"Six hundred."

Kabuta stayed silent, and that worried Mike.

The auctioneer said, "Do I hear six hundred one?" and no one responded. "Going once, going twice," and Kabuta said, "Six one."

"Six Two, six two, six two. Do I hear six two?

"Sold to the big Black in the big hat."

The auctioneer looked at Pat and said, "Sorry, Mr. Donahue, its worth a lot more."

Pat said, "I know, but Molly wants a bigger one. Now that our seventh one has come she thinks this one isn't big enough. You know Molly, what Molly wants, Molly gets."

Mike said, "Maybe she thinks she needs the back seat for a nursery, Pat."

He turned and said, "That's just what she said." His eyebrows lifted and his eyes got a little bigger as the fat rolled back. "Michael Ross!" Then he stuck out his pudgy hand and said, "Have you come back to stay, or to sell? I'll give you a handsome price for the place. Molly fancies it, you know."

Mike said, "And what Molly wants, Molly gets."

"That's about it."

"We may stay—we're not sure yet what we'll do. Who do I make the check out to? You or the auction barn?"

"Did you buy my rig, Michael? I thought the Black did."

"He was bidding for the both of us. He's my partner and best friend, from America."

"Well, Mike, I was glad to see you leave, and I hope you don't stay, I want that place of yours. You haven't changed much though. A little broader in the shoulders maybe."

"Hard work, Patrick."

"Nobody calls me that anymore, it's Pat, to my face anyway."

Mike realized that he was looking into the face of an unhappy man. He paid for his purchase and was told he could leave them in the auction barn until morning.

In the morning when Kabuta drove the carriage up to where they were waiting Peg, said, "Those are the prettiest horses I've ever seen."

Mike said, "They're easy to handle too. I imagine you and Katy will drive them all over County Kerry."

A little prick of fear entered Katy's heart. Has he changed his mind and intends to stay here after all, she thought.

Two days later they were driving on the road that ran along the shore of Upper Lake Killarney. Memories were flooding the canyons of Mike's mind and his heart was so full it felt like it might explode. It was getting late in the afternoon and the rain that had been coming down all day stopped, and the clouds rolled away.

Mike pulled the team up to the hitching rack in front of the Ross cottage and slowly got down. He didn't help Katy down from the coach like he usually did, but she understood. He walked ahead of them and placed one foot on the ancient step and rubbed his hands lovingly up and down the pine rail that had worn smooth from the many hands that had slid up and down it, or the seat of pants of the children sliding down. How many times had he done that in his youth? He could almost hear Gabriel laugh and Esther squeal with glee as she would slide down this slick rail, hit the ground on both feet, and then roll across the thick carpet of green grass, to plunge into the clear blue-green waters of the lake.

He could hear his mother say, "How do you kids expect me to get the grass stains out of those clothes?"

And Riley saying, "Oh, Mother, bother the stains, look at the fun they're having."

When Gabriel started to run to his dad, Katy caught him by the arm and said, "Wait, son, let your father be for a while."

They all stood there a long time, watching.

Mike ascended the steps, stopped at the door and knocked several times, but there wasn't anyone here. He ran his hands lovingly over the door post, lifted the latch, and entered the cottage.

He went through every room. Nothing had changed since he was a boy except for Callie's spinet that she insisted she couldn't do without. He went from the parlor to Gabriel's room, and it was clean and just the way he'd left it so many years ago. Mike shook his head. For a fleeting moment he thought he saw Gabe smiling up at him, with an arrow in his hand that he was wrapping a head onto with rawhide. His spirit was definitely present. They had been making arrows just before he was killed. The wax pot was still on the table with the lid on. No one had disturbed this room except to clean it for over seventeen years.

Then he went to Esther's room, and it was the same. Then to his old room, and it was just the way he'd left it.

Then he went into his mother and father's room. The furniture was the same, but the clothing was the O'Casey's.

Finally, he came out of the house and motioned them to come up on the verandah. He still didn't trust his voice, so he motioned them to sit and they did, in the rocking chairs that Riley had made with his own hands from hard maple he cut from his own land.

He took Gabriel and Peggy by the hands and led them toward the milk barns. There was change here. They were much bigger, and so was the chicken house, and as his gaze swept back over the fields he could see they were growing good crops, and the horses and cows in the meadows were slick and fat. This was obviously a prosperous farm, but he was perplexed that there was no one here.

He could see the cow's coming down the lane from the upper meadow to be milked, but there wasn't anyone to milk them.

He was telling his children how much he loved growing up here.

Shaking off his melancholy, he went back to the verandah and said, "Folks, we have work to do. Come in the house." He showed Kabuta and Peg, Gabe's room and said, "This will be your room as long as we stay here." Then he took Katharine and Peggy into Esther's room and said, "This will be your room," and he told Katy they would take his old room. "You boys will have to sleep on the floor in the parlor, or in the hayloft on the hay, it's your choice."

They decided they'd rather sleep on the hay.

"I can't imagine where the O'Casey's are, or the people who work this farm, but if those cows aren't milked their udders could be ruined."

"There must be a wedding or a wake; if there is, none of their friends would miss either of those.

"I'll go drain the separators and pour the cream into cans and clean the separators. And Kabuta, when you get changed will you help me fill the trough with feed, and Katy, you and Peg can help us milk the cows, if you will. It looks like we have about fifty cows to milk." It turned out to be fifty-two.

They had about half of the cows milked when a wagon came down the lane from where the Culpeppers lived. Three men got out of the wagon and they were surprised to see half of the cows milked and in the overnight feed lot.

Earl Culpepper stuck his head in the door and he saw the backs of two big men and two slim women milking the cows, and they were singing as they worked. He could see right away these people were no stranger to milking.

Kabuta got up and turned around to pour a three-gallon bucket of milk in a cream can and Earl backed out of the door.

Kabuta hollered, "Mike, you'd better come and tell this fellow who's stealing his milk," as he emptied his bucket.

Mike emptied his bucket and went out to where the men were conversing. He said, "Aren't you Earl and James Culpepper?"

Earl said, "Yes sir, and this is our brother, Pete."

"I'm Michael Ross, where are the O'Casey's?"

The Culpeppers shook Michael's hand and Earl said to his brothers, "You two get to milking and I'll bring Mr. Ross up on current events."

When the Culpeppers told Kabuta and the ladies they would take over, Kabuta said, "I'm enjoying myself, I'll help you finish, if you don't mind."

Mike took time to introduce them all around and Katy and Peg went to the kitchen to see if they could stir up something for supper. Mike and Earl went to the verandah to discuss business.

When they were seated Earl said, "Mr. Ross, the O'Caseys are gone. But I'm sure you'll find enough food in the house for a day or so. The O'Casey's didn't go into town often, but when they did they set in a good supply."

The lake was calm for a change and the four children were skipping rocks on the water.

Earl said, "Let me start from the beginning. Both of our parents died in the past year and Mother Callie died a month ago. Willy was never the same and he grieved himself to death, and we buried him today.

"He and I went over the books a week ago and he gave them to me. I have them at home and you'll find them in perfect order.

"The O'Caseys said you were a wealthy man and didn't need what they had. We became very close. They had no folks of their own, as you know, so they left what they had equally to my brothers and me.

"The O'Caseys were wonderful folks and we've been happy here. If you can use us, we sure would love to stay."

Mike said, "If we stay, you stay, but I must tell you we've only been back in Ireland two weeks and we're already sick of this constant rainfall. We may stay, but we more than likely we'll sell and go back to America."

"If you do sell, I think the O'Caseys left us almost enough to offer you a fair price. And we'd sure love to have it."

"Patrick Donahue has already told me he'll top any offer I get by five thousand pounds."

Earl's shoulder slumped. "We can't compete with the banker, and we won't work for Pat Donahue."

"I've never been too fond of Mr. Donahue myself. Don't lose hope, Earl. I'm sure we can work something out."

"Well, I see the boys have finished, we'll be here bright and early in the morning, and thank you, Mr. Ross."

"My name is Michael, Earl, and my friends call me Mike. I would like to think we're friends. I'm calling you Earl, and I'll expect you to call me Mike from now on."

"Thank you, Mike, I'll see you in the morning."

Katy called everyone in for a supper of pancakes, eggs and bacon, with sweet buttermilk, and syrup made out of brown sugar. When Mike said grace he thanked God for their safe journey and their good fortune of finding the place so well kept. And he prayed for wisdom in what to do about selling the place.

After supper they all went out on the verandah just as a thin cloud swept slowly over the setting sun, with the different colors of blacks, blues, and white, mingled with the bright rays of the setting sun causing every color imaginable. Then with the craggy mountain and the farm setting mirrored in the blue-green waters of the lake, a double picture was painted by the Master's hand, which held them in awe. Once again Katy burst out, "Oh! Michael, how could you ever have left? But I'll be forever thankful that you did!"

They all expressed their wonder at the beauty of it all, and as the quiet of night gathered around them; the peacefulness that crept through them was captivating.

Mike said, "I've been so happy in our Valley of the Smokes I'd forgotten how beautiful and peaceful it is here. Wait until you see Fort Ross—there's something about that place that's almost haunted, but the whispering of the wind through the pines is like music.

"Wait a minute, there's something in Gabriel's room and in mine that I often wished I had at the gathering of our people in the meeting hall." That thought brought a wave of loneliness to his heart.

As he went through the door he heard Katy say, "Oh! How I miss our people, especially Running Springs and my Chief," and Peg said, "Me too."

Hearing that made up Mike's mind—they would go back. He suddenly realized you can't ever really go home, or where home was when you were young. He'd loved it here in Ireland, and a part of him always would, but the valley was his home.

When he rejoined the family he handed the harp to Kabuta and said, "See what you can do with that. I notice you threw your old cheap one away. I tried to buy you one in St. Louis, but I couldn't find one."

Kabuta tapped the dust out of the harp and started playing a sad, haunting tune of Africa. It sounded so sad that Katharine started to cry and said, "Please don't, daddy."

Then he started playing a gay ditty that Mike knew and he joined in. They played well together and took one request after another until bedtime.

When they went into the house Mike told Kabuta and Peg to take his mother's room and said the boys could have Gabriel's room after all.

The next morning they all, except Mike, saddled horses and rode along the lake front for miles, just looking over the country.

Mike and Earl went into the bank and met with Pat Donahue and went over the accounts. Mike was pleased with the profits that had accumulated over the last twenty-three years, but he didn't think the O'Caseys had paid the Culpeppers as much wages as they should have. There had been only two small raises since he set their wages in the beginning.

After Earl had left the bank and went home, Mike mounted his horse and visited a number of horse ranches and a few small dairies and inquired what they were paying their help. He discovered that all of them were paying better.

When he returned late in the afternoon the Culpeppers were milking and Kabuta was helping them.

He called Earl aside and said, "I did some checking today and discovered that you haven't been getting the going wages that you should have been receiving."

Earl said, "We're aware of it, but that's the offer we made Willie because we raise our own chickens and hogs and feed them with the grain we raise here on the farm. We have a garden and a few fruit trees also. So we've been satisfied with those arrangements. I have a son that we had agreed would go on the payroll when school is out this year."

"Earl, after you left the bank Pat offered me far more than this place is worth, and he said the first thing he was going to do was run you Culpeppers plum out of County Kerry. What's the cause of the bitterness between you and pat?"

"He thinks I'm the father of his first son."

"Are you?"

"I don't know. I could be, but I know a number of men that lay with her before she married Pat. Some of us thought you had. She bragged that she could have married you, because you liked what she had."

"I assure you she made the offer, but I never touched her except to dance with her. I always prayed that I would marry a virgin, and I decided if God was going to give me one, I should be one myself. I am so thankful that Katy is the only woman I've ever known that way, and I'm the only one she has ever had, too. God has richly blessed us, and I believe it's because we have tried to live a clean Christian life, and to share that belief with others.

We're sharing it with an Indian village in the valley where we live, and we are beginning to see a tremendous change in their way of living."

Earl said, "I admit the boy favors me a lot. I told Helen all about it before we got married. I told her if she didn't love me enough to marry me for what I was and what I would become, she didn't love me enough. She forgave me and said, 'As long as you're true to me, I'll never bring it up,' and she never has. I have been true and I always will be. I love Helen and she's a good wife and mother.

"I ride over to Limerick in County Cork to do my banking. It's a nuisance for me, but I just don't trust Pat. I really don't blame him for feeling the way he does, and there's not a day goes by that I don't wish I'd never known Molly."

The next morning Mike told the family that he and Earl would be gone for two days. "We're going to Limerick. I'm going to sell the farm to the Culpeppers."

Katy rushed to hug and kiss him and Gabriel said, "Oh boy, did you hear that, Peggy? We're going home."

When Mike and Earl reached the bank and found out how much money the Culpeppers had, Mike said, "That's not near as much as Pat offered me."

Earl said, "I'm sorry Mike, but there's no place we can get more without getting a mortgage on the place, and we just don't want to do that. Your neighbor, Mr. O'Callaghan, wants to sell his place and we have enough to by it with all his stock and equipment. We just don't want to go into debt."

"I respect that, Earl," Mike said, "and I'll sell you my place for four hundred pounds less than what you have. That will make up for the wages you should have had. I would give that much just to see Pat's face when he finds out you own our place free and clear.

"There's some memorabilia in the house I'll take, everything else goes with the place."

The papers were drawn up and signed and the bank gave Mike a bank draft for the full amount of the sale.

With all his business done Mike took a week to just walk with his family over the old trails he traveled as a boy, pointing out to them where he had killed wolf, deer or elk. He took them fishing at his favorite boyhood spots.

Mike had been putting off going to his family's graves, but finally he asked Kabuta to help him clean the spot and divide the Iris bulbs for replanting.

They took tools and picnic baskets and sailed for Fort Ross on the little island on Lower Lake. When they tied up at the dock, Mike realized that someone had replaced the old dock with a new one. The underbrush had been cleared away and someone was turning the place into a beautiful park. He was pleasantly surprised to see that the Irises had been thinned and replanted all around and over the graves. It was evident that this was to be the main attraction in the park. There was a plaque, telling of the tragic death of his family.

Kabuta, Peg and the children stayed around the old fort and let Mike and Katy go on to the grave site. Mike removed his hat and lowered his head and let the memories of his childhood flood his heart and soul. Tears flowed softly down his cheeks as Katy held on to his arm, weeping softly.

After a while, Mike shook himself and led Katy deeper into the woods, where they sat down on a log.

"Listen to the wind blowing through the trees and let your imagination run free," he said.

They sat there for a few minutes. Then Katy said, "Music, it sounds like an orchestra playing softly."

"Yes, you hear it, too. Katy, when I let my imagination run wild I can hear my mother singing my favorite Irish lullaby."

After they showed the children where their grand parents and uncle and aunt namesakes were buried, they returned to the cottage.

The next day they packed what they would need in the buckboard and Mike went to see Earl and said, "We're going to see some of the historical places and then come back to spend one more night here and pick up the things I wanted. Then you can occupy the house."

It took them three weeks to see the things they wanted to see, but it rained so much they didn't enjoy it as much as they had anticipated. It only increased their longing to return to their valley that nestled high in the mountains of north central North America, and the beautiful people that had become their family.

* * * * *

When they returned, they boxed up the things that Mike wanted to take. Then they went into Dublin and rented rooms to wait until Captain Bill put into port. Mike had made inquiries and found out that he would dock in a week and sail a week afterward, so they had two weeks to kill.

The Culpeppers came to milk the cows the morning they left in time to tell them good-bye, and the other two brothers thanked Mike profusely.

They went to every theater production in town and ate at the best places. Having finally realized the extent of their fortune, they spared no expense.

One night after they had come in from an evening of pleasure, and Katy laid beside him with her breast rising and falling in gentle slumber, Mike started thinking about all the things he could do with his wealth. Maybe he could go into politics and become the leader of Ireland—and perhaps be the one to gain their independence from England. He had all the money he would ever need and the only thing left for him to gain was power.

The vision of Pat Donahue's fat face floated in front of him and he remembered how unhappy he looked. He had become the most powerful man in

County Kerry, and what had he gained? Mike decided that what he had gained was weight, a wife who didn't love him, and the hate of almost everyone he met.

Then he started thinking about the hours he would be away from his family, and what it would do to them if he tried to become the most powerful man in Ireland. He could see Katy's smile fade away, he saw himself become a stranger to his two beautiful children. He would lose the respect and love of Kabuta and Peg. Then he thought of the Scriptures that said, "What doth it profit a man if he gains the whole world and loses his own soul?" He knew he couldn't lose his soul, because he committed it to Christ long ago. But he also knew that he could push Jesus off the throne of his life, and push Him into a corner of his heart. No, he would gain nothing. He would lose all he loved and held dear. He slipped out of bed onto his knees and asked God to forgive him of his self-indulgent thoughts. Then he said, "This is the day the Lord has made, I will rejoice and be glad in it."

His mind was made up, he would continue to live the peaceful life and let others strive for the power.

The next morning at breakfast Katy said, "Mike, there's a new play at the theater tonight and Peg and I want you and Kabuta to take us to see it."

Kabuta said, "You take them, Mike and I'll stay with the children."

Peg said, "No, Thank you. I'm not leaving this place without my man after what happened before. Kabuta, haven't you noticed that we are an oddity here? Have you seen any other Black people?"

"No, but they have treated us with respect, haven't they?"

"Yes, except for that big redhead where Katy and I had lunch yesterday. I'm not about to go out again without you."

"What did he do to frighten you?" Kabuta asked.

"You tell him Katy, I'm too embarrassed to talk about it."

Katy said, "He was a big fellow, and rather handsome. Actually, you could see he was interested in Peg from the moment we sat down to eat our lunch. When he approached our table and started making advances, Peg showed him her wedding band and said, "I'm married."

He said, "That doesn't matter, I just wanted to have a little fun with you for a little while in the back room."

"We both stuck our hands in our bags and pulled out our double-barrel derringers. We paid our bill and backed out of the place, with him laughing at us."

Kabuta said, "Mike, what would happen if I broke this redhead's neck?"

Mike said, "You won't have to if I get to him first! Kabuta, there's nothing the Irish like better than a good fair fight. If he insults Peg again in your presence, you can beat the hell out of him; the others will respect you for it. I'll make sure his friends won't get into it. We'll see it's a fair fight. But if he says he's had enough and apologizes, they'll expect you to forget it.

"Don't take a weapon with you, if you kill an Irishman I might not be able to get you out of Ireland alive. You know I'll be armed and I'll take over if he draws a gun. Agreed? We may be just borrowing trouble, he probably won't show up, and if he does, when he sees Peg with us he won't cause any trouble."

Kabuta said. "I hope he shows. I can't stand anybody insulting my little dove."

Mike had heard of a pub that was supposed to have the best food in town. They couldn't take the children there so they got a woman to come in to entertain the kids until bedtime. They went to the pub, and it was the same one where the man had insulted Peg.

They had donned the buckskins the Indians gave them, with the knee-high moccasins and their big cowboy hats, and everyone noticed them when they came in the pub. They planned to have their evening meal there before going to the theater. There was no place to hang their hats while they were eating, so they kept them on.

They had just sat down when the redhead came in and ordered a tankard of ale. Looking as though he'd already had too much to drink; he took his drink and started for a table when he saw Peg. He acted like he didn't see anyone but her as he approached her table.

Mike stood up and said, "Friend, we're strangers in Dublin and we're not looking for trouble, I understand that you insulted Mrs. Kabuta yesterday. I'm sure you've had time to think about what you did, and being the gentleman you are, you've come to apologize to her and her husband. If that is your intention, I'm sure they will accept your apology. But if it's not your intention, as his best friend I have spoken to the local officer on the beat and he has assured me that he will not interfere when Mr. Kabuta beats you to within an inch of your life."

Everyone in the pub heard this exchange, and when the redhead burst into laughter they all joined in. The man bent over with laughter and when he could get his composure he said, "Man, I'm the heavyweight champion of the British Isles!"

Kabuta hadn't said a word, but now he rose from his chair and took off his hat and handed it to Peg and said, "Would you hold this for me, my little dove?"

This brought another roar of laughter. Kabuta removed his buckskin shirt to reveal muscular arms and chest. He said, "We should go outside so I won't bust this place up with you, Red."

As the redhead looked at Kabuta he realized that his announcement that he was the heavyweight champion of the British Isles hadn't impressed him at all. Perhaps he had insulted the wrong woman. But it was too late to back out now.

Shannon, the innkeeper said, "The bar is closed." He took charge, saying, "Now men, there'll be no interference by any bystander. The fight will end when one or the other can't, or refuses to get to his feet, and there will be no time outs. Is this agreeable with you, men?

They both assured him it was.

They stepped out into the street and Mike saw that the officer he had spoken to before had called for reinforcements and they had blocked the street. He shouted, "Silence. Now that I have your attention, I want to inform you that if anyone interferes in this fight, in the paddy wagon you go.

"Shannon, we've blocked off the street so nothing will interfere with the proceedings."

There was a big man standing up in a cart, trying to get someone to bet on the Black, but he wasn't getting many bets until he offered three to one, then he got a few small bets. Mike said, "Mister, how much can you afford to lose?"

"Twelve hundred pounds," he replied.

Mike said, "I only have two hundred on me. I'll cover that much."

Peg said, "Katy, will you loan me a hundred? I want to show Kabuta that I have confidence in him."

Katy gave her the hundred and said to the man, "I'll take a hundred of that, and Mrs. Kabuta has a hundred that says her man will win."

The man had no trouble getting small bets after the crowd saw the confidence the Black's friends and family had in him.

Shannon held the bets.

There were many other small bets between other men around the circle of onlookers.

Shannon said, "This is a fight to the finish, and anything goes, except there will be no gouging of the eyes. Let the fight begin."

Red stepped to the mark and struck a pose. Kabuta hit him on the chin with a straight right that shook him down to his heels. He went staggering backwards and would have gone down if the crowd hadn't held him up.

Red shook his head and came in pumping his hard fists. Kabuta covered up behind his own big arms and let Red punch himself out. He caught most of the blows on his strong arms, but a few of them got through to his massive chest, and one caught him high on the forehead. Though strong himself, Kabuta was aware that his opponent was tough and experienced, and one false move could be disaster.

The crowd was going wild and the big man said to Shannon, "You might as well give me the purse now."

Kabuta keep bobbing and weaving, sticking a stiff left into Red's breadbasket once in a while, but mostly he let Red punch himself out. No man could keep up that pace for very long, especially one that had drunk as much ale as Red had. Kabuta keep covering up, getting in a punch here and there. When Red stepped back and took a deep breath, Kabuta stepped in and stuck a stiff left into his gut and followed it with a left hook to the rib cage. He followed that with a left and right to the face that left Red stunned and dazed, but he was game.

He came back with a straight right flush on the chin that made Kabuta blink. Red hit Kabuta with every punch and hook he had in his repertoire, and Kabuta absorbed it all and refused to go down. No other man he'd ever faced had taken that kind of punishment without being knocked out. Red had given about all he had, but he had taken more than he ever had and he knew he didn't have much more to give.

When Red's punches started to lose their sting, Kabuta walked in with three fast, stiff punches to Red's chin and he threw a right that caught him square on the chin. That punch lifted Red off his feet and he found himself lying on his back in the middle of the street, looking up at the stars.

He rolled over on his stomach and started to push himself up. Then dropped back down, rolled back on his back and looked up at Kabuta and said, "That's enough, I'm not getting a shilling out of this."

The crowd that had been going crazy a few minutes ago was now strangely quiet at the sight of the fallen warrior.

Kabuta stood with his legs spread apart, standing like a mighty rock, looking down at his fallen foe. When he reached down and took Red's hand and pulled him to his feet, and these big men hugged one another, the crowed roared their approval. They had seen the fight of their lives and it didn't cost them a penny.

"Red, are you ready to apologize to my wife now?"

Red nodded, and Kabuta motioned Peg to come forward.

When she stood before them, Kabuta said "Red, meet my wife, Mrs. Peg Kabuta."

Red responded by saying, "Mrs. Kabuta, I've never been more sorry for anything in my life than I am for the things I said to you. Will you accept my most sincere and humble apology? And I promise you, I'll never make that mistake again."

Peg nodded and rejoined her friends. She and Katy went with Mike to collect their winnings.

Kabuta shook Red's hand and said, "I was glad to hear you say you'd had enough. I know you had much more in you, and I'd had enough of you, too, redhead. I sure hope I don't have to go through this again to protect my wife's honor. I don't want to take another beating like that."

Red lowered his voice and said, "You're right, I could have continued, but I wasn't getting a shilling for this fight, and I knew I was getting beat. I don't want to get my jaw broken, or my brains beaten out for nothing. Mr. Kabuta, you are quite a fighter."

Kabuta called Mike forward and said, "Red, meet the man that taught me all I know about fighting. You'd better be glad it was me and not him you were fighting."

Mike shook Kabuta's hand and said, "Congratulations, you just made us twelve hundred pounds richer, but no thanks. I want no part of him."

And he shook Red's hand.

The man Mike collected his bets from walked up and said, "If you men want to make some real money fighting, I can direct you to the right people."

Kabuta spoke through swollen, bleeding lips and said, "Look at my face— one eye nearly closed, both lips split open and my body feels like I've been kicked in a dozen places by a horse. I can't speak for Mike, but no sir, I don't intend to get my brains beat out for money. Protecting my wife's honor is another thing."

Mike said, "That goes for me, too."

When they got back to their room, Peg gave Kabuta a bath in a steaming tub of hot water that she had poured a lot of salt into.

"What are you doing to me, woman?" he screamed, "that hurts worse than the beating I just took out in the street."

"You never took a beating, and I never want to hear you say so again. You were magnificent."

"You tell my body that and make it believe it, and then I'll believe it. I'm hurting in every muscle in my body, and some I don't have."

After she took care of his hurts she poured more hot water in the tub. He lay in the tub until his tight, aching muscles finally relaxed, and then he crawled into the cool white sheets.

Katy and Mike knocked on the door and when Peg let them in Mike said, "We're ready to go to the theater."

Kabuta said, "Mike, I'm going to trust you to take care of our girls tonight, I'm not getting out of this bed."

Peg said, "You go ahead and I'll stay here and keep my hero warm."

Mike said, "I have time to pick up two more tickets, so we'll take the kids."

CHAPTER THIRTY-ONE

When they boarded Captain Bill's ship for the return trip for Richmond three days later, Kabuta's face was still swollen and sore.

Captain Bill said, "All Dublin is buzzing about that fight. I'd have given free passage to have seen it."

"I'd accept, too," Kabuta said.

A few weeks later they were lounging on deck, discussing what they would do when they reached Richmond. They decided they would winter over there and head for the valley as soon as the snow melted off the Blue Ridge Mountains of Virginia. They would hunt and fish some and get their supplies ready for the long haul home.

As they sat there Peg spied a ship following way off in the distance. She said, "Look!" and she pointed at the ship. It was just a dot on the horizon when Peg first saw it, but as they watched it they realized it was closing in fast.

Mike watched it for a while until he was sure it was overtaking them rapidly. He went to tell Captain Bill.

Bill said, "Yes, our watchman in the crow's nest spotted it and there is some concern. It's not flying a flag. I have just given orders to raise every sail we have to try to outrun them. We're heavily loaded and I seriously doubt we can. I hope we can get so close to Richmond they won't dare fire on us. We haven't worried about pirate ships for some time now, but I just heard in England there's a daredevil working these waters.

"So far they haven't dared fire on a ship as well fortified as ours. If they board us, we'll fight to the last man to protect your wives and children. Keep them below deck. If they see women and children aboard it will make them more determined to take us."

Mike went and told the women to take the children below deck and keep them in the cabins until further notice and to close the portholes. He explained what Bill had told him.

They all went below and Mike and Kabuta cleaned and oiled their guns and strapped on their pistols. Then they sharpened their sword, broadsword and knives. They were as ready as they could be.

Kabuta went up on deck and Bill said, "I've called a meeting of the men and I think you and Mike should attend. After all, you have more to lose than we do.

Kabuta took Mike the message and asked, "What do you think he meant about us having more to lose than they did? Does he know how much money we're carrying? Would he rob us?"

"There's no way he could know how much we have, and Bill wouldn't rob us if he thought we had a fortune. He was thinking about our wives and children. Kabuta, just think what a bunch of pirates on a ship at sea would do with them!"

"Over our dead bodies," Kabuta replied.

"That's why Bill wants them to stay out of sight. If they see women it'll make them more determined to take the ship."

After every sail they had was catching all the wind they could, Bill gathered his men and told them that a ship was bearing down on them and that it wasn't flying their colors. "This might mean nothing, but it may be the pirate ship we heard about in England. It's obvious that we can't outrun her, and she probably has us out-gunned and out- manned. You're all good men and you know what you have to do. If they attack us, we'll let them know they've been in a fight."

He issued every man a musket and a pistol, and each man went to his post to be ready for the attack they were sure would come.

When night closed around them they entered a dense fog and put out all lights. The ship following them fired a cannon shot at the spot where they disappeared, but it fell way short. Bill changed directions a little bit and headed straight for the mouth of the James River.

The other ship fired again, but the ball fell a hundred yard north of them and was still short.

They could not be seen and they could barely see the lights of the other ship. When the ship overtook them it was three hundred yards off to their right.

All of a sudden the wind died and the sails hung limp and the ship slowed to a crawl. Both ships were barely moving.

Kabuta called Mike out on deck in the middle of the night, and when Mike appeared Kabuta said, "Mike, we can't outrun them. I have an idea. It's as dark as it can be in this thick fog. The Pirates know we're running, and they would never suspect someone might board them. If we could slip aboard and slit their sails and a good wind came up, it would rip them to shreds and we would sail away."

Mike said, "I think it's worth a try."

They went to the Captain's quarters and Mike said, "Bill, we have an idea that we think will work, and if a stiff wind comes up we have a chance to get away."

Bill interrupted and said, "I fail to see how that would help us. Wind will benefit them more than it will us."

Kabuta said, "Not if they have no sails. Aren't the sails all attached to the mast?"

"Yes, and they have two large mast poles on a ship of that size."

Mike said, "Give us two sharp saws and a grab hook, and some burlap we can wrap around the hook so it won't make much noise when we throw it over the rail. We'll saw the mast poles almost through and when the wind hits those sails they'll come tumbling down, and we'll sail away. As you said, we have more to lose that any man on this ship. Let us do it, we make a good team."

Bill said, "I like it, but the oars from a longboat are pretty noisy. The longboat will take you within a hundred yard of the ship and one man will row you alongside in a dinghy; Less noise, less danger."

They brought Mike the iron hook and he wrapped a thick layer of burlap around it. Mike and Kabuta strapped on their pistols and swords.

Bill said, "Mike, Kabuta, come to my cabin." When Kabuta and Mike were sitting across the desk from Bill, he said, "Let's pray." They removed their hats and bowed their heads, and Bill prayed, "Dear Father God, bring Mike and Kabuta back safely to us, In Jesus' name. Amen."

When the longboat pointed its bow toward the pirate ship its last light flickered out. The fog socked in to where they couldn't see from one end of the boat to the other. Bill's first mate was in command of the longboat and when he calculated they were a hundred yards off, Mike, Kabuta and the oarsman slipped into the dinghy.

When they came to the ship it was just to their right. The oarsman said, "We almost missed her." He paddled alongside of the ship where they had seen the light, and the oarsman said, ""Do you hear that noise of something striking the side of the ship? They've made it easy for you. That's a rope ladder. Some sailor will catch hell for forgetting to pull that in."

Kabuta said, "Yes, too easy, and they might have a dozen men waiting for us to stick our stupid heads up so they can whack them off with a broadsword. Row us around to the other side."

When they got around to the other side Mike threw the hook over the rail and it made a slight thud when it hit the deck. Mike drew the rope slowly to him and the hook caught.

Kabuta said, "Let me go up first, I'm heavier than you are. If it holds me, you know you're safe to come up."

Kabuta slipped quietly over the rail and Mike was on his way up as soon as Kabuta disappeared.

It was so dark they got down on their hands and knees and crawled to find the masts that they wanted to weaken. They discovered that there were a few grain sacks stacked around each pole, probably placed there so the men could sit on them and lean their backs against the poles when they were taking a break. They set the sacks aside and paused to listen, but hearing no noise they started sawing slowly to keep as quiet as possible.

Sailors that serve on a ship any length of time know where everything is and can move in the dark with ease.

Kabuta saw the glow of a cigarette come out of a doorway and heard the door slam shut. The glow of the cigarette was coming straight to where he had stacked the bags of grain. Kabuta moved quietly in front of the bags. He couldn't see the man but the glow of the cigarette showed him where the man's chin was. Kabuta hit him so hard on his chin that his neck snapped like a reed. He was dead almost by the time he hit the deck. Kabuta felt for a pulse alongside of his neck.

When Mike heard the thud when the man hit the deck, he drew his sword and waited. Kabuta did the same. When they were satisfied the danger had passed, they resumed sawing. When Kabuta had his pole cut two-thirds through, he swept the sawdust with his gloved hand close to the base of the pole and stacked the sacks back around the pole, hiding the cut and sawdust. Then he dragged the dead man to the rail just as Mike joined him.

Kabuta said, "I'm afraid I killed this gent. We'll have to take him with us; you go on down, and I'll lower him down to you."

When they were all aboard the dinghy they rowed quietly away.

When they got to where they thought the longboat would be waiting, they missed it. The oarsman started rowing around and around in ever-widening circles. The ocean waters were so calm it seemed as though they were gliding on a glassy sea. Before they saw it they almost bumped into the longboat. When they finally boarded it the first mate said, "We were about to give you up. What have you here?"

Kabuta said, "I had to kill a man, and we had to bring him along so our surprise would work."

It was thundering and lightning east of them and it seemed to be coming closer. Kabuta said, "I hope that storm hits us before daylight, or before this fog lifts. If it doesn't, we're going to be sitting ducks for their big guns."

Mike said, "If the storm hits us, they won't be following us, that's for sure."

They had no more than gotten the dinghy and longboat on board and battened down when the storm hit and swept the fog away. The ship shot forward and Mike and Kabuta stumbled right into two women that had been concerned, but when they saw their husband's safe aboard, that concern turned to seething anger.

"You're never, no never, to do something like that again without our knowledge!" Katy said.

"We have every right to know when our husbands are facing danger," Peg added. "At least we could be praying for you."

Day was just breaking when the storm hit and they could see the pirate ship start forward, and then the masts came crashing down.

Bill said, "Praise the Lord, we'll be in Richmond before they get that repaired. That was quite an idea you had, Mike."

"Kabuta suggested we slip aboard and slit their sails first, but I thought this would be easier, and not so dangerous. It worked, that's the main thing."

Clearly, two minds are better than one.

They weathered the storm and after it passed they had smooth sailing, and a week later they sailed peacefully into the mouth of the James River.

The children had the run of the ship. The cabin boy, Will Clark, taught them all the knots they used on the ship. Peggy had taken a shine to him, and she had told him all about the valley and how nice the Indian people were.

Will went to Mike and said, "Mister Ross, I've ridden, and worked with horses all my life. And this is my first voyage, and I hate it. Peggy and the others have been telling me about your valley. Would it be possible for me to go with you to your valley?"

Mike said, "We'll see," and he went to find Katy. Mike said, "Will Clark wants to go with us to our valley. What do you think?"

Katy surprised him when she said, "I've gotten to know the boy very well on this long voyage across the sea, and I like him. He's a nice boy, and Peggy's going to need a husband some day."

"Next you'll be telling me that Peg wants to take Sterling along for Katharine."

"Could be," she said, imperiously.

"Where are we going to get girls for Gabriel and Riley?"

"We haven't crossed that bridge yet. But there are plenty of beautiful Indian maidens for them to choose from."

When they entered the mouth of the James River Mike and Kabuta joined their wives as they stood along the rail, looking at the green fields of corn and cotton and the cows and horses grazing along the hillsides.

Mike noticed the tears slipping down the girls' cheeks and said, "Girls, what's wrong? Are you missing Ireland already? We can go back if you want."

Katy hit him gently on the arm and said, "Oh Mike!" as she hugged him tightly, "I've never been so happy to see cotton fields in my life."

Peg, said, "Yeah, and to know we'll soon be straddling horses, headed for our Valley of the Smokes. I didn't know I could be so happy."

Katy said, "Mike, we were so scared you'd want to stay in Ireland. Peg and

I had resigned ourselves to be happy there, but we're sure glad we won't have to make the effort."

Kabuta said, "I'm just as glad to see Virginia as you girls are, but I don't want to stay here long."

Mike said, "Girls, Kabuta and I think we should spend the winter here and leave in the early spring."

"It would be good to spend some time with mom and dad," Katy said."

Kabuta said, "And it'll give us time to decide exactly what we want to take back with us, and to buy the things we need. We'll buy our horses first and start breaking them right away."

As soon as they docked Mike rented a carriage and Kabuta drove their families out to the plantation.

Mike took the cashier's check from the sale of his farm and deposited it in the bank. Truitt Day was just a few years older than Mike when they had met when Mike first came to America, and he handled Mike's money back then. After a few pleasantries Mike said, "As you know, I had all my assets transferred to St. Louis to your establishment out there. We're going to spend the winter here and I want what Captain Alcott left me and what I just deposited, to stay here for the time being; put seven hundred pounds in a checking account, and the rest of it in a market account. We'll be leaving here in the early spring, and at that time I'll transfer all of my assets to St. Louis."

Truitt said, "I'll set it up for you, and I'll be going to St. Louis to head our operation out there as soon as the snow melts next spring."

Mike said, "Good, then we'll see one another once in a while, Lord willing."

"Our trustees think St. Louis is going to be one of our most economic booms for us and you'll be one of our largest investors. I appreciate your confidence in our establishment, and I'll assure you I'll guard your investment well."

Mike took the checkbook and went out to Mr. Whitlock's and bought a young stud and gear and rode out to the plantation to join his family.

Mike's family would spend the winter with Katy's folks, but the following day Kabuta's family moved into the house he and Mike built across the river, next door to Ellis and Lola.

When Ted Chambers finished setting up his retirement the way he wanted it, he said, "Ellis, would you go into town with me and pick out the four horses you think I need, a good saddle and two pack saddles? As you well know, I always had your dad drive me around, and I've never been much of a horseman. I'm pretty good with a shotgun or rifle, but I've never shot a pistol or bow and arrow. You have to teach me a lot this summer. Mike told me to ride some every day to get my butt toughened up, so I'm depending on you to get me in shape."

Ellis said, "It'll be a pleasure."

They went to Paul Whitlock's place the next morning and bought everything Ted wanted except the packsaddles. They decided to wait and get Mike or Kabuta to pick out the other things he'd need.

Ted's training started the next day. He could shoot the shotgun and rifle accurately already, but Ellis taught him how to increase his speed in bringing them into play. The side arms were more difficult for him, and he would never reach the speed of Ellis, Mike and Kabuta, but he worked hard and became quite capable.

He bounced in the saddle until Ellis taught him how to use his legs and learn how to let his body flow in rhythm with the gait of his horse. At the end of the first day of riding he was so sore he wasn't sure he wanted to go west after all. But after a month of hard work he liked the fact that he was getting tough, and the flab he had was disappearing and being replaced with firm muscle. And the day finally came when the soreness faded away and he found himself looking forward to saddling his horse and riding for miles. He and Ellis had taken camp gear and ridden over the mountains to the village of Hope and back, and Ted was beginning to really enjoy this sense of freedom that came from being out in the fresh air and doing just what he wanted to. Long before Mike returned he knew he would be ready for anything that lay in front of him, and he was eager for the adventure.

Sterling had just turned thirteen and he became fond of Ted, and when he didn't have to work on the farm he went with him everywhere. He wasn't happy on the farm. He hated everything about farming except working the horses and cattle. He read everything he could get his hands on about the frontier. He said, "Mr. Ted, if mom and dad gives me permission, would you let me go west with you?"

Ted had become just as fond of Sterling as Sterling had of him. He said, "Sterling, nothing would make me happier, but it would break your mother's heart."

A few days later Sterling went to his father and said, "Father, you know that I love you, mom, sis and Arthur, but you know how I hate farming. Would you talk to mom and convince her to let me go with Mr. Ted when he goes west with Mr. Mike and Kabuta?"

Ellis and Lola spent some sleepless nights discussing this.

Ellis said, "Darling, he hates farming and he'll run away when he gets a little older, anyway."

"But Ellis, he's so young."

"Mr. Ted, Kabuta and Peg will look after him. I know it's going to hurt you, darling, it hurts me too. But it's going to hurt a lot more if we wake up some morning and he's run away. If we let him go with our blessings he'll be with friends that will take care of him and we won't worry so much. He'll run away if we refuse to let him go. Then he'll be alone out there, and we'll worry ourselves sick to bed."

Lola said, "You have a talk with Mr. Ted, and if he says he'll look after him, he can go."

The next morning Ted was helping Ellis and the boys weed the cornfield. Ellis said, "Mr. Ted, Sterling wants to go west with you. And if it's all right with you, I'll have a talk with Mr. Mike and Mr. Kabuta, and if they agree, we're going to let him go.

"It hurts us something awful that he wants to leave us, but we're afraid he'll run away and try to find you if we refuse to let him go."

"Ellis, that's a wise choice. I've become very fond of Sterling, and he's a fine young man. But surely you can see his heart isn't in weeding corn. He has big dreams about the west. I'd be happy to become his surrogate father, and I'll make it my business to see he comes to no harm."

"Lola and I are happy that Arthur doesn't want to leave us. He said he was going to be the best farmer in Virginia, just like Mr. O'Flannery, across the river.

"Mr. O'Flannery is buying all our extra corn and hog meat, as well as chickens and eggs. He's a big cotton farmer and he buys a lot of food for his slaves.

"Arthur and our baby girl will have a house to live in if they marry and choose to stay with us. Thanks to the Captain, you, Kabuta and Mr. Mike, we're doing real good here."

Ted hollered, "Sterling, will you come here a minute?"

Sterling came running.

Ted said, "Sterling, if I bought you four horses and gear, with all the supplies you'll need, would you go west with me and Kabuta and Mike's families?"

Sterling rolled his eyes up to his father and said, "Could I, papa?"

"Sterling, your mama and I talked it over last night, and it will hurt us to see you go. We want you to promise that you'll mind Mr. Ted, just like you mind your mama and me. Mama said if you promised to do that, you could go."

"I promise, papa!" He dropped his hoe and hugged his papa and ran to the house to hug his mama and to tell her he would mind Mr. Ted, "And mama, I know you and papa will pray for me, and I promise I'll pray for you, too. I love you, mama, now I've got to go help papa."

She hugged him close to her breast for a long time and said, "Wait a minute." She gave him a cool jug of milk and a sack of cookies to take to the field with him, and as soon as he was out the door she sat down and let the tears flow. She prayed, "Dear Lord, our boy is leaving us. Dear Jesus, keep him in the hollow of your hand. I ask it in your precious name, amen."

* * * * *

Kabuta decided to ride out to see Ellis and Lola while Mike was conducting business, but he told Peg he would be back before bedtime. He wanted to eat Lola's good cooking. As he rode up the James he hoped she'd have ham hock and pinto beans, cornbread and sweet milk. They couldn't get that in Ireland. Boy! How he'd missed that.

Mike reached the plantation just in time to sit down to a good meal with the family.

After they were in bed Mike said, "Truitt Day, the man who has been taking care of our assets here, is going to be transferred to St. Louis in the spring and at that time he'll transfer the rest of our assets to our account out there."

Mike was never one to waste time, so the next morning he, Kabuta and Will Clark went to Whitlock's horse ranch. When Paul recognized Mike and Kabuta he said, "It's good to see you two again, and I still have the best horses and mules in Virginia."

Mike said, "It's good to see you too. We want nothing over four years old and we prefer three. We want three mares to ride, with saddles and bridles for them, and ten more mares with pack saddles."

"I have that many broke for riding, but two of them are just over two years old the others are from three to four. They're all ready to ride, but none of them has ever had a packsaddle on. The three and four-year-olds are carrying foals. If that's a problem, I can give you three two-and-a-half-year-olds that haven't been broken yet."

"We'll take them instead; we have time to break them our way. If you can get them in a corral we'll come back around one o'clock to look them over. We have to meet Ted Chambers for lunch," Mike said.

"They'll be waiting, and you'd better bring your check book. If you need horses you won't be able to pass these up. I'm confident of that."

As they rode toward town Kabuta said, "Mike, would you have any objections in taking Sterling to the valley with us?"

"No, not at all, Katy told me that Peg wanted to take him along, if his parents would allow it and he wanted to go."

"Ellis said that he and Ted have become close friends and Sterling has been begging them to let him go, and after Ted assured them that he would be happy to become Sterling's surrogate father and watch out for him, they decided to let him go, if it was all right with us. He said Ted bought himself and Sterling four each good geldings, and all the weapons we suggested each person would need. He also said they had been practicing horse riding, and with those weapons, until Ted has reached his capabilities, and he thinks Sterling can outdraw any of us with the pistols."

When they were seated in the cafe waiting for their food, Ted said, "Mike, Kabuta, would either of you have any objections to my taking Sterling with me?"

Mike said, "Kabuta just told me that Ellis said that you were so sure we wouldn't, you went out and bought practically everything he would need."

Ted laughed and said, "All except the supplies you think we'll need."

Kabuta said, "To answer your question, we're delighted. Will is going with us too."

As they rode back to pick up their horses Mike said to Kabuta, "When Ted first approached us about going west with us I doubted that he would really get himself in shape to make the trip, but after seeing him today, I have no doubt."

Kabuta said, "I've never seen such a change in a man. He doesn't even look like the same man, he looks ten years younger."

They looked over the horses and gear and Mike gave Paul a check and they took the horses back to their old place and put them in the corral near the waterfall.

The next day Peg and Kabuta moved into the cabin and that morning, Kabuta, Mike, Will Clark and Sterling started breaking horses. A few days later Mike went into the mercantile store and ordered all the things they would need in the spring. Mike said, "We don't want this delivered until the snow melts off the Blue Ridges. But I wanted to place the order now, so you would be sure to have them at that time."

"I'll have it, and Mr. Ross, it's good to have you back. When you left here I figured that red hair of yours would be decorating some Indian brave's lance. How are the Captain and Ted Chambers, I haven't seen either of them in ages?"

"The Captain is dead. Ted is fine."

"The Captain's dead? Hard to believe, he seemed to be a sturdy chap."

"Over a year ago; He left his place to the Fullers, and Ted and I and Kabuta sold them our places." Mike glanced upward and whispered, "Forgive me, Lord, for that little lie." He just figured if the man thought they bought the place he would respect them more.

"Those niggers are riding high, aren't they?"

"I don't know any niggers," Mike said, rather sharply, "and I wouldn't take it kindly if my good friends, the Fullers, were treated unkindly."

"No sir, Mr. Ross, not by me they won't. Live and let live, that's my motto."

Mike said, "I'll pay you for these things when they are delivered."

Almost every day, weather permitting, everyone who was riding west in the spring, including the children, rode and trained their horses. By the time the snow melted off the Blue Ridge Mountains, the horses obeyed their masters' every command. They were ready.

CHAPTER THIRTY-TWO

On a cold spring morning Katy and Peg said a tearful good-bye to Katy's mother and father. They were all aware of the fact that they probably would never see one another again.

They crossed the river to meet the rest of their party, and Lola was clinging to Sterling, moaning softly. When she finally released him he ran and hugged his little brother and sister, ran and hugged his dad and said, "Thank you, papa, for understanding and getting mama to. I'll love you always."

He jumped on his horse; picked up the lead ropes of his other horses, and led them up the road, with tears blinding him.

Ted Chambers caught up with Sterling and rode silently beside him. When Mike started to mount his horse, Ralph rode up and said, "Wait, Mike, I have something for you." He stepped down from the buggy and handed Mike the jewel- studded sword that was shoved down into a new leather scabbard. Mike drew it out and ran his hands lovingly along its fine blade and said, "Thank you, Ralph, I'm thankful to have it back."

The end of the day found them camped at the little lake nestled in the canyon, with the creek flowing out of it, where the big cat almost got Peg when she was a young bride. She took the children there and told them the story. Gabriel, Riley, Peggy and Katharine went fishing while everyone else got busy taking care of the horses and preparing supper.

Sterling and Will Clark were determined to prove their worth to the adults, so they worked hard, even though they would have been much happier fishing.

After they had all the packs off and their horses staked, they managed to get their poles and pull in a few trout.

Mike walked up and said, "That's enough for breakfast. Clean them and put them in a bucket, and we'll hang them high in a tree so the pesky coons can't get them. Then we'll go eat."

They were on the trail by sunup the next morning and, due to the fact they were using packhorses instead of pulling heavily loaded wagons, they reached the little Quaker village of Hope, where they had stopped for the night many years ago.

Katy said, "Look how it's grown!"

Peg said, "Look, Katy, a cafe, maybe we won't have to cook tonight."

"We won't if Mike and Kabuta brought any money with them," Katy replied.

Ted heard this bit of conversation and said, "Girls, I can't help with the cooking, but supper is on me tonight. I brought quite a bit of cash money because I didn't know what to expect out here."

Ted Chambers practiced drawing and dry firing his weapons every day, especially his bow. He was feeling better than he had for a long time. The fresh air of the great outdoors and the rays of the sun had given him twice the energy, and a ruddy complexion instead of the sickly pallor he once had. After he'd lost his wife he had no desire for the social life they had led in Richmond. He didn't even tell his best friends where he was going, or what he was going to do. He knew they would think he was crazy and try to talk him out of it, and he just didn't want to argue the point.

Looking back on it, he was glad he did it the way he did. He was really a happy man for the first time since his wife passed away. He was doing what he had wanted to do since he was a little boy. How thankful he was that he had hooked up with some young people that let him carry his own weight and treated him as an equal instead of an old man. He was also pleased that they said grace at every meal, like he and his wife had.

When they reached St. Louis they laid over for a few days for a good rest before they hit the plains. It had been a wet winter with a heavy blanket of snow covering the land. Now the snow was gone and the green grass was waving high, and the plains were loaded with large herds of buffalo, and there were many deer and antelope. The streams would be teeming with fish. There would be no shortage of food. Mike bought two more packhorses so they could divide the schoolbooks they were carrying.

If they ran into any hostile Indians they intended to try to outrun them and the horses that might slow them down were the ones carrying the books. By relieving them of half of this weight, Mike felt more at ease. He went to the mercantile store, looking around, just killing time, and he saw one of the first side-cutting mowers for cutting hay, that was ever invented, and a high-wheeled rake that would rake a wide swath of hay. It had a foot lever to dump the hay. He took Kabuta to see them and said, "What do you think of these? Do you think they'd be worth purchasing a wagon and four mules and the extra time it would take to get home?"

"Mike, if we had those in the valley," Kabuta said, "it would make the cutting and stacking enough hay to carry our stock through the winter an easy job."

"True, but we don't need any more mules and wagons. It would really slow us down."

"Maybe, but the Indians we ran across on our trip across the plains from here to our valley have always been friendly, and you know that our people will eat all the mules we don't want to keep."

Mike thought for a moment before saying, "You're right. We'll buy a good wagon and four good mules to pull it. We'll have to set in more supplies too. But the wagon won't be overloaded and by changing teams at the noon hour they can move at a good clip all day. We can reach the valley long before the snow covers the mountain passes."

As an after thought Kabuta said, "Let's bolt a cook stove in the tail end of the wagon."

"Good idea, I wish I'd thought of that." That was the last thing they bought before they left town.

Mike dropped by the bank and to see Truitt Day. After a few pleasantries Mike said, "Well, how do you like St. Louis?"

"It's not Richmond, but it's a growing town and I'm glad to be a part of it. We've found a good church and the wife likes the pastor and his wife.

We miss our family and friends, but Louise makes friends easily and we're settling in."

"We're moving out in the morning and we won't see you for at least two years. We bring in a load of furs and hides and stock up on supplies every two years."

After they purchased everything they needed they rolled out of St. Louis on a bright sunny morning.

Katy said, "Peg, I'm going to miss the cafes."

"Yes, we both will, but I'm glad we're moving again. I want to get my arms around Running Springs."

The first night out Kabuta said, "Everybody get some rest, I'm cooking tonight." He did himself proud when he sat juicy porterhouse steaks in front of them, with creamy white gravy poured over baked biscuits. And he topped that off with coffee and apple pie.

That night Peg held Kabuta's head against her breast for a long time as she told him how proud of him she was. "What you did tonight showed everyone how thoughtful and caring you are. I sometimes lay beside you when you're asleep, looking at the twinkling stars, and I wonder what I ever did to deserve such a wonderful man. I thank Almighty God you found me."

"Woman, you talk too much", Kabuta said, as he claimed her soft, responding lips. "If I were any happier, I swear this heart of mine would explode. Now, let's get some sleep, I'm tired and we have another hard day tomorrow."

* * * * *

Ted turned out to be quite an artist: he painted a picture on each side of the wagon of Mike and Kabuta facing two Indians and they were all holding their hands out, palms up, in a gesture of peace.

Many days later they were traveling through the foothills when they saw two mountain men with their pack mules loaded with furs. The men came up out of the bottom of a creek that ran into the river, moving as fast as they could get their mules to run.

When they saw the wagon and all the packhorses being led by Mike's small group, they swung in their direction.

Kabuta pulled the wagon to a halt and the others gathered around him as the two rode up.

A small man introduced himself as Bob Archer, "And that long, tall drink of water is Homer White. Folks, you are riding straight into about twenty Apache braves, led by a young chief, and they're wearing war paint. They're far north of their own country. If they could take back these fine animals and your scalps on their lances, they would be considered great warriors. We circled their camp last night and I'm sure they didn't see us, but they're coming this way and they'll see our tracks and be after us.

"We were headed for a rocky point that we know of, where we were going to enter the river and travel down the center of it and leave it on another rocky point on the other side, to try to lose them.

"That little creek back there comes out of a shallow canyon and there's a place right ahead where you can get down in there. When you cross the creek turn left and go along the face of the cliff back about a half-mile. There's a small box canyon where this little creek flows from up top, causing a good pool of water there. You can throw a couple of ropes across the canyon where it's very narrow to keep your animals from scattering. The banks of the canyon are high enough that the Indians can't see you until they're are very close.

"They'll surely see your tracks and come looking for you. Folks, you have a fight on your hands.

"Homer, I figure we have a better chance with them than just the two of us, and I wouldn't leave women and children to such a fate, anyway. Besides, we're about out of ammunition, as you well know."

Homer said, "You folks follow me, I don't think we have any time to lose."

Mike said, "Kabuta, I think we should defer to these men's wisdom; they know these Indians far better than we do."

Kabuta said, "Lead on, Homer, if you please."

When they reached the small pool of water in the back of the canyon Mike could see at a glance that it was a perfect place for them to defend themselves. But if they lost the battle, it was a perfect trap, also. There was no running away—they would have to fight to the end.

They quickly turned the animals loose in back of the canyon and stretched the ropes across it. Mike was sure the horses wouldn't run, but the mules he bought in St. Louis might.

Bob Archer said, "My horse is about all in, but if you'll give me a horse I'll scout back up the river and see if I can locate the Indians."

Mike said, "Take my horse; he's the best we have. Everyone else, check your guns and make sure they are all loaded and fill your belts with extra shells."

Mike and Kabuta found a place where they could climb to the top of the canyon. When they reached the top they found some brush about four feet tall where they could weave through in a number of places.

Mike said, "Kabuta, if we lined everyone up here behind this brush and laid low with our double barreled shotguns, and built a big fire at the base of the cliff, making sure that plenty of smoke rises, the Indians would come through this brush to look over in the canyon. If they're a bunch of young braves, they might think we're not so bright as to give ourselves away so easily. They just might walk right into our trap. Ten shotguns would get ten of them with the first barrel, and the second shot might get the rest."

"Do you think the girls could really, absolutely, shoot a man though?" Kabuta asked.

"With what those Indians did to them shortly after we were married, they'll pull the trigger just as quickly as any of us will.

"I don't like the thought of killing again either, but it's their lives or ours, and if they take our families, it will be after I'm dead."

Homer White and Ted Chambers came up and Kabuta ran the plan by them. "Mike and I were just coming down to ask you two if you thought it would work."

Homer scratched his head and thought it over, and said, "I like it. Those shotguns will put the fear of the Almighty into them, and if you get the young chief, the others will break and run."

Ted said, "Sounds foolproof to me. But I think it's important to get them all. If one gets away we might have the whole tribe down on us."

Mike said, "That's my thinking, also. With the element of surprise we should get ten of them with the first barrel, and there's a good chance we could get the rest with the second. You did say there were twenty of them?"

"That's what Bob said. He was the one that scouted their camp."

They went back to the wagon and built a large fire right against the base of the cliff, and Kabuta piled some green juniper boughs on it to cause it to send a plume of dark smoke high into the sky.

They emptied the water barrels and filled them with the clear sweet spring water, and Katy and Peg started cooking a pot of ham hock and pinto beans.

They would show the Indians exactly where they were, hoping they would think they didn't know they were near. Katy gave the four younger children cane poles and told them to catch a mess of fish from the little water hole in the shade of the wagon.

Bob Archer thought his partner and the rest of them had gone stark raving mad when he rode toward the canyon and saw the smoke billowing up over the rim. He rode up the canyon as fast as he could and jumped off his horse and said, "What in blazes do you think you're doing?"

Kabuta started to laugh. "You think we're crazy, do you? That's what we want the Indians to think."

Katy handed Bob a plate of food and a cup of hot coffee and said, "Mr. Archer, enjoy. Then come up on top and join us and you'll see what we're up to."

Kabuta said, "Did you find them, and how many are there? And if so, how long do you figure we have to wait?"

"Twenty and I figured maybe two hours, but with that smoke, they'll be drawn like bees to their honeycomb."

He watched Kabuta and Katy climb up a winding, steep trail and disappear up on top. He ate quickly and followed. When he got near the top he saw the four younger children hiding in a hollow just under the rim.

Gabriel and Riley wanted to fight with the others, but Mike said, "I want you men to keep your pistols handy and protect your sisters."

When Bob reached the top Mike handed him one of the three double-barreled shotguns he was holding and said, "It's loaded, and here are two more shells." Then he called the others to gather around him. As they stood in a circle Mike prayed this simple prayer, "Dear Heavenly Father, may your will be done this day, in Jesus' name, Amen."

Then he said, "Bob, we're going to line up here behind this brush and when I give the command to fire, we'll all rise at once and start firing. We'll line up this way: Bob, you take the left side, then Homer, Will, Katy, me, Sterling, Ted, Peg and Kabuta. I'll get the chief, and the rest of you get the man closest to you. With the element of surprise, we might get them all. Now get comfortable until we hear them coming."

"That won't be long," Bob said, and then he said, "Homer, these young folks will do to ride up the valley with."

"Yes, and anywhere else you might care to go," Homer remarked; as he sat down to rest his back against a sturdy bush.

Suddenly Kabuta said, "Here they come!"

They got to their knees and waited in silence while the braves made their way toward them. When they got close enough, Mike said "Now!" They all screamed as loudly as they could, as instructed. Seven shotguns blasted away, in seconds the chief and six of his men were dead and the others broke to run, but only four sprang on their horses and sped away down river.

Once they all settled down, Mike said, "Ted, you and the boys drag these bodies to where those large boulders are sticking out of the cliff. Roll them over to roll down against those boulders. Then take shovels and break the bank down and cover them as deeply as you can. Bob, Homer, if you'll go with us, Kabuta and I will go after the four that got away. We don't dare let them get back to their village."

They saddled the fastest horses they had and started after them. They rode hard until dark, and then rested their horses until the moon came out.

Sterling and Will told Ted they were ashamed of themselves because they froze and couldn't pull their triggers on the first volley, and when they did fire, it was too late and the four they should have gotten were the ones that got away.

Ted said, "Everyone was so busy none of us noticed, let's keep this to ourselves. You'll do better next time. Right now; let's get this job done."

They got all the bodies placed against the rocks and about two feet of dirt over them, and it got so dark Ted figured it was too dangerous to work here. They would finish the job in the morning.

They all ate little and went to bed trusting the dogs to warn them if danger approached. The children were in their bedrolls as close to their mothers as they could get. Peg and Katy were having problems of their own. The killing weighed heavily on them, and their heart's ached for the wives and mothers that would never know what happened to the men they loved.

Ted was fifty-one years old and he had just killed two men; something that he never dreamed he would do. The thought of it so sickened him that he lost his supper, but he was glad he'd been able to defend the women and the children.

Mike and his companions knew they were catching up with the four young braves. They had just come up on an Indian pony that one of them had apparently ridden to death.

Shortly after the moon and stars came out, giving them some light, Bob said, "There's a cave about five miles further on where they're probably heading in hopes of finding others from their tribe. It's used a lot by Indians. Homer and I sat out a storm there one time with some friendly ones."

As they rode slowly on they saw another dead pony lying across the trail. When they came to where a large sycamore hung over the trail Homer said, "We should leave our horses here. The cave is just around that point of rock up about a hundred yards."

They tied their horses to some low hanging branches and moved cautiously forward.

When they slipped quietly up to the mouth of the cave in the dark shadows of the bluff, they stopped and listened. They could hear voices but they were too deep in the cave, too muffled to recognize or understand.

Mike said, "Let's go get them."

Kabuta said, "No, Mike, it's too dark in there. If we all go in we might find ourselves fighting one another."

"Right; You three stay out here and I'll go in and flush them out. When they come out, get them."

"Good idea," Kabuta said. "But I'm the one to go in there." He paused a moment and continued, "Well, we have to do this, so I'm going in."

He slipped into the cave, immediately bumping his head on the low ceiling. Then he got down on his hands and knees and began feeling his way back into the dark depth of the cave. When he got close enough to understand the language that he'd heard, he realized they were Apaches, as Bob had said.

He understood the tongue and he heard one young brave say to another, "Stop talking. We'd better get some sleep and slip out of here before sunrise. Two of our horses are dead and the other two are spent. We'll have to walk many miles to our village."

Kabuta moved quietly against the wall and sat still and waited for them to sleep. When he'd heard no conversation for nearly an hour he moved deeper into the cave, stopping to listen every few seconds. He finally located three of the braves by their deep breathing.

He worked his way around them, but he couldn't locate the fourth man.

Then he heard something just behind him. Kabuta froze in place.

The young man came at Kabuta and when he did Kabuta grasped him by his long hair, sinking his knife into the young man's side. The young man screamed and Kabuta let out a mighty roar in his booming voice.

The brave fought like a tiger. He cut Kabuta several times, and Kabuta felt blood pouring from his wounds. The brave jumped and landed on Kabuta, knocking the breath out of him. Kabuta fought for breath, and the brave momentarily and accidentally shifted his weight. Air rushed into Kabuta's lungs, and with strength ebbing he put his hands around the brave's throat and squeezed with all his might. The brave kicked and flayed. Then he was still.

The other three dashed toward the faint light at the mouth of the cave. Kabuta heard shots. Then silence.

Mike hollered, "Kabuta!"

"Get a fire going, I'm cut bad," he yelled back. Bob and Homer started hunting dead wood. With his strength almost gone Kabuta crawled out of the cave, dragging the dead body of the brave. He rolled up on his right side and said, "Mike, my left arm and side."

Bob got a fire going, and Mike tore Kabuta's shirt to his waist and examined his wounds. He was bleeding badly from a stab wound in his left side that had gone between his collarbone and the muscle of his shoulder.

"Homer, go look in my saddlebags and bring me that flask of whiskey and the white rags you'll find there."

Mike soaked one of the rags with the hundred proof whiskey and pushed it into the wound, stopping the flow of blood somewhat. Then he poured the cut on his arm full of the burning liquor and pulled the cut together and bound it as tightly as he could. He said, "Kabuta lay there as quietly as you can. Don't move any more than you can help it."

Bob had brought up the horses and Mike got Kabuta in the saddle and swung up behind him. He said, "I have to get Kabuta back to the wagon where I have the supplies to stop this bleeding, or he'll die. I trust you to bring these bodies in so we can bury them along with the others.

Ted couldn't sleep so he was standing watch with his pistol on his hip and a shotgun in his hand when Mike rode in. He challenged them and Mike said, "It's Kabuta and me, Ted. Help me get Kabuta off this horse, he's been wounded badly."

When Mike eased Kabuta down to Ted, Kabuta could barely walk to the wagon tongue and sit down. Katy started a fire in the stove and started boiling water and Peg got a campstool for Kabuta and hovered anxiously over him. Mike threw all the wood they had on the fire. He had to have all the light he could get to see to stop the bleeding from the two serious wounds on Kabuta, the small ones he didn't worry about.

As soon as Katy had water boiling Mike dropped his needles and the horse-hair that Ted had removed from Mike's horse's mane into the water to kill any germs that might be on them.

Peg had gotten Kabuta onto his bedroll.

Mike shoved his knife into the coals of the fire and let it get red hot.

He said, "Kabuta, my friend, I wish you were completely out. This is going to hurt mighty badly. I have to cauterize the wound on your shoulder to stop the bleeding."

Mike folded a rag and said, "Bite down on this." Then he removed the rag from the hole and the blood gushed out. When Mike started to put the red-hot blade against Kabuta's flesh, Peg screamed, "No, Mike!" and she fainted and Ted caught her as she fell and carried her to her bedroll.

Kabuta was almost unconscious from the loss of blood when he said weakly, "Do it, Mike," and he bit down hard on the cloth. When the hot blade was pushed into the wound he passed out. Mike left it there until the bleeding stopped.

Mike cleaned the slash wound on Kabuta's arm, sewed it up and poured a drink down his throat soon after he regained consciousness.

Katy patted cold water in Peg's face, bringing her back to reality.

Peg went to lay beside her husband, careful not to touch him, but letting him know she was there.

Mike had just cleaned his scissors and needles and put them away when Bob and Homer came with the four bodies and Ted showed them where to put them until morning.

It was a weary bunch when they finally banked the fire and went to bed. It had been a hard day for all of them, especially for Mike. He felt responsible for their party and the worry and dread of the battle and the killing of all these young men, and it was still possible he could lose his best friend. His emotions were running wild and his body was trembling with weariness when he finally went to bed.

Katy was the last one to come to bed and when she laid down beside him she whispered, "Thank you, Father, that we all came through this alive, and please heal Kabuta." When she put her arms around Mike and drew his head down on her breast she realized tears were streaming down his face. She knew that he was worn out and she understood his tears.

He said, brokenly, "Kabuta will have two horrible scars for the rest of his life for what I had to do to save his life. Katy, I had to do what I did today to save you, Peg and the children. But those men we killed today were so young."

"We've all being traumatized with what happened today, and thank God you had the wisdom to direct us the right way. We all understand, Mike, and Kabuta will thank you. Kabuta will be fine, thanks to you. Sleep, my love."

But no one slept much that night.

They buried the other bodies the next morning, and Mike sent Sterling and Will and all the children out to gather grass seeds to scatter over the burial place. They had just finished scattering the seeds when it started raining gently.

They cleared a place in the wagon and made a bed for Kabuta.

Bob said, "Mike, we had better get your wagon and stock out of this canyon. That storm looks bad west of here and a flash flood could sweep through this canyon and wash away everything you have. We'll help you get out of the canyon and then we'll be on our way. Homer and I want to thank you for saving us and for the ammunition you gave us to see us through to St. Louis."

"No need for thanks; you did as much to save us as we did to save you. Go with God's blessings."

They had just cleared the canyon when the headwaters of the flood hit it. The storm proved to be a fast moving one that soon passed over them and the sun came out to brighten their spirits. When they came to a clear-running stream they camped for the night, not more than five miles from the canyon.

They had traveled for days and Kabuta seemed to be getting over his injuries better than Peg was. She was strangely silent for days, hovering over her love, and quick to grant his every wish.

Peg had not spoken to Mike or Katy any more than she had to for days, but the first day Kabuta mounted his horse after his ordeal, Peg came and hugged

Mike and Katy and said, "Mike, I hated you for the horrible scars that my Kabuta will carry, but he said they would always be reminders of the day you saved his life. Thank you, Mike, and can you ever forgive me for hating you for even a little while?" Then she burst into tears as Mike held her in his arms. She had held it in too long.

Three days later they ran into Running Deer with a scouting party looking for buffalo. After a warm greeting he said, "The young people of the tribe are camped up on the Bighorn River for their annual buffalo hunt."

Crazy Horse said, "Five more and we go home, but we haven't seen a buffalo all day. We camped where we always do and you can be there in time to cut a chunk off of a roasted buffalo calf for your supper."

Katy said, "Get up mules; that sounds good to me."

She and Peg had been riding the spring seat of the wagon all day. Kabuta had ridden his horse longer than usual that day, but he was lying in his bed now. Mike said, "Running Deer is the Chief with you?"

"He won't leave the old people; Crazy horse is in charge of the hunt this year. Running Springs is back in the valley too. She is expecting. Crazy horse said this morning that if we didn't find buffalo within three days we'd head back; if we got five more it would be at least a week. If you're going on in the morning, I'd like to go with you, if Crazy Horse thinks he can do without me."

Mike said, "Kabuta's been hurt pretty badly and Peg wants to get him home as quickly as possible. So we'll move on early in the morning."

"Five or six days, Mike, and the Chief will be glad to see you. We all will. We've missed all of you and your fiddle and harps."

Mike said, "We have a surprise for you. We'll have a real get-together when Kabuta gets back to normal. He's a little short of breath these days."

Running Deer escorted them back to camp where their friends warmly and enthusiastically received them.

Mike told Crazy Horse they would press on to the valley in the morning.

Crazy Horse said, "I'll have the butcher carve some steaks for you to take along."

"We would appreciate that, and Running Deer would like to go with us. He's concerned about Running Springs and the baby that's due."

"I'll tell him he's free to go."

Five hard, grueling days later they drove up to their homes, and their hearts were full of joy. The journey was over. Now they could settle down to a more peaceful life.

Running Deer had ridden on ahead to alert the village that the Ross and Kabuta families would be there in a few hours.

Chief Big Thunder gathered his people behind him to greet their friends as they drove into the village.

When they came in a great roar went up from the crowd and Katy, Peg, Katherine, and Peggy couldn't hold back the tears of joy. And the men's hearts were full.

The Chief wanted to run and wrap his arms around them all, but he maintained his dignity, and said, "Welcome home, my children."

He was pleased when Katy, Peg, Katherine and Peggy couldn't restrain themselves and ran and hugged their beloved Chief.

Mike called Ted Chambers, Will Clark, and Sterling Fuller forward and introduced them to the Chief and said, "You three must understand that Chief Big Thunder's word is the law here, and he must be obeyed."

The three assured him they would.

"Welcome to our village. We know that Mike and Kabuta wouldn't bring anyone unworthy here."

After the buffalo hunting party returned they had a meeting in the lodge for a night of feasting and merrymaking.

Kabuta was regaining his strength quickly and when the Chief said, "Mike, get your fiddle and play for us," Mike called Kabuta forward. Mike had bought the finest harps money could buy while they were in Richmond and he and Kabuta had practiced playing together for months.

They started out playing haunting music, and then sad, melancholy music. Then Kabuta started mocking birds of all kinds, and it sounded just like the birds themselves were singing. When they started playing gay, happy tunes the people started to sway to the music. Katy and Peg sang a duet together and told everybody how happy they were to be home. Peg said, "We don't want to ever leave the valley again." And Katy said, "No, not ever."

Then they danced to the music of Mike's fiddle and Kabuta's harp.

They settled into tribal life and Mike and Kabuta assembled the mower and rake and put Will Clark to mowing hay, and Sterling raking it up in rows, then some of the teenage Indian boys loaded the hay on wagons and hauled it to the large corral next to the shed where they kept the cows and horses through the winter months. They stacked enormous stacks of hay to feed the stock when the snow covered the valley.

Ted had noticed a long-legged dun mule running free with the mules and the horses, and when they would frolic across the valley the mule would always be out in front of all the others.

He mentioned it to Mike one day and said, "I'd like to have that mule to ride."

Mike said, "Once in a while you'll run across a mule that can outrun many horses and are just as sure footed. They're even better than a horse in the mountains or forest."

"Mike, do you think anybody would object if I broke that mule to ride?"

"Ted, all the work mules belong to the tribe. Go talk to the Chief, and he'll tell you what you have to do to earn the mule. And if he gives him to you, I'll break him for you."

"Thank you, Mike, but I'd like to break him myself."

The Chief gave his consent, and said, "If you bring in an elk to roast for the tribe after you break the mule, he will be yours."

Ted went to a clearing and dug a deep hole and put a post in it and tamped it in tight. Then he saddled his horse and went after his mule. He left early one morning because he didn't want anybody see how awkward he was with the lariat rope.

He threw loop after loop before he got a rope around his neck and the mule led easily. Ted took him to the post and took a rope and tied him to it with a loop so he wouldn't run around and around the pole and draw himself up close to it. He ran him around the pole for about two hours that afternoon and left him there for the night.

Katy and Peg watched this activity for a while and Peg said, "What are you doing?"

He said, "You just watch me for a few days and you'll see."

The following morning Ted snubbed him to the post and put a saddle on him. The mule sidestepped and kicked at Ted a few times, but he was snubbed so close to the post, that try as he would he couldn't keep Ted from strapping the saddle on his back.

When Ted removed the snub rope the mule went stumbling backwards to the end of the rope. Ted was standing on the rope and he went catapulting backwards when the rope went taut. He was embarrassed when Katy and Peg laughed at him. The mule started around the pole, pitching for all he was worth, but he couldn't get rid of the saddle. He slowed to a trot and finally stopped and looked back at the contraption on his back. Ted repeated this process, occasionally slipping a bridle on him, for ten days before he climbed into the saddle. After the fifth day the mule didn't pitch at all.

On the eleventh day Peg and Katy were watching as they had every morning since he tied the mule to the post. When he mounted, the mule shivered, crow-hopped a few times, and then started trotting around and around. This gait jarred Ted's insides so he kicked the mule into a lope. Then he dismounted and gave his mule another taste of sugar. He removed the rope from the mule's neck and mounted him and rode across the valley. He didn't come back until late in the afternoon and he was leading a gentle pack mule that the girls recognized as one they had packed many times.

Ted left the village early the next morning. It was a crisp fall morning and it had snowed high up on the mountain during the night. By the time the sun came up he had crossed the valley and was well up in the foothills, looking for the elk that the Chief said he had to bring in if he wanted the mule he would name Mouse.

He had heard somewhere that elk love to lay on the snow. He started climbing toward the snow-covered peaks, up a slow-running, twisting creek that wound its way down the mountainside. Just as he decided he couldn't go much farther, the creek ran around a point of rock, and a small valley that seemed to just hang up here in the mountain opened up before him. He rode out into the middle of the valley and he saw him, a buck about a year old, just entering an aspen grove, with its golden leaves rustling in the early morning breeze.

Ted had brought his rifle and the pistols he always wore around his waist, but he wanted desperately to bring him down with his bow. He was out in the open, so he turned back and tied his mules to trees.

He took his rifle out of the boot, picked up his bow, threw a quiver of arrows over his back and started briskly toward the aspen grove, hoping he could enter it before the elk saw him. When he reached the grove he paused and leaned against the largest tree he saw to rest a minute. The high altitude made him short of breath and his heart was pounding so hard he realized his hands wouldn't be steady. So he slipped down on the ground with his back resting against the trunk of the tree and rested for fifteen minutes.

He rose and saw the elk pushing through the smaller trees. He couldn't actually see the elk, but he could see the top of the trees parting as it pushed slowly through them

Ted placed himself where he thought he should be, got his bow ready and waited. He saw the elk come out of the thick trees and stop to scratch his side on a big tree. He couldn't get a shot because the tree trunk was between him and the spot where he knew his arrow had to go. Ted was so eager to get his shot off he had great difficulty keeping still. Finally the elk stepped forward. Ted took a deep breath and drew his bowstring back to where the tip of the arrow lay just over the bow. He let his breath out slowly and let the arrow fly. He watched in amazement as the huge animal dropped in his tracks. Ted walked to where the elk fell, almost under the only branch strong enough in the grove where he could hang it to bleed, and he gutted it.

When he had completed the task he had some difficulty getting the pack mule to stand still so he could lower the animal onto his back, but he finally got it in place and tied firmly on the mule. It was a slow process coming back down the mountain, but he was a proud man when he rode up to the Chief's teepee and presented the elk to him.

Big Thunder said, "Ted, you've earned your mule. Take the elk to the butcher block."

He followed Ted and said to the butcher, "Prepare the elk for a feast for the whole tribe for the next evening meal."

The next evening Katy and Peg praised Ted for the way he broke the mule.

The Chief made a great fanfare when he said, "Ted has paid his dues to become a full member of the tribe by supplying this elk for our weekly feast, and in appreciation, the tribe is giving him the mule he wanted."

Mike slapped Ted on the shoulder and said, "I remember when you were afraid you wouldn't measure up and fit in. Well, man, you fit real good."

Kabuta said, "All the fellows back on the dock in Richmond wouldn't believe it if they could see us now, Ted. I still have a hard time believing it. I have Peg pinch me once in a while just to let me know I'm not dreaming."

"Kabuta," Ted said, "I wouldn't go back to that life if they gave me the whole state of Virginia. I'll be content to live out my life right here."

CHAPTER THIRTY-THREE

The men got busy and built the schoolhouse and Peg and Katy started their long-awaited school. They were overjoyed at the eagerness of the children to learn to read and write the English language.

Katy was thrilled when Big Thunder came to their house and said, "Katy, I have a burning desire to learn how to read and write like my little daughter has. But I would lose face with my people if I sat in with the children."

Katy said, "If you would come to our house after supper each evening, Peg and I would be honored to teach our great Chief all we can."

The Chief was highly intelligent and soon learned all Katy and Peg could teach him. He read every book that Katy and Peg had brought with them so many times he could almost recite them from memory.

When Katy and Peg were sure they had taught him all they could they went to Mike and Kabuta and asked their advice about something they wanted to give the Chief for a graduation gift.

Katy showed them a leather-bound Bible that she had bought in Richmond. "Mike, this was to be your Christmas present, but if you don't mind we'd like to give it to the Chief. He's devoured all the written material we have but this. Do you think it will offend him?"

They both thought it would be a fine idea. Mike said, "I've come to love our Chief like a father, and I've been praying how I could present Christ to him. I think he's sincerely seeking the truth about everything, and being as intelligent as he is, he'll be drawn to the Master by the reading of His word."

The following morning Peg and Katy went and asked to see the Chief. When they were seated in front of him, he said, "What can I do for my teachers?"

Katy said, "Chief, you were such an outstanding pupil Peg and I want to give you a graduation present." She handed him the beautiful Bible and said, "This book tells the truth about the Great Spirit you worship."

For days the chief could be seen riding away from the village in the early hours of the morning, and he would return late in the afternoon.

Then one day he called a meeting in the great lodge and he asked everyone in the tribe to be present. They met Christmas day and the Chief asked Mike and Kabuta to play their harps, and they played a number of hymns, and then he asked Katy and Peg to sing.

After they had sung he got up to speak. Mike, Kabuta, Katy, and Peg were speechless when he said, "My people, I love you, and I ask you to bow your heads while I pray." And he ended his prayer in Jesus' name.

Then he read them the Christmas story. He went on to say, "You may have wondered where I have gone and what I've been doing these many days away from the village. I have read this book and many passages many times and again, and I have come to believe that this is the word of the Great Spirit. I will not demand that you come to the meetings, but from this day on we will meet once a week in this place to read and study this book.

"Katy and Peg taught me how to read and write; now I would like to read you something that I have written by my own hand."

He described their homeland; from the top of the snow-capped mountains to the floor of the valley, the waterfalls, the lakes and rivers. And the geysers that shot their steaming winds and waters up out of the bowels of the earth. He described the roaming of the bear, elk and other animals they all knew about. He told how the large flocks of geese flew in to land on their lakes and rivers. He described the camp on the Little Bighorn River and the buffalo hunt in vivid colors. "Now, my people, we should all thank our great God and Heavenly Father for this great land He has given us. And I will be forever grateful for what Katy and Peg have done for me."

When he sat down his people cheered him long and loud. Mike, Kabuta and Ted were the first ones to congratulate him on what a fine job he had done.

But he was far more pleased when Peg and Katy came and hugged him.

Katy said, "You were our smartest pupil, I could not have described your country and your beautiful valley as well. You should be proud."

"Our valley, Katy," the Chief corrected, "I'll always be grateful for all that you and Peg have done for me; especially for teaching me who the Great Spirit really is."

They had truly come home.